American Gilt

Book III

SCANDAL

J.D. Peterson

"American Gilt"

"Scandal" Volume Three

American Gilt Trilogy

Copyright © 2016 by J.D. Peterson

Revised Edition – 2023

First Edition 2016

Printed in the United States of America

Sources and photographic credits are located at the back of this book.

ISBN-13: 978-1533379252

ISBN-10: 153337925

Library of Congress Control Number: 2016908684

© J.D. Peterson Media

© 'New Moon Music' – B.M.I.

Published by J.D. Peterson Media

Laguna Niguel, California, U.S.A.

www.americangilt.com

Formerly published as 'Swan Song Trilogy'

This book is dedicated to the women of the world.

Sara Swan Whiting Belmont
June 22, 1861 – May 20, 1924

Chapter One

December 24, 1883

Newport, Rhode Island

The window panes rattled against the winter wind, the sills already laden with several inches of holiday snow. A taper candle on the vanity flickered in response. Caught in the invisible current of a cold draft, it sizzled as hot wax dripped onto the table, escaping the fate of the burning flame.

The pounding of horses' hooves emanated from the street. Sara looked out between the panes of the frosted window, ice forming on the glass. She told herself she wasn't interested, watching as a sleigh loaded with riders bundled together against the cold plodded down Bellevue Avenue. The accumulated snow was making it a challenge for the horses to keep up a proper pace. The soft yellow light of streetlamps shimmered on snowflakes, blowing haphazardly around the travelers in the harsh wind. Shadows and light competed for dominion over the scene as a cadence of laughter and sleigh bells echoed over the quiet Newport street.

"I'm being shunned," Sara whispered, moving away from the window. "Any fool can see that." The news of her impending divorce had splintered her reputation in the set, leaving her an outcast among the ranks. She had not received an invitation to tonight's ball, and Sara expected this new trend to continue into the foreseeable future.

Aching from an unrelenting weariness, her mind slowed, searching for any solution that would arrest the thief of her peace and return easy contentment to her life. She twirled the laudanum bottle in her hand again, wondering how large a dose would be needed to achieve her simple goal. She could bear no more of the scandal and desperately needed this nightmare to end.

"In three days, it will be the first anniversary of my marriage to Oliver Belmont," she thought sadly. *"I should be making preparations for a celebration."* But that was not to be. The honeymoon had turned disastrous after the arrival of her family in Paris, who were there to announce the newlyweds to polite society in France.

Oliver had begun drinking absinthe in excess, which influenced his personality in a very nasty manner. *"He'd grown sullen and argumentative, and I could do nothing to improve his demeanor,"* she remembered. The conflict had escalated into a violent argument. In his rage, Oliver had slapped and beaten Sara, all the while shouting that *"she was not his wife."* He'd stormed out of their Paris apartment, leaving her a victim of his vicious temper.

Absent for weeks on end, he'd finally surfaced in Spain. Word had it that Oliver had gone to Barcelona with a French 'dancer' as his traveling companion, and the rumors had brought unforgivable humiliation and embarrassment to Sara.

Looking back now, she couldn't help but wonder if Oliver had only married her to escape his father's constant pestering over a career. She knew the marriage had also entitled him to a larger allowance and other rewards, like a house of his own. "Did he ever love me?" she quietly mused.

Soon after their horrible argument, Sara had discovered she was pregnant with Oliver's child. Mindful of the health of mother and baby, Mrs. Whiting had called for a doctor who'd ordered Sara back to the States before the pregnancy was too far along to permit travel.

When Sara had return to Newport without Oliver, a huge scandal had erupted, publicizing the condition of their short marriage in the newspapers. *"Everyone is talking about it,"* she thought bitterly. *"Debating my private situation in a very public way."*

A battle had ensued between the Whiting and Belmont families, each blaming the other for the responsibility of the disastrous marriage. The two families rallied friends in support, and people took sides. Prominent families drew lines in the sand, and Sara felt the eyes of judgment on her everywhere she went.

With the Belmont family supporting him, Oliver had maintained his innocence to the charges of abandonment and abuse, and his parents had begun a propaganda campaign to destroy Sara's good name while protecting Oliver – and themselves, from the effects of the scandal. Mrs. Whiting had launched a similar campaign to protect her daughter, incessantly urging Sara to seek counsel with a lawyer for the dissolution of marriage. Finally, Sara followed her mother's advice. *"What choice do I have?"* she'd asked herself.

In September, with the divorce papers filed, Sara had given birth to a baby girl that she'd named Natica, after her friend Lady Lister-Kaye. Angry and heartbroken, Sara had forbidden Oliver to visit her or the child. In retaliation, he'd denied his paternity to the baby, leaving the little one to grow up in the shadow of illegitimacy while he went about his privileged life as if nothing had happened. "He even has the audacity to claim he is a bachelor!" Sara fumed in the empty room.

Shaking her head in despair, Sara gripped the rubber plunger on the opium bottle and squeezed with new determination. Filling the glass dropper to the top, she extracted it from the amber phial and watched dispassionately as a single drop of brown liquid dripped back into the bottle, returning to its source like a refugee seeking escape from its captor.

Reconciliation had become impossible, and ultimately Sara knew she had been left with no choice but to file for divorce. Now, with her first anniversary just a few days away, she found her name erased from invitation lists where she should have been an honored guest. She'd fought against the stigma, but as an impending divorcée with a child, she'd been left with a reputation nearly as bad as a harlot. Her friends rallied around her, but Sara avoided them, knowing they would be tainted by association.

Sara's hand moved in slow motion as she focused on the laudanum. Time expanded, each second swelling in magnitude, her mind racing with the reality of the option she was considering. The challenges of her relationship with Oliver had been going on for years and years, almost from the time they'd met, and she was frazzled by the battle. Sara wanted it to stop – now! What better way to escape the tragedy of her life than to take a long nap? A nap from which she would never awaken. Peace held an allure that coerced her toward action.

In the distance Sara heard her baby cry and faltered, weighing the veracity of her solution. "What good is an outcast for a mother?" she whimpered, growing angry at her lack of courage.

A glimmer of hope filtered through her mind. Perhaps, she considered, she could draw from a well of strength deep within her, a courage that possessed the fortitude to face her tormentors. Could she summon the bravery needed to stand tall, using the truth to empower her against the gossip? But what strength did she have to fight against decades of social propriety and regulations? She felt exhausted – weak, and powerless against the forces of society.

Raising the dropper to her lips, she squeezed the bulb and released a small dose of the opiate on to her tongue. The bitter tast swished in her mouth, and she paused, gathering her determination to continue.

Filling the dropper again, she lifted it toward her mouth to repeat the process. Loud voices rose from the parlor below, surging into shouts of panic erupting from her family in the sitting room.

"What in the world is going on..."

Sara looked up, catching her reflection in the vanity mirror, dark circles under her eyes tainting her twenty-three-year-old visage. A knock sounded at the door just as the terrified shrieks of her infant daughter reached her ears, accented by a loud crash. The noise reverberated like thunder through the halls of *Swanhurst*, and her door flew open without preamble.

"Come quick, miss," Bridget cried, her red hair flashing in the lamplight. "The Christmas tree has caught fire!"

Shoving the phial onto the dressing table, Sara buried it amid the collection of medicine and perfume bottles. Running from the chamber, she followed her maid down the steps to the parlor, concern for her baby's safety now paramount in her mind.

Chaos greeted Sara as she entered the sitting room, just as the Whiting's houseman, Owen, threw a pail of water over the smoldering pine limbs. The toppled tree lay crashed on its side, a jumbled mess of popcorn strings and ornaments, while the acrid smell of burnt evergreen filled the smoky room, irritating her throat and eyes.

"Get the baby out of here!" Mrs. Whiting ordered Bridget. The maid lifted the infant from the cradle and threw a receiving blanket over the child's face as she left the room for the other side of the house.

"What happened?" Sara demanded, though it was obvious one of the candles had kindled the tree limb to flames.

"Everything's under control," Owen announced, throwing a canvas tarp on the wet carpet. "Everyone calm down." The tall, lanky man worked at covering the damaged rug, soot floating in his blond hair.

Mary, the Whiting's housekeeper, opened the windows wide, allowing the frigid air and snowflakes entry into the parlor. Walking to the sofa, she lifted a pillow and began fanning the smoke from the room.

"Thank goodness you saw the fire before it got too large," Milly said to Jane.

"Yes, it was lucky indeed," Jane agreed, wrapping her arms around herself tightly.

"Indeed," Mrs. Whiting echoed. "We very nearly had a catastrophe on our hands."

"Very nearly," Sara repeated, trembling from the ramifications of the evening.

Two weeks later
January 11, 1884
New York, New York

Standing in front of the parlor fireplace Mrs. Whiting confronted her youngest daughter. "You simply must go to the ball," she insisted. The matriarch of the family, Mrs. Whiting was dressed in a stylish violet-lace gown, her graying hair arranged in a fashionable coiffure. Still attractive considering her years, she ruled the Whiting family with a firm hand. Clearly, she wasn't in the mood to take 'no' for an answer.

"In spite of the fact that everyone has been treating me absolutely horridly?" Sara kept her voice even, speaking as calmly as she could. She had dressed in her finest French gown and was ready to go, but now at the last minute, she was having second thoughts at the wisdom of attending tonight's Patriarch Ball. "You've seen for yourself the way they scowled at me in church on Sunday. The whispers and stares – they're wearing on my nerves!"

"Mrs. Olerich and Mrs. Wilson are very polite – and don't forget Mrs. Astor. You know full well that Mrs. Astor is a strong ally among the Four Hundred. It would be a mistake to underestimate her influence. And there are plenty of others sympathetic to you, Sara." Her mother pointed at her vehemently. "You just can't let a few gossiping old biddies get the best of you. They thrive on the misfortune of others. Where's your pride?"

"My pride has been trampled and stomped into the ground," Sara said bluntly, her voice dull. "Put yourself in my shoes."

"That's exactly what I'm doing!" her mother cried. "Not only for your sake, but for Natica's sake as well. She won't always be a baby, you know. Do you want her to have to sulk around in the shadows all because her father is a cad?"

Her mother's words pierced the veil of Sara's misgivings, striking a chord of truth, and she turned to Mrs. Whiting, resignation filling her eyes.

"You can't just give up and go into hiding," Mrs. Whiting continued, sensing she was winning the argument. "Or let Oliver and his family destroy your life with their lies and gossip. You must hold your head up and carry on."

Sara sighed. "Of course, you're right, although it's a challenge much more easily said than done." Gathering her strength, she took a deep breath and slowly raised herself from the sitting room chair. "I'll go. But it's for Natica's sake, not my own. We both know there isn't a gentleman in town who will be seen dancing with me."

Mrs. Whiting (from top)
Jane Whiting, Amelia 'Milly' Whiting

"Then don't dance. But you must put in an appearance to save face. Do it for your honor. Do it for the honor of the Whiting family."

"To the devil with honor," Sara muttered miserably as she followed her mother outside to the carriage where her sisters waited.

Taking her place in the coach Sara noticed Jane, her oldest sister, wore her usual frown of disapproval, but said nothing. Milly, sitting next to her on the bench seat, looked lovely as she fiddled with her lace gloves, seemingly impatient to leave.

It was an uneventful ride to Delmonico's up Fifth Avenue, and no one talked much. Sara was glad for the quiet. It gave her time to gather her confidence for the evening. She took comfort knowing that she wasn't going it alone, but had the company of her family, even if she was presently annoyed with them.

Arriving at the venue, Sara followed her mother and two sisters upstairs to the second-floor ballroom. The Patriarch Ball was one of the most splendid events of the season, and invitations were highly coveted. As was usual, Mrs. Astor was among the organizers for the event.

When the Whitings reached the ballroom, they were greeted by the scent of red and yellow tulips, purple hyacinths, and white lilies arranged in vases throughout the room. More flowers were wrapped around mirrors and threaded through chandeliers. Large pots filled with leafy ferns and Ficus trees accented the colors of the blooms.

"The decorations are simple but lovely," Mrs. Whiting noted as they moved into the ballroom.

"They seem somewhat bland compared to the lavish decorations at the Christmas ball," Jane returned.

Two footmen dressed in Astor-blue regalia and powdered wigs welcomed the guests. The men passed out dainty dance cards to the society crowd as they entered the party. Taking a program from the footman, Sara followed Jane and Milly into the main ballroom behind Mrs. Whiting.

The newspaper had announced that over three hundred people were expected at Delmonico's tonight. Scanning the faces, it became clear to Sara that the party was attended by the usual congregation of elite guests, although there were many in attendance she did not recognize. Happy for the large crowd, Sara hoped it would afford her the option to fade into the scenery if need be. She watched the laughing dancers finish their polka while silently praying she would not have to endure too much disdain during the evening.

The Landers orchestra entertained the guests; the melodies paused while the musicians prepared their next tune. Sara and her sisters trailed their mother as she perused the ballroom in search of friends. Moving around the dining tables Sara caught the disapproving glances of Mrs. Edwards, who was chatting with Mrs. Robbins, their voices suddenly dropping to a whisper as she passed. A hush seemed to ripple through the crowd as they walked, but Sara held her head high with all the pride she could rally. Her daughter's face flashed in her mind, reminding her what was at stake, and Sara renewed her vow to be strong against the gossip created by her divorce. Mrs. Whiting spotted Mrs. Wilson seated at a table with Mrs. Endicott and Mrs. Webb. The sight of her mother's friends brought Sara relief from the tension as the Whitings joined them at their table, taking seats in the empty chairs.

"I'm so glad you've arrived!" Mrs. Wilson greeted. "I was beginning to worry you would skip tonight's event." The aging woman welcomed Sara from under the brim of a wide picture-hat, her smile bringing creases to the wrinkles at the corner of her eyes. "My daughter Grace is here, just returned from England where she was a guest of the Prince of Wales." Clearly pleased, Mrs. Wilson continued, "She's currently off dancing with Mr. Crandall."

"How lovely," Mrs. Whiting said, flinging a sidelong glance at Sara. "I'm certain there are plenty of gentleman looking for a partner to join them in a waltz."

"Indeed, there are." Mrs. Endicott smiled, intuiting the situation. Plump and of small stature, the woman would be attractive if not for a nose too large for her tiny face. The eldest of the group, her white hair was smoothed into a tight bun at the nape of her neck. "Sara, I'm sure you'll be happy to know your friend Edith Jones is here along with Miss Astor."

"I look forward to visiting with them." Sara smiled, spotting Edith and Carrie across the ballroom – although she wondered what type of reception her friends would offer in such a public arena.

"It appears Miss Jones is escorted by a gentleman this evening," Mrs. Webb stated with interest. Dressed in black, the widow continued to wear the mourning color, although it had been many years since her husband had passed away. "A Mr. Edward Wharton."

"His friends call him Teddy," Mrs. Wilson chimed in. "After Mrs. Stevens postponed Edith's engagement to Henry, Mrs. Jones set to work getting her daughter a new suitor."

"Mr. Wharton certainly seems to be an eligible bachelor." Mrs. Endicott smiled, a distinct tone of approval in her voice. "He's handsome enough and comes from a good family."

"So, I've heard," Mrs. Whiting concurred, enjoying the conversation.

A butler appeared and offered champagne to the guests. Taking a glass, Sara sipped the fine vintage and distracted herself by watching the bubbles spritzing in the glass. The ladies chatted on around her in animated conversation, discussing the upcoming balls that would continue in an ostentatious manner until Lent, at which point they would cease until after Easter.

The conversation suddenly dwindled, and Sara looked up to notice everyone staring behind her. Turning, she followed their gaze to Mrs. Astor moving through the ballroom toward them. Dressed in the most gorgeous magenta silk gown Sara had ever laid eyes upon, Mrs. Astor looked like a European royal. Trimmed in fur and intricate French lace, the gown was completed by an opulent display of large glittering diamonds adorning every available space on her frame – including a tiara and her famous stomacher – an expensive belt constructed primarily of diamonds, believed to have once belonged to Queen Marie Antoinette.

As Mrs. Astor neared, Sara caught her eye, but the matriarch seemed to look right through her, giving no acknowledgment. Instead, Mrs. Astor greeted a bubbly débutante newly introduced into society, then continued her promenade to the table at the front of the room. A flurry of ebullient young débutantes followed at a proper distance, anxious to earn favor with America's queen.

Nothing more needed to be said. In a flash, Sara realized Mrs. Astor's fondness for her was ebbing. A lifetime of friendship destroyed by her divorce – by Oliver! Shame washed over Sara, and she struggled against the urge to run from the ballroom and escape the judgment diffused by the social barrage of her persecutors.

But she'd never thought Mrs. Astor would turn against her.

"Just don't you worry over Mrs. Astor," Mrs. Wilson leaned in and whispered from under her hat. "She supports you very much privately. Publicly, she has standards to uphold for the set."

"Of course," Sara murmured. "She has standards to uphold." But Sara knew without Mrs. Astor's support, her days among New York's elite would vanish like a dream in the morning light.

Chapter Two

Four days later
January 15, 1884
New York, New York

Etiquette for a married woman was far more complicated than that expected of a débutante, as Sara well knew. After the ball, she was required to call on her hostess within a few days, in this case, Mrs. Astor, to extend her gratitude for the invitation.

"I'm not looking forward to this visit one bit," Sara confided in Bridget as her maid helped her dress for the afternoon. "After the cold reception I received at Friday's ball, I'm not sure what to expect."

"There's only one way to find out," Bridget said with encouragement. "If Mrs. 'A' has truly turned against you – which I doubt – she won't receive you."

"That's what I'm afraid of." Their eyes met in the mirror as the maid finished arranging Sara's hair into a lovely coiffure. "Which is why I'm going without my family. If there's shame to bear, I'll bear it alone."

Placing the brush on the dressing table, Bridget smiled with reassurance.

Sara reached for a spritz of perfume. Finding the delicate French bottle, she applied just a touch, and returned it to her vanity. Her eyes searched for the laudanum – just in case she needed it – but the bottle was absent from the mirrored tray. Pushing around a few jars and bottles, she gave a cursory search but failed to find the laudanum.

Turning, her eyes locked with Bridget's. Sara thought the maid's cheeks colored when she turned away, busying herself tidying up the bedchamber.

In a flash, Sara realized Bridget knew the depths of her melancholy and to what end she would go to alleviate her suffering. Clearly, the maid had seen the laudanum bottle in Sara's hand and had intuited her intentions on Christmas Eve when she'd burst into Sara's bedchamber due to the fire.

Embarrassed at being discovered, Sara said nothing. Evidently, Bridget had removed the laudanum from her room to avoid any future temptation to permanently end her misery.

"You better be off now. I'm sure you mean to be prompt."

"Yes, of course." Sara smiled.

"Good luck, miss."

It was a short ride down Bellevue Avenue, but for Sara, the moments dragged by with a subtle dread. Arriving at the Astor home precisely at two o'clock – the proper hour for visiting – Sara offered her calling card to the butler. Wearing a fine suit and bow tie, the man disappeared into the house while she awaited the verdict of her visit from society's queen. When the servant reappeared, he led Sara to the parlor, requesting she wait there for Mrs. Astor.

Taking a seat on the divan, Sara released a silent breath while fidgeting with the tassel on her handbag. Catching her nervous preoccupation, she pushed it aside just as Mrs. Astor entered the room.

"Hello, Sara," Mrs. Astor said, her powerful presence filling the room. Impeccably dressed in navy blue, the woman was clearly prepared for afternoon visitors.

"Hello, Mrs. Astor." Sara rose from the chair and curtsied.

"I'm so glad you came by today," Mrs. Astor said, taking a seat adjacent to the divan. The massive gilt chair was suitable for a monarch. "I wanted to talk with you."

"To be honest, I wasn't sure if I'd be received."

"I can understand your apprehension. Your visit affords us a chance for a necessary discussion."

The matriarch gave Sara a direct look. Resisting the urge to squirm, she was suddenly glad for her training in poise.

"I wanted to explain my actions at the Patriarch's Ball. You must understand, in spite of my fondness for you, there are certain long-standing parameters to one's conduct in society."

"Of course." Sara smiled nervously. "Have I done something to offend you?"

"Not directly, dear, but there is the matter of your divorce. The scandal has delivered a most unfortunate stain on your family's good name. If I weren't so fond of you, I'd be forced into the position of removing you from my guest list." Their eyes met in common understanding. "Of course, the Whitings have a long pedigree of respect in America, and as Carrie is the godmother of your daughter, my affection for you runs deeper than most. So, in your case, I've made an exception."

"I'm most appreciative of your consideration."

"It was not a decision I made lightly." Mrs. Astor revealed sharply. "I'm not at all pleased with the way divorce is growing commonplace among the set. But, there are extenuating circumstances in your case – very distasteful ones at that. Most coming from the general direction of the Belmonts." Mrs. Astor paused, shaking her head in obvious aversion. "Rest assured, your family will continue to receive invitations. But keep in mind dear, that does not mean I can openly approach you when we're out amongst the ranks. What kind of message would that send? I can't be seen condoning something as utterly shocking as divorce, no matter what the circumstances."

The words sunk into Sara's mind with clear comprehension. "I understand."

"You are still a welcome guest among the Four Hundred, but please don't be offended if I fail to acknowledge you upon occasion. In your heart, rest assured my fondness for you remains strong." Offering Sara a warm smile, Mrs. Astor continued, "You're still young, dear. I'm certain as time goes by, the whole affair will fade from people's minds, and life will resume a normal routine for you and your daughter. New scandals are always waiting in the wings to captivate people's attention, quickly dispersing old tales with new. So, taking everything into consideration, I think your future is bright."

"When you put it that way, it certainly would appear so."

Gathering her handbag, Sara rose from her place on the divan and politely curtsied. "I won't take up any more of your time."

"I'm glad we had this chance to talk," Mrs. Astor affirmed, signaling the butler to show Sara out.

Once outside, Sara climbed into her carriage on a slow step. Bundled against the winter cold, she worked to keep warm, her mood somber from the sentence decreed upon her social standing. As the coach wound through the streets of New York, her broken heart was too numb for tears.

Six months later
July 15, 1884
Bowie, Maryland

The pasture rolled over the lush hills of Belair Stud Farm, located fifteen miles east of Washington, DC. The farm had sired many champion racehorses, but when Oliver caught the news of a stud descended from the winner *Lexington*, he was tantalized by the possibilities of owning a champion. It had been a long and arduous journey, and he was anxious to stretch his legs when his coach finally pulled up in front of the manager's office in time for the afternoon meeting.

The divorce from Sara had been finalized a few months ago, and Oliver hadn't skipped a beat, moving on with his life as carefree as ever. *"Auggie and Perry are busy making their mark on the business world,"* he reflected on his older brothers. *"While I continued to search for a career that holds my interest – and finds favor with my father."*

At first, he'd decided on farming, focusing on viniculture as a specialty. Oliver toyed with the idea of starting his own winery, imagining delicious bottles bearing a Belmont label. The plan had its merits, but after some consideration, he returned to his original idea of farming crops. But that idea lost its allure in a short time, as well. "It just seems like too much work," he murmured.

After a visit to Lexington, Kentucky, Oliver was bitten by the racing bug and finally decided on raising racehorses. *"I want to settle in the bluegrass state,"* he'd told his father. And August Belmont had quickly squelched the plan. Years before, August had been looking into leasing a farm in Kentucky and was all too familiar with the rough and hard-drinking set, lounging about in the towns and on racetracks, gambling and betting on races. He feared the influence upon Oliver would be fatal.

Oliver chuckled aloud at the memory. Why did his father always insist on being so dramatic? As a consolation, August had offered him the Nursery to pursue his interest. The family farm on Long Island was a magnificent equestrian property. His father had purchased over 13,000 acres of land years ago and built a twenty-four-room mansion, cottages, stables, and his own racetrack. The place even boasted a bowling alley. Although it was a generous offer, Oliver declined the gift, preferring to build a place of his own. *"I want to escape the shadow of Papa,"* he thought. *"Taking up residence at the Nursery would surely keep me under his thumb."*

The door to the office opened and a gentleman dressed in dungarees and cowboy boots emerged from the shadows of the interior. "Mr. Belmont?" he asked while smoothing a Stetson over his thick head of hair.

"Yes," Oliver replied, moving toward the man. Short of stature, with wavy brown hair and matching eyes, his good looks kept him a favorite with the ladies. "I'm here to see about the stud."

"Of course. I'm Jake Brandt," he said, holding out a hand in greeting. "I'm the ranch manager."

"Nice to meet you, Mr. Brandt." Oliver smiled, shaking his hand.

"If you'll follow me to the barn, we can get down to business."

"Fine," Oliver replied, wondering if perhaps he should reconsider the merits of viniculture.

Four months later
November 18, 1884
New York, New York

Following the inscrutable footman toward the art gallery, Sara knew she'd never seen the Astor mansion on Fifth Avenue decorated so profusely – and that was saying something! There were flowers of all types, everywhere! Roses and lilies and orchids and violets were arranged throughout every inch of the home amidst ferns, ivy, and a multitude of palm trees. Flowers seemed to grow from the very wall where they framed the expansive foyer mirror. Yards of blooms were woven into garlands and wound over stair railings and candelabras. The entrance to the art gallery was adorned with massive gold vases overflowing with ferns and ivy and *La France* pink roses.

Stepping into the art gallery Sara viewed even more flowers, their scent sweetly cascading throughout the room. Flowers were even hanging from the ornate chandeliers in immense bundles of colossal pink roses and greenery. The beauty made Sara take pause in awe.

Today was Carrie's wedding day. She was marrying Marshall Wilson in front of one thousand guests. Instead of exchanging vows at the church, the bride had decided to hold the wedding in the opulent art gallery of the Astor mansion.

Escorted by her mother and two sisters, Sara followed an usher to their chairs at the back of the room, where they were seated next to her brother Gus, and his wife Florence already arrived for the ceremony. Florence caught her eye and smiled, her blond hair curling under a lovely day hat that matched her kelly-green gown. Gus looked handsome in his formal suit, a lock of his chestnut hair falling casually over his forehead. Settling into her place, Sara thought they made a handsome couple.

While Milly and Jane took chairs next to Mrs. Whiting, Sara glanced through the assembly of high-profile guests bearing witness to the social event of the season. Taking mental inventory, Sara's thoughts drifted back to when she and Carrie were young girls. They'd been the dearest of friends and close allies when they'd débuted into society, confiding every secret in each other as they embarked on their search for the perfect husband. Now, it seemed, Carrie had succeeded in achieving that goal. *"While I failed miserably,"* Sara silently anguished.

The two ladies had promised each other a position as bridesmaid when the time came. *"Carrie had fulfilled the duty as my maid of honor."* Sara thought back to when she'd married Oliver several years ago. But now, in light of the scandal caused by her failed marriage and subsequent divorce, Sara had not been surprised when a reciprocal offer failed to arrive from Carrie. *"I can't blame her,"* Sara thought, and she'd made peace with the situation. *"Nonetheless, it hurts to be relegated to the position of guest. But after my conversation with Mrs. Astor..."* Sara frowned. *"I'm grateful to have received an invitation at all."*

Curious, Sara examined the guests seated for the ceremony, casually looking around for familiar faces. Her friend George Rives sat a few rows in front of her, accompanied by his wife, Kaye. The Vanderbilt family was together: Alice and Cornelius, as well as William and Alva. So many feathers bounced out of Alva's hat it looked like she had a full bird resting on her head.

Chuckling to herself, Sara turned her attention to the other guests. It was then she spotted the Belmont family on the opposite side of the gallery. Her stomach churned at the sight, and she shifted in her chair, meeting her mother's eye. Mrs. Whiting simply shrugged, frowning her response. In spite of Mrs. Astor's dislike for the family, Mr. and Mrs. Belmont were seated among the guests, along with Auggie Jr., escorted by his wife, Bessie, and Perry Belmont, the congressman, who appeared to be without a guest.

"Oliver's missing," she thought. *"Thank goodness for small favors."* His presence would surely add insult to injury, causing more stress than her nerves could bear.

Strains of the bridal march began to play, and the guests fell silent. An adorable flower girl dressed in white silk and layers of tulle stepped down the center aisle, draped off with a wide satin ribbon for the bridal party. Throwing fuchsia-pink rose petals over the white carpet runner, the bridesmaids, and ushers followed the child in the matrimonial procession.

Caroline "Carrie" Astor Wilson
Edith Newbold Jones Wharton

Finally, Carrie appeared, looking more lovely than Sara had ever seen her. Her gown was magnificent with a silver brocade bodice and acres of flowing train, delicately carried by an attending maiden. Carrie's face was covered by a veil that looked to be old point lace, held in place by gorgeous diamond stars and orange blossoms. She carried a bouquet of rare and costly orchids accented with lily-of-the-valley.

Watching her friend speak the vows of marriage, Sara quietly wept. Tears of joy mixed with tears of sadness, her emotions creating an abyss of dreams and hopes for her dear friend through the filter of her own experience. *"I wish you many, many years of happiness, Carrie,"* Sara prayed silently as she dabbed a handkerchief to her eye.

Five months later

April 29, 1885

New York, New York

Wedding bells would ring today for Edith and Teddy Wharton. Surprised to hear Edith was having only a small family wedding, Sara nonetheless shopped for a spectacular gift for her dear friend. As she browsed her way through Tiffany's, memories of the hopes and dreams they'd shared as young débutantes flitted through her mind like a folktale long repeated.

"It is made of the finest silver, as is the standard for every Tiffany tea set," the clerk said in a knowledgeable tenor.

"Of course," Sara agreed with a nod. "Have it wrapped and sent to the newlyweds." Reaching in her handbag, she handed the man a card. "Here's the address. Make sure it's sent today."

"Of course, ma'am. I'll see to it at once."

Five months later

September 25, 1885

Newport, Rhode Island

Stitch by stitch, Sara pulled the needle through her embroidery sampler, but her thoughts were elsewhere, to be sure.

"I don't even like sewing," she murmured, fighting with a knot in the silk thread. She grabbed her scissors and snipped off the offending strand.

Alone in the *Swanhurst* parlor, her only companion was the loud tick-tock of the mantle clock echoing through the room. Impatiently, Sara glanced at it, wishing it could be silenced.

"Time cannot be stopped," she mumbled while pulling the needle through the cotton fabric again and again.

"It's been nearly two years," she thought. *"Two years since my separation. Two years since I filed for divorce. Two years as a single mother and two years on the periphery of the set. I've been shamed by a man who slapped and tormented me, drunk and crazed by absinthe."* She reflected on her decision to divorce. *"What choice did I have but to leave the untenable situation behind? But how long will this penance continue while my youth slips away?"*

The sewing grew tedious. Frustrated, Sara pushed away the embroidery and rose from the wing-backed chair. The incessant sound of the clock was really getting on her nerves.

"Perhaps I *should* have gone with my family to the party at Atlantic House." She sighed, knowing full well she was not up to the challenge tonight. There seemed no point in going through the trouble of dressing only to sit with the old women and widows.

Her former acquaintances were usually in attendance with husbands and tales of children – and they all knew why she was without a husband or escort.

Each season, a new bevy of débutantes was introduced, and Sara began to feel much older than her twenty-four years. "I've been spending too much time in the company of the older women," Sara whispered. Which was one of the reasons she'd decided to skip tonight's party.

Besides, best to surrender herself to her fate. Tainted by scandal, it was clear no man wanted to be seen dancing with her. Well, no man her age. She thought back to the elderly men seeking her company, their breath foul with drink, their eyes barely veiling obscene preoccupations.

"Pretending I have a future will only set me up for more sadness," she silently decided. *"I can't compete with the new débutantes. And I don't belong with the old women."* Time to face up to the fact that regardless of her youth, she'd most probably spend the rest of her life alone.

The clock continued to mark the seconds, the loud tick-tock echoing over the parlor as she climbed the steps to her bedchamber, seeking escape from the maddening sound.

Chapter Three

One year later
October 28, 1886
New York, New York

Liberty was a right Americans had fought hard for in their new country, and the gift from France was a testament to this enduring dream for all countrymen. Sara and her family had ventured into Times Square to watch the parade and festivities celebrating the unveiling of the Statue of Liberty. With a glance at the morning skies, she saw they threatened rain on this chilly October day, and she tied her scarf snuggly around her neck for warmth.

"Let's try to get closer to the podium," Mrs. Whiting urged the family, pushing their way through the crowd of New Yorkers. "I want to hear the speeches."

The procession, led by the Commander-in-Chief himself, traveled down the street with much fanfare, urged on by the loud music of a marching band. A throng of citizens crowded the city streets waving flags in support, clamoring for a view of the stage. Police corralled people to the sidewalks while children, carried on the shoulders of their fathers, took in the scene from their high vantage points.

Reaching their destination, the parade paused so President Cleveland could address the public. Loud cheers rose from the crowd in a deafening roar of support. Pride pulsed through Sara as she listened to him commemorate the occasion from a platform erected near the bandstand.

"A stream of light shall pierce the darkness of ignorance and man's oppression until liberty enlightens the world..." President Cleveland's voice was dwarfed by the immense crowd as he delivered his pontification over New York.

"I read in the newspaper that the Statue of Liberty was designed by Frédéric Auguste Bartholdi," she thought to herself. *"Certainly, a testament to his artistic skill."*

After years of work and preparation, the statue had finally been completed and presented to the United States. The sculpture portrayed a woman who had been dubbed 'Lady Liberty.' Wearing regal robes, she held a torch high in one outstretched hand and a tablet in the other inscribed with the date July 4, 1776. Standing on a broken chain, the statue symbolized freedom for all Americans.

"This is quite a historical day," Mrs. Whiting noted. "I'm glad we decided to fight the crowd to witness it."

"Me too." Sara nodded. "I know the statue has been in the works for many years, but I heard the project ran out of money. It's said Mr. Pulitzer stepped in to raise funds for the pedestal, but even his efforts were stalled for a while in his attempt to gain support."

"I'm glad to see the committee was able to raise the cash they needed to complete the project," Milly said, her brunette hair blowing in the breeze.

Chanting from a group of suffragettes rose above the babble of the crowd. Turning, Sara saw they hoisted signs demanding 'Votes for Women' while congregating together near the bandstand. Working women joined ranks with well-dressed ladies, shouting above the din to be heard. The police moved in to subdue the disturbance, but the women only grew louder, more determined to gain notice for their cause.

"What's that all about?" Jane asked, narrowing her eyes with disapproval.

"I think it's over the procession to Bedloe's Island," Milly answered. "Apparently, only men are permitted to sail over for the final dedication and unveiling of the statue."

"You must be joking!" Sara said, angry at the thought of segregation.

"The organizers felt women could be hurt by the crush of the crowd." Milly informed her. "Only dignitaries are allowed on the island. I read it in the *World*."

"It appears the suffragettes are properly outraged by the decree," Sara said. "I almost feel like joining them myself. After all, the statue *is* of a woman!"

Jane turned to her with wide eyes. "I didn't know you were a feminist."

"I wasn't, but the older I get, the more I know. And the more I know, the more I agree with their cause!"

The speeches concluded, and the band started playing again, the loud music conquering the shouts from the suffragettes.

"Let's get back to the house," Mrs. Whiting instructed. "The best is over."

Weaving their way through the bystanders, the family escaped the noise and fanfare of the parade just as the President headed down Fifth Avenue for the port at Battery Park.

⚜

Three months later
January 31, 1887
New York, New York

Leaning back in the plush chair, Raymond wished Oliver was there to join them for dinner. His older brother was otherwise occupied tonight, so Raymond had invited his friend, Jim Tremont, visiting from Boston, to meet for a meal.

Small in stature, the twenty-three-year-old Raymond had made a name for himself in the usual amusements of a young gentleman; namely, polo and sharpshooting, of which he was an expert. Like Oliver, the brown-haired youth's small build gave him a fawn-like appearance that he fought to dispel by indulging in women and wild behavior, which usually included large quantities of liquor.

The Knickerbocker Club was a favorite meeting place for the Belmont brothers, and a club Jim enjoyed as well.

"Let's stay behind and enjoy a cigar, and perhaps a few more cocktails," Raymond suggested.

"That sounds good," Jim agreed. "Most of the dinner crowd has made their way home for the evening."

The two men talked of frivolous matters as they finished their drinks. The hour grew late, and the building, emptied of dinner guests, now grew quiet. With a final swallow, Raymond finished his scotch, giving a quick glance at his watch. Midnight.

"I suppose it's time to call it a night," he said to Jim. Rising from his dining chair, he pushed away from the table. "I'm glad we had a chance to meet while you're here in New York."

"Me, as well." Jim nodded, standing beside Raymond. Tall and stocky, Jim towered over Raymond, the two men creating a picture of opposite physiques. "Maybe we can get together for some target shooting later in the week?"

"I would enjoy that," Raymond readily agreed.

"I hear you're friends with Buffalo Bill. He seems like a fun chap."

"He is, indeed." Raymond smiled. "Oliver and I are going to Nebraska to visit him at his ranch at the end of February. I'm looking forward to it."

"Sounds like a great adventure," Jim said as the two men walked out into the dark New York street. "Well, my hotel is down this way." He pointed in the opposite direction of the Belmont home. "Send a note, and we'll practice up on our sharp shooting."

"Until then," Raymond replied. He stumbled on the curb and released a drunken laugh, regaining his balance. "Ah, I do enjoy the effect of good scotch."

"Are you okay to find your way home? Do you want me to hail a cab?"

"Perhaps we should," Raymond agreed.

The two men waved down a passing taxi and jumped inside for the short ride. After dropping Jim off at his hotel, the cab delivered Raymond to the Belmont mansion. Whistling a happy tune, which suited his carefree mood, Raymond climbed the steps to the entrance and rang the bell, as he never carried a key. The shadow of a man loomed into view through the small window beside the carved front door.

"Hello, Mr. Baehr," Raymond greeted the uniformed man. The watchman was employed by his father for added nighttime protection against burglars and the growing number of hoodlums prowling the New York night.

"Hello, Mr. Belmont," the watchman replied, his bushy mustache wiggling as he spoke. "Had too much to drink tonight?"

"No, no. Of course not!" Raymond chuckled. "I believe I've had just enough to drink."

"Of course." Mr. Baehr shook his head in agreement, making no argument. He was well aware of the young man's penchant for liquor.

"In fact, I feel wonderful." Raymond winked. "It's much too early to go to sleep, don't you think? Why not join me in the cellar for some target practice?"

"If you wish, but only for a minute or two. Then I've got to get back to my duties."

The watchman lumbered after Raymond, his heavy boots following as the younger man led the way to the back of the house. Nearing his fiftieth birthday, the guard had little interest in shooting at this time of night, but felt obliged to comply, regardless.

"I'm an expert marksman," Raymond bragged as they entered the basement. Rummaging through a shelf in the laundry room, he pulled out the .32 caliber pistol he kept hidden there specifically for the purpose of target practice. Cracking the gun open, he inspected it for ammunition.

"The pistol is ready to shoot," Raymond said, giving the watchman a cocky grin. "I'm certain I can hit the smallest target from across the room." Raymond pulled a pearl-stud pin from his shirt and held it up for the night watchman. "Do you have good nerve?" Not waiting for an answer, Raymond continued. "Stand over there." He motioned to the far side of the basement. "And hold this pearl between your fingers so I can demonstrate my expertise."

Raising a gray eyebrow in objection, Mr. Baehr took the stud from Raymond while shaking his head to the contrary. "I'm certain you're an expert marksman, but I rather like my fingers, Mr. Belmont." Walking to the coal bin, the man inserted the pin into a wooden board. Turning back, he caught Raymond staring down the barrel of the pistol as though it were a toy. Rumors had been flying regarding the young man's penchant for testing fate in this way. Now, the watchman saw for himself the gossip was true.

Focusing on the target, Raymond cocked his gun, then stopped. "Be a good sport and close the cellar door, will you? It's drafty. Besides, I don't want the noise to wake the family."

"Of course, sir," Baehr replied. Doing as requested, he reached the top of the stairwell and pulled the door closed as the deafening boom of a gunshot reverberated through the basement.

Rushing back down the stairs, he stumbled in his haste to return to the cellar. With a jolt of horror, the watchman found Raymond slumped in a chair, blood gushing from a hole in the right side of his head. The gory sight of Raymond's splattered brains made the man gag, but he quickly regained his composure. Running to the main floor, he collided with a family servant, roused by the noise.

"Get a doctor, quickly, man!" Mr. Baehr shouted. "There's been an accident." Although he felt Raymond was already dead, he knew a doctor was needed to make the final proclamation.

"Yes, at once!" The bleary-eyed servant grabbed a coat from a nearby closet and disappeared out the front door to summon the physician.

"What's happened?" A second servant appeared in the foyer wearing a nightcap and brown chenille robe.

"Wake Mr. Belmont!" Baehr ordered. "There's been a horrible accident. Tell him to come at once."

The man rushed to the second floor, leaving Baehr alone again. Turning, he wiped the sweat from his forehead with his shirtsleeve, repulsed at the thought of returning to the horrific scene that waited in the cold basement.

Chapter Four

Eight months later
September 5, 1887
Newport, Rhode, Island

"Birthdays are so much fun!" Natica exclaimed, tearing the colorful tissue paper from the gift. "Oh, Grandma, she's so pretty!" In awe, she lifted the porcelain doll from the box.

"Not any more beautiful than you, little girl." Mrs. Whiting laughed as she hugged her granddaughter. "Happy Birthday!"

"Look, Mommy," Natica said, holding the doll.

Sara picked up her four-year-old daughter and gave her a big hug over layers of petticoats that fluffed her pinafore. Long brunette spirals fell to the little girl's shoulders, tied back with a pink ribbon. Her brown eyes were wide with excitement for her birthday party.

"You are getting so big, so fast!" Sara said, returning Natica to the carpeted floor.

"And quite the little lady, too," Milly added proudly.

"Aunt Milly and I bought you another gift," Jane said, handing her a dress box wrapped with pink calico fabric.

"Remember your manners," Sara prompted.

"Thank you," Natica said. Taking the gift from Jane, Sara helped her daughter untie the ribbon as the youngster eagerly opened the package. Pushing aside the tissue paper with tiny fingers, she revealed a gorgeous white tulle dress. Dainty pink flowers accented the bodice and floated over the lacy skirt.

"A princess dress!" Natica's face lit up. Sara helped her lift the garment from the box and held it up for her to view.

"Do you notice anything special about the dress?" Milly asked, eyes dancing with surprise.

The little girl gave her aunt a questioning glance, while Jane lifted the doll, holding it up beside the new outfit.

"Oh!" Natica gasped. "My dress matches my dolly's! We can be like sisters!" She took the doll from Jane with a gleeful smile.

Mrs. Whiting laughed with pleasure, watching the obvious joy on her young granddaughter's face. It was wonderful to see the family happy again.

"Can I put on my new dress, Mother?"

"Of course, you can. It can be your party dress." Sara agreed, glad for this cheerful scene that had been so long in coming.

The divorce from Oliver had taken almost a full year, and even though a generous monetary settlement had been worked out, the most important thing was that Sara had retained full custody of their daughter.

The Belmonts had responded by continuing to deny Oliver's daughter any connection to their family bloodline, ignoring the fact that she bore his surname and an uncanny resemblance to her father. In essence, the Belmonts had divorced themselves not only from Sara and the Whiting family but also from Natica, born as a result of the short marriage to Oliver. Sara had been deeply offended by this denial, but after a few years she'd actually seen it as an irrefutable way to prevent Oliver from calling to see Natica. *"He certainly can't demand visitation if he claims he's not her father,"* she thought.

Sara tried not to dwell on the fallout from the scandal that overshadowed her life. Even though it had been three years, sometimes things still got a bit catty among the women of the set. Divorce continued to be frowned upon, and left with a child to raise, Sara often found herself an outsider to many of society's events in spite of Mrs. Astor's promise of inclusion.

On the other hand, the Belmont brothers had developed quite a notorious reputation as audacious playboys, but no one really cared much. It was a fact Sara had learned years ago. *"Men can get away with a lot more impropriety than women and emerge unscathed."* 'Boys will be boys' was the common sentiment, and most folks turned a blind eye to their escapades. Besides, with their wealth, the Belmonts could buy public opinion if they so desired. And in the end, they had succeeded in doing just that.

Divorce from the Belmonts had almost become welcome when, in February, they'd all been shocked to read in the *New York Times* that Raymond, the youngest of the sons, had come to an untimely death.

"Raymond seemed preoccupied with the afterlife," Sara mused, "not to mention his penchant for taking unnecessary risks." She reflected how he'd often been seen drunk – and even passed out in the city streets, frequently carrying a firearm of one sort or another. In the end, it had been the gun that killed him. No one was sure if it was accidental or if he'd chosen to meet his demise from some macabre sense of adventure.

The papers said the funeral had been a large and somber affair, with the Belmont family insisting on privacy. *"Raymond's death came as a frightening reminder of the unpredictable moods I'd been forced to endure while married to Oliver."* Though she was sympathetic toward the family, Sara was glad to wash her hands of the drama that constantly surrounded them.

Watching her young daughter play with the new baby doll, Sara noted the little girl's deep brown eyes, an unmistakable cloning of her father's features. *"The Belmont bloodline will always be connected to us by this child,"* she thought. *"Even if they don't acknowledge Natica as one of their own."*

"There. You look beautiful," Jane said, as she finished tying the bow on Natica's new dress.

"You and your doll are a perfect match." Mrs. Whiting smiled.

"You look like a little doll yourself!" Milly cooed.

"I'm going to name my doll 'Annie'," Natica announced to the family.

A chuckle escaped Mrs. Whiting. "Why don't you and little Annie go play while we get your birthday cake ready."

"Remember, you've got to make a wish when you blow out the candles." Jane advised her niece.

"A very special birthday wish," Milly added, enjoying the fun.

"Okay," Natica murmured, much too interested in 'Annie'.

Carrying the doll over to the parlor room window, Natica talked to her all the while like a little mother. Standing the doll on the windowsill, she seemed to be showing her the *Swanhurst* grounds and instructing her on the ways of propriety.

"I think she's practicing to be a débutante. She's such a little miss." Jane declared, a warm smile dispersing her usual stern expression.

"And you are quite the doting aunt!" Sara laughed, happy to see her sister enjoying herself for a change.

Ever since Natica was born, Jane had been much happier. The baby seemed to fill an unspoken maternal need that had been buried deep inside her sister. Or, more succinctly, had been misdirected at Sara, especially in her younger years. Now, with Natica around, Jane was much too preoccupied with the child to be bothered with any of Sara's dilemmas, much to her relief.

Mary carried a tray in from the kitchen loaded with plates and silverware. Her plump figure was covered with a floral-print apron as she moved on a sure foot, heading for the dining room. Bridget trailed her carrying small candles for the cake, napkins, and glasses. Placing the items on the dining room table, the two servants busied themselves getting things ready for the family celebration.

A giggle arose from Natica, still playing near the window. "Mother, who is that man? He just keeps looking at me," she said innocently, breaking into new laughter. "He's making funny faces at me."

Mrs. Whiting hurried to the window and pulled the curtain aside. Sara stepped up behind her and quietly gasped. A figure was lurking under the evening shadows of a beech tree by Webster Street. It didn't take long for Sara or her mother to realize that it was Oliver's short silhouette. He was obviously stalking the house – and they both knew the reason why.

Natica.

Sensing that something had gone awry, Jane and Milly came to look through the window with the others. Oliver's intrusion on the birthday party caused a bitter mood to descend upon the room, quelling their happiness by his very presence.

"Come into the dining room, dear." Jane ushered the child away from the window.

"It's almost time for you to blow out your birthday candles. Have you decided on your wish?" Milly helped escort Natica toward the cake table, hoping it would distract the child.

A scowl covered Mrs. Whiting's face, pale with anger. "For all his insistence that she is not his daughter," she seethed, "he certainly seems to know what day it is!"

Much too indignant to speak, Sara could only stare through the glass, anger sparking from her eyes. The audacity of that man to come snooping around their estate like a common thief! His lack of manners knew no boundaries.

"I should go out there and give him a piece of my mind!" Mrs. Whiting growled. "Or better yet, let's send for the police and have him arrested for trespassing. That will teach him a lesson."

"He's leaving," Sara told her, watching Oliver's shadow disappear into the encroaching night. "I think he knows he's been spotted."

"Arrogant fool!" Mrs. Whiting spat. "How dare he show his face here!"

"Enough, Mother. He's gone." Sara turned from the window. "I don't want to upset Natica on her birthday. Forget about Oliver. Let's just have cake as if nothing has happened. I don't want to give him the satisfaction of ruining our party."

Pausing to collect herself, Mrs. Whiting worked to dismiss her foul mood. She released a huff, then offered Sara a resolute smile. "You're absolutely right." Regaining her composure, she waved her hand toward the dining room as if leading the way.

"After you."

The next day
September 6, 1887
Newport, Rhode Island

"How have you been coping with your wife's death? Is your son okay?" Sara handed George a glass of scotch. She noticed worry burrowing new lines in his face, his blond hair and mustache showing tale-tell signs of gray from his recent hardship.

It had been almost six months since Kaye Rives had succumbed to pneumonia in the spring. Frequently ill, Mrs. Rives was of a weak constitution. Although dismayed by the news of her death at such a young age, it really came as no surprise to Sara.

"He is handling it the best that he can," George replied, offering an ineffectual smile. "His aunt has been a great help, but it's no substitute for his own mother."

"The pain of her death will diminish with time."

"I know. I know..." He rubbed his forehead as if to erase the awful reality from his life. "At least that's what I've been told. But Junior seems just as lost as I am without her. Maybe even more so, as I'm frequently away traveling on business."

"Try to remember George, he will be a young man soon." Sara counseled. "Junior will marry and have children of his own before long. The loss of his mother will be replaced by concerns for raising his own family."

"That day cannot come quickly enough for me. I'm exhausted from trying to cope with life in her absence."

Sara's heart ached to see her friend in such despair. She searched for words of comfort, knowing deep inside her soul there was no escaping the finality of death.

"I wish I could do more," she said helplessly.

"It helps just being here with you. There aren't many people willing to talk about such an unfortunate affair."

"You're welcome here at *Swanhurst* anytime you want to talk. Or not talk. I'm here to help in any way that I can."

"Thank you, Sara. After all you've suffered at the hands of Oliver, I feel as though you understand what I'm going through in some small way."

"Divorce is a far cry from losing a spouse to illness."

"It's a loss, nonetheless." He grew quiet, then reached over, boldly taking her hand. The parlor grew silent, and after a moment George spoke in a soft tone. "Do you remember the afternoon in my apartment?"

Taken aback, she whispered, "That was a long time ago." So long, she thought, it seemed like a dream.

"I know. And much has happened since then," he said gently, his blue eyes meeting hers. "Yet, I've never forgotten those stolen moments, alone together."

Sara wondered why he was bringing up this incident from their past. "You're grieving George. Please, give yourself some time to get over your loss."

"Grieving or not, you must know how fond I am of you." His words were insistent. Still holding her hand, he searched her eyes. "I can only hope you share my sentiment."

Trepidation mixed with hope, churning like a riptide inside Sara. "It's too soon to speak of such things, George. You'll be in mourning for at least the remainder of the year. Perhaps then we can talk more freely about such sentiments."

Considering her words, George gave her a steadfast look. "I suppose you're right. But it does help to know that you're open to such a discussion in the future."

With sudden realization, Sara became cognizant that she was indeed up to a conversation about a future with him. It occurred to her that they could be the answer to each other's marital woes.

"I should be getting on my way," he said, rising from the chair. "I've taken up enough of your time."

She walked with him through the foyer and politely opened the front door.

"Do you mind if I call again?"

"Not at all. But I must remind you, it takes time to get over such a loss. Not to mention the propriety of such a situation."

"I appreciate your concerns." He placed his bowler hat on his head with a practiced hand.

But Sara couldn't help feel a bit enchanted as he raised her hand to his lips and gave her palm a gentle kiss, his mustache brushing against her skin. He paused, allowing her a sincere look, then quietly turned and walked down the porch steps to his waiting carriage.

George Lockhart Rives

Chapter Five

Three days later
September 9, 1887
Middletown, Rhode Island

Oliver fell into stride beside William as they ambled through the open field. The crisp morning air whispered of autumn, ripe with a smell of fresh cut hay that tickled his nose. Goldenrod rustled in the gentle wind next to wild purple asters and Queen Anne's lace, serenely dotting the pasture far into the horizon.

"I'm really glad I sold Oakland to your uncle last year. Gray Craig is much more suited for an equestrian center. And I've got my eye on a few new horses I'd like to add to my collection."

"It could use a nice house," William noted as he gazed across the estate. Tall and lean, William's clean-shaven face was handsome, his hair blown awry by the wind. "A large cottage would be great. Imagine the parties we could have out here."

Laughing, Oliver nodded his agreement, his short stature boosted by his braggadocio. "We could fit all of Newport and New York on this property. But seriously, it was a great idea for us to join together to purchase this land for a nature preserve. The way they're building things up along the beach, it's only a matter of time before everything is bought up."

William Kissam Vanderbilt (top)
Oliver Hazard Perry Belmont

"All it takes is money."

"Money certainly helps. That, and a little imagination," Oliver added. "Perhaps we should start a club of sorts and invite others to join in the fun – all in the name of preservation, of course. Along those lines, I'm thinking of expanding my interest in animals beyond horses."

"Oh?"

"I'm considering taking a trip to Africa or maybe India," Oliver told Willie. "And bringing some exotic animals back with me. You should come along. We could start a type of zoo. One where the animals can roam free in large pastures resembling their natural habitat." He let out a laugh. "Can you imagine the entertainment we could provide for the set?"

"You get more eccentric with each passing day." William chuckled, his eyes shining in amusement. "But I must admit, you've piqued my interest. Have you considered what you'd do with the animals in the wintertime? Exotic creatures usually enjoy a more temperate climate than Rhode Island can provide."

"Oh, I don't know..." Oliver's voice drifted as he glanced around the seventy-seven acres of the Gray Craig property. He could see Nelson Pond, and in the distance, the Atlantic Ocean. "You make a good point. I suppose we'd have to go about constructing a few buildings to house them. They'd freeze in the cold, which would not be a good thing."

William let out a laugh. "No. That would not be good. I can hear the women sobbing now."

"I'm sure you'd be able to comfort them." Oliver wiggled his eyebrows and laughed. "If you know what I mean." The two continued their stroll toward the barn.

"Hmmm... I'm liking this idea more and more." William winked while following his friend into the stable.

_____

Six months later
March 14, 1888
New York, New York

Winter had hit with strong force this year, delivering one storm after another. With spring a few weeks away, many had hoped for an early break in the weather, only to be disappointed by another bad turn. Snow had been falling since after midnight the previous day, and still, it showed no sign of slowing down. Sara pulled her shawl tighter from the cold while watching Owen haul in another load of firewood, his arms strong from many chores.

"I want to get as many logs in here as possible to dry," he said, placing the wood in a pile near the fireplace. "If this storm continues, the snow is going to bury our wood supply in the drifts. I'll stack some into the basement, as well."

"How much coal do we have?" Sara asked the houseman.

"We had a full load delivered last week, so we have plenty to keep the furnace going for the month."

"Thank goodness for that much," Sara replied, fighting off a shiver.

Joining them in the parlor of their New York home, Mrs. Whiting made a beeline for the window. Her hair was hidden by a dark blue day cap, her arms buried under layers of wool sweaters. "In all my days, I have never seen such a blizzard," she said, viewing the snow covered landscape. "It's like a great white hurricane."

A knock at the front door brought Mary hurrying from the kitchen. Jane and Milly came into the parlor, along with Bridget, who was tending after Natica.

"Mommy, can I go sled riding?" the youngster asked eagerly, tugging at her skirts.

"Maybe another day – it's much too fierce outside for you now."

Voices carried from the hall as Mary brought their caller into the sitting room. "An officer has come about the storm," she announced.

"Mrs. Whiting." The policeman nodded to the family members as he removed his hat. The officer's blue uniform coat was dusted with snowflakes, as were his mutton-chop sideburns. "Mr. Rives asked me to check on your family and see how you're faring through the blizzard."

"That was very considerate of him," Mrs. Whiting said.

"Yes, very thoughtful," Sara agreed. "We've got firewood and coal to last a while," she briefed the officer.

"And thank heavens the pantry is full," Mary added, entirely in charge of the kitchen inventory. "We probably have enough food for a week, maybe longer. Although I think we'll be eating a lot of noodles and rice if the meat runs out."

"Is there any word when the storm will let up?" Mrs. Whiting asked, anxious for news.

"No, ma'am," the officer replied. "I expect it will last the rest of today, although it could be longer."

"The weather was so warm before this hit," Sara commented. "I thought perhaps springtime would make an early appearance this year."

"The Central Park Observatory is currently recording temperatures of six degrees." The policeman informed them in an even voice. "We have a state of emergency on our hands. The government is mobilized, but there isn't much they can do. The snow is already reported to have accumulated over eighteen inches, and the drifts are blowing up to thirty feet in some places. Some of the smaller homes are completely covered, with people trapped inside."

"How terrible," Sara sympathized, concern etching her face.

"With snow that deep, it's got to be causing problems for travel," Mrs. Whiting noted.

A strong gust of wind shook the entire house, the windows, and doors groaning from the blast. Natica's eyes grew wide in fear, and she snuggled closer to her mother for safety, burying her face in the folds of Sara's gown.

"Indeed, it has," the officer agreed. "The railroads are shut down completely, and the telegraph system is also disabled. Even the stock exchange has closed. It seems the entire eastern seaboard is paralyzed by the storm." The family circled the public official to better hear the news of the blizzard. "You should know that fire response is impossible as the hose cars can't get through the streets. There are quite a few fires burning out of control around the city, so please be extra careful."

"We will," Sara told him. "Thank you for the report."

Replacing his cap, the officer headed to the foyer. "I'll let Mr. Rives know you're all safe," he said. "And I'll check in with you tomorrow, if possible."

"We appreciate that very much," Mrs. Whiting thanked him.

A quiet fell in the sitting room as Mary showed the policeman out. Sara returned to the sofa, pulling Natica onto her lap. Her sisters took seats, as did Mrs. Whiting, while the house rattled from the ferocious blizzard raging outside. No one spoke. Lost in thought, they each contemplated the seriousness of the situation.

Raising his tall figure to full height, Owen broke the silence. "I'm going to see how much kerosene we have," he said, pulling his hat on tight.

Looking up, Mrs. Whiting gave him a cheerless smile. "Thank you, Owen. I don't know where we'd be without you."

⚓ ⚓

Two months later
May 13, 1888
Atlantic Ocean

The bitter cold of winter had fought the shift of seasons, refusing to release its power over New Yorkers. But spring had inevitably won the battle in a vibrant burst of blossoms and blooms. Society was slow to resume its routines, as the harsh blizzard had brought many deaths and lasting damage to the city. Telegraph lines, downed by the snow, were now buried underground to prevent a future loss to communications in the event of another natural disaster.

The days grew longer, and springtime grew into summer. The brutal storms of winter were soon lost in the memories of the set, now focused on the activities of the social season. The ranks among the *nouveau riche* had swelled in number with the advent of new inventions and industrial growth. Seeking acceptance among the established families, the newcomers joined the yearly pilgrimage to Newport with aspirations of being accepted into the higher ranks of society.

But the old guard quickly tired of the crowds and sought new entertainment in other locales, including Tuxedo Park, the Adirondacks, and Europe. Such was the case with William and Alva Vanderbilt, who'd invited four guests to sail with them to the Mediterranean aboard their personal yacht.

The Vanderbilt's luxury liner, *The Alva,* was arguably one of the finest private ships ever built. William had commissioned the ship, named as an homage to his wife, in 1886. Complete with a modern steel hull, saloon, and elegant staterooms, the yacht was over two hundred and eighty feet long and more than thirty feet wide, requiring a captain and crew of fifty-two men to operate the vessel and tend to the comfort of the guests.

The Vanderbilts were wonderful hosts, treating their fortunate companions to fabulous meals prepared by a personal chef while enjoying the pleasure of card games and other amusements as the yacht sailed across the Atlantic to their destination.

Peering through the porthole of her elegant stateroom, Alva decided to take a stroll outside, yearning for a breath of fresh air and a breeze on her face. Assessing her appearance in the large mirror, she placed a stylish straw bonnet over her hair, the brim adorned with a plethora of silk blossoms, and firmly tied the rose-colored ribbon under her plump chin. Smoothing her pink linen gown, she grabbed the matching cloak and left her room, headed topside. Rounding the starboard deck, she noticed a few bathing chairs. Stepping nearer, she saw only one chair was occupied.

"Why are you sitting out here all alone?" Alva surveyed Oliver lounging lazily with a magazine. A close friend of Willie's, he'd been invited to join them for the year-long cruise. "The party is in full swing below."

Oliver raised his round eyes to meet hers. "I could ask you the same question."

"William was beginning to bore me. That always happens when we're together too long."

"Is that why you spend so much time with Mr. Hunt?" Oliver asked, a mischievous lilt in his tone evident as he referred to the architect. "Does his wife mind?"

"Of course not," Alva said, releasing an unbridled laugh. "Our relationship is strictly business. You shouldn't believe all the rumors you hear. You, of all people, should know that, Oliver."

"It's not a rumor, it's a fact. Your house on Fifth Avenue is a testament to your partnership. Besides, you know I never spread gossip," he quipped.

"Well, in all honesty, I do enjoy Mr. Hunt's company, regardless of his wife's concerns. I suppose that's why I've decided to have him design me another cottage in Newport. It helps to enjoy one's architect when undertaking such a tremendous feat."

"I'm certain that's an important consideration, aside from talent."

The ship rocked from a rogue wave under a sky of gathering dark clouds.

"Do you mind if I join you?" Alva asked. Uncharacteristically demure, she eyed the lounger beside him.

"It's your yacht, Alva, you can do as you wish."

"Only if my company is welcomed. I don't want to make my guests uncomfortable."

"I don't believe that's possible." He laughed. "You must know you're the belle of every ball – or cruise, in this case."

"You certainly know how to charm a woman, Oliver," she said, settling into the deck chair beside him. "I wish you'd give my husband a few lessons."

"Trouble in paradise?"

She just rolled her eyes.

"Unfortunately, I must remind you about my lack of expertise when it comes to matters of matrimony." He attempted some humor in regard to his short-lived marriage to Sara.

"I'm more concerned about *extramarital* protocol," Alva said with chagrin. She paused, then decided to confide in him. "Ah Oliver, it's no secret that every young débutante that crosses William's path enchants him. I'm not that naïve – nor am I blind. Perhaps I'm at fault. Maybe I've busied myself too much with being a mother at the cost of poorly fulfilling my duties as a wife." She gazed absently at the low, gray clouds. "And if the truth be told, I suppose I've been preoccupied with gaining the Vanderbilts their rightful place among society. *Nouveau riche* indeed! Although I've succeeded in my efforts, what good will it do me if my marriage falls apart?"

"Of course, you're aware that Willie is my best friend, and I won't speak ill of him," Oliver gently admonished. "But it does make me sad to hear of troubles between the two of you. Where is he now?"

"He's in the middle of a high-stakes poker game with the other gentlemen."

"He doesn't seem to mind our spending time together."

"Why should he!" She grinned coyly. "We're only two friends keeping each other company." An idea struck her, and Alva perked up. "You must join me at the racetrack one day. It's a lot more fun enjoying the spoils when you have someone to share it with. Willie is always too busy to come along, although he seems to have time for the sport when I'm not around."

"Horse racing is a wonderful pastime," Oliver said, turning to her. "I'd enjoy spending time at the track with you. But I don't have to tell you our association may create a few rumors."

"Oh, let them say what they will." Alva shrugged indifferently. "I enjoy your company, and I won't apologize for it. But I should confess, I hope the rumors will make Willie just a teeny bit jealous." Her lips turned up in a smile. "Regardless, you must join me at the track."

"Should I be offended by your ulterior motives?"

"Only if they work!" Alva scoffed. "I suspect Willie likes you too much as a friend to turn on you. Or else he dislikes me enough as a wife to ignore our friendship."

"Come now, Alva. Give yourself more credit." Oliver could read the dismay on her face and decided to change the subject. "I'm thinking of devoting my career to horse racing. Maybe I'll build a new house with a stable, like the Nursery my father built in Long Island."

"Horses are a valuable commodity, and racing can prove lucrative."

"Indeed." He nodded. "Perhaps I should speak to Mr. Hunt about designing *me* a new home – maybe I can find a nice building lot on
Bellevue."

An enormous wave descended on the boat, causing it to pitch dangerously to the side, interrupting their conversation.

"Looks like a storm is blowing in." Alva grabbed ahold of her lounger, sliding precariously with the boat. "Maybe we should go below deck."

Oliver agreed, rising from his chair. Another swell forced him to grip the boat rail for balance. "Let me help you." He took her hand, carefully leading her inside, when suddenly the boat slammed into another wave. The force knocked Alva into Oliver's arms. Their eyes locked, and the two exchanged a lengthy look of palpable desire.

Chapter Six

That same day
May 13, 1888
Newport, Rhode Island

The Newport papers printed daily announcements of new guests arriving from surrounding cities for a holiday. As the season progressed, the weather grew delightful,
reminding the crowds why they'd made the sojourn to Rhode Island in the first place.

"I can't help but reminisce about our débutante days," Edith murmured. Strolling
across the yard, her cotton-lace gown cascaded in layers of fabric around her slim figure.
"Little did we know then how simple and wonderful life was."

"I know what you mean. Our only concern was to become wives." Sara agreed, happy
for her friend's visit to *Swanhurst*. "But to what end? To live our lives in the shadow of our
husbands? Looking back, it hardly seems worth the effort we invested." The two walked
leisurely across the grounds and settled on a bench under the old copper beech tree.

"I've got to tell you, Sara, in some ways I envy you."

"Surely, you're joking! I was a divorcée at age twenty-two and left with a child as a
constant reminder of my failure at marriage. Hardly
enviable."

"You shouldn't think of it as a failure," Edith admonished. "You should think of it as
correcting an error. Look at me... After my engagement to Henry Stevens was broken,
my mother pushed me right into this marriage with Teddy Wharton. She didn't care
that there was little fondness between us. The marriage was a matter of convenience and

social propriety. It's brought me nothing but indifference. I would be much happier to be unmarried than burdened with a loveless marriage."

"I'm sorry you're unhappy, Edith. But at least you're still a welcomed member of society."

"Society is a bother." Edith scowled. Brushing a wisp of hair under her half-bonnet, her eyes took on a distant look. "Sometimes I dream of finding a place to disappear from society entirely – but I doubt if such a place exists. Instead, I concentrate on my writing in spite of the criticism it brings me. Women are supposed to foster children, not books, you know."

"You wouldn't condemn society so much if you were on the outside looking in. I try to downplay all the balls and parties I'm not invited to as inconsequential, but it really does hurt my feelings. For over five years now I've shared the Belmont name but none of its privileges. It appears that an unmarried woman has no place in our modern society."

A warm breeze blew across the lawn, billowing her gauze skirt in its wake.

"Sara, you remain a welcome guest throughout the Four Hundred. You're a private member of the Casino Club and the Coaching Club," Edith reminded her. "And if someone is rude enough to omit you from their guest list, I should think it a party you wouldn't want to attend anyway."

"Perhaps... But Carrie is too busy for me anymore. I never see Anita, and who knows what's happened to Elizabeth."

"I don't think that has as much to do with your place in society as it does with us just growing up and growing apart. I rarely see them myself, although that's probably due to the hours I spend on my writing. Not to mention traveling back and forth to Europe."

"I suppose you're right." Pausing, Sara continued by changing the subject. "Any hopes of having your new works published?"

"As a matter of fact, there is. I'm working on a book of interior design with Ogden Codman, Jr., but we won't be ready to publish for a while. It's an extensive work with lots of photographs. In the meantime, I've finished several stories for *Scribner's Magazine*."

"I look forward to reading them."

"The publisher still wants me to use a man's name for a pseudonym." Edith's expression turned defiant. "And I still refuse! Why should I pretend to be a man for the sake of upholding some ludicrous patriarchal tradition? Men act as if women have no minds, no intelligence, and no view on matters of the world. It's absolutely ridiculous."

"I couldn't agree more. It irks me the way Oliver's moved on from our divorce unaffected by the scandal. He actually refers to himself as a *bachelor*! Divorcé and father is more apropos. And he's always throwing parties or picnics, trying to impress everyone with his wealth. Worst of all, it appears he's been very successful in his efforts. There's no question a double standard exists between the sexes."

"For all our complaining about men, I suppose life would be dull without them." Leaning toward her, Edith asked, "Have you given any thought to finding a new husband? I know things haven't gone well, but you're much too young to give up on love, Sara."

"I do daydream about it occasionally," Sara admitted. "I find myself wondering how my life would be if things had gone right. But honestly, I don't think I have the heart for romance anymore."

"Perhaps you should try harder." Edith grinned. Meeting Sara's glance, her eyes were insistent. "Put your mind to it with more effort."

"You make it sound so easy."

"And you make it too complicated. Love can heal a broken heart." Edith chuckled, "That's my prescription, Sara. A new husband."

"Okay, doctor."

The ladies erupted into laughter, their peals rippling over the lawn. Looking up, they caught sight of Natica running down the porch steps. The two watched as the little girl scampered toward them across the grass and threw herself into Sara's arms.

"Are you up from your nap?"

"Yes. Grandma said I should come and call you to lunch."

"You remember my friend Edith." Sara introduced her with a nod.

The little girl curtsied clumsily. "Hello, Mrs. Edith."

"Well, hello Natica." Edith smiled at the youngster's whimsy. "You're getting to be such a grown-up little lady."

Natica smiled shyly. "Grandma says you should stay and have lunch with us."

Edith was obviously delighted with the invitation. "Well, if your grandmother insists, then how can I refuse?"

Tugging at Sara's hand, Natica pulled her up from the chair, with Edith following suit. "Perhaps you can show me the way to the dining room?" Edith cajoled.

"Of course," Natica said and proudly led the way to the house.

———

One month later
June 15, 1888
Newport, Rhode Island

"I'm so glad you agreed to join me for tonight's ball. I think you're spending too much time alone at *Swanhurst*," George admonished. Looking dapper in his evening suit, he held her hand under white dinner gloves. Beard and mustache neatly trimmed, George was self-assured and handsome in a stately way. "You need to get out more often."

"I must admit, I was grateful for your invitation," Sara confided. Giving special attention to her appearance tonight, she'd worn her newest, most fabulous Worth gown, newly arrived from Paris. Layers of silk and lace fell around her figure in flounces, the bodice accented with seed-pearls that exposed ample décolletage. Bridget had finished her hair in a new up-do style of curls that she found quite pleasing. "But I think it's a little unseemly for a divorced woman to attend a ball unescorted, so I've stayed away."

"Obviously, you haven't tried to get an escort," George noted, assessing her elegant gown. "A woman of your beauty and talent would easily find a companion if you had a mind to, regardless of your divorce."

The music ended, and he took her hand, leading her off the dance floor. "You certainly have sustained your flair for the waltz, but I never hear you sing anymore, Sara. Have you given up on your music?"

"No, not at all," she said. "But I don't sing for others too much these days, just at home for my own enjoyment." The orchestra began the strains of a new song, and a fresh group of dancers replaced them on the floor.

"Well, perhaps I could persuade you to enchant me with a melody one day soon." George led her toward the door to the wraparound porch. "Shall we get some fresh air?"

"Yes. It's gotten quite warm in here."

She followed him outside, where the crowd had thinned. Sara liked Ocean House. It was a popular hotel in the middle of town that hosted many of society's events, including frequent fancy dances throughout the summer. When she'd received the note from George requesting she join him for the ball this evening, Sara had gladly accepted his invitation.

They strolled around the porch into the evening shadows, where they interrupted two young lovers stealing a moment alone. Although it was a sweet scene of innocence, Sara had to resist an overwhelming urge to warn the young woman about the follies of losing herself to marriage. But she knew her words would fall on deaf ears, just as sure as summer follows spring. Besides, who was she to give advice? In spite of being a single mother, if she were honest with herself, she often yearned for a companion. There was no doubt that life was more challenging when faced alone, yet prospects for a woman like herself were few, which made tonight's outing with George all the more enjoyable.

George sat on the porch swing and motioned for Sara to join him. She daintily gathered her skirts and accepted the seat close beside him. Breathing deeply, she took in the evening air scented by the trellis roses and honeysuckle curling and twisting around the porch balustrades. The pitch-black sky above Newport revealed a glittering expanse of stars that seemed to sparkle specifically for their pleasure.

"I'm glad for this quiet moment," George confided. "I've been so busy lately in Washington, I was beginning to think I'd miss the entire summer working." He glanced at her cautiously. "I must confess, I hoped to get you all to myself for an evening. I was afraid some of the wealthier widowers would be occupying your time."

A skeptical laugh escaped Sara. "Although I'm flattered by your admission, I can assure you that few gentlemen are beating a path to my door. I'm not the young débutante I once was, George, and my experience with Oliver has taught me to be cautious in matters of the heart."

"I hope not *too* cautious."

Gazing at the stars over the rooftops, she only sighed, giving him a resigned look.

"I'm actually glad to hear no one's been courting you," he stated unapologetically. "If I were to be perfectly honest, I jealously want your affections for my own."

Watching him closely, Sara had the distinct feeling he was going somewhere with the conversation.

"I have a matter of importance to discuss with you." He paused, faltering for words, and chuckled. "I hardly know how to begin," he said, growing sheepish. "I suddenly feel like a schoolboy."

A nervous giggle escaped her. "Then we shall be a perfect match because you're making me laugh like a silly schoolgirl. I must admit, I enjoy the feeling," she divulged.

"I don't know why this is so hard to say. I suppose I'm afraid of rejection," George admitted with a shrug. "It's been many years since I've asked a woman to be my wife."

Sara gasped. Had she heard him correctly?

He seemed to wait for her to say something, but she only stared at George, dumbfounded. The orchestra grew silent, laughter drifting onto the porch from the merriment inside. A breeze blew off the sea, rippling over the roses climbing the porch railing. A blossom fell gently onto her lap, and Sara picked it up, smiling. Lifting it to her nose, she inhaled its delicate perfume while her imagination played with the idea of remarriage.

"I didn't want to drop this on you unsuspectingly..." he began. "But over the years, I've been frank about my attraction to you, Sara. It was hard to stand by and watch Oliver ride roughshod over your emotions. Toying with your life and your reputation like a heartless rogue."

"George, you were a married man yourself when you kissed me in your apartment," she quietly reminded him. "That was hardly a proud moment for either of us."

"Perhaps not," he acknowledged, his lips sealed in a quick frown. "But I can assure you, my intentions were very sincere." He turned and gazed into her eyes, gently taking her hand. "Seriously, Sara, I'm not as adept at this as I was when I was a younger man. But in the spirit of that first kiss, it would be my fondest wish that you become my wife."

Sara began to speak.

"Don't give me your answer now." He stopped her, holding up a hand. "Take some time and think about it. There could be many advantages to such a relationship. You would once again be welcomed wholeheartedly into society as my new wife. I could help you raise Natica, and you could help me with my son, Junior. Perhaps we could even have children of our own one day?"

Silence enveloped the two as Sara let his words seep into her mind. Marriage? After five years alone, she'd thought her prospects for matrimony dubious, at best. Could it really be possible for her and George to piece their lives together again after having both been dealt such unfortunate fates?

The scent of cigar smoke floated in the air, drifting across the porch from the direction of two gentlemen smoking together in the pleasant darkness. George got up from the swing and offered her his hand.

"Think about it," he repeated. "There's no hurry. The Secretary of State is sending me to Cuba for a month." George smiled, proud of his position as assistant to the cabinet member. "I'm being sent on a mission to investigate the financial prospects of trade between our two nations." He guided her back toward the ballroom. "Perhaps we can meet when I return, and you'll let me know what you've decided?"

Unable to resist the excitement fluttering through her, Sara blushed. Admittedly, George was nearly twelve years older than she, but that was hardly an argument against matrimony. And although she'd never felt the tingle of excitement for him that she'd felt when she'd first met Oliver, there was no denying her fondness for this man. Perhaps she would develop a deeper attraction toward George over time – a more mature affection, different from the débutante infatuation she'd had for Oliver.

Suddenly haunted by Mr. Waterbury's face, she recalled his surprise proposal so many years ago at the Bachelor Ball in Manhattan. Sara had delayed giving her response to him in hopes of hearing from Oliver. Ultimately, she'd lost them both for one reason or another. Maybe it wasn't so wise to wait and give George her answer? Yet, she was hesitant to accept his proposal without at least sleeping on it for the night. She didn't like making important decisions hastily.

Slipping her arm through his with newfound affection, they started the stroll back toward the ballroom. Without warning, George swung her around in one quick motion and pulled her into a close embrace. In the low filtering light from a lantern, he gave her a deep, passionate look, then leaned in to kiss her lips.

Surprised by his spontaneity, Sara nevertheless submitted to his advances. It'd been so long since she'd kissed a man she silently wondered if she'd forgotten how. The heat of her desire had been imprisoned inside her soul for many years, but now, she felt it suddenly spark to life, and she released herself to the passion. George felt her acceptance and pulled her tight in his arms, kissing her deeply. Sara sighed and drifted into a wave of bliss. Overcome by the warmth of his kiss, she breathed deeply of his masculine scent. After a long moment they paused, but his eyes continued to focus on hers.

"Would you like to dance?" he finally asked in a soft voice.

Sara smiled and nodded 'yes'.

Five weeks later
July 25, 1888
Monte Carlo, Monaco

The roulette wheel whirled as the ball spun around and around in high-speed circles. Waiting for the dealer to call the winner, Oliver sipped his absinthe, hopeful of regaining his lost money. "Lucky thirty-three deserted me last night," he mumbled, his hair disheveled. Tugging off his bowtie, he opened the collar of his shirt in a very bohemian way.

"Number eight, black," the dealer called to the players at the table.

His money was lost again.

"Perhaps I should consider a new number," Oliver muttered to the player beside him. The man only grunted while fiddling with his betting chips.

"Or maybe I should quit now before I lose even more," he thought, knowing his father would complain vehemently over his gambling debts. Pulling his watch from the pocket of his jacket, Oliver saw it was nearly three o'clock in the morning. The crowded gambling casino held no evidence to the late hour, filled with wealthy patrons trying their luck at the tables.

Cheers rang from a craps game adjacent to the roulette wheel. A gray-haired man laughed heartily as the dealer pushed a large stack of chips his way. Encouraged by the win, Oliver decided to try his luck one last time.

"Three thousand francs on number thirty-three," he said, pushing his cash into the center pot. Watching the table through bloodshot eyes, Oliver finished his absinthe.

The men around him placed their bets, and the croupier gave the wheel a hard spin. Tossing the ball into the tray, it whirled, circling at full speed, until finally coming to rest.

"Number thirty-three," the dealer announced.

"Victory!" Oliver cheered. "Thirty-three has not deserted me after all." Collecting his cash, Oliver realized he'd recovered his previous losses and was now fifteen hundred francs in the black. "Well, gentlemen, my faith has been restored in my lucky number," he announced, taking leave of the table. "Good luck!"

Chapter Seven

Four months later
November 25, 1888
Newport, Rhode Island

The church was cold yet packed full of mourners assembled for the funeral. Sara watched her mother straighten, dressed from head to toe in black, standing strong beside her son in the front pew. Florence, Gus's lovely wife, had been too young to succumb to death; and the shock of her loss was worse than any of them could've imagined. The somber mood in the sanctuary was both physically and emotionally exhausting, hanging in the atmosphere like a shroud.

Wearing a blank stare, Gus watched the proceedings of his wife's funeral unfold in the chapel, his face pale, his eyes swollen from tears of grief. With his little daughter Charlotte under his arm, he seemed to be trying to shield her from the reality of her mother's death. But no one could do that.

Wiping the tears from her eyes, Sara was overcome with sadness – and anger! How could this have happened? The doctor had been unable to reduce her sister-in-law's fever, and the grip of her illness grew tighter.

The family had stood by helplessly, watching as the energy drained from Florence, finally bringing her to her last breath. The day she'd passed, Florence had called for Sara and Mrs. Whiting only hours before her final moment, begging them to watch over her little girl as she grew into a woman.

Augustus 'Gus' Whiting

"Hush, now. You're going to get well very soon, Florence," Sara had assured her sister-in-law that she'd recover. Although Sara had insisted that the entire conversation was nonsense, Florence seemed to know more about her fate than Sara had been prepared to face. Unable to watch Gus's wife suffer, Sara had willingly promised Florence anything and everything she'd requested, if only she would get better.

But Gus's wife had not recuperated, and now the family was somberly assembled to pay tribute to her short life amidst the sympathy of their friends. Cold and numb, Sara gazed at the coffin, covered with dozens of flowers. White lilies, carnations, and roses, sent from family and acquaintances as far away as London and Paris, filled the sanctuary in a testament of condolence for Gus. His prominence in the business world brought him recognition throughout America and Europe, and the shocking news of his wife's untimely death had spread quickly across the continents.

Dabbing at her eyes, Sara clung to her composure with effort. The light in the church grew dim from an apparent cloud blocking the early winter sunshine. Reverend Magill recited the closing prayers for Florence's blessing in the afterlife, his voice low and somber. The church fell quiet, save for a gut-wrenching sob escaping Gus. Mrs. Whiting reached to take her son's hand in a weak attempt to comfort him.

But Sara knew there was no comfort to be found. Her little niece turned, staring at her with hollow, blue eyes. The child seemed to plead with Sara to make it all go away, the truth too heavy for the little one to bear. Sara took her hand and squeezed it gently, silently vowing to do

everything in her power to help Charlotte deal with this horrible blow. Although only eight years old, she appeared to fully comprehend the finality of losing her mother to illness.

The church grew still, and no one spoke as the pallbearers surrounded the casket. Weeping echoed through the sanctuary while the black-suited men carried the coffin to the hearse waiting outside. Taking Charlotte's little hand, Gus and his daughter followed the funeral procession to the waiting carriages on the street.

Right then and there, Sara decided to marry George. Amidst the appalling scene playing out before her, she realized how quickly life could pass by. The acuity of her awareness forced her to realize how suddenly life – or death – could intervene in any plans made for the future, and Sara made up her mind to live her days with new determination.

Marrying George would be the beginning of a fresh chapter. With this newfound certitude, she lifted her head and joined the others outside for the funeral procession to the cemetery.

Five months later

March 20, 1889

New York, New York

"I do," Sara answered Reverend Chambers decisively, meeting George's eyes.

"And do you, George, take this woman to be your lawfully wedded wife, forsaking all others. Through sickness and in health, for richer or poorer, for so long as you both shall live?"

Sara's heart pounded as she heard him respond, "I do."

"Then, with the powers vested in me, I now pronounce you husband and wife." Reverend Chambers lowered his prayer book and addressed George. "You may kiss your bride," he announced, removing his frameless spectacles from the bridge of his nose.

With a serene smile, George leaned in and gave Sara a sweet and gentle kiss, sealing their marriage before the few witnesses gathered for the ceremony.

In the wake of his return to New York from Washington several weeks ago, George had sent a note to Sara. The Whitings had been in the city spending the long winter among friends. The letter had announced George's return to New York and contained an invitation to meet him for dinner at Delmonico's.

In the days following George's marriage proposal, Sara had thought long and hard about a life with him, and she stood by the decision she'd made at Florence's funeral to marry George. *"Yes, he is older,"* she thought, *"But he's genuinely fond of me, and I believe he will be a good husband and more importantly, a good father to Natica."* The youngster was growing bigger every day, and George's experience as a husband and parent was certainly a vast improvement over Oliver's indifference and selfish escapades. And after George's passionate kiss at the Ocean House dance, she knew they could be happy together.

"Marry me, Sara," George implored over dinner and wine that evening. He'd looked so handsome to Sara that night, his blond hair gleaming under the lamplight. "My term as Secretary of State ends on March 6th. Let's not delay. Let's marry right away." And he'd presented her with a lovely diamond ring to make the engagement official.

"George, these things take time to arrange," Sara reminded, catching the shimmer of the diamond sparkling on her finger.

"Yes, engagements can take years when you're a young débutante. But we're older now, and both getting remarried. Why don't we get a few witnesses and have a small ceremony? That way, we can keep this quiet from the gossipers and the society columns. What do you say?" He'd paused for a moment, giving her time to consider his plan, his sapphire eyes sparkling at the prospect. "We can take a short honeymoon afterward, maybe somewhere in upstate New York. I have family in Albany that I'd like you to meet. We could vacation and visit at the same time."

What George tactfully failed to tell her was that the Rives family had been less than thrilled when he'd announced his engagement to Sara. Aware of her divorce, his relatives had made it clear they'd prefer he remarry someone unscathed by scandal. The fact that she had a daughter born of this marriage strengthened his family's misgivings. But George hoped they would soften in their opinion once they met Sara and had a chance to get to know her.

At first, Sara had suggested they marry in Paris, but George thought that appeared too much like an elopement. Employing his skills as a lawyer, he'd made a strong case for a quiet New York wedding. In the end, Sara had decided he was right. Why should they run off and risk starting more rumors than necessary?

So Sara had agreed, and before she knew it, they had their marriage license and plans for a ceremony in the parlor of the Collegiate Reformed Dutch Church at Fifth Avenue and Twenty-sixth. They'd kept the wedding small and private, with only four guests. George's oldest son, Junior, was his witness. The young man was approaching his fifteenth birthday and was deemed mature enough to fulfill the duty. And Sara's mother had quickly agreed to be her witness. Her sisters, Jane and Milly, had stayed behind to look after Natica and Charlotte.

Mrs. Whiting had been jubilant at the announcement. Clearly happy to see her daughter remarry, she'd hoped it would bring an end to a formidable episode in Sara's life. Now approaching her twenty-eighth birthday, Sara was far from becoming a spinster, but Mrs. Whiting was relieved to see Sara wed, escaping such a fate, with only two years to spare before her daughter's thirtieth birthday.

The small group moved outside into the cool spring sunshine amidst hugs and congratulations. George Jr. and Mrs. Whiting threw rice over the couple, upholding the nuptial tradition. Junior, tall and lean, seemed genuinely happy that his father was remarrying.

"Well, Mrs. Rives," George said warmly. "Are you ready for a honeymoon?"

"Yes." She beamed, nodding. "I'm more than ready."

Sara Swan Whiting Belmont Rives

Wearing a simple but lovely gray traveling gown, Sara had finished the outfit with a matching hat. The veil, now lifted onto the brim, revealed her eyes shimmering with joy. Cuddling her bouquet of roses, Sara was half-tempted to tease him by stating that her mother would *not* be joining them on their holiday, but she resisted, not wanting to dredge up that old conflict.

"I still wish the two of you would stay in town for a few days and let me throw you a wedding breakfast, or at least a dinner party to announce your marriage," Mrs. Whiting offered, unable to restrain her delight. "Our friends and family here in the city would love to cheer you on your way."

"I know they would." Sara gave her an appreciative smile. "But I'm sure you understand that we want to keep the wedding private, at least for now. Besides, everyone will hear about it soon enough, as an announcement will appear in tomorrow's *New York Times*."

"Well, maybe when you return from Albany, you'll have a change of heart," her mother urged. "There's no shame in remarrying, Sara. Everyone knows the circumstances of your divorce, and the set is even more aware of George's loss. I know they'll all be very glad to hear the two of you have found happiness together."

"We can talk about it when we get back," Sara assured her. Smoothing out her gray gown, she looped her free arm through George's.

"We'd better get off to Grand Central Depot. We don't want to miss our train," George said, leading her toward the carriage.

She gave her mother one last quick hug.

"You have a wonderful honeymoon in Albany," Mrs. Whiting whispered. "And don't you worry one bit about Junior or the girls. They'll be fine, and I'm sure everyone will adjust nicely once things settle down."

Sara noticed a tear in her mother's eye as she'd placed a protective hand on Junior's shoulder. With a nod, Sara climbed into the surrey behind her new husband. Waving a happy goodbye, the couple turned the page to a fresh start in their lives.

Later that evening
Albany, New York

The bellman set the bags on the suitcase stand. "Thank you," George said, handing him a few coins.

"Let us know if you need anything else," the young man replied as he left the room.

"What a beautiful hotel." Sara sighed, pulling the curtains aside to take in the view. Dusk was falling over the mountains, and the sky was painted pink and orange with sunset.

The journey had been pleasant and thankfully uneventful, but it had made for a long day. Now, settling into their honeymoon suite, the couple relaxed.

No longer the naïve débutante who'd been shy in the mysteries of intimacy, Sara embraced the thought of sleeping with her new husband. She was well aware that Natica's birth had changed her in many ways. Some good. Some not so good. But she was a woman now, and although nervous, she was looking forward to enjoying the company of a man after years of forced celibacy.

"You know the World's Fair is opening in Paris this May. Perhaps we should go," George suggested, while removing his topcoat. "They're calling it *Exposition Universelle*. I understand Eiffel has built a tower over Paris specifically for the fair. It's supposed to be quite spectacular." He gave her an amused look and added, "Of course, if your family attends, we'll insist upon separate suites."

A chuckle rippled through Sara. "I would love to go to Paris with you, but let's leave my family to make their own travel decisions, shall we?"

He laughed in agreement, his eyes dancing with humor. "You must be tired," George said, his voice turning gentle. "Did you enjoy your dinner?" He walked to a small table and lit a large columnar candle with the swish of a match.

"Very much so." Sara gave him a warm smile. "The entire day has been lovely."

Winter darkness fell quickly, and the candlelight flickered silhouettes through the suite. George loosened his tie, removing it as he walked

over and gently took her hand.

"Why don't you sit down?" he suggested. "And relax a bit."

Sara did not resist, coquettishly allowing George to lead her to the brocade-covered bed. Daintily sitting on the edge of the mattress, she indulged herself in the warm glow of his romantic ardor.

"Perhaps I should slip into something more comfortable," she said softly.

"Perhaps I can help you with that."

With a tender and amorous mien, George knelt on the floor in front of her. Slowly, he lifted her foot into his hand and began to unlace her button boots. One by one, he removed them from her dainty feet, gently massaging her stockinged toes. Sara responded with a flush of quiet murmurs.

Passion enveloped her with each caress, and George delighted in her sighs, letting his hands move higher up her legs as he caressed them. Sara fell back onto the bed in a sweet surrender to his advances, beckoning him to join her.

Removing his shirt, George laid beside Sara, pulling her into his arms. Skillfully and seductively, he began undressing his wife – and she let him.

"Well, Mrs. Rives..." he whispered, gently kissing her. "At long last, you are mine."

"Yes," Sara said. "I am yours – and you are mine."

And the newlyweds allowed the candle to burn down deep into the night hours.

———

A few days later
March 23, 1889
New York, New York

Rifling through the newspapers, William absently searched for the stock page. The family shipping company and railroad businesses were doing very well as they expanded into the new territories of the growing country. *"America has certainly brought my family opportunities for more wealth than even the savviest politicians could have predicted,"* he reflected smugly. In fact, it appeared that the government might be approaching the Vanderbilts for a loan to the country's treasury to aid in the financing of its burgeoning industrial growth.

Many were calling it a new age, while author Mark Twain had dubbed it the 'gilded age.' Great fortunes were being amassed by resourceful men willing to invest in modern inventions and new business opportunities. A wealth unlike any seen before became obvious through the opulent new homes and skyscrapers being built by successful companies and prestigious American families.

As the riches grew, so did the extravagance of the parties and balls as the members of the set engaged in a show of one-upmanship. *"Although, to date, none have succeeding in outdoing Alva's Fancy Ball."* William smiled at the thought. Many had tried, but their efforts had only resulted in complaints and criticism from the commoners of the city, leaving the party hosts embarrassed instead of admired.

Turning the pages of the newspaper, his eye was caught by a headline of recent nuptials. "George has gotten married!" he whispered in surprise, and quickly read the article. *"Such a tough blow to lose a wife."* Taking a sip of his coffee, he almost choked as he read the name of George's new bride.

Sara Swan Whiting Belmont.

"Oh my God!" he whispered. But re-reading the article, he saw there was no mistake. George had taken Sara for his wife, and they'd gone to upstate New York for a honeymoon.

"I hope she leaves her family behind this time," he muttered, rubbing his eyes. Carelessly throwing the newspaper on the desk, William's thoughts traveled to his own wife.

In spite of his business success and a marriage that had produced three children, Alva and he had grown distant over the years. Busy building new mansions, Alva spent a tremendous amount of time alone with the architect, Richard Hunt, planning the building designs. But William hadn't really minded. He'd grown accustomed to the routine. Besides, it freed him up to chase the newest assortment of beautiful débutantes.

Like he'd once chased Sara when she was a young woman.

Oliver had let her slip through his fingers, for whatever reason, and now she was Mrs. Rives. For as much as William had teased her, he knew it was really because of his wounded ego, a response to the way she'd spurned his attention, something he rarely encountered. *"She was young and innocent at the time,"* he thought. *"And I'd clearly frightened her by my advances."*

Still, he couldn't help but wonder if Sara had married George for love or to escape the stain of scandal she'd been forced to face after Oliver had abandoned her, pregnant, in Paris.

His own marriage was in a state of decay, but Alva didn't seem to care any more than he did. They busied themselves with family and other matters of social preoccupation, like actors playing out their separate roles. Reviewing the years in his mind, William thought back to their cruise with Oliver. Alva and his best friend had spent quite a lot of time together, and rumors began to fly about an extramarital liaison between the two.

"I'm not quite sure why I don't care too much," he mused.

Perhaps it was guilt over having stolen an afternoon kiss from Sara, even though he felt certain no one knew about it except the two of them. He really wasn't the kind of man prone to a guilty conscience. And if he was, his sins in business were far greater than any improper tryst with a young débutante – who just happened to be in love with his best friend at the time. Maybe in some simpler world, Oliver and he could have just swapped ladies, but that was not a matter for consideration now, with Sara married to George.

"My, my…" he said with new realization. "It's amazing how quickly things can change." Taking another sip of his coffee, he turned to the stock pages, quickly burying thoughts about Sara and George into the far reaches of his mind.

Chapter Eight

One week later
April 1, 1889
New York, New York

After a lovely afternoon visiting friends in the city, Carrie was expected at her mother's home. The skirts of her daffodil-yellow gown swished as the butler showed her into the parlor where Mrs. Astor awaited her arrival. As mother and daughter settled into conversation, the maid served them Darjeeling tea and finger sandwiches.

"How are Mr. Wilson and my grandson?" Mrs. Astor asked. Dressed in her usual finery, her wig, now an essential accessory, covered her thinning hair, sitting slightly askew on her head.

"Just fine." Carrie smiled, her eyes shining at the mention of her son. "Little Marshal is growing so fast I have to constantly fit him for new clothes. I don't mind telling you; it's a full-time job."

"Another generation of robust Astor men." Mrs. Astor chuckled, every bit the proud grandmother.

"By the way, we're thinking about joining the migration up Fifth Avenue."

"How lovely. There seems to be quite a boon of new homes in those parts."

"Indeed. This area of town is filling with merchants and professionals. It's much quieter uptown. Marshall and I are meeting with an architect next week to discuss house plans."

"I'd enjoy seeing the drawings once you settle on a design."

With a dainty nibble, Carrie enjoyed a cucumber sandwich. Tactfully, she changed the subject, keeping her tone casual. "Have you heard about Sara? It seems she and George Rives have married."

Blinking, Mrs. Astor turned. "Yes, I've heard. I'm very happy to know she's found a new husband. And the Rives are a most respectable family."

"Yes, they are," Carrie agreed. Mentally formulating her words, she cautiously continued. "I couldn't help but notice you've been giving her the cold shoulder since the divorce. Perhaps now that she's remarried, you can find it in your heart to be more welcoming to her."

"Perhaps..."

"We both know she's suffered terribly over the situation. Even the worst criminal gets a reprieve after they've served their sentence, Mother."

After a moment's contemplation, Mrs. Astor replied unfazed, "Point taken."

Mother and daughter grew silent. The maid returned with a fresh pot of tea, curtsied, and left the room as sunlight broke through the clouds burnishing the elegant parlor in colorful illumination.

Nearly three months later
June 22, 1889
New York, New York

June was the height of the racing season, and the Jerome track was one of New York City's finest. Climbing the stairs to the luxurious clubhouse, Oliver strolled past the ballroom and the dining room, headed for the seats overlooking the track from the bluff, specially reserved for the most elite guests. His father, August, had built the track with his friend, Leonard Jerome, many years ago to promote and pursue their mutual love of horse racing.

Crowds were gathered, filling the stands surrounding the track to capacity while a current of excitement moved through the sport's enthusiasts.

As he walked, Oliver caught sight of the tote board displaying the betting odds. *"This should be a great race today,"* he thought. *"The running of the Champagne Stakes always features great horses from champion bloodlines."*

Looking dapper in his tailored suit, Oliver was ready to spend some money on an afternoon of betting. Actually, that was his second priority, his first being a visit with Alva. Oliver had received a note from her inviting him to join her for the afternoon's competition.

"I didn't think you'd miss today's contest," Oliver said, walking into the private Vanderbilt box.

Alva looked up, her face breaking into a smile. "Oliver! I'm so glad you made it! I just received the brandy and cakes you sent over for me." Dressed in a fine satin gown, her large touring hat was adorned with the colorful feathers she favored so much. "I hope you'll help me enjoy them?"

"If you insist," he acquiesced with a smile. Taking the chair beside her, Alva ordered a nearby servant to open the bottle of brandy.

"How are your horses doing? Have you won?"

"No. Two losses so far," she said glumly. "And you know how I hate losing, but they're only the preliminary races. The main event is just getting started. I bet on *Ebony Shadow*. He has a strong record of wins." Alva smiled as she made a notation on her track sheet.

Their attention was arrested by the clanging of the bell, signaling the start of the race. The horses bolted from the gate, and Alva watched in dismay as her mount stumbled, but quickly regained its footing. The jockey appeared to push the stallion hard as the group rounded the first turn. Vying for the lead, it started to look as though Alva's horse was advancing. The rider skillfully veered the animal toward the rail and charged ahead in a quest for the win. *Ebony Shadow* rounded the second turn, making great strides against the challengers.

Cheering her horse on, Alva yelled with a wild abandon she seldom exhibited in a public setting. Oliver joined in the spirit of the race, shouting right along with her. As the flag went down, it was announced that *Ebony Shadow* had taken first place. Jumping up, Alva clapped exuberantly.

"Good show, Alva!" he congratulated, applauding beside her. "You picked a winner!"

"I knew it! There was something about that horse that smelled of victory."

"Would you like me to collect your winnings for you?"

"That would be wonderful. And perhaps we should toast with some champagne?" A naughty laugh escaped her. "After all, it is the Champagne Stakes."

"I think that's a fabulous idea," Oliver said, enchanted by the woman. Alva knew what she wanted and made no apologies or excuses for her whims, and he liked that. "I'll have a bottle sent over right away."

He left the seating area and headed for the cashier, feeling as victorious as if he'd won the race himself. But it was enough that he'd captured the interest of this self-assured woman. Alva seemed dauntless and independent, unlike Sara, who would do nothing without her mother's consent. He found himself steadily drawn to Alva's company.

After he collected her winnings from the race, he ordered a bottle of *Dom Perignon* and headed back toward the Vanderbilt's box for their private celebration.

Six months later
January 16, 1890
New York, New York

Cuddling her newborn son, swaddled and fed after a nap, Sara headed to the parlor for some time with the family. Gazing at the gurgling baby in her arms, only five days old, he felt so tiny and more precious than all the money in the world. They had named the boy Francis Bayard Rives. Sara really wanted to name him Francis *Whiting* Rives to carry on her own family surname, but in the end, George won out by giving the baby his family's Bayard title.

Growing bored with her bedroom confinement, Sara felt strong enough today to leave her room. Overriding Jane's objections, she carefully descending the staircase while taking in their New York home.

She just loved the house she and George had bought on Thirty-Seventh Street. The place was large and roomy, with plenty of space to start a new family. He'd given her carte blanche to decorate any way she chose. It had been a lot of fun but also a lot of work, especially as her pregnancy progressed. Sara had hired an interior designer that came highly recommended. Jane and Milly helped, too, happily enjoying the task. The end result of their decorating efforts proved to be very successful, meeting everyone's approval, including her husband.

"There's the new mother!" George beamed as she came in with the baby. "Let me see how handsome he is."

Sara walked over and showed him their son. "I've decided he's got your nose and my eyes," she announced, taking a seat in the upholstered rocking-chair.

"I want to see new baby Bayard, too!" Natica ran over, her pigtails bobbing on her head with each step. "Ooh. He's sooooo tiny," she cooed softly. "Will he want to play 'house' with me?"

Chuckling at the little girl, George said, "He'll probably want to ride horses and play army, like most little boys."

"I can ride horses, too!"

"Of course, you can." Sara patted her shoulder. "You and your little brother will have plenty of time to play lots of games."

Sara smiled at George, who was admiring his son with the pride of a new father. He turned his sapphire eyes to his wife in undisguised adoration. Sara bathed in the moment, enjoying the joy and contentment now surrounding their growing family.

She'd given him a son – their son. He already had George Junior from his first marriage, but Junior was nearly sixteen and fast becoming a young man. Plans had been made for Junior to attend Princeton at the end of next year, and he would be leaving home to board at college.

Taking this into consideration, Sara knew her husband wanted more children to continue the Rives family lineage, and she had succeeded in making his wish come true.

"You've made me a very happy man, Sara," George said softly. "In case you aren't already aware of the fact." He leaned in for another peek at Bayard. "Very happy, indeed."

Ten months later
November 24, 1890
New York, New York

The news spread through the financial district like wildfire: August Belmont had died during the night. Without question, the fiduciary world would be affected by the change in guard, and the stock exchanged rippled from the announcement. Brokers stood ready, anticipating new influence in the banking industry, while ticker tape flowed onto the trading floor without so much as a pause.

Seventeen months later
April 27, 1892
New York, New York

Hyacinths and daffodils were displayed throughout the Astor mansion to celebrate the return of spring, but the tense mood around the parlor was palatable as Mrs. Astor discussed the new order with her nephew.

"Now that both my father and Uncle William have passed on, I am the rightful patriarch of the Astor family," Willie said. "I am the first son of the first son in line for the top seat. And it seems only fair that my wife, Mary, should be known as 'Mrs. Astor'."

Willie Astor gave his powerful aunt a pointed look. Wearing the garb of an established gentleman of the set, he stood proud and stern, confronting his aunt with piercing brown eyes.

"I think you should begin prefacing your name with uncle's first name to avoid any confusion."

Amusement filtered across Mrs. Astor's face. "I find it rather entertaining that you feel you can march into my home and dictate such a verdict to me. Need I remind you I am still at the forefront of society, and everyone knows that I am the one they are referring to when they speak of 'Mrs. Astor'. There is only one, and that remains to be *me*!"

"Aunt Lina, must you insist on being so disagreeable in this matter?" Willie demanded, anger reddening his cheeks. "I'm simply asking you to continue calling yourself Mrs. *William* Astor, as you always have."

"But now that your mother has passed away, I am the senior Mrs. Astor. There is no confusion to that title. None at all, as far as I can see. You are the one who is complicating the issue. I suppose your wife will have to wait until I'm dead to be known as *the* Mrs. Astor."

Rising from the sofa, Willie grabbed his hat and headed for the entry. Pausing at the doorway, he turned, lips tight with anger. "I can see there is no point conferring with you on this matter. Apparently, you're set against being amenable to such a discussion. Well, you haven't heard the last of it," he threatened, leaving the room.

Mrs. Astor heard him walk through the foyer, slamming the front door as he left the house. "It will be a cold day in hell when I relinquish my name and all the respect I've garnered over the years to *anyone*," she vowed to the empty room. "Especially to Mary Paul Astor."

Three months later
July 25, 1892
Nantucket Shoals, Atlantic Ocean

The Atlantic Ocean provided a slower route to Newport from New York than the train, but aboard the Vanderbilt yacht, it was pleasurable just the same. With four gentlemen along for the journey, William thoroughly enjoyed the poker game tonight – particularly since he'd won. Turning in just after midnight, he looked forward to resuming the pastime tomorrow, knowing the other gentlemen would want a chance to win back their money.

Sleeping peacefully in the luxurious stateroom, William lurched awake in sudden panic. The ship rocked violently, and he was thrown to the floor in the heave of her pitch.

The door to his suite flew open, and his valet, wearing only his pajamas, shouted wildly in the darkness, "The *Alva's* been hit, sir; she's taking on water fast. You must hurry to the lifeboat."

"What the devil has happened?" William demanded, scrambling to his feet. Holding onto the bed frame, he brushed the hair from his eyes with his free hand.

Portholes burst open with a horrible crash, allowing seawater to gush into the room in fast, unrestrained torrents. Shouts from the crew could be heard above deck as the boat tilted precariously forward toward the bow.

"Please hurry, sir. The situation is dire!" the valet cried, grabbing his employer's arm.

Rushing to the deck, the large crew was already working to release the five large lifeboats into the dark water. Fire was raging from below, smoke billowing out the portholes with a stench.

Thick fog coated the seas, making visibility extremely poor, but in turning, William saw the huge hull of a steamship looming above him, clearly the source of the collision. Lumber and metal railings from his yacht bobbed in the ocean water, wrenched loose from the main hull.

"This way, sir," yelled a sailor. "Quickly!"

With the assistance of the crew, William and his four guests were hastily transferred to a lifeboat as *Alva's* nose drowned deeper under water.

A rescue team from the steamer responsible for the accident approached in a rowboat to assist in the recovery of men. The first lifeboat, carrying William and his friends, reached the steamer, and they were pulled aboard. Amidst the mayhem, sailors continued to rescue crew members from the cold water, hauling them onto the rowboats and escorting them to the safety of the *H.F. Dimock*.

The captain personally greeted the beleaguered evacuees climbing on to the steamer's deck. "Get the medic out here, now!" the captain shouted, "See to these men's injuries."

Watching the flames and water battle for his boat, William teetered on the deck.

"No one's been hurt, sir," the first mate of the *Alva* informed him. "Everyone has been recovered."

William nodded at him, relieved to hear the news, although it was clear the yacht had sustained major damage. Standing helplessly on the deck of the *Dimock*, William watched as the *Alva* sank beneath the black waves, disappearing into the depths of the sea in an awful heave of surrender.

Four months later
November 20, 1892
New York, New York

The dark silence was airless and heavy, somberly cloaking the mansion, heedless of the early morning sunlight. Oliver climbed the staircase slowly, making the journey to his mother's bedroom. He'd received a note from Perry alerting him that their mother had fallen ill. Dr. Polk had been called, as well as Dr. Barrow and Dr. Hanlen, but regardless of all their expertise, the prognosis did not sound good.

"How is she?" Oliver asked Perry as he neared the bedroom.

"The doctors are with her now," Perry said, a faraway look haunting his weary eyes. "They've assured us they're doing everything they can, but they don't seem very optimistic."

The bedroom door opened, and Auggie quietly joined them in the hallway with Bessie at his side, her eyes red from tears. Their clothing was disheveled, evidence of the night they'd spent without sleep. Oliver watched his brother put an arm around his wife, working to comfort her.

"Oliver, I'm so glad you're here," Auggie said in a whisper. "I just hope it isn't too late."

Eager to know more of his mother's condition, Oliver looked up to see Dr. Barrow and Dr. Polk come out of the sickroom. Graying, Dr. Polk was the elder of the men. The two doctors paused in front of the closed door, looking grim, quietly talking to each other before walking over to join the Belmont brothers.

"How is she?" Oliver asked anxiously, his brow furrowed with worry. "Is she recovering?"

Dr. Barrow gave all three brothers a direct look from behind his horn-rimmed eyeglasses. "I wish I had better news. Your mother has fallen unconscious. Hopefully, she will rally, but I think it more prudent to advise you to prepare for the worst."

"We've done everything possible," Dr. Polk added in a subdued voice. "Now, all we can do is wait and see if she regains consciousness. We should know by the end of the day."

"Where is Dr. Hanlen?" Perry asked.

"He was called back to the hospital for an emergency operation," Dr. Barrows said. "The three of us conferred over the treatment for your mother, but again, all I can tell you is that we've done everything we can for her at the present time. Our only hope is that she has the strength to recover."

"Excuse us," Dr. Polk said, leading his colleague to a private side of the hallway to discuss the patient.

Oliver fought the hollow emptiness winding through his heart like a cold serpent. His sweet Little Mo, lying unconscious. She'd been so heartbroken when his sister Jeanne had died. Years later, when she finally seemed to be recovering from the loss, Raymond had been tragically shot in the pistol accident. It seemed as though a part of her had died again. Raymond was her baby, and Mrs. Belmont had been overcome with a sorrow that drew deep lines on her lovely face. Fighting a stab of guilt over his little brother's demise, Oliver wondered again if he was responsible in some small way for Raymond's senseless death.

After his father's passing several years before, his mother had become a vacant shell, displaying no desire to participate in any of their gay parties or dinners. She withdrew from society, growing more and more reclusive. Although Oliver and his brothers had tried to persuade her to attend balls or the opera, she'd insisted on staying home with only her novels for entertainment, leaving them unsuccessful in their efforts to break through her grief.

Oliver walked up to Dr. Barrows. "May I see her?"

"She's unconscious," he reminded Oliver, catching the worry in the young man's troubled eyes. "But if you'd like to sit with her a moment, I can see no harm in it."

Nodding his understanding, Oliver walked to his mother's door. Taking a deep breath, he gathered his wits and entered the darkened room.

Lying motionless on the bed, his mother was silent in the dim chamber. For one terrifying moment, Oliver thought she might already be dead until he heard her fitful, labored breathing. Relief surged through him, and he trembled, taking the chair near her bedside. Reaching for her hand, so tiny and delicate, Oliver held it in his own. She felt unnaturally cold, and he realized the specter of death was waiting in the shadows ready to descend and claim her soul at any moment. Wishing for a miracle – or at least a miracle medicine, Oliver battled the frustration that assaulted his hopes for her recovery. *"For all the family's wealth,"* he thought, *"when it comes to matters of life and death, there is no negotiating a payment to spare the life of a loved one."*

"There's so much I wanted to tell you, Mother..." Oliver choked on his words, fighting back the tears that threatened to devour him. "But all I can say is 'thank you' for always being there for me. For taking my side even when you weren't convinced that you should."

He thought back to his years in the navy and then in Bremen. His mother had been his only ally against his father's orders, and it was she that had finally capitulated to his marriage with Sara. Memories of his childhood floated through his mind unbidden. Happy memories of opening gifts with his sister, Jeanne, at Christmas time and his early years at St. Paul's School. His mother, sweet and strong, was always there to guide him as he grew to be a man.

"I know I've disappointed you in so many ways." His voice broke with raw emotion. "But I have loved you, my Little Mo, with a devotion as strong as any son could feel for his dear mother."

For a moment, Oliver thought she'd responded by squeezing his hand, but he realized it was only his hopeful imagination. She lay still and quiet, the only movement her labored breathing, growing softer and shallower.

Gently, he laid her hand back on the sheet and wiped away a tear. His chest ached with the agony of a breaking heart, the pain filtering into his soul.

The bedroom door opened, and his brothers entered with Bessie, and his sister Fredericka, who'd recently arrived. Taking seats, the solemn group kept vigil around the bed.

And together, they somberly waited.

Chapter Nine

Five days later
November 25, 1892
Newport, Rhode Island

Settled on the ornate French sofa with her husband Teddy, Edith conversed with Alice and Cornelius Vanderbilt. Invited for an early evening visit at The Breakers, the group fell into an easy discussion revolving around the balls and fox hunts of the past summer in the resort town, and prospects for amusements during winter in the city.

"We'll be entertaining Mr. Henry James and several other writers at our home in New York around Christmas. We hope you'll join us," Mrs. Vanderbilt invited. Pretty and petite, Alice's honey-colored eyes were warm and genuine. "I really enjoy Mr. James' novels, and his visits provide a refreshing break from the boredom of winter."

"Speak for yourself, my dear," her husband teased. "I prefer discussions of a business nature." Handsome and dark, Cornelius was clean-shaven, his eyes shining with amusement from under bushy brows.

"Of course, dear." Alice grinned. "But all work and no play will make you very dull." She turned back to Edith. "I'm sure you've heard Alva's finished building Marble House. Have you seen it yet?"

"No. We were abroad when they had the housewarming party," Edith answered. "Is it wonderful?"

"You know, Alva." Alice's voice dripped with criticism. "Always intent on building the bigger and better birdhouse. That woman has an ego the size of the moon."

"How are your children?" Edith chuckled, politely changing the subject. "I haven't seen them in several years. They must be getting quite grown-up these days."

"The girls are outside playing on the lawn with Will." Alice smiled at the mention of the youngsters. "And, indeed, they are growing up fast – too fast if you ask me. Our oldest son, Neily, left for college just yesterday." She sipped from a cup of tea. "How is your mother doing, Edith?"

"She's well, thank you," Edith replied. "She and Father are in France now. I think they'll be staying until springtime."

"We were considering a trip to Paris, but we haven't made any firm plans," Teddy added. Slim and tall, Teddy's hair was parted down the middle. His thick mustache gave width to his narrow face but added a sternness to his demeanor. He could have been a handsome man, if he'd only smile more often.

A sudden commotion among the servants roiled through the house with growing distress. The Vanderbilts and their guests turned to each other alarmed, suspending their conversation mid-sentence.

"What in heaven's name is going on!" Cornelius' voice began to rise, objecting to the ruckus. But his question was quickly answered when a servant ran into the room yelling at the top of his lungs.

"Fire! Fire!" the young man screamed in terror. "Run for your lives!"

Panic arrested their pleasant visit amid gasps of disbelief. Jumping from their seats, everyone began moving quickly for the exit. Chaos ensued, and Edith hurriedly followed Teddy and the Vanderbilts into the foyer, already consumed by thick and dirty gray smoke. Coughing, the group made it to the front door and escaped outside to the lawn, where they discovered utter pandemonium.

"Call for the firemen!" Cornelius shouted urgently to a servant. "Make sure there's no one in the house!" he yelled to another as people scattered helter-skelter.

Running as fast and as far from the building as their feet would carry them, Teddy pulled Edith away from the house. The two reached what they considered a safe distance and stopped to catch their breath. Impulsively, they hugged each other, then turned to witness a full view of the cottage, quickly becoming consumed by flames.

Edith's blood ran cold at the sheer horror of the sight. Like a hungry animal that would not be appeased, the flames sparked with vicious destruction. Flaring from room to room, the blaze spread through the building, quickly conquering the structure. Fire licked the roof, casting a surreal orange light over the approaching darkness of night, while the toxic, chemical odor of the black smoke rained soot over the acreage in cloudy plumes. The power of the fire was terrifying, and Edith silently prayed everyone had escaped safely.

"How could this have happened?" Alice wailed with tears in her eyes. Her three children huddled around her, frightened, and she drew a protective arm over them. "Our artwork and antiques! My jewelry!" she moaned through tears.

"None of that matters, Alice," Edith said. Pushing her own fears aside, she worked to comfort the woman. "Your family is safe – I just hope none of the servants have been injured."

Forced to shout above the roar of the flames, Edith was silenced when the large beam supporting the main roof thundered to the ground in a torrent of fire and sparks.

The firemen arrived, and a pump and hose were taken to the ocean's edge. The crew worked to douse the flames with seawater, but even Edith could see the fire was moving much more quickly than the men trying to rescue the home.

Witness to such raw power, the ladies stayed well out of the way, watching helplessly as the fate of The Breakers became imminently clear to all.

Irrespective of the efforts to save the building, the flames had definitely won.

⚜

Two days later
November 27, 1892
Newport, Rhode Island

The noon light poured through chintz curtains covering the windows, conveying a cheery mood over the youngsters' playtime. The attic in *Swanhurst* had been turned into a playroom for the girls, complete with a child-sized table and chairs.

Picking up the miniature teapot, Natica pretended to fill her cousin's cup. "Here is your tea," she announced in a proper tone, brown curls framing her cherubic face. "Would you like a scone or cake?" She held up a tiny platter filled with miniature-baked goods, specially prepared for the youngsters by the Whiting's cook.

"Yes, please," Charlotte answered politely, her blonde hair tamed into a long braid. Although three years older than Natica, she nonetheless enjoyed playing with her little cousin. "A scone would be delicious."

"I've heard Miss Post will be joining us later for the ball. I've chosen the loveliest yellow gown to wear."

"I'll be attending tonight, too," Charlotte said. "My gown is scarlet red. I want everyone to notice me when I walk onto the dance floor."

"Scarlet red?" Natica giggled. "How shocking. And do you have long matching gloves that go past your elbow?"

"Of course," her cousin boasted. "Gloves, a lace hat, and a gorgeous fan to show all the interested gentlemen that I am free to marry."

Moving to a trunk, Natica picked up a petticoat and pulled it on her head like a veil. "I have received a proposal from Mr. Archer. I simply adore my wedding dress. Say you'll agree to be my bridesmaid."

"Certainly!" Charlotte helped Natica arrange her 'veil.' "Mr. Archer is a very lucky gentleman."

The young girls walked over to the full-length mirror and admired their handiwork. Their game of pretend was more a rehearsal for future courtship than either presently realized.

"Don't I look perfectly lovely?" Natica chirped, while Charlotte looked on at her reflection.

"You certainly do."

After a moment, Natica pulled off the petticoat. "Your turn," she said and began arranging the lace garment on her cousin's head. "You will make a most beautiful bride."

Charlotte adjusted the veil, letting it fall over her shoulders. "We're going to Paris after Christmas, you know," she commented, breaking from the role of bride.

"Yes, I know." Natica pouted unenthusiastically. "I do like going there, but Mother has gotten us new tutors. Now we'll have to study French even harder."

"I know. It seems like all we do is study anymore. Not only history and mathematics, but all those charm classes in boring etiquette." She grimaced at Natica. "Who cares which fork you use to eat salad or fish?"

"I don't care, that's for sure." Natica frowned. "But it seems to be very important to Mother."

The girls were interrupted when Bridget entered the attic, quickly assessing the girls' activity. "Mrs. Clement is here for your piano lessons." Bridget informed them. "The two of you are wanted downstairs."

"Okay," Charlotte answered, her voice glum as she pulled the petticoat from her head. "We'll be right down."

Meanwhile, in the parlor...

"It must have been perfectly horrible," Sara said, listening to Edith with rapt attention. "The entire house was burning within minutes! It was utter chaos!" Edith's eyes were distressed as she relayed the events to Sara.

"How did the fire start?"

"I'm not certain, but it appears to have been caused by the furnace, which is directly under the foyer. We were almost trapped!" Edith turned pale as she talked. "I have never been so frightened in all my life."

"Thankfully, no one was injured." Sara leaned forward with rapt attention, adding, "But I heard the house was completely destroyed."

"Without a doubt. But can you believe the timing? It was like a bad omen! Of all the days to call on the Vanderbilts!"

"Now, Edith, you shouldn't take it so personally."

Reaching for her teacup, Edith drank the contents dry in one quick, unladylike gulp. "Perhaps not," she agreed, placing her empty cup on the side table. "But it's going to be a long time before I forget that visit!"

<hr />

Two weeks later
December 10, 1892
New York, New York

Milly moved through the ball like a young débutante, swishing in her cobalt blue satin gown. Sara watched her with a surreptitious eye from across the dance floor while her sister chatted with banker John Davis. She couldn't recall ever seeing Milly look so lovely, despite her forty-seven years.

Her hair was layered on the crown of her head in a swirl of curls, encircling her face with an attractive allure. The bustle of her colorful gown was gathered in fashionable flounces, swaying gently from her tiny waist as she moved in the orbit of Mr. Davis.

Mr. Davis appeared equally enthralled by Sara's sister. His posture erect, he stood a few inches above Milly, easily meeting her eye. His expensive suit was perfectly tailored, and he wore it with a confidence that lent him an aura of power.

"Here's your punch." George interrupted her thoughts as he handed her the drink. Noticing her preoccupation, he followed her gaze. "Your sister looks quite intrigued with Mr. Davis."

"Yes, indeed. Nothing like a New York Christmas party to bring people together."

"Don't I know it?" George teased, his smile nearly hidden under his trimmed mustache. "You've got our social calendar quite full, my dear, until well after New Year's Day."

Sara turned to him, feeling a little penitent. "I suppose I'm making up for a few lost years from society. But would you prefer we isolate ourselves from the fun?" She grinned at him endearingly.

"Of course not." Shaking his head at her efforts to appease him, he gave a reluctant smile. "But you should really consider scheduling some time for sleep."

She laughed at his good nature while watching Milly blush at something Mr. Davis whispered in her ear.

"I wish I could get closer and hear what they're talking about," Sara brooded.

"Now you sound like your mother."

"Hardly that bad, George! Those two seem to be engaged in a discussion of some importance. You can't blame me for being curious." She smiled and batted her eyelashes at him.

"Hmmm..." He arched a brow. "I'm sure you've heard what they say about curiosity killing the cat."

Raising her punch glass to him in a toast, Sara laughed. "Touché," she said, taking a sip of the drink. "Do you think it's possible my sister could actually have a chance at marriage?"

George regarded the couple across the room. "Women older than she have managed to secure a husband. Your sister is sweet enough and still attractive for her age. For her sake, I hope that's exactly what the two of them are whispering about."

"It really would be exciting to have another marriage in the family. Or even two. Not only for Milly but for Gus as well," Sara finished, contemplating the possibility for her brother.

Gus had seemed lost and lonely since Florence's death. But happily, Sara had discovered that a lady had caught his eye, a Miss May Clagett, and Gus was going to Washington, DC, to visit her. The only drawback was that he wouldn't be joining the family for Christmas dinner.

Sara's thoughts were distracted when Auggie Belmont, Oliver's brother, entered the ballroom, his commanding presence drawing attention. Auggie was surrounded by a few of New York's most powerful men, all of whom were subscribers to tonight's ball. The list included Carrie's brother, John Jacob Astor, along with James Roosevelt and her very own husband, George. Finally, Sara was a welcome guest at society's balls, but she didn't often cross paths with the Belmont family. Thankfully, Oliver had not put in an appearance tonight, although Sara noticed Perry, the congressman, flanking his brother, Auggie. The two men shared quite an allocation of power between them.

The orchestra began the strains of the next waltz, and George took her glass, placing it on the table. "Would you care to dance?" He offered his hand.

Thinking it might move her closer to her sister, she accepted. "Only if we dance on that side of the room," she answered, with a discreet nod in Milly's direction.

He rolled his eyes at her with mock impatience. Shaking his head, George led his wife onto the dance floor. "As you wish, detective."

<hr />

That same night
December 10, 1892
Washington, D.C.

Rows of stately homes were the only scenery passing by the carriage window, and Gus took note of the architecture as they rolled down the city street. Rubbing his hands together for warmth, he decided Washington was lovely in the night-glow of the gas lamps reflecting light off the white of a fresh snowfall.

"I would have preferred to stay in New York for the holidays with my family," he thought. *"But I can't seem to stop thinking about Miss Clagett."* May had a delicate beauty that had won his affection from the first time they'd crossed paths at the Dignitary Ball last autumn. Tiny of stature, she exuded spunk and strength in spite of her diminutive size. When she'd sent him an invitation to her family's Christmas dinner, Gus thought perhaps May shared his attraction and had quickly decided to attend in an effort to court the young woman.

Life had been empty since Florence's death, and he'd kept very busy, occupying his time with business matters in an effort to distract himself from his grief. His young daughter was in the good care of his mother and sisters. "That's best for Charlotte's upbringing," he muttered. "Especially since I don't have the slightest clue how to raise a daughter, especially in this modern age." Natica was only three years younger, so at least the two girls had each other to play with, which Gus thought good for Charlotte right now.

If he remarried, that would change. *"Miss Clagett certainly has the pedigree necessary for such a union."* She belonged to an old Maryland family and was a direct descendant of Bishop Thomas John Clagett, the very first bishop of the state. She also claimed Ethan Allen as her uncle, the ex-district attorney of the county. *"Of course, none of that will matter if we can't find affection for each other."* Gus took heart, hoping this wouldn't be the case, as the carriage rumbled to a stop in front of her parent's home on the quiet metropolitan street.

Climbing from the coach, he pulled his silk top hat snuggly over his light-brown hair. Nervous over his appearance, he brushed the shoulders of his heavy woolen topcoat, then stood tall and headed for the house. Trudging through the snow up the path to the door, he let the brass door-knocker fall hard, praying he had not come in vain.

Chapter Ten

One month later

January 10, 1893

New York, New York

The Astor parlor was under assault, the clamor of hammers and construction noise from next door seeping into the elegant room like an unwanted plague. Sipping tea from the dainty hand-painted cup, Carrie politely listened to her mother's complaints regarding the hotel construction.

"I can understand your displeasure. It must be difficult to live with so much ruckus."

"It's horrible! I'm certain your cousin did this purposely to make my life miserable," Mrs. Astor said, her hands shaking from anger as she drank her tea. "How could he tear down his father's lovely mansion and replace it with a hotel! *A hotel!* It's a crime against the family, I say!"

"So it seems... The family homes have stood side by side on Fifth Avenue for many years," Carrie agreed from her seat in the large easy chair. "It's a shame relations between the two of you have deteriorated to such a low point. What did you do to make him so angry?"

"Me?" Mrs. Astor harrumphed. "I did nothing. It was Willie who strutted over here and demanded I begin referring to myself solely as Mrs. *William* Astor – and I refused! Now that your father is gone, I am *the* Mrs. Astor. Simple and succinct. He wants his wife, Mary, to have the title. Well, she's got a few more years and a lot more entertaining to do before she gets to don a name I've earned from many seasons at the forefront of the social scene."

"Of course, she has." Carrie smiled, finding it easier to be agreeable when her mother was in a fighting mood. Still, she thought, her cousin and his wife had to be out of their minds to make such a demand of her mother. The scruples of the younger set were swiftly degrading due to the entitlement of their inherited wealth, but out of respect, she considered, the young men should at least wait until the elders had reached the end of their days before vying for their crowns.

"The hotel is going to open in March. When will your new house be ready?"

"They're starting construction in March, so I'm doomed to live with this racket for a while yet. Of course, I could go to the house in Newport. Either way, I've hired a watchman to patrol the grounds." Mrs. Astor asserted. "I don't want anyone trespassing."

"That's always a good idea," Carrie said with a nod of her head. "Try to look on the bright side, Mother. With all the new development in this part of the city, I think you'll be happier moving to a quieter part of town. Besides, we'll be neighbors."

"I hope you're right, but this couldn't be happening at a worse time." Mrs. Astor gave her daughter a sad look. "We're still in mourning over your father's death, and now your sister is vying for a place in *Town Topics*."

"If you ask me, she *caused* Father's death!" Carrie huffed, her mood quickly shifting to displeasure. "Carrying on with her neighbor Mr. Borrowe like that – and then abandoning her husband and children to chase him to Europe so she could continue the affair. I do believe she's lost her mind!"

"When your father caught up to her in London, he found her husband James and Mr. Borrowe in a heated argument – it nearly came to a duel. He managed to mollify the situation long enough to get Charlotte to Paris and try to talk some sense into her."

"Well, the strain was too much for him," Carrie spat. "Or he wouldn't have collapsed in the hotel suite from heart failure."

"At least he didn't live to see her love letters printed all over *The Sun*." Pinching the bridge of her nose, Mrs. Astor continued. "The shock would have certainly killed him. The notes left little to the imagination."

"Such betrayal by one of Mr. Borrowe's friends," Carrie said, biting back her outrage. "Giving his private letters to the press like that. I'd hate to meet the man's enemies."

"Your father and I arranged the marriage between Charlotte and Mr. Drayton ourselves. It was the perfect union, with his well-paid position in the Equitable Life Company, she was amply provided for. They have four healthy children and a good standing among the set. Why she had to ruin it all and deliver the Astor name to scandal is beyond me. Now she wants a divorce! Can you believe it? A *divorce*, for heaven's sake!"

"Oh dear..."

"Indeed." Mrs. Astor brushed a hand over her forehead as if to wipe away the turmoil. "I've always frowned on divorced members of the set. How will I handle my own daughter joining the ranks of such women? She's left me in a most untenable situation."

"A situation of her own making!" Carrie insisted. "Unlike Sara, who was forced into divorce because Oliver refused to own up to his responsibilities. Everyone wanted to blame her mother and sisters, but we all know Oliver agreed to their honeymoon visit. He even rented an extra-large suite to accommodate everyone! Once he got what he wanted – a reprieve from his father and a larger allowance – he ran off with a dancer and used her family as the scapegoat!"

Pausing, Mrs. Astor turned to Carrie. "Why are we talking about this now? It's been years since Sara's divorce."

"Because I've never felt the set was fair to Sara. And because I'm Natica's godmother! Now my sister's filing for divorce because she indulged her fantasies in an affair! If it were anyone else, you'd reject her from the set without a thought."

"I can't argue that point. By rights, I should disown her, as her conduct goes against everything I've ever stood for. It is public knowledge from the printed letters that she's at fault," Mrs. Astor lamented. "She's placed me in a terrible position. But I don't know if I can turn my back on my own daughter."

It was unusual to witness her mother grapple with her conscience. "Divorce is growing more common these days." Carrie pointed out. "If we cut every divorced woman from the set, there may be very few left standing."

"I hadn't thought of that, but regardless, divorce will never be acceptable!" Sipping her tea, Mrs. Astor grew quiet, lost in contemplation over the threat of scandal.

"And, of course, all the men will carry on just fine," Carrie added, joining her mother in contemplation.

<hr />

One month later
February 2, 1893
New York, New York

Clearly, the year was going to be one for weddings, Sara thought happily, watching as Milly took her place beside her fiancé in the parlor of the Whiting's New York home. She'd told Sara of the engagement last month, and the news had hit the society page very quickly. Most of the set had assumed the wedding would be a large formal affair, but Milly had thought that a bit gauche considering the couple's age.

"I can't believe this is really happening!" Milly whispered earlier as Sara helped her dress in the bedchamber. Her gorgeous sky-blue gown accented Milly's complexion and sable-brown eyes, showcasing her beauty. "John is so wonderful to me – I feel like the luckiest woman on earth." She set her hairbrush on the table and turned to look at her sister. "I suppose Jane was wrong about me after all. I did manage to find a husband."

"Jane was very wrong!" Sara laughed, reassuring her sister. "Mr. Davis would have been foolish not to propose to you. And I think you were both wise to have a quick ceremony without all the hoopla. George and I were really glad we'd made the same decision."

"And after me, Gus will be marrying Miss Clagett in May. What a festive year it's shaping up to be."

"This is definitely a year for celebration."

"Oh, Sara! This is a dream come true!" Milly's face glowed with joy. "I was resigned to being a spinster until John started showing me favor last summer at the Atlantic House. In my heart, I'd hoped he was pursuing me for marriage, but I was still surprised when he proposed at Christmas."

Pushing her recollections aside, Sara returned her focus to the present day. Standing quietly next to George, she slipped her gloved hand in his, a witness to the wedding in the parlor. A simple affair; there were no flowers except for Milly's rose bouquet, tied together with a white satin ribbon. Listening as Reverend Huntington, the rector at Grace Church, officiated over the ceremony, Sara smiled at the happy sight, simultaneously fighting back tears of joy. Life was full of unexpected surprises, and this wedding was a much-needed happy occasion that she was glad to celebrate with her family.

The past few years had been fraught with deaths among the Four Hundred, including both of Oliver's parents. If he'd grieved over their loss, it wasn't evident. Oliver was as conspicuous as ever, flaunting not only his newly inherited wealth but also his flirtatious relationship with William's wife. Rumors were wild with speculation over the two, including scuttlebutt about them marrying – before Alva and William were even divorced! That was Oliver's typical disregard for propriety, Sara thought unkindly. He did what he wanted without any consideration as to how it would affect others.

Vows were spoken between Milly, and Mr. Davis and rings were exchanged, ending the short ceremony. Standing tall over the couple, Reverend Huntington congratulated the newlyweds. His warm eyes exuded joy as he wished them many years of wedded bliss.

The small group filed outside into the chilly February air. Gus and Jane, along with Mrs. Whiting, congratulated the newly married couple, as did George and Sara. Mr. Davis' only guest was his daughter Flora, from his first marriage to Miss Chapman from St. Paul, who'd succumbed to illness while in Paris over five years ago.

Giving her sister a long hug, Sara said, "You and John have a wonderful honeymoon in Washington. Enjoy yourself and promise me you won't worry about a thing. I'll make sure to send out your wedding announcements this very afternoon."

"I really appreciate your help." Milly beamed, blushing in her new role as bride. "And I'll send a note once we get settled and let you know how our trip went."

Mrs. Whiting hugged Milly again, then turned to the new husband. "What a happy day," she said, shaking Mr. Davis's hand.

"Thank you so much for everything," John said to his new mother-in-law, the sparkle in his eyes lending the groom a youthful look. "I plan on taking very good care of your daughter."

"What more could a mother ask for?" Mrs. Whiting smiled while patting a handkerchief at joyful tears.

"I wish you a world of happiness," Gus said, shaking John's hand.

George joined in, echoing the sentiment. "We'll celebrate with a dinner party when you return."

"That would be very nice," Mr. Davis thanked him. Taking Milly's hand, he asked, "Are you ready?"

With one last wave to the family, Sara watched her sister climb into the carriage and drive down Fifth Avenue, a new bride.

⚜

Four months later
July 31, 1893
Newport, Rhode Island

Comfortable in the rocking chair, Sara softly sang a lullaby while cuddling the sleeping baby in her arms. It had been nearly ten years since Natica had been born and three years since her son's birth, but still, she'd almost forgotten how tiny new babies could be!

George had been overjoyed when she'd told him she was pregnant again, and Sara truly hoped that as their little family grew, it would make her marriage even stronger, like it had when Bayard was born. Looking down at the sleeping child, she was grateful for George. He'd proven to be a good husband as well as a good father to the children.

Fondly, Sara wished for Mary. The elderly housekeeper had retired last month and gone to live with her sister in Providence. With her departure, Sara felt a lasting emptiness. Mary had been like a member of the family, raising Sara and watching over her as she grew into a woman.

"I suppose we'll have to find you a new nanny," Sara cooed to the baby.

The door opened, and Mrs. Whiting led Natica in to meet her new half-sister.

"What's her name?" the little girl asked, peering curiously at the tiny bundle.

"We've decided to call her Mildred." Sara smiled warmly. "Mildred Sara Rives. Do you like that?"

"Yes." The little girl nodded. "But she's too little to play 'house,'" she commented, examining the small baby in her mother's arms.

Mrs. Whiting chuckled at her granddaughter. "Not for long. Babies grow up faster than you know."

"She's as little as a dolly." Natica gingerly touched the baby's miniature fingers. "And so soft. Bayard is not the baby anymore, is he, Mother?"

"No. Bayard is a big boy now. Mildred is the baby." Sara got up from the rocking chair and laid the newborn in her cradle while Natica watched every movement. Returning to her chair, Sara held out her hands to the growing girl.

"Come and sit with me."

Natica obediently shimmied onto her mother's lap. She seemed unsettled by another new addition to their family. "Do you love her more than me?" Natica asked with the candidness of a child.

"Of course not!" Sara exclaimed. But as she looked at her daughter's face, Oliver's brown eyes stared back at her, reminding Sara of the pain he'd brought to their lives.

"There is plenty of love to go around for all my grandchildren," Mrs. Whiting assured the girl.

"And the baby will love you back, just like Bayard does," Sara told her. "You and your brother will have your own little sister to play with at Christmas time, and in the summer, you can build sandcastles on the beach. It will be wonderful, you'll see."

Natica seemed happy with the idea and smiled at her mother as a soft knock sounded at the door.

George peeked his head inside. "Is it safe for the gentlemen to enter?" he asked in a velvety voice.

"Yes, come on in," Sara answered.

He entered the room with Bayard toddling at his side. Natica was the first to greet them.

"Come see our new baby sister," she whispered, ushering them to the cradle.

With a delighted smile, George followed the little girl to the bassinet for his first glimpse of his new daughter.

"She's too little," Bayard declared woefully. "We can't play with her – she'll break."

The adults chuckled, charmed by the young boy's innocence.

"She'll grow up faster than you know," George assured him with a pat on his little head.

Warm contentment melted Sara's heart as she watched them all admire the new addition asleep in the cradle. After a moment, George glanced up at Sara, his eyes filled with a tenderness and love that soothed her to the depths of her very soul.

"I've sent a telegram to Junior at boarding school. I'm sure he'll be delighted to know he has a new sister." George placed a protective hand on Sara's shoulder. "How are you feeling?" he asked her gently.

"I'm tired, but I could not be happier," Sara answered warmly,

knowing it had never been more true.

Chapter Eleven

One year later
July 20, 1894
Middletown, Rhode Island

The ocean breeze blew against the tall grasses with a gentle swooshing sound. Birds sang cheery songs, adding to the peace and sweetness of the afternoon.

"Most travelers return with trinkets and artwork," William stated flatly. "But not you, Oliver. You bring home a zoo full of animals."

"If I didn't know you better, I'd think you were complaining."

"I'm just saying." William chuckled as they walked the grounds of their estate in easy companionship. "The menagerie will be a great amusement for our friends. They'll most certainly want to visit Gray Craig to see your new collection of birds and beasts. Kind of an extreme way to get them out of Newport and into Middletown, don't you think?"

"Perhaps." Oliver smiled, his boyish features lending an air of immaturity to his face. "Once we get the animals settled in, let's throw a big party, shall we?" He paused, considering the logistics of his mission. "I have to pass the animals through customs and quarantine first, then they'll be shipped up here on the Fall River Line."

"When do you think that will be?"

"Probably by the beginning of August. Most of society will still be in town for the summer. It will be a great ending to the season."

"It very well could be." William shook his head in agreement while taking in the azure summer sky. "Might I ask exactly what type of creatures you've brought back from India?"

"Well, for starters, over a hundred beautiful birds. You should see them, Willie. They're quite spectacular, and a few were very expensive, I might add." Oliver squinted his eyes while taking mental inventory of his purchases. "Bull, deer, monkeys, and sacred cows." He raised his chin, and announced, "Cows are hallowed in India, you know."

"So I've heard." William chuckled, unable to restrain his amusement.

The gentlemen strolled into the Gray Craig stables as they talked and were quickly met by the smell of straw and hay pungently mixing with the scent of the horses.

"India is much warmer than Rhode Island," William reminded him. "Some of the animals can roam free on the grounds, like the deer and bull. But you're going to have to build some type of enclosures for the more exotic creatures, as we discussed before. And their pens are going to need to be heated."

"I've already got workers on the project." Oliver smiled smugly. "I have cages ready for them now, and plans have been drawn up for new animal houses. They won't take too long to build. Everything should be ready for them before winter." He turned to William. "You worry too much. It's going to be great fun."

"I suppose horses couldn't contain your interest."

"I love my horses, Willie, but why limit oneself? Wait until you see these incredible animals – especially the monkeys. They're very entertaining."

"Hmmm..." William couldn't resist the opportunity to tease him. "I suppose women aren't enough entertainment for you?"

Oliver laughed outright. "You're awful to compare the fairer sex to monkeys! Better not let your wife hear you talk like that."

William let out a disapproving grunt but wisely refrained from commenting.

"Oh, I almost forgot to tell you," Oliver announced matter-of-factly. "I've also returned with several men to care for the animals. We'll have to find them rooms here on the grounds. The one chap always wears his native clothes, and he'll only sleep on the bare floorboards because of some religious belief."

"Sounds uncomfortable, but to each his own, I suppose."

"It's hard to know what's going on in the man's head, though, as he speaks no English. I had to hire an interpreter as well." Oliver laughed carelessly, then changed the subject. "Did you see my new carriage? It's quite fabulous. I'm driving it into town for *Le tout Newport*. Would you care to join me?"

"The daily three o'clock parade down Bellevue – definitely the place to show off your ride. I'll have to arrange my most extravagant coach to keep up appearances."

"You'll be glad you did after you see my new carriage." Oliver nodded.

Leaving the stable, the pair jumped into the coach and headed for Newport, leaving in plenty of time to join in the evening parade.

———

A few days later
July 23, 1894
Newport, Rhode Island

Tossing a white rose on the coffin, Sara uttered a soft prayer while the ropes were prepared to lower the casket into the ground. Island Cemetery was becoming much too familiar for her taste. Certainly not a place where she wanted to spend her summer season.

Sara wanted to be strong. She had to be strong. But her mother's death from a sudden heart attack a mere six weeks earlier had been a horrible shock. There'd been so much to attend to in settling her legal affairs. Gus had been named executor, along with George. As a lawyer, George was a great help to Gus, and the two had worked together settling Mrs. Whiting's estate.

Her mother's death had been sudden. She took ill shortly after returning to *Swanhurst* from Pau, France, where she'd rented a home. As the years passed, Mrs. Whiting had taken to spending her entire winters there.

Upon her return in May, Sara thought her mother looked frail. *"You're looking a bit pale, Mother. Are you feeling well?" she'd asked. "Perhaps you should visit the doctor for a checkup."*

"I'm quite fine, Sara. Just weary from traveling,"Mrs. Whiting had vehemently assured her.

But as spring gave way to summer, her mother seemed to grow listless and tire easily. In June, Mrs. Whiting fainted in the sitting room at *Swanhurst.*

"Get the doctor!" Sara had shouted to Owen, who'd been chopping wood behind the house.

While they'd waited for the doctor to arrive, Sara had berated herself for not following her instincts. *"I should have insisted Mother have a physical. Or at least summoned the doctor to Swanhurst. I should have done something!"*

"She's had a heart attack," the doctor had said. *"You'd best make sure all her matters are in order."*

Dr. Robinson didn't think Mrs. Whiting had much time. And he was right.

Sara had gone to her mother's bedside, hoping she'd regain consciousness if only for a moment, no matter how brief. Her prayers had been answered when her mother had opened her eyes to find Sara sitting in the chair, keeping vigil in the sickroom. Their conversation streamed through Sara's mind.

"Sara..." Mrs. Whiting's voice was dry and weak as she tried to talk.

"Shhhh, Mother. Don't exert yourself."

"Please," Mrs. Whiting whispered, "I need to say this... Sara, I never meant to be the undoing of your marriage to Oliver."

"Why are you bringing up old news?" Sara gently reprimanded. "That's all in the past."

"No, Sara, let me talk," Mrs. Whiting insisted, taking her daughter's hand in her cold palm. "Now that I'm an old woman and the scandal is behind us, I have many regrets. Regrets that I took your sisters to Paris to join you on your honeymoon – in the same suite, no less." The old woman closed her eyes for a moment with a sad nod. "I don't know what I was thinking... We should have stayed home and left the two of you alone. And I'm ashamed of myself for intercepting your telegrams in London. How presumptuous of me to have pretended to be you, demanding a divorce." The old woman closed her eyes again as if to blank out the memories. "I should have stayed out of the way, and now it's much too late. Too late for you and too late for Natica to share the Belmont name she so rightly deserves."

"Shhhh... Mother, please forget about all that." Sara fought against tears welling in her eyes. "In truth, you saved me from a life of misery with Oliver. You were right about him all along. I don't share your regrets. George has been a blessing sent from heaven. He's more than made up for those problems. Besides, Oliver doesn't deserve a daughter as wonderful as Natica."

"The two of you could have worked things out. And now, you would still be Mrs. Belmont and Natica would share the family lineage." With watery brown eyes, Mrs. Whiting gave her daughter a penetrating look. "I'm sorry, Sara," she whispered.

"I insist you stop this nonsense, Mother."

Sara couldn't prevent the quiet sob from escaping her throat when she watched her mother close her eyes for the last time. Mrs. Whiting's breathing grew lighter, then stopped completely, leaving the room perfectly still. A quiet fell, like an airless bell jar, and Sara had yielded to the grief of her tears.

And now this.

Pulling her mind from her memories, Sara shivered from the icy emptiness draining her soul. Once again gathered at Island Cemetery, the family was assembled for the second funeral in less than seven weeks.

Gus, her wise and dear big brother, was now also dead.

No one could have predicted that Gus would pass so soon after their mother, and from the same cause: heart disease.

"How could this be happening?" Sara wept, as the small ceremony came to an end. Milly and Jane, pale with grief, each took their turn placing a white rose on their brother's coffin.

"He seemed to be in perfect health." Milly sobbed, her eyes rimmed red with grief. "He was staying with us – he seemed to be fine. He even went out coaching in the afternoon."

"No one can predict a heart attack, Milly," Sara assured her sister in a meager effort to comfort her.

"After dinner, he took ill. I called for Dr. Robinson, and then you sent Dr. Cleveland." Milly whimpered, wringing her gloved hands while recalling the turn of events. "The doctors stayed at his bedside until morning, but Gus only grew worse."

Taking young Charlotte by the hand, Sara's heart ached for the girl. Only a few days from her fourteenth birthday, and she'd already lost both of her parents. Staring into the child's innocent blue eyes, Sara fought against a growing anger with God. Wasn't it bad enough he'd taken Charlotte's mother from the family? And now to take her father as well! Never in her wildest dreams would Sara have guessed her niece would be orphaned. Nor had raising Charlotte ever been part of the equation for Sara's life, but giving the young girl an earnest look, Sara squeezed her hand reassuringly.

"I will watch over you as if you are my own child," she promised her in a gentle voice.

Charlotte nodded slightly at her aunt through a tear-stained face, clutching Sara's hand as if it were her only lifeline.

Nothing would ever be the same.

"*Oh, why does life have to be full of such tragedy?*" Sara wondered silently. It'd been hard enough to try to make it through the day without her mother's wise guidance, but now her brother was gone as well. The fact that they'd both passed away within two short months of each other only added to her burden of grief.

And there was no Whiting heir to carry on the family name, she noted with resignation.

Set to marry Miss Clagett, Gus had received a note from her unexpectedly postponing the wedding, claiming illness. And then Gus was stunned to discover Miss Clagett had coldly announced a new engagement to Mr. Clifford Perin from Chicago directly to the press.

"How tactless of Miss Clagett not to speak directly to Gus about the matter," she whispered wearily. "Especially as the engagement notice had already been printed in the *New York Times.*" Sara knew it'd hurt Gus terribly to see the notice, not to mention his embarrassment among the set. But his friends rallied around him, assuring him he could do better for a wife.

And now he was dead.

Watching the procession to the hearse, Sara knew that *Swanhurst* and much of her mother's wealth now belonged to her. The estate had been passed from mother to daughter for two generations, and now it would pass to her. "I am the matriarch of the Whiting family now," she realized.

What was left of it.

"It's the end of an era," Sara thought with sad clarity.

Walking up beside her, George placed a compassionate hand on her shoulder. Their eyes met in a moment of affinity, drawing their hearts closer while Sara struggled to cope with this new loss. Looking at him through the black veil of her hat, she smiled wanly, glad she at least still had George to count on.

Chapter Twelve

A few weeks later
August 1, 1894
Newport, Rhode Island

The family gathered at the entrance to the Newport Casino, along with most of the townsfolk. Today's tennis match really didn't interest Natica too much, but she knew her friend Cathleen Neilson would be there with her family, and she was eager to see her. Passing under the brick archway, the family headed straight for the box seats above the outdoor tennis field reserved for members of the Casino Club. Tourists were relegated to lawn seats, which lacked a clear view of the field.

"Maybe your mother will let us go for an ice cream cone," Charlotte suggested to her younger cousin. The two had grown very close, becoming partners in mischief despite their age difference. Natica was coming up on her eleventh birthday, and Charlotte had just turned fourteen. The two girls stuck together like glue, helping each other come to terms with the deaths in their family. *Swanhurst* had seemed empty without their grandmother, and Natica knew her cousin missed her father, although she didn't cry as much anymore.

Her own father was a curious subject that upset the grown-ups. She really didn't understand any of it, but Natica couldn't help wondering about him even though her mother told her George had adopted her – whatever that was, and that he was her dad now. Natica had a sneaky suspicion they were keeping a secret from her, but she couldn't fathom what it was.

At least Charlotte knew her dad was in heaven.

"Oh, ice cream would be wonderful!" Natica quickly agreed. "Maybe we can buy a pinwheel, too. I don't really enjoy watching tennis matches, although I do love playing."

"Me either," Charlotte said. "But there's a lot to do around the casino."

Her mother glanced back at the girls as the family found their way to the viewing box.

"What are you two whispering about?" Sara asked, taking her seat next to George. The girls looked so grown up to her compared to the younger children, home under the watchful eyes of Bridget and their new nanny, Anna.

"Can we go get ice cream?" Natica asked with pleading eyes.

"You don't want to watch tennis?" Sara asked the girls.

"Not really, Aunt Sara. Do you mind if I take Natica over to the ice cream stand?"

"And can I get a balloon – or a pinwheel?" Natica implored, her voice full of excitement.

"Maybe," Sara said, distracted by the aristocratic crowd that'd convened for the afternoon sport. Everyone was dressed in their finery, smiling and laughing as they took seats in the casino boxes and bleachers. It promised to be a fun afternoon.

Overhearing the conversation, George reached into his pocket and

Pulled out a fat money clip. Leafing through the bills, he handed the girls

a whole dollar.

"You can have one of each if you'd like." He smiled generously. "A pin-wheel *and* a balloon."

"You're going to spoil them!" Sara admonished half-heartedly.

"And ice cream, too!" he added, with a mischievous glint at Sara.

"Thank you! Thank you!" Natica squealed with delight.

"Don't wander too far," Sara instructed. "Stay close to the casino grounds, and be sure to check back."

"We will. I promise," Charlotte said, taking charge of the money. She was wearing her long hair in a bun covered by a straw sun hat. Assuming a more mature style than her little cousin, Charlotte was at the in-between age of child and woman, and she frequently struggled between the urges of both behaviors.

In a rustle of petticoats, Natica followed her cousin back to the ice cream man stationed at the front of the casino. Winding their way through the crowd, they were in a merry mood, laughing and waving at friends they saw along the way. Finally, the sight of the red and white striped umbrella came into view, shading the cart where ice cream cones were being doled out to the wealthy families attending the tennis match.

"What flavor would you like?" Charlotte asked her little cousin.

"Chocolate, of course."

"Strawberry for me," Charlotte said. "It's my favorite."

Natica watched as her cousin told the round-faced gentleman, tending the cart what they wanted. He opened a silver cooler and scooped the ice cream high on cones for them, handing it off to their eager hands.

"Better eat fast, little ladies." He smiled, giving them a bunch of paper napkins. "The ice cream will melt quickly in this heat."

"Yes, sir," Charlotte said, paying him.

Taking the cones, they wandered over to an empty bench on the sidewalk in front of the casino. The girls sat down, shaded from the sun by an old elm tree, and zealously licked at their treats.

Then Natica spotted him.

The same man that had been hiding under the tree at *Swanhurst* on her birthday. And she'd noticed him other times around town, too. He always seemed to have his eye on her, but it didn't make her nervous or uncomfortable – just curious. Handsomely dressed, his face was half hidden by the shadow of his top hat, but Natica was certain it was the same man. A couple of times, she'd overheard her mother and grandmother call him 'Absent Absinthe Oliver.' And here he was, looking straight at her, watching her every move.

Shyly, Natica smiled at him from behind her ice cream cone. He smiled back and winked but didn't approach them. He just stood near the side of the casino entrance, leaning against the building while observing the two girls enjoying their cones.

"Oliver," Natica whispered. Impulsively she turned to her cousin. "Do you know who Oliver is?"

Charlotte stopped eating mid-lick. "Oliver?" She followed Natica's gaze and saw the man in question on the fringes of the casino crowd.

"Oh him," she grunted, growing protective. "You shouldn't talk to him. Your mother will be upset if you do. I know she wants you to stay away from him."

"But why? Who is he, Charlotte?" Natica asked. "Why is he always watching me?"

Her cousin ignored the questions, but after a minute, Charlotte got up from the bench.

"Come on," she ordered Natica, leading her back inside the casino. "Let's go find your parents."

"What about my pinwheel and my balloon?" Natica wailed.

"We'll get them later," Charlotte promised. "Now, just come on!"

Charlotte threw an anxious glance over her shoulder in Oliver's direction. He was still there, watching them intently.

Obediently following her cousin, Natica could tell Charlotte was nervous, and it was clear that this 'Oliver' man was the reason.

But no one would tell her why.

Two weeks later
August 15, 1894
Newport, Rhode Island

Men and women perched on wagons and chairs competed for a clear view of the auction block. The large crowd had convened this afternoon for the sale of the Whiting's surplus of beautiful carriages and horses. Leaving a large estate, Gus had been the horseman in the family, and his collection was extensive. Much more than they needed.

"I'm sad to sell them off," she'd confessed to George.

"I know, but the family only uses a few of the carriages. And four or five horses are sufficient to haul them," George had wisely pointed out.

In the end, Sara had agreed with George to put the majority of the stable contents up for auction to settle Gus's estate.

Now, working her way through the buzzing crowd, Sara sensed the excitement building in the enthusiastic townsfolk. Keen for the sale to begin, they evaluated the horses as they were led from the stalls to the front of the group for bidding. Sara noticed Mrs. Astor, as well as Mr. and Mrs. Burden and Mrs. Stevens. *"All in all,"* Sara thought, *"there must be at least one hundred people in attendance."*

And everyone was hoping to secure a good bargain on the Whiting's excellent animals and equipment.

The sale began promptly at the stroke of noon. William Easton, the auctioneer brought in from New York, began calling out prices in a booming, singsong voice.

"One fifty, here," Mr. Easton called loudly. "Who'll give me two? Two Hundred dollars for this amazing mare."

When the Whiting's coach wheelers *Marquis* and *Baron* were brought up for sale, the crowd responded in spirited bidding to the reasonable starting prices. James Stillman bought them both at a cost of $850. Fred Sheldon bought the bay gelding *Bismarck* for $425. The bay geldings *Nobel* and *Jim* were sold to Mr. Flagler for the bargain price of $525 and $250, respectively.

"I can't bear to part with Charlie," she'd told George, referring to her favorite bay gelding. So George bought the horse from Gus's estate for $375. *"Perhaps we should keep that fine coach, too,"* he'd suggested.

And the carriage was reserved from the sale. But the tandem cart was put on the auction block, and Sara's cousin, Mrs. J.A. Swan, bought it for $285.

As the afternoon wore on, the auction drew to a close. One by one, people departed the stables, leaving only a few folks milling around to secure their purchases. Weary, Sara decided to walk back to *Swanhurst* to check on the children. Strolling down the Newport sidewalk under the branches of tall trees, she was shaded from the hot sun, leaves flickering shadows over the sidewalk.

Lost in thought, she reviewed the afternoon sale in her mind. *"An entire lifetime of Gus's work has been dissolved in one single afternoon,"* she thought.

In spite of the picture-perfect weather, Sara fought back the feeling of loss that echoed through her, like an empty house that'd been abandoned to ghosts.

Only she felt like the ghost now, left to find her way among the living.

⚜

Five months later
January 4, 1895
Newport, Rhode Island

Newport was an empty town in winter, except for the local residents. A cold snap had passed through New England, leaving a light dusting of snow over the grounds of Marble House. The beveled-glass door leading to the courtyard opened, and Alva quietly welcomed a man inside.

"No one saw me, I'm certain," Oliver informed her, slipping into the back entrance of Marble House.

"Are you absolutely sure?" Alva asked. "We've really got to be careful. With Willie in New York for the next couple of days, it seems everyone is suspicious of our association. If I end up in divorce court, I want to have the upper hand for a settlement," she fretted. "And it would be disastrous if I were seen cavorting with you in my home in his absence."

"Somehow, Alva, I don't really think you care who sees us together," he chided, following her upstairs. "Besides, the servants know everything. You're only fooling yourself if you believe otherwise."

Easy laughter trilled from her lips. Wearing her favorite dress, she hoped the gold tones of the thread highlighted her hair, which she'd given special attention to in anticipation of Oliver's visit. Taking him by the hand, Alva seductively led him to her room. Once inside, she closed the door, lowering her lashes flirtatiously.

"Mr. Belmont..." she teased, falling into his embrace. "It's very improper for you to be alone with me in my bedroom."

Wrapping his arms around her, Oliver kissed her deeply. "Whatever do you mean, Mrs. Vanderbilt? I can think of no better place to be except here with you."

They kissed again, falling onto the bed in a tangle of arms and legs.

"I don't want to go anywhere or do anything except stay here with you," Alva whispered, melting into his caresses.

"Then we'll stay here until the world comes to an end," Oliver promised, thinking himself a poet.

"That would suit me perfectly," she answered, kissing him deeply.

The clock ticked by, and the two lovers lost themselves in their insistent passion, indulging in the forbidden sweetness of their affair. Bit by bit, the clothing came off until they were making love like a married couple. Neither seemed to care about the propriety of such an arrangement, especially since Alva's marriage was in a shambles due to Willie's constant flirtations with women half his age.

And Oliver, used to having his own way, was much too enamored with this confident woman to refuse her attentions. Lately, making love to her seemed to be the focus of his existence, and he delighted in satisfying her.

The minutes turned to hours, and they finally paused, tired and exhilarated from their intimate liaison. Laying amidst a jumble of sheets, they held each other in the waning sunlight, satiated from the afternoon's passion.

"Things can't go on this way much longer." Alva sighed, worried. "I've got to get out of this marriage, and the sooner, the better. I just can't bring myself to upset the children."

Listening as she spoke, Oliver stroked her hair. "Children are resilient," he said. "But you must do things the way you see best. I admit I'd like nothing more than to have you all to myself. I hate all this skulking around, but if I have to sneak to be with you, then so be it."

"What was that?" Alva shot up in bed. "I thought I heard Willie calling me. He's supposed to be in New York until Monday."

"Alva..." The sound echoed through the halls of Marble House. Oliver recognized William's voice, and the two lovers jumped into action, throwing their clothes on as quickly as they could move.

"He must have returned to Newport on the last ferry," Alva gasped in panic. "Quick, Oliver, hide in my dressing room. He'll never find you in there."

Oliver grabbed his shoes and hurriedly pulled the door closed behind him. Pushing behind Alva's clothing, he hid among the ruffles and flounces and grew silent, straining to listen.

"What are you doing in your chambers at such an early hour?" William asked, entering the room. "The sun hasn't even set." He looked around suspiciously, sensing that he'd surprised his wife.

"I had a headache and decided on a nap," Alva answered, keeping her tone nonchalant. If Willie discovered Oliver, her chances to sue him for infidelity would backfire.

Tilting his head skeptically, her husband assessed her demeanor. Experienced at extramarital affairs, William was dubious of Alva's headache excuse. Infidelity was usually endorsed by the gentlemen of the set, but he was well aware that his willful wife liked to blaze trails in areas usually reserved for men.

Opposing each other in a stand-off of wills, their discourse was interrupted by a loud crash coming from the direction of her closet.

Turning toward the disturbance, William threw her a stern gaze. "A headache, eh?" he scoffed. Spinning on his heel, he stepped toward the dressing room.

"Don't go in there!" Alva bellowed, moving to stand between him and the doorway. "That's my personal room."

Ignoring her objections, Willie pushed her aside and entered the closet. Riffling through the hangers, he pushed apart the skirts and gowns, only to discover Oliver hiding behind Alva's clothes.

"I knew it!" William exclaimed.

"Hello, Willie," Oliver said, offering him a contrite smile.

Alva stood by helplessly, debating her next move.

"Get out of there!" William ordered, flustered at being on the receiving side of an affair. "You know I could have your head for this." But he only half meant it. Secretly, William thought the entire scene rather comical. Oliver was his good friend, and admittedly he'd lost his affection for Alva. In a way, the old chap had done him a favor by keeping her occupied. Besides, the attraction between Alva and his friend was no secret to Willie, and Oliver knew of his personal dalliances with young débutantes.

William was hardly in a position to criticize him for sneaking into bed with his wife.

Particularly when he'd just spent the past night with his latest love interest in New York.

The three returned to Alva's bedroom and stood staring at each other, each at a loss for words. After a few speechless moments, William shook his head in disbelief, then moved for the chamber door.

"I need a drink," he announced.

"Wait!" Alva shouted, her voice ringing through the room. "It's clear this farce of a marriage has reached a low point."

Stopping, William turned back, evaluating the pair.

"I'll be filing for divorce in the morning," she informed him in a commanding tone. "And if you make one mention of this incident, I'll drag your name through the mud – which will be an easy matter, as everyone's aware of your philandering."

Opening his mouth to respond, William stopped himself mid-breath. With a vexed glance at his wife, he shook his head and stomped from the

room, slamming the door behind.

Chapter Thirteen

Four months later
May 18, 1895
Kent, England

"Oh, Sara, I'm so glad you were able to join me on this trip. It's so exciting to be staying in a real castle." Milly glowed, clearly delighted, as they toured the halls of the old fortress.

Walmer Castle was the home of Milly's daughter-in-law, Flora, who was now Lady Blackwood. After her marriage to Terrence Blackwood, also known as Lord Dufferin to the locals, the couple had moved to Kent, England.

"It is exciting," Sara said. "Thank you for inviting me. I only wish George could have made the trip."

"I'm sure there will be other invitations to Walmer in the future." Dressed in a finely embroidered gown, Milly had stepped into her role as Mr. Davis's wife with poise and ease.

Following Milly through the rooms, the two continued exploring the castle, passing through a long, arched corridor paneled with dark wood.

"When will John be back? Is he going to be joining us for dinner tonight?"

"He's in the city today, working on a legal proposal for an associate." Milly's voice filled with pride as she spoke of her husband. "But he'll join us tomorrow, just in time for Lord Dufferin's fancy ball on Saturday night. It's being held in honor of our visit, and the guest list is filled with important names."

"I'm looking forward to meeting everyone," Sara said enthusiastically.

"Me too. It's going to be wonderful fun! And quite different from New York parties."

At the end of the hallway, the corridor opened into a wide, circular room with hardwood floors and wainscoting. High ceilings rose above Sara and Milly, and they stepped up to the glowing fireplace to warm their hands against the chill.

"This must be the Lantern Room I've heard about," Milly said, leaning her head back to view the rotunda.

"It's lovely." Following Milly's gaze, Sara looked up and saw the glass dome, a skylight delivering bright sunbeams into the room.

"I hear there are several greenhouses, too. They have a kitchen garden for vegetables and herbs, as well as a greenhouse just for flowers."

"We should take a walk through it."

"That would be nice if we can find it! I'm having a hard time keeping my bearings with all these corridors and winding hallways."

"I'm sure it's near the kitchen."

"I'm sure you're right." Milly nodded. "Oh, Sara, just being here makes me feel like a queen."

"It certainly does give one the effect of being a royal."

"Did you ever think this would be in my future? Not only marrying a wonderful man, but being related to an actual British lord. How perfect that John's daughter, Flora, married Lord Blackwood. Now, I'm traveling at John's side to distant castles and hobnobbing with European socialites – it's beyond my wildest dreams."

"Such a wonderful turn of events," Sara said. "I know there were many who said you'd live your life as a spinster. But you've certainly had the last word Milly, now, haven't you?"

"I suppose I have." Milly chuckled. "But you always encouraged me, Sara. Inspiring me to dress in beautiful gowns and attend parties and balls as if I were a younger woman. You've shown me that love isn't reserved exclusively for the junior members of the set. I may not have been a teenage débutante, but I've certainly found happiness, despite all the speculation that it would never happen for me."

"But it did happen, Milly! And here we are in England, being entertained as the guests of honor, thanks to your new husband's family."

"Yes…" Milly spun in a circle, looking at the decor as if to soak up the magnificent castle. "What a great adventure! I've learned to have new faith. I want to breathe in every single moment and live my life anew."

Watching Milly, Sara admired her sister's confidence. "I think I'll follow your example. Come on, let's go up to our chambers and get ready for lunch. I have a feeling the next couple of weeks are going to be very busy."

"And very exciting!" Milly added, with a flourish of her fancy gown.

⁂

The next week
August 16, 1895
Newport, Rhode Island

The citizens of Newport seemed as proud of the new Breakers as if it were their own personal palace. Conversations in the casino and clubs centered around the majestic new cottage. Clearly, Richard Morris Hunt had created yet another masterpiece in the new home, as the lavish mansion was more like a palace than any cottage.

Shown in by the butler, William stood in the grand entrance, pondering the fact that few would have guessed The Breakers to be Mr. Hunt's last and finest effort. When the newspapers announced that the architect had died several weeks before, the cottage stood as his very last architectural triumph. Undoubtedly, the building would last for many years as a tribute to Hunt's talent and skill.

Following the butler through the Great Hall, William examined the palatial room, towering fifty feet over his head. He was duly impressed by the five-story home. The luxurious cottage boasted over seventy rooms and took up an entire acre of land. William knew Cornelius had insisted the home be made as fireproof as possible, and as a result, the cottage was constructed of steel and limestone, with virtually no wood except for the imported paneling. The chambers were finished with marble walls in addition to intricate mosaics, making the home easily comparable to a royal residence. Gilt and gold were employed lavishly in the interior design, which had been contracted to Jules Allard and son, in conjunction with Ogden Codmen, Jr.

This new Breakers, rebuilt, was a glittering, opulent reinvention of the original.

Chuckling quietly to himself, William took in the surroundings. "I wonder," he thought aloud, "if my brother isn't trying to outdo Alva's architectural achievements?" He noted that the limestone fortress was clearly an improvement over the original house, not only structurally but in its splendid interior as well. Perhaps the original home's destruction by fire was a blessing?

"William! You're late." Alice glided into the Great Hall and led him toward the library, smiling. "The party was last night."

"I know. I'm sorry I missed it. I had to be in New York for a meeting." he apologized to his sister-in-law while settling comfortably in a bergére chair. "But I wanted to stop by and congratulate you on your new cottage. I must say it is superb!"

"Thank you. We're very pleased with the design," Alice said, taking the chair across from him. Attractive and self-assured, Alice was dressed in a simple gray gown, her dark-brown hair pulled to the top of her head in a popular style. "Cornelius and I received the fabulous Faberge egg you sent for the housewarming! It will look beautiful in the morning room."

"I'm glad you like it. I understand it once belonged to a Russian empress."

"How lovely. Perhaps I'll start a collection."

"That would be a nice pastime. How was your ball last night?"

A maid entered the library carrying a silver tea tray. Placing it on the center table, the servant poured two cups, served them, and silently excused herself.

"I decided the house opening would be the perfect opportunity for Gertrude to make her début." Pride was unabashedly written over Alice's face. "It's a shame you missed it. But I intend on entertaining on a regular basis now. Last night's guest list was wonderful, although I think we may have inadvertently created a situation."

"Oh?" William looked up. "Anything I can help with?"

"Your brother?" Alice frowned.

"Hmmm... I'm not sure I can be much help there. What happened, if I might ask?"

"Well, Gertrude looked beautiful, and as you know, most of the family was here, including your nephew, Neily." She referred to her son, the third 'Cornelius' in the Vanderbilt family, nicknamed 'Neily' to tell them apart.

"That doesn't sound like a problem."

"It wasn't," she sighed. "Until Grace Wilson caught his eye. My

husband doesn't approve of her, and I must admit I have some misgivings about the girl as well. She's been around a bit too much to preserve her innocence. Parties throughout Europe with foreign cooking and fine wines have made her too worldly for her age, not to mention the rumors surrounding her and the Prince of Wales." Alice raised a brow and continued, "Did you know she goes yachting in her best gowns and picture hats! Can you imagine? But worst of all, we think she's more interested in money-hunting than husband-hunting, a skill well-honed by the Wilson family. It looks as though she's set her sights on Neily. And he fell for it hook, line, and sinker."

"All that at one party?" William fought back an amused smile while remembering similar comments he'd heard about Sara Swan Whiting when Oliver had first courted her. "Perhaps it's just a passing fancy, and the two of you are making a mountain from a molehill? Sometimes, if you give these matters too much attention, you create a fire where there was once only a spark."

"Perhaps." Alice raised her teacup to her lips. "But if the situation begins to heat up too much, Cornelius and I are seriously considering sending him to Europe. In his absence, Grace would surely be captivated by other courting gentlemen and forget about Neily – and he'd forget about her."

"The way Oliver forgot about Sara when his father sent him to Bremen?"

Alice grimaced, considering his comment. Her eyes grew distant as she set her cup on the table.

"I hear the ninth Duke of Marlborough is courting your daughter," Alice commented, directing the conversation to a new topic.

"I suppose you could say that." William shrugged. "It's more like an arranged marriage by her mother. Alva doesn't seem to care that Consuelo is not in love with him. She wants a royal marriage for the family, and you know how she behaves when she wants something."

"Well, even though you're divorced, I should think you would have some influence over your daughter's future. What do you think of Sonny?"

"What does it matter what I think?" William blurted. "I'm not the one that's going to have to live with him for the rest of my life." He paused, collecting his thoughts. "I just want Consuelo to be happy, Alice. In all honesty, I wish Alva would back down and let the girl marry Mr. Rutherford, whom she claims has captured her heart. He's a nice enough chap and comes from a good family. But Alva wants a royal title, and she is terrorizing the poor girl into complying with her wishes. Consuelo has appealed to me for help, but there's not much I can do for her."

"Alva can be stubborn," Alice said. "She's certainly not one to cross when it comes to getting her way. I'm sure it will all work out for the best."

"Where's my brother?" William didn't want to discuss his ex-wife anymore.

"Cornelius went down to the harbor to check on the yacht. He'll be back in an hour or so. Would you like to stay for dinner?"

"I wish I could," William apologized. "But I've already made plans."

She gave him a curious glance but was too polite to question him. Which was a good thing because he had a secret rendezvous with Mary Ann Hoffman, one of the season's newest young débutantes. And why not? He was no longer married, and the children lived with Alva now, so he didn't have to worry about setting an example.

"Maybe another time then."

He got up from the chair in an easy move. "Yes, of course. I would enjoy that." Alice led him into the Grand Hall. "Give my best to Cornelius, will you?" William called.

"I'll do that." Alice waved, watching as the butler showed him out of the glistening new cottage.

Two weeks later
September 3, 1895
Newport, Rhode Island

It was already September, yet summer refused to surrender its heat to the cooler evenings of autumn, just like many in the set who refused to relinquish their hold on the Newport party season, happy for one last chance to dance the night away at Belcourt.

"Well, Oliver, this is quite a ball you've thrown together," William praised his friend, while touring the home in an easy gait. "I'm glad to see you're feeling better. The ladies were quite disappointed the other day when you postponed the event."

"I don't know what hit me, but I was really sick for a day or two," Oliver said, strolling with Willie through the gothic-style mansion. "Luckily, I began to feel better, so I decided to throw the party after all. But I don't think I'll be up to leading any dances tonight. I'm going to stick to receiving only."

"I'm certain your guests won't mind."

"Does it bother you that your ex-wife is hosting tonight's party with me? Alva really has been a tremendous help with the preparations."

"No." William shrugged off-handedly. "She has a real flair for entertaining. I'm glad she could assist you."

Oliver smiled at his congenial friend as they ambled toward the staircase leading to the balcony over the ballroom of Oliver's new home, Belcourt.

"I took Alva's lead and hired Richard Hunt to design the cottage, with special attention to my interest in matters of an equestrian nature. The entire first floor is devoted to horses with stalls constructed entirely of teakwood."

"Your horses live better than most people," William joked.

"These aren't just any horses, Willie. These are prize winners."

"Then I suppose they deserve such luxurious stalls." Following his friend up the stairs, he said, "I'm guessing you were one of Hunt's last clients."

"What a shame to hear of his passing. I'm glad I didn't delay in building."

Reaching the balcony, the men stood quietly, watching the dancers make good use of the fabulous ballroom. Laughing and waltzing guests filled the hall, and it seemed everyone was there, from wealthy Americans to titled Europeans.

Massive beams divided the hall ceiling into elegantly carved archways, curving skyward the entire length of the ballroom. Instead of plaster walls, large and ornate stained-glass windows lent intricate designs and brilliant colors along both sides of the room, leading the eye to focus on the immense fireplace taking up the entire wall on the opposite end of the hall.

As the waltz ended, Mullally's orchestra, brought in from the casino for the evening, filled the room with discordant sounds as the musicians retuned their instruments. Dancers searched for new partners and assembled in groups waiting for the cotillion to begin.

"It looks as though the Dom Pérignon is taking their minds off the humidity."

"Apparently so." Oliver laughed. "Come on. Let's go back downstairs."

Leaving the balcony, the men headed to the main ballroom. Oliver gestured towards the potted greenery and trees as they walked into the hall.

"My florist threw these palm decorations together at the last minute. The original order was lost. I couldn't very well use wilted, dead flowers. But what I'm lacking in roses, I've made up for with spirits – and electric lighting. Edison did my house himself, you know."

"That man is simply a genius." Willie grinned.

There was no jealousy or rivalry between these two men. They both had anything and everything they desired and enjoyed sharing news of modern inventions with each other.

"You'd better be careful, or you might start a new trend with these electric lights," William advised him.

"Me? A trend setter?" Oliver asked. "Well, if the electric lighting isn't impressive enough, I'll dazzle my guests with these fancy party favors." Oliver pointed to the table near the opposite wall of the ballroom. "They cost me over seven thousand dollars. But it's only money." He finished with a laugh.

As they arrived at the table, William reviewed the offering of gifts for the guests. Ash receivers, wide and gorgeous satin sashes with rhinestones and real pearls, and satin caps in color and form like those worn by the Belmont's jockeys; all made a rich display for the guests. More gifts for the ladies included Parisian flower fans, satin bags hung with jewels, and small satin slippers filled with natural flowers. But to William, the coup de grâce were the birdcages with real singing canaries.

"Your father would roll over in his grave if he knew the way you were spending his money." William chuckled. "I feel certain he'd throw a conniption." The two laughed heartily at the remark. "Your collection of shining armor is getting to be quite large, too." He teased Oliver as they passed the display. "Do you think you might be getting a bit carried away with your hobby?"

Statues of four horses bearing as many styles of ancient armor were conspicuous figures in the hall, displayed beside four more styles of

chainmail from ancient times.

"If you keep adding to your collection, you may have to build another house with a larger ballroom." William laughed good-naturedly. "Or start a museum." He liked Oliver's eccentric interests, although there were those that criticized his colleague as being queer. The Whiting family usually led the crowd in that department.

But William thought Oliver made life a lot more interesting. His picnics and parties had blown a fresh wind into society's gatherings, where conversation usually revolved around fashion or engagement news. Matters Willie considered boring – unless they were being explained to him by a beautiful young woman.

"Are you still planning on going down to New York for the boat race?"

"Absolutely," Oliver said. "I wouldn't miss the *America's Cup* for anything."

"That's good news, because I plan on winning this year with my fabulous new yacht."

"You are the favorite, but you're going to have some tough competition," Oliver cautioned. "All the best boats in Newport are lifting anchor now and heading for New York."

"I know," William said, his tone growing cocky. "And I don't care who's entering. I'm going to win this year."

"There's no question *Defender* is a fine ship, especially with the aluminum hull," Oliver agreed. "You make for some serious competition in the sport, Willie."

A flurry of dancers regrouped the moment the orchestra started a new waltz. Laughter and gaiety permeated Belcourt's ballroom, much to the joy of its owner.

"Let's step out for a cigar."

"I'd like that," William agreed.

"I think I'm going to turn in early," Oliver announced with a shrug. "The party is a success and will continue quite nicely without my presence. Besides, I'm sure you'll keep an eye on things for me."

"Of course. Come on then." William started for the entrance. "We'll have a smoke, and then you get some rest. We don't want you passing out on us like a young débutante."

"Watch who you're calling a débutante." Oliver frowned, giving him a light jab.

The two chuckled and slipped from the ballroom, unnoticed by the guests.

Chapter Fourteen

Two days later
September 5, 1895
Newport, Rhode Island

Reading the newspaper account of Oliver's extravagant new mansion built at the bottom of Bellevue Avenue made Sara bristle. The house was typical of his over-the-top tastes and personal indulgences. It was easy to see the circus her life would have become if their ill-fated marriage had endured.

Instead, Alva Vanderbilt had hosted the new home's first ball with Oliver. "I'll never understand how that woman managed to avoid the scandal of her divorce," she whispered. Sara threw the newspaper aside and went to check on the children studying with Anna, working hard to keep her lingering aversion toward Oliver at bay.

Walking through the foyer, she heard a knock on the door. Not waiting for the maid, Sara greeted a delivery man waiting on the porch. Wearing a brown uniform and a matching patrol-style cap, he smiled politely.

"A package for Miss Natica Rives," he said, holding up a box.

"That's my daughter," Sara said, signing for the package. "Today is her birthday."

Taking the box from the man, she bid him 'good day' and carried it back into the parlor. Inspecting the package, she gave it an easy shake
while noting there was no return address identifying the sender.

"Perhaps I should open this before I give it to Natica," Sara thought, anxious to see the contents.

Gently undoing the ribbon, she lifted the top off the box. Pulling aside the tissue paper, Sara saw a beautiful Swiss cylinder music box tucked inside. Intricate wooden inlay was accented with colorful enamel in a lovely geometric design. A card lay on top and she opened it quickly, curious to see who had sent the expensive gift.

Happy 12th Birthday Natica

Love,

Uncle Oliver

A wave of anger flushed over her. "Uncle Oliver, indeed!" she hissed. "The nerve of that man!" Sara threw the delicate music box back in the package, breaking the hinge, and shoved it out of sight behind the sofa with plans to dispose of it as quickly as possible.

She couldn't be bothered returning it.

⚜

Two months later

October 4, 1895

Poughkeepsie, New York

Perched on the seat inside the ornate carriage, Oliver surveyed the view of the New York countryside. Open fields met with forests in acres of verdant land, colorful in the crimson and orange hues of autumn foliage. Haystacks were gathered in the fields, ready for harvest, while livestock dotted the pastures, lazy and content. Clear flowing streams splashed into ponds nestled in the crook of the hillsides while the sun glowed warm over the idyllic scene.

The team of horses pulled together in unison, their hooves pounding a steady rhythm on the road, exhilarating Oliver. Coaching was one of his favorite hobbies. "*These trips across the countryside keep life interesting,*" he thought, catching sight through the window of their caravan. A parade of fine carriages met his sight, full of friends and family on a pleasure ride from Manhattan to Tuxedo Park.

Gazing at the scenery, Oliver's reflections turned to his parents, bringing him mixed emotions. "*I miss having my Little Mo to talk to,*" he thought. "*But not so much my father's constant pestering for a career.*" Since their passing, Oliver had resolved to live his life to the fullest and let the dead rest in peace.

"*One good thing has come from all the changes,*" he decided. Alva had met with a lawyer the very day after they'd been caught alone together by William at Marble House. In her usual take-charge manner, she'd been able to secure a divorce in record time. Only one month later, the judge ruled in Alva's favor, giving her full custody of the children, a ten-million-dollar settlement, plus one hundred thousand dollars a year in alimony – as well as ownership of Marble House. *"All's well that ends well."* He grinned.

Oliver had worried the affair might drive a wedge between Willie and him, but to their credit, the friendship had been strong enough to endure the breach of trust. *"It's obvious William has lost any fondness for Alva,"* he reflected, which was fine with Oliver. He'd come to realize the woman was able to captivate his interest at the expense of all others. Although the press was constantly full of speculation about a possible marriage, they were happy just to be able to enjoy each other's company unencumbered.

"The horse has lost a shoe, sir," the driver hollered, interrupting Oliver's contemplations. "We'll have to stop and get it taken care of."

"Signal the Vanderbilt carriage," Oliver yelled back. He turned to Alva beside him on the coach seat. "I'm sure it's nothing to worry about," he assured her as the driver reined the four-horse team to a stop in the town of Poughkeepsie.

Oliver watched the Vanderbilt carriage slow to a halt behind them, carrying Alva's daughter Consuelo, and her fiancé, Sonny, the Duke of Marlboro. Mr. and Mrs. Jay were also traveling in the Vanderbilt coach, tagging along for the adventure.

The carriage stopped in front of the town square, and the duke quickly alighted from the coach to stretch his legs. Wearing black slacks and a double-breasted jacket, the man headed to the side of the cobblestone street.

"How serious is it, Ollie?" Alva joined him while he inspected the horse.

"At this point, it's merely a nuisance. He lost a shoe back by Wappinger Falls. He's a fabulous animal, and I don't want him to go lame." Oliver shrugged and gave her a resigned look. "I'm afraid we'll be delayed a while until the blacksmith can take care of it."

"How long will it take?" Her face showed her displeasure with the delay.

"An hour or so, but we should still make Staatsburg by this afternoon, as planned."

The driver separated the horse from the team and disappeared around the corner, leading the animal to the farrier's shop.

"Well, at least it's a beautiful day," Alva said, taking in the clear, cerulean sky. "All things considered, I suppose the situation could be a lot more troublesome."

"I was happy to take a break anyway," the Duke said, sauntering over to join them. "I asked Consuelo to walk with me, but she says she's fine waiting in the carriage. I don't know how she can sit for so long without stretching."

"Good breeding," Alva joked, noticing a crowd gathering to watch the travelers.

"I suppose," Sonny answered with a shrug. "I, for one, prefer getting a little exercise when the opportunity presents itself." The Duke sauntered across the street, oblivious to the growing commotion.

"I think our arrival has been noticed by the locals." Oliver surveyed the group assembled on the sidewalk.

"It's not because of us." Alva discreetly pointed at the Duke. "Royalty has arrived in their small hamlet. You'd think Consuelo would want to share the limelight." Alva regarded her daughter sitting alone in the carriage, appearing bored and disinterested.

"She doesn't seem to enjoy the attention." Oliver laughed, watching the young lady peer at the crowd from the coach window.

"Nor does the Duke realize he's become the subject of scrutiny," Alva said, watching the man strut in front of the Nelson home, blind to the crowd he was attracting.

Soon the entire street was filled with nearly a hundred bystanders trying to get a look at the visiting royal. Apparently, word of his arrival had moved through the town like wildfire.

"This is exactly why I urged Consuelo to marry the duke," Alva announced smartly. "All the money in a world doesn't buy the bloodline of European royalty."

Oliver laughed, amused by her preoccupation with the town's interest in the duke's visit. "A bankrupt royal is no better than a bankrupt commoner," Oliver noted in a soft voice. "I'd rather have the money than the title any day of the week," he said, just as the local police moved in to contain the crowd.

Chapter Fifteen

One month later
November 6, 1895
New York, New York

The silhouette of the city buildings cast long shadows against the morning sun. The days were getting shorter, and the trees had dropped their colorful leaves, yielding to winter. Today the weather was a little warmer, and Sara was glad for the bit of sunshine to chase away the chill, if only for the day.

George had been putting in long hours on an important legal case for the firm and had decided to stay at his mid-town apartment, so he could focus on his work. Sara hadn't seen him in several days and missed his company more than she cared to admit. On a whim, she'd spontaneously decided to go to his suite this morning and surprise George.

Quickly dressing in a fashionable royal-blue cashmere gown, Sara donned a matching cloak. It hung from her shoulders in a charming way, swaying around her frame as she moved. Her half-bonnet was a darker shade of blue, the ribbon tied under her chin in a large bow. Checking her appearance in the mirror, Sara had found it quite pleasing and left the home to hail a cab.

Stopping first at a French bakery, she bought George's favorite chocolate croissants, hopeful the two of them might be able to steal an hour together before he had to be at his downtown office. Excited at the prospects of surprising him, Sara peeked in the bag of pastries and smiled.

Taking in the view through the carriage window, she saw the morning shops opening for the day, watching as proprietors placed crates of fresh vegetables and fruit along the sidewalk for sale. Her mind drifted to the current talk making the rounds among the set. Everyone was gossiping about a story the newspapers had printed regarding the sorry state of the Vanderbilt marriage. Alva ignored the twitter, wearing her divorced status like a badge of honor instead of shame. She'd actually gone around New York claiming to be the very first divorced woman in society! What an insult to Sara – and to Mrs. Slater before her! Alva simply had to be the center of attention, and it was clear to Sara that she would bend the truth if necessary to meet those ends. *"In spite of her claims of being scorned, it appears Alva is still receiving invitations to the most exclusive parties,"* she thought.

Except for the Vanderbilt soirées, where she continued to be shunned.

"The Vanderbilt family has their own drama these days." Shortly after the new Breakers was opened, Sara heard Cornelius Vanderbilt had suffered a seriously debilitating stroke. Apparently, his condition was the result of a terrible quarrel with his son, Neily. Cornelius had forbidden the young man to marry Miss Grace Wilson, indifferent to their claims of true love.

"Neily ran off and married her anyway," Sara thought. *"Even though he was faced with the threat of being disinherited from the Vanderbilt fortune."* She couldn't find fault with the young lovers, quite aware herself of the force propriety could wield on a courtship.

Still, it made Sara sad to know the stroke had left Mr. Vanderbilt quite incapacitated, and now, The Breakers had become a convalescent home. *"With Cornelius bound to a wheelchair now, Alice's plans for entertaining in their new palace have been abandoned,"* Sara mused. She was disappointed to know there wouldn't be any parties or dinners held in the beautiful home after all.

Concluding her short ride, the cab pulled up in front of the Brunswick Hotel and drew to a stop. The driver quickly jumped from his seat and came around to open the door for Sara. She paid him and added a generous tip before heading to the building's entrance.

Entering the lobby, Sara thought back to her visit to George's suite so many years before as a young débutante. Life had fallen short of fulfilling the dreams she had designed for herself, and she wondered at the way things had turned out with the two of them now married.

Passing the elevator, Sara made her way to the staircase, relishing the exercise, while shifting her focus to more pleasant events. In all fairness, Sara admitted to herself that life with George and the children was wonderful.

"Would we ever find the courage to live our lives if we knew what the future held for us?" she murmured.

Reaching the apartment door, Sara paused and listened, hearing faint conversation filter from the walls within. "I must be mistaken," she whispered, glancing at her delicate diamond watch. *"Eight o'clock in the morning is much too early to be entertaining guests."* Sara knocked softly on the door. The delicious smell of the chocolate croissants wafted from the paper sack she carried, and she enjoyed the excitement her surprise afforded her while waiting for George to answer the door.

A rustling and scurrying emanated from inside his apartment, and Sara wondered what was taking him so long. Finally, he opened the door; his face flushed as if he'd been hurrying to answer her knock.

"Sara!" George was clearly surprised, just as she'd hoped, but something about his demeanor made her hesitate. His usually well-combed hair was mused and disheveled. Wearing a crisp, white dress shirt and brown suit pants, Sara noticed his bow tie was missing, and his collar was unbuttoned.

She had the distinct impression she'd interrupted something, and an uncomfortable mood was fast descending on her cheery disposition.

"What are you doing here at this hour?" George inquired, his tone solicitous.

"I missed you," she replied in slow, measured words. "I thought I'd surprise you with your favorite pastry." She held up the bag of croissants and entered his suite. A thick uneasiness hung between husband and wife, a veil dividing the room. They stood facing each other, but George did not meet her eyes.

"Tell me, George, why do I feel like an unwelcome guest in my husband's apartment?"

He smoothed his hair back with a hand and laughed nervously. "Don't be ridiculous. I was just getting dressed to go to the office. In fact, I was planning on coming home tonight to see you and the children. I thought we could take in the theatre or maybe have dinner at 'Sherry's'?"

Suspicion poured through Sara, and she found herself doubting his words. Looking around the room, she searched for a clue to support her discomfort. She'd never felt this way around George before and had always trusted him implicitly. But her trust seemed to evaporate in the morning light of his suite.

"You're acting strangely," Sara said flatly, studying him.

"I'm just a bit weary," he replied. "I've been working very hard on this case."

"Indeed," Sara answered. That was when she smelled it: the unmistakable scent of lilac perfume. A quiet gasp escaped her, and she suddenly realized they were not alone in his room.

The couple stared at each other in silence, each standing their ground.

Sara's attention was caught by an almost indiscernible shuffling emanating from behind the closed door of the bathroom. She nonchalantly walked over to a window near
the water closet, feigning a glimpse at the city skyline. With a quick move, she threw open
the door to the small chamber.

A young woman recoiled, stepping back from the door as though she'd been trying to
listen. Adjusting the bodice of her dress, she stumbled, staring meekly at Sara.

Stunned into silence, Sara felt her heart break. It was a fast, clean wound, delivered with
the sureness of a Samurai's sword.

Well aware that most aristocratic men had mistresses – even Mr. Astor – Sara was
nonetheless shocked. It was quietly accepted for a man to have a lady on the side – some
even carried on publicly. Yet, knowing this did nothing to stop the crush of pain. Sara had
thought George was happy and devoted to only her. Apparently, when it came to men,
she was still much too naïve for her own good.

Numb with shock, Sara turned and rushed for the door, unable to face the truth. She
had to escape his apartment.

Escape him.

Escape *her*.

The identity of the young woman hiding in George's bathroom was unknown to Sara,
and she didn't want to know, either. What difference would it make, anyway? Her trust
and faith in her marriage was broken, shattered in an instant like fragile crystal – and like
so many of her dreams.

"Wait!" George rushed after her. "Sara, please! It's not what you think!"

He reached for her hand, and she spun around angrily, throwing the paper sack of
croissants directly in his face. He jerked back from the blow, and she escaped into the
hallway, slamming the door behind her.

Hot tears burned her eyes as she rushed down the corridor, moving so fast she momen-
tarily stumbled on her petticoat. George appeared in the hotel hallway shouting after her
to return, but she could not.

She would not.

When she finally hit the street, the fresh air smacked against her face, allowing her to
gain a small degree of composure. Quickly, Sara flagged down an approaching cab and
jumped inside, not waiting for the driver to open the door. Now, in the privacy of the
taxi, she did not fight her tears but allowed them to flow with the pain of her heartache.

What should she do?

What *could* she do?

Another divorce?

Sara's stomach lurched in repulsion at the thought as the coach carried her home. Her mind churned, working to understand why George would take a lover. She had thought he was happy, bitterly realizing that her fondness for him had turned into real love.

This was just too much to take. Her heart was broken, yet again, this time by George. Sara had never imagined he would step out on her like so many other husbands. The humiliation she felt was familiar, and it tasted of the shame Oliver had brought down on her when he'd taken off for Spain, leaving her behind in Paris.

"I'm not a young woman anymore," she thought. A second divorce would most certainly guarantee her a life as a spinster. She had to think about the children. With a young son, as well as three girls who would eventually début and marry into society, she *needed* George – like it or not.

Pulling a handkerchief from her pocketbook, she dried her tears, all the while trying to breathe into the hollow space in her stomach. Her heart ached with a terrible force, a sharp knife in her chest. Fighting against the pain, she worked to regain her composure before reaching home. *"I'll be greeted by the children,"* she thought. *"They'll be waiting my return."* At all costs, she did not want them to see how distraught she was.

Desperately needing time alone, Sara decided she'd bluff a headache and escape to her room until she'd calmed down. As the house came into view, she weighed the future of her niece and two daughters and their prospects of a happily married future in a patriarchal society.

It occurred to her that the 'happily ever after' of books was a myth created by storytellers and writers like her friend Edith. *"Does such a thing even exist?"* she wondered. Climbing out of the carriage, Sara realized with great sadness that, in reality, there was no such thing as a happy ending.

Two months later
January 11, 1896
New York, New York

Winter's cold did nothing to quell the heat of excitement surging through the house on Fifth Avenue, though there were no fancy decorations and would be no elaborate ten-course dinner for the few friends gathered today in the home's salon.

"I suppose everyone knew the two of you would eventually marry." Mrs. Jay smiled across the bedroom at Alva, happy to be one of few invited guests for today's nuptials. "It was only a matter of time."

Standing a couple of inches taller than Alva, Mrs. Jay wore a deep-purple gown for the civil ceremony. Her gray eyes were covered by a small tulle veil draping from the top of her velvet leghorn hat.

"I wanted to make sure to get Consuelo married before I made plans for myself," Alva stated magnanimously. Sitting on the bench in front of her vanity, she blotted her face with *papier poudré*. "But now, she's the Duke's bride and gone off to England to start her new life, leaving me free to indulge in my own romantic ambitions."

"Are you certain you're going to be happy with such a small ceremony?" Mrs. Jay asked. Stepping up behind Alva at her dressing table, she met her friend's eyes in the mirror's reflection. "I know how you like to throw grand parties."

"I'll be happy enough to finally marry Oliver," Alva assured her. "We couldn't find a minister from any church that would perform the ceremony because of our divorces. For a moment, it looked as though we wouldn't be able to remarry. Oliver finally went to the mayor with a special request for a civil ceremony Friday night!"

"As long as it's legal, who cares?" Mrs. Jay offered congenially. "What time does the train leave?"

"We have to board by one o'clock," Alva said. "Newport will be empty this time of year, which suits us fine. We'll have lots of privacy at Belcourt for a honeymoon."

"What about Marble House? I know you received it as part of your divorce settlement."

"I'm seriously considering closing it up for now. Except for the laundry facilities," Alva added with a laugh. "They're far superior to Belcourt's."

"Do you still have plans to go to Europe?"

"We do." Alva nodded. "Oliver bought tickets for Italy. We sail on the twenty-ninth to meet Consuelo and the duke. Together we're going to holiday in Egypt for a month, then the four of us are returning to England for an extended visit." Alva smiled at the plans. "We'll return to Newport in the spring."

"Won't that be wonderful!" Mrs. Jay said, glancing at the crystal desk clock on the vanity. "We should join your waiting groom. It's nearly ten o'clock, and Mayor Strong must be here by now."

With a quick and final glance in the mirror, Alva followed her friend down to the second-story drawing room of her New York mansion. The only guests were her two sons, Harold and Willie Jr, Colonel Jay and his wife, her sister, Jennie, and her dear friend Miss

Duer. Walking across the salon, Alva joined Oliver on the east side of the room where he stood between the two windows.

"Are you certain you don't want to invite your brothers?" she asked him, taking her place at his side.

"No. Let's just keep this simple, shall we?" Oliver implored her. Wearing a black frock coat over his tan waistcoat and matching trousers, he looked quite handsome. "After all the effort it took me to get the mayor over here this morning, I'm not going to worry about a guest list – or even a best man, for that matter." He gave her a straightforward look. "Is this small ceremony going to be okay with you, Alva? I know how you like to celebrate with large soirees."

She tilted her head, wearing a sultry look. "It'll be perfect. Short but sweet, and not a moment too soon. We'll have a celebration with our friends another time."

"If you're sure. In any event, you look lovely," Oliver said, fumbling with his lily of the valley boutonniere.

"Thank you. I'm glad you approve." Alva smiled, smoothing a hand over the skirt of her dress. Her powder-blue traveling gown was trimmed with mink fur on the collar and sleeves. Taking the flowers from his hand, she attached them securely to the lapel of his suit.

"You always look lovely, Alva," Oliver complimented. "It's one of the reasons I'm in love with you. That and your spunky charm," he added with a wink.

Mayor Strong hurried into the room, shown in by the butler. The officiate carried a little black booklet, apparently containing the text of the

civil ceremony for marriage within its pages.

"Hello, Oliver. I'm sorry to keep you waiting," he said apologetically. "Good morning, Alva. I've got the marriage certificate right here." He held it up proudly. "Are the two of you ready to tie the knot?"

"Absolutely," Oliver answered without hesitation. Giving Alva a long, lingering look, he knew he really was ready for this marriage.

The woman beside him was so different from Sara. Alva didn't criticize him when he drank too much wine or liquor at parties. A few months back, he'd gotten so drunk at a masquerade party he'd actually passed out inside one of his heavy suits of armor. Sara would have complained loudly over such an antic, but Alva simply found it amusing.

The small group assembled together in front of the parlor's fireplace as Mayor Strong recited the marriage ceremony from the pages of his book. Within a few short minutes, it was over, and the handful of guests that had gathered to witness the occasion cheered wholeheartedly when Oliver kissed his new bride.

And that was the extent of the fanfare.

"I'll have this document filed with the Bureau of Vital Statistics immediately," Mayor Strong assured them. "And we'll keep the entire matter private, as you wish."

"Thank you, Mayor," Oliver said. "Now, if you'll all excuse us, we have a train to catch."

In a whirlwind of activity, the newlyweds exited directly to their waiting coach, bound for Grand Central Station and, ultimately, Newport.

The new Mr. and Mrs. Oliver H. P. Belmont.

One month later
February 11, 1896
New York, New York

Many had been anxious to see the new Astor home at 841 Fifth Avenue, although the reasons were two-fold. The first, of course, was to witness the grandeur of the new house. Everyone wondered if it would be as fabulous as the Vanderbilt's castle. The second reason was to see how Mrs. Astor would deal with her daughter Charlotte's divorce.

Publicly shunning those who had legally dissolved their marriages, the set was poised to know what fate society's queen would declare over her own offspring. The added scandal of Charlotte's love letters to her paramour splattered all over *The New York Sun* would most certainly seal her fate in the eyes of the ever-proper Mrs. Astor – daughter or not. Speculation was rampant, and newspaper reporters squirreled away in the shadows of the street, showing a special interest in the matter.

As guests walked into the home, the answer was clear to everyone present.

Charlotte stood beside her mother in the receiving line, smiling as people entered to attend the ball. Dressed in a resplendent gown accented by fabulous jewels, she went about her duties, welcoming friends as if scandal had never touched her fashionable life.

Chapter Sixteen

Two months later
April 10, 1896
Newport, Rhode Island

The month of April was early to return to Newport for the summer season, but Sara had been feeling nostalgic and decided to go to *Swanhurst* before the rest of the family for some quiet time alone. *"Most of society won't arrive for another month,"* she thought. The town was still empty, which suited her perfectly.

Sara had sent a note last week to have the house opened for her arrival, looking forward to the familiarity of her bedroom at *Swanhurst*. Natica and Charlotte, as well as the younger children, would be working with their tutor in New York for another week.

"Why don't you go ahead of us," Jane had encouraged Sara. "I've got Bridget and Anna to see to the children's care, and all the schoolwork will be completed next week. We'll join you in Newport directly afterward."

In the end, the thought of a week alone had an appeal Sara couldn't resist.

Swanhurst looked beautiful when she'd arrived a few days ago. Fresh, green buds emerged from tree branches while daffodils and hyacinths popped up in the dirt of the flowerbeds. Sara was happy for the familiar comfort of her family home. A piece of her heart would always remain here at *Swanhurst*.

This morning the sun had risen bright and warm, and on a whim, Sara decided to go for an outing, ordering the carriage to be readied for a ride to Easton's Beach. She hadn't been down there in years, and Sara thought a walk in the sea air might be a refreshing change, affording her a chance to clear her mind from the cobwebs of winter.

"Owen, head down to the far end of the beach. Close to Sachuest Point," she called to the driver. As the carriage moved in a gentle rhythm, Sara searched the shoreline for an appealing spot through her view from the window. She wanted to be alone for a while. Completely alone.

"That looks like a nice place for a walk," she announced, as they rounded the corner. "Can you drop me off over there?"

Owen pulled the coach into the lower end of a makeshift parking area. The spring wind had blown a thin layer of sand over the ground, and the beach itself could only be viewed between several high dunes.

The driver jumped out and came around to open the door, assisting Sara down from the ride. Throwing a wool cape over her simple lavender-colored morning dress, Sara clambered to the sandy ground. She'd skipped wearing a hat, instead tying a brightly colored Chinese silk scarf over her hair. It was unlike her to reject the bonnets and veils she'd been taught to wear as a young girl to preserve her pale complexion. Only servants had sun-tanned skin, from long hours toiling under the hot sun.

But today, the sea breeze made it a challenge to keep a hat on. Besides, these days Sara gave less and less credence to the social restrictions and requirements she'd followed like the gospel for most of her life – at least during times when Charlotte, Natica, and Mildred weren't around. Mindful how important it was to set a good example for the girls until they were married, Sara stuck to protocol while in their company.

"Why don't you come back in an hour or so and pick me up," she excused Owen.

"No, ma'am, I'm afraid I can't leave you here on the beach alone." Towering above her, his feet shifted in the sand as he gave her an apologetic look. "There might be vagrants or the like hanging around. I'd prefer to stay with the carriage and wait for you here."

Touched by his protective nature, Sara acquiesced. "I suppose you're right. Although I'm sure I'll be perfectly fine."

"Yes, ma'am," he said. "But if you don't mind, I must insist on waiting for you. It's not proper for me to leave you here alone," he repeated.

"As you wish." She smiled and stepped out onto the sand, heading toward the waves.

As she walked around the mountainous dune to the open beach, the carriage disappeared from her sight. Sara breathed in the isolation of the deserted shoreline. Strolling in the sand to the water's edge, she gave a steady gaze up the long beach, stretching from town all the way to the end of the point. There wasn't a soul in sight, and that was exactly how

Sara wanted it. The sky was crystal blue and sunny, but the strong ocean wind brought a chill to her bones.

Reaching the rocky shore, Sara discovered tide pools filled with sea foam, harboring snails and crabs that scooted under stones to hide. She stooped to inspect them more carefully before moving on over the rocks down the coast.

A fresh wind hit the shore, and on an impulse, Sara took off her headscarf. Pulling the pins from her long hair, she shook her head, allowing the wind to blow through her tresses. *"I suppose I'm being improper,"* she thought with a chuckle. *"But honestly, I don't care one bit."* Not today, anyway. This simple act of freedom gave Sara a feeling of liberation she seldom experienced.

A memory surfaced in her mind of the day she'd met Oliver at Bailey's Beach. The day he'd told her the Belmonts had agreed to their marriage. What a happy day that had been! It'd seemed that all her dearest dreams were finally coming true. Sara's heart began to beat fast with the memory of the love she'd once felt for Oliver that long ago day on Bailey's Beach. It was a love she'd refused to acknowledge for many, many years, buried under layers of humiliation and heartache.

"Once upon a time, my love for you was true," Sara whispered into the sea air. "But you did not love me. You did not love me..."

Her eyes welled with tears meant for a bygone era. Impatiently, she wiped them from her eyes. *"I've cried more than enough tears for you, Oliver Belmont."* Sara realized that as much as she now deplored Oliver, she had once loved him dearly.

"Yes," she announced to the sea. "I loved you, Oliver. Once upon a happy time. But I will never open my heart to you again. Never ever. Not after what you've done to Natica and me."

But none of that matter now. Oliver was married to Alva.

And Alva had secured her daughter a royal wedding and a title as Duchess. *"Now, that was a very sad situation,"* Sara thought. Everyone knew the girl did not love the Duke of Marlborough – nor did he love Consuelo – although he did seem enamored with her wealth. She and George had attended the wedding, and it brought Sara great sadness to hear the bride weep terribly, with misery instead of joy. *"Alva had arranged the marriage with no thought or concern to her daughter's happiness,"* she reflected. *"Only to her position in society and what the marriage could accomplish in that regard, not only for Consuelo but for the Vanderbilt family."* Sara noted the similarities to her own Mother, who'd been keen on her marrying into the Belmont family.

In the months leading up to Consuelo's engagement, gossip had been ripe with talk of Alva threatening suicide until her daughter agreed to the marriage. She'd even locked herself in her chambers at Marble House without taking meals. Finally, in a dramatic scheme, Alva feigned a heart attack. Consuelo, fearing for her mother's life, relented and agreed to her wishes.

"Poor girl," Sara said. Once the marriage was a *fait accompli* – as Alva always got her way – Alva made a miraculous recovery, and Consuelo was packed off to England.

Sara's attention was drawn to a blur of white bouncing in the breakers. Thinking it sea foam, Sara was startled to realize it was a white swan.

"What on earth…" she whispered, watching the bird fight against the surf. "Where is your partner?" she called, knowing swans mated for life.

The swan eyed her while tossing against the rough breakers. It was as though the lovely bird had a message for only her, some long-lost secret, but what that message was remained a mystery to Sara. There was a stillness in the moment, and frosty chills trickled down her spine. Such a strange sight to witness – a pond bird thrashing in the ocean waves. Sara wondered again where the swan's mate had disappeared to, while another wave sent it whipping in the surf.

The sound of church bells reached her ears, blurred into the wind's song. An eerie cognizance heightened Sara's perception, and she had the oddest feeling she'd done this before. The moment swelled, the swan steadfast, watching her.

"Déjà vu," Sara said softly, mesmerized by the swan bouncing in the surf.

"So peculiar…"

Fascinated, she watched as the bird took flight, heading toward Easton's Pond, home to a large colony of white swans.

Breaking from the spell, Sara blinked, and continued her stroll down the beach, her thoughts drifting in a free-flow cascade of ideas and images.

George's proposal entered Sara's mind. Their short courtship, quick marriage, and quiet honeymoon were in stark contrast to the extravagant society wedding to Oliver held at *Swanhurst*. Sara wondered what would've happened if she'd never met Oliver, instead courting George from the start. But he'd been married…

A sudden wave of guilt passed over her, like the chill of the ocean wind, and she found herself comparing the two men. Maybe she hadn't been fair to George by marrying him when she was only fond of him. Perhaps he knew all along that she didn't have the same fervency for him that she'd felt for Oliver. But what twenty-year-old had wisdom in such matters when overcome with the raptures of passion?

A familiar melancholy filled her heart, and Sara realized that most of her life since her first honeymoon in Paris had been lived in subtle discouragement. She'd lost her dreams and ambition after her divorce, focusing instead on raising her daughter and then her niece. Now she had two more children.

A flock of seagulls squawked overhead, clamoring for attention, and she glanced up at them, watching as they headed out to sea. Fading into the white clouds, the sea birds disappeared, and Sara lingered in the moment.

Striving to be objective, Sara acknowledged to herself that perhaps she'd kept her fondness for George in check since the beginning. In light of what had happened to her first marriage, maybe she'd done so to protect herself from further heartbreak. Who could blame her? Conceivably, that could be why George had sought the companionship of another woman.

"And maybe I've inadvertently punished him for Oliver's crimes," she said aloud to the clouds. It suddenly occurred to her that perhaps she'd hurt George's pride, and that had been the impetus that drove him to find comfort with another woman.

A loud wave crashed on the shore sending its spray high into the air. "Or maybe George never really loved me..." Maybe his only concern was to find a mother for his son after Kaye died.

Sara didn't really believe that, though. George seemed genuinely contrite, and he'd been very attentive since that awful morning.

Sara's hurt and anger had been slow to ebb, but now, she decided that she'd punished her husband long enough. *And to what end? To destroy her marriage completely?*

"No," she decided in her private soliloquy. "I won't allow that to happen." She pondered her life, watching as the waves receded. And in that quiet moment, she decided to somehow find forgiveness for George and open her heart to him anew.

A quick look at her watch told her she'd been on the beach for well over an hour. Turning around, she headed for the carriage, chilled from the weather.

Traipsing through the sand, Sara pulled her hair up in a quick bun and covered it with her headscarf. She realized the day was fast approaching when she'd hold a party for the girls' débuts. Sara desperately hoped they'd find true love and a happy marriage, as well as social prominence. She had a few more years before Bayard would court, and even longer until Mildred would début. But it was time to make plans for Charlotte's presentation into society, with Natica following soon afterward.

Natica.

She'd grown so lovely. Oliver could claim she was not his daughter until his dying breath, but no one could mistake the resemblance. Natica had Sara's mouth and Oliver's eyes, and even the most casual observer could see it.

It had been hard for her to watch the little girl suffer for her father's behavior. Sara had made up for it by giving Natica every possible opportunity to flourish. She'd made certain Natica received excellent schooling, including tutoring in French and German, as well as teaching her all the finer points of etiquette, a necessary skill for a lady in today's society. She'd done the same for Charlotte and would follow suit with Mildred when the time came, and she blossomed into a woman.

Sara let out a judgmental laugh.

Today's society, indeed.

Today's society was nothing like her days as a new débutante. The burgeoning growth of industry and modern technologies had brought exorbitant amounts of wealth, the likes of which had never before been seen by Americans. And with that wealth came great power.

And with power came corruption. The lifestyle among the set was becoming more excessive and eccentric every day if one were to believe the gossip in *Town Topics.* Unfortunately, more often than not, the stories turned out to be true. And Sara couldn't help but worry over the effect such attitudes of excess would have on her children as they entered society.

Owen stood near the coach like a sentry, waiting for her return. "Did you have a nice walk, ma'am?" he asked, helping her inside.

With a sigh, Sara realized her outing had accomplished quite a bit beyond just a chance for fresh air and exercise. "Yes, thank you. I think I'm ready to return to *Swanhurst.*"

"Yes, ma'am. At once," he said. Taking the reins, he called out to the horses, who quickly rambled into motion toward Middletown Road.

Chapter Seventeen

Six months later
June 10, 1896
Newport, Rhode Island

Time is undefinable, although it can be measured. The setting sun. The rising moon over the ocean, waning and waxing, atop stars that spin across the sky with regular precision – these constant transits lend humankind a template from which science measures the progression of time.

Craftsman with gears and delicate tools breathe life into mechanisms, creating the ever-ticking heartbeat of the mantle clock – a soldier and companion of the home. Passing the trade from father to son, their skills are evident in a gentleman's pocket watch or a lady's broach timepiece, pinned so near to her heart – just so, on the bodice of her day dress.

Some clocks are simple, some carved or embellished with delicate jewels. Gears spin, hands move over numbers, and in this way, time is measured, but remains undefined. Mysterious and illusive, time is familiar, as day by day, week by week, month by month, it drifts ever forward, mostly unnoticed, until time has run out.

"Mrs. Rives, you must come at once." The voice on the telephone was crackly and distant. "Your sister has suddenly taken ill."

Sara tried to stay calm as she fettered out the news from New York.

"You must be mistaken," she told the caller, who'd informed Sara he was a physician. "My sister is on her way to Newport as we speak. She just opened Rhua House for the summer and has a host of parties planned for the season."

"Is your husband there? May I speak with him?" the doctor asked impatiently.

"Yes, of course." Sara moved away from the mouthpiece and urgently called for George. He hurried from the sitting room where he'd been relaxing with the evening newspaper.

"What's wrong?" he asked her, taking the telephone from her hand.

"I'm not sure. Something about Milly taking ill," she blurted, letting him take the place by the telephone.

"Hello? This is George Rives."

Sara watched him, anxiously trying to determine the seriousness of the situation.

"Yes. I see." George kept his voice low. "Yes, of course. I'll have the matter taken care of right away. Yes. Thank you," he said and replaced the earpiece on the telephone hook.

"What is it, George? What's happened?" Sara fought against her growing panic. From the pained expression on his face, she wasn't so sure she wanted to hear the caller's message.

In a somber voice, he said, "Sara... you'd better sit down. The news is not good."

Doing as he said, Sara found the nearest chair, a chill of fear moving through her body. "Don't leave me hanging like this! What's happened to Milly?"

George took a deep sigh and paused. "She's gone, Sara."

"What do you mean, *gone?*" Her eyes welled with tears. "You're not saying Milly *died,* are you? She's too young! I just talked to her. She's fine. She's just ill," Sara rambled.

"I'm afraid she is not fine," George said, gently taking his wife's hand. "I'm sorry, Sara. Milly has passed away. They suspect a heart attack, same as your mother and Gus."

"No!" Sara cried in denial. "She can't be dead! She's on her way to Newport right now. She's opening Rhua House. It's going to be our best season since we lost the others."

Sara allowed George to pull her into his arms, working to console her.

"Yes. I know..." He tilted her chin up to meet his eyes. "But I'm afraid those plans are going to have to be changed to another Whiting funeral. I'm so sorry, Sara." He glanced back at the telephone. "I have to visit the undertaker and take care of the preparations," he said gently.

"This can't be happening." Sara struggled to accept the truth of her sister's death. But if it were true, that meant she and Jane were the last living members of the Whiting family. And now, there was going to be yet another funeral.

Profuse tears flowed as Sara wept in George's arms, trying to come to grips with the sad news. Her grief seemed insurmountable, and Sara cried bitterly while memories of Milly's wedding mixed with visions of their younger years, emerging from Sara's mind like a misty dream.

But dreams turn into nightmares. Sara floundered, desperately hoping the future would bring new joy, as she grieved the loss of her dear sister.

One week later
July 17, 1896
Newport, Rhode Island

Finding his wife writing a letter in her suite, Oliver interrupted the activity. "I have a surprise for you," he said impishly. Looking the perfect gentleman of leisure, he was dressed in a fine waistcoat and trousers. "Something new for us to enjoy."

"I can't imagine what."

"Come with me down to the stables," he cajoled. "I promise it will only take a few minutes of your time."

Curious, Alva did as he asked. Leaving her letters unfinished on the desk, she followed him to the stables. When they got to the driveway, Alva could not believe her eyes.

"A horseless carriage! What fun!" she exclaimed with obvious delight. This was sure to get them noticed in the evening parade!

"Do you like it?"

"Like it? It's wonderful! And the perfect addition to your already well-appointed collection of fine carriages."

"I suppose it was the obvious next step. One must keep up with modern inventions." Oliver chuckled. "I just hope the contraption works as well as they claim. I detest the thought of getting stuck in the middle of nowhere."

"Nonsense!" Alva laughed. "No carriage, horseless or not, would ever dare break down on a Belmont."

"Well then…" He bowed his head. "Mrs. Belmont, would you care to accompany me for a joyride through Newport? I think we should join the coaching parade in new style tonight."

"I would love to, Mr. Belmont. I just hope it doesn't scare the regular trotters out for a jaunt."

"You can't stop progress, Alva," Oliver pointed out. "This is the way of the future, so the horses and Whips will simply have to get used to us in our automobile."

The idea held great appeal for her, as Alva got a tremendous thrill out of flaunting her wealth.

"I must go and change into something more suitable," she fussed. "I want this to be an appearance to be remembered."

Oliver grinned at his wife. "I'd have it no other way," he said, leaning in to kiss her cheek. "Afterwards, I'm taking you to the casino. We'll park right in front where everyone will notice our fabulous new machine."

"Oh, Oliver, that sounds like such fun! Newport will be so envious of us!" she exclaimed, turning to go back into the house. "I won't be long, I promise. This is going to be a very entertaining evening, after all."

<hr />

Two weeks later
August 1, 1896
Newport, Rhode Island

Carrie and her husband were staying at her mother's Beechwood mansion in Newport for the summer. Convening for a visit in the Morning Room, Carrie and Sara sat beneath a large wooden rose carved into the ceiling. An ancient symbol of secrecy, the rose sheltered their conversation in privacy.

"It's been ages since we've had time for a proper visit," Carrie said while sipping iced tea. Her lace gown was a pretty blue that set off the color of her eyes.

"Yes. And so much has happened." Sara smiled at her friend. "We're married with children of our own."

"The years seem to go by so quickly," Carrie agreed. "Tell me, how are things with you and George?"

"Fine, thank you. And you and Marshall? Have you been happy?"

"Happiness is fleeting, but we are very content. Perhaps that's the most one can hope for."

"Perhaps," Sara murmured. Shifting in her chair, her satin tea dress reflected the light. "It's certainly not the picture of happiness they promised us as little girls."

The two ladies laughed easily together as though they'd not skipped a step in their friendship.

Growing quiet, Sara debated sharing her problem with Carrie.

"Have there been any disturbances in your marriage?"

"Disturbances?" Carrie eyed her with curiosity. "Ah... You mean, have there been any dalliances with roving women."

Shrugging, Sara hesitated, ashamed of revealing George's extracurricular activities.

"I suppose there have been one or two." Carrie played with her teacup. "I try not to pay attention to such dilly-dallying. Gentlemen seem to think they're entitled to enjoy women, much as they would pluck an apple from the tree."

With a simple nod, Sara let the room fall quiet.

"Why do you ask? Has something happened with George?"

"I'm not certain," Sara said. "But I do have my suspicions." There was only so much she could openly admit, even to a friend.

A breezy laugh escaped Carrie, sprinkling mirth over the parlor like flower petals. "Oh, Sara! Don't be such a prude. Let the men have their affairs. The way I see it, it's one way to keep from getting pregnant more than is necessary."

"I suppose that's one way to look at it."

"As long as he's sleeping with you at night and providing for you and the children, why be bothered? As you know, my mother was well aware of my father's mistress down the avenue."

"I don't believe my mother had an awareness of such a problem."

"Well, if we women make a fuss every time a man looks at a woman other than his wife, I'm sure we'll all be left old maids – or be forced to be mistresses ourselves."

"What a horrid thought!" Sara exclaimed, her mouth a moue of objection. Catching Carrie's eye, she caught the joke, and the two ladies chuckled at the vision of society's lovely débutantes degraded to a life as lonely old spinsters.

Tilting her head, Carrie fondly scrutinized Sara. "I can see you've been hurt. You must genuinely love George."

"Yes, I suppose I do. I don't think I would have taken this so hard if I didn't love him."

"There were many who thought you'd married him for convenience. I'm relieved to see it isn't true."

Sara met her eyes and smiled.

"Trust me, Sara," Carrie said. "With a little time, all will be well. Besides, a marriage could have worse problems."

"I'm sure you're right." Sara nodded. Finishing her tea, she set her cup on the table while giving consideration to Carrie's advice.

Ten days later
August 12, 1896
New York, New York

George knew Colonel Mann would be eating his dinner at Delmonico's this evening, as always. It was the day before his gossip newspaper *Town Topics* went to print, and Mann would be waiting for him, George felt certain. He clutched the letter sent from the publisher, knowing he had to deal with this matter – and deal with it now.

After receiving the note from Mann at work, he'd gone directly to the restaurant. Still wearing a suit reserved for the office, George stuffed the letter into a pocket of his tweed pants and gathered his resolve.

How did he get himself into this situation? Memories of Sara surprising him at his apartment brought new regrets, and George felt certain one of Mann's newspaper spies had spotted him out with Miss Mason. George had slipped into the brief affair, heedless of his nagging conscience. He'd really tried to keep the matter hidden, but this ruthless publisher hated society's ills and was hell-bent on reforming America's aristocracy. His methods were well known; expose any form of misconduct, be it adultery, drug addiction, or gambling. And expose it publicly by printing it in his weekly newspaper for all to read. In this manner, Colonel William D'Alton Mann held power through fear over anyone in society guilty of even the smallest transgression.

Entering the restaurant, George told the maître d' he was meeting someone and headed directly for the dining room and Colonel Mann's regular table. Sure enough, there he was, the maggot. George scowled as he approached the Colonel's table.

"Good afternoon." George tried to muster a polite tone.

The Colonel looked up. Tall and thin, Mann's face was covered by a bushy, white beard and full mustache, leaving his piercing brown eyes the main point of focus. A smirk crossed his face when he recognized George.

"Good afternoon, Mr. Rives. I've been expecting you." He motioned to the chair. "Won't you sit down?"

George hated this man's arrogance, but, keeping his guard up, he sat in the chair. Looking across the table, George knew Colonel Mann's opinion of fashionable society was low, describing the set as worthless fools and jackasses in print. George felt the description more fitting for the Colonel himself. The man seemed void of a conscience.

"I think perhaps you've come to discuss business?" Mann furrowed his thick, white eyebrows.

"I don't appreciate receiving threats, Mr. Mann. I can only imagine where you dug up this ancient gossip." George fumed. "But you will *not* print this trash in tomorrow's paper."

"I must insist you call me 'Colonel Mann'," he gently reprimanded. "I suppose whether or not the story goes to print depends upon you, Mr. Rives." The Colonel's tone was deep and venomous. "My reporters are hard at work, and they must be compensated for their employment. Publishing can be an expensive vocation, you know. Typeset machines, ink, paper..."

"How much do you want?" George interrupted him mid-sentence. Mann's bribery and extortion were no secret; neither was the solution any great mystery.

Placing his napkin on the table, the Colonel moved slowly. Drawing out the moment, he watched George squirm from his threats of exposure.

"How much is it worth to you?"

"I don't have the resources of William Vanderbilt."

"True. But you are still a very wealthy man, Mr. Rives."

"Just tell me how much you want so I can wash my hands of you."

"Now, now. No need to get nasty." Colonel Mann sat back in his chair and rubbed his white beard, thinking the matter over. He could easily have been mistaken for Santa Claus, but in appearance only. His demeanor was heartless and cruel, impeccably aimed at the people of the set whom he universally detested for their lifestyle of excess.

"I should think a thousand dollars will cover my expenses."

George reeled from the number. "You have got to be joking!"[1]

"Actually, I'm not. My usual amount is upwards of three thousand dollars." He gave George a slight sneer. "So you see, I'm actually giving you a discount."

"I'll give you five hundred."

A low, malevolent laugh came from the Colonel as he shook his head.

---

1. *approximately $36,000 In 2023

"Five hundred dollars comes nowhere near covering my expenses. I assure you, the price is one thousand dollars." He surveyed George and continued.

"Please try to remember, Mr. Rives, my reporters are still hard at work all around the city. If they should happen to find another story about your mistress..."

"She's not my mistress!"

"If you insist. Then we don't have a problem, do we?"

"I want immunity!" George growled, straining to keep his voice low.

"That's precisely why the price is one thousand dollars. Five hundred for my expenses, and another five hundred for your continued protection from my reporters."

Glaring at the evil man, George took out his checkbook and hastily scribbled a draft for a thousand dollars. At the bottom of the check, he made a memo for 'advertising'. He signed his name and passed the check over to Mann.

The publisher picked up the note and examined it for accuracy. A sardonic smile crossed his face. "Advertising indeed." He nodded at George. "Or should we say, a *non*-advertising fee?"

Putting his checkbook away in his breast pocket, George could barely disguise his disgust. "You swear none of this will ever be printed."

"I'm an honorable man, Mr. Rives," Colonel Mann responded in feigned offense. "I assure you, your digressions will never be printed or published. You have my word."

"I'm not sure how much value I place on your word, Mann." George rose from his chair to leave the restaurant.

Entertained by George's conundrum, Colonel Mann released a nasty laugh. "It's been a pleasure doing business with you," he smirked.

Standing over the pompous cad, anger pumped through George's veins. He fought against an overwhelming urge to punch the Colonel. Taking a deep breath, he corralled the urge and turned away, quickly leaving Delmonico's.

Chapter Eighteen

One year later
August 16, 1897
Newport, Rhode Island

Finishing a light lunch, Sara, Charlotte, and Natica exited the café. Turning up Bellevue, Sara urged them to hurry.

"Come on, ladies. Your gowns have arrived from Paris, and we've got an appointment. I decided it would be easier to go down to the dress shop for the fitting since we had lunch plans in town anyway."

"I can't wait to see how the dresses look!" Natica said.

"Me too! The fabrics we chose were so lovely," Charlotte chimed in.

The three ladies entered the seamstress' shop on Thames Street with happy anticipation. Bolts of fabric lined the shelves, while notions and other sewing tools were displayed on nearby tables.

"Are you sure I need new dresses?" Charlotte asked. "I've already got a beautiful gown I can wear to the Vanderbilt's dinner, Aunt Sara."

"Nonsense! A lady can never have enough stylish gowns. Every woman in society must take special care to dress with taste and fashion." Sara answered without hesitation. "A woman's wardrobe is essential to her success in society. Never forget that!" She glanced at her niece. "This is your first party without the family. It's not your début, but I think we should treat it as such until we can plan your official coming out, which, I'm thinking, will be in the spring." Sara had promised the girl's mother on her deathbed that she would take care of Charlotte, and Sara fully intended on keeping her word. Charlotte was now a young woman of eighteen years, and prospective suitors were taking notice.

Alice Vanderbilt had not entertained since Cornelius's stroke, but this summer, she'd announced a party for fifty young people. And the invitation list included young Charlotte Whiting. Sara had been relieved when the note arrived, knowing that any hint of scandal remaining from her divorce so many years ago seemed to finally be fading from the memory of society's hostesses.

"Good afternoon." A petite woman with graying hair greeted them. "I'm Mrs. Marseille."

"We have an appointment for dress fittings," Sara told the woman. "Ordered from Mr. Worth in Paris."

"Yes, of course, Mrs. Rives. If you'll follow me to the fitting area, I'll get your gowns." The shopkeeper led them to the rear of the building, where they heard the whirl of sewing machines coming from behind a door. "Are you excited to see them, my dear?" she asked Charlotte.

"Yes. Very much so," the girl replied shyly.

"We'll try them on and take care of any necessary alterations," Mrs. Marseille assured her. "I worked for Mr. Worth in Paris for many years, so I'm familiar with his techniques."

The woman disappeared for a few moments, then came back with an assistant pushing a wheeled rack filled with their new gowns.

Charlotte's face lit up at the sight of the beautiful collection of dresses. Silk, taffeta, and satin gowns were hung in a display of every hue; pink, purple, and blue – all of Charlotte's favorite colors. The gowns were accented with the finest lace, seed pearls, beads, and sequins.

"Which are mine?" Natica asked her mother.

"These are for you, young lady," the clerk said, pointing to a new rack being wheeled in by a second assistant, a perky young brunette with a measuring tape hanging around her neck.

"You're almost fifteen now," Sara told her daughter. "And we have to put together a new wardrobe for you as well."

Charlotte and Natica smiled, whispering to each other with delight as they examined the gowns.

After a few minutes, the two young ladies were ushered into the changing room to try the garments on for fit. Sara found a chair and relaxed, looking forward to the fashion show.

Her mother's face popped into her mind, and she fought against the sadness brought on by the memory. She still missed Mrs. Whiting very much. Her mother had left big shoes to fill. Now preparing the girls for the next phase of their lives, Sara had a new appreciation for her mother's work as the family matron, a role she now endeavored to assume in her absence.

The shopkeeper and her assistant were helping the girls into the gowns, the sound of laughter emanating from the changing room. After a moment, Natica emerged in a robin-egg blue satin evening dress that Sara had to admit looked beautiful on her teenage daughter. The outfit made her appear more mature than her age, and Sara wondered at how quickly she'd grown.

"So lovely!" Sara sighed proudly. Natica was looking more like a woman than a teenager every day. Undoubtedly, the girl was going to be one of society's beauties. And those brown eyes she'd inherited from her father lent a captivating aura to her appearance.

"Oh, I simply adore this dress," Natica cooed, viewing herself in the three-way mirror.

"I can understand why. It looks beautiful on you."

Charlotte came out of the dressing room and joined her cousin before the mirror. Wearing a dainty pink silk gown, layered with crepe-de-chine and embroidered with seed pearls on the bodice, her niece looked lovely. The dress was as stylish as any Sara had seen promenading down Bellevue Avenue.

"This is absolutely gorgeous," Charlotte murmured, her voice filled with awe. Gazing at her reflection in the mirror, Charlotte seemed curious at the image of the young woman reflecting back at her, almost as if she were seeing herself for the first time.

The shopkeeper grinned at the scene, aware that this shopping trip was heralding a rite of passage for the two young ladies approaching the day of their débuts.

"Both dresses are lovely," the woman announced. "And they look like a perfect fit. Why don't we try on the others?"

Charlotte and Natica happily agreed, following the clerk back to the dressing room while Sara waited for the next modeling session.

She remembered how much fun this time in her life had been. Nothing was more exciting than coming out, and Sara intended to do a much better job marrying the young ladies off than she'd done with her own poor choice for a husband.

And she knew it all started with the perfect dress.

Ten months later
June 28, 1898
Atlantic Ocean

The scent of the sea reached Oliver, along with the musty smell of the ship. Once again, he was on a naval battleship, not as an ensign taking orders this time, but as a respected naval officer. The warship barreled through the waves full speed ahead, rocking as it traveled through the choppy Atlantic waters.

Gazing out over the afternoon horizon, a smirk crossed his face. *"The newspapers are so easily manipulated,"* he thought. Oliver had planted an article in the *Times,* and he couldn't resist wallowing in an exaggerated sense of power. Pushing away errant thoughts of his parents, Oliver suspected he'd become exactly the kind of man they'd wished to avoid. *"I'm sure they'd consider me eccentric and self-indulgent."* But Oliver didn't see himself that way at all. He considered himself rather clever and resourceful.

"Sir." a young man saluted him. "The captain has requested you attend an officer's meeting at sixteen-hundred-hours."

"Thank you." Oliver returned the seaman's salute. He had to disguise his amusement at the situation. In a way, he wished his parents *were* alive to see him volunteering for duty. But his motivations were not a selfless act for his country. In fact, there was little Oliver did that could be called magnanimous.

"I must hate jury duty more than I hate the navy," he mused. He'd been called to the Common Pleas Division of the Supreme Court in New York and was expected there yesterday to serve as a juror.

Could anything be more boring? Sitting there all day listening to dull repartee.

Instead, Oliver had devised a plan that would not only allow him an excuse from court but would cast him in the light of a naval hero, like his grandfather on the Perry side of the family.

In a shrewd and speedy move, Oliver had contacted his uncle, Admiral Rogers, whom he'd not seen since his ensign days over ten years ago. Oliver offered to serve in Cuba to assist with the conflict going on between the small island country and the United States. His uncle, although aware of his nephew's military shortcomings, realized that the Belmont name would bring attention to the skirmish, so Oliver had quickly been reinstated into the navy and assigned to the battleship *Iowa,* now on its way to Santiago to join in the battle.

"Perhaps I should be fearing for my life," he thought with a smile. But the dapper appearance of his naval uniform, complete with the stripes of an officer, gave him an air

of supremacy that was even greater than that brought about by his vast wealth. For a moment, he understood why his parents would have chosen such an honorable career for him.

"It could have been a wonderful vocation," he decided. Except for one little detail: he hated naval life. Too many rules and regulations for his taste. But a quick trip to Cuba to escape jury duty while bringing him some military prestige – now that was an option he couldn't refuse – if only for the excitement.

Walking around the deck he quietly chuckled at his own cleverness. *"What a victory to see the article printed in yesterday's newspaper about my naval assignment."* He took special delight in the report of the sheriff being unable to find him to serve papers for missing court! Oliver smiled anew at the image of the sheriff's frustration. *"And how nice to see the newspaper commenting about my extensive military honors."*

Indeed.

He kind of liked the ring of it. It was nice to know propaganda was working in his favor again.

"My, my, wealth can buy a person just about anything." Only his family knew the truth: that he'd dropped out of the navy. The general public was unaware of the great lengths his parents had gone through to protect the Belmont name from the embarrassment of his escapades. Strutting around the deck, Oliver examined the modern artillery equipment on the boat while pondering the printed words.

"It will be recalled that Mr. Belmont graduated from the Naval Academy with honors and resigned from the navy in 1882 as Ensign, and ever since he has carefully maintained his knowledge of naval tactics, and today is an excellent seaman. His offer to build and equip a torpedo boat destroyer will be recalled."

It was a Belmont family secret that he had not graduated, let alone with honors. He might be an excellent seaman, but in his mind, that only meant avoiding seasickness. Hired sailors and captains were the ones who actually took care of running yachts for a man in his position. Sailing was more about reclining lazily on deck or engaging in gambling while drinking spirits with guests, happily cruising the world's most exotic ports-of-call.

Heading below deck to prepare for the captain's meeting, he savored a sense of antic-ipation in regard to reaching Santiago, while at the same time, Oliver wondered exactly how long this little naval diversion would last.

A few weeks would be fine. That would be just enough time to get him excused from jury duty, he decided, basking in his gloriously good mood. Maybe he should consider running for political office as Perry recommended. This was just too easy. And maybe, just maybe, he'd get himself an honorable place in the history books after all.

Five months later
November 21, 1898
New York, New York

As much as she enjoyed Sherry's and other New York restaurants, Sara had a special place in her heart for Delmonico's. She'd attended countless parties and balls at the famous eatery, but tonight was special, as she'd decided to include Charlotte and Natica in the festivities in response to Mrs. Gallatin's invitation.

It was a coming-out party for their hostess's daughter, Elizabeth, and Sara thought it gave the perfect opportunity to further acquaint the girls with the ritual of the ball. This particular crowd was a mixture of old and young people, and they mingled together in the restaurant's second-floor salon in easy repartee. Society had begun referring to young débutantes as 'buds' and looking around at the youthful faces of the season's newest offerings, Sara could understand how the term had been chosen, even if she did find it a bit vulgar.

"Our table is over here." George motioned, leading the way. The ladies followed him while greeting friends and acquaintances. A footman assisted with the heavy chairs as the family was seated at the well-appointed table. Catching George's eye, Sara smiled, remembering her vow to forgive him. To date, this was a task that had proven easier said than done.

"Why don't you sit here, Natica." He pointed at his seat. "And let me sit next to your mother this evening."

"That's fine." Natica slipped into the chair too quickly for Sara to object, distracted by the excitement of the party.

Sara smiled congenially as a waiter filled their glasses with lemon water and turned her attention to the merriment in the room.

A handsome young man approached the table and invited Charlotte to dance. Sara was pleased to see her niece's dance card fill quickly with names. But when another gentleman invited Natica to dance, Sara intervened. She thought her daughter too young and was not enamored with the idea of Natica's dance card filling up with appointments. Natica looked older than her years, and some of the young bucks just couldn't wait to court her.

Coming to attention in her chair, Natica noticed her friends across the room. "There's Cynthia and Isabel! Mother, do you mind if I go and chat with them?"

Aware that she had an open view of the room, Sara acquiesced, intent on keeping an attentive eye on the teenager. "That's fine," she answered simply, and Natica excused herself from the table

Charlotte was right behind her. "Do you mind if I join you?"

"Come on!" Natica called over her shoulder. And that left her and George alone, something Sara had tried to avoid since her visit to his apartment that fateful morning.

"I know you hate the thought of being alone with me," George echoed her sentiment in a low voice. "But we simply cannot continue with this void between us."

Turning, Sara gave him a stern look. "I suppose you should have thought about that before you took up your dalliances."

A waiter stepped up to the table. "Can I get you a drink? Lemonade or champagne?" he offered.

"Champagne would be wonderful," Sara said sweetly.

"I'll have a scotch, neat," George told the young man, all the while keeping his eye on Sara.

After the waiter left the table, George tried again. "I've apologized profusely, and I meant every word, Sara. Are you ever going to find it in your heart to forgive me?"

"I'm trying, George, but it's proving to be a difficult challenge. I can't

just snap my fingers and make the hurt go away." A sad laugh escaped her lips. "I've become acutely aware of how naïve I've been regarding men. Not just you, George, but all men."

"I don't care how other men behave," he interrupted her. "To be perfectly frank, I'm ashamed of myself and absolutely sick about hurting you so deeply."

"Perhaps your apology is extended not because you believe you did anything wrong but because you got caught! You had to have known such escapades would cause disharmony between us."

George rubbed his forehead, searching for a way to make peace with his wife. "May I make a suggestion?"

"If you'd like."

"As you know, Pierre Lorillard, Jr. started a community near Poughkeepsie. He's calling it Tuxedo Park. They've built a clubhouse and added amenities for hunting and such, renting out cottages. I've heard some of the set are even buying their own cottages."

George watched Sara's face for any sign of enthusiasm. "Pierre has invited us to visit. He has a lovely home there with plenty of room for house guests. Newport is getting so crowded in the summer. I thought we might take a trip to Tuxedo and see what all the hub-bub is about. It would give us some time alone, and we might think about buying a place. It could be a fresh start for us, Sara, and we could finally put this debacle behind us."

The idea appealed to her, and Sara met his eyes, cautiously releasing her defensiveness. George looked contrite, and she felt a flicker of forgiveness open her heart. "I think I might like that. But it's going to take more than a trip to Tuxedo Park to heal my trust."

"I understand. But you must know how much I love you. And how important our family is to me. What I did was unforgivable, and I assure you, Sara, I've learned my lesson. The thought of losing you over such a meaningless dalliance is distressing." Reaching across the table, he took her hand in his and gently kissed it. "Sara, please, tell me how to heal your hurt. I'm willing to do whatever it takes to return to your good graces."

A ring of truth filled his sincere words, and Sara considered the power of compassion. Taking Carrie's advice to heart, she realized George had been a wonderful provider and an even better father to the children. Weary from the tension that had descended over their relationship, Sara yearned for the closeness they'd once shared as husband and wife.

Like a rose blossoming in the morning sun, Sara offered him a lenient smile. "Alright, George. I'll try. I'll try very hard. It might be fun to join the set in Tuxedo, and we can give our marriage a fresh start. But I assure you, if something like this happens again, the heartache will surely kill me."

"I won't allow that to happen," he promised, his face showing relief. "Now. Tell me you'll share a waltz with me."

Nodding, Sara rose from her chair and followed him to the dance floor, pledging to embrace a new future with George.

Later that evening.

"I'm going to the powder room." Natica interrupted Charlotte, who was busy chattering away with her girlfriends at the table.

"Okay." Charlotte nodded. "I'll be right here when you get back."

Natica left the ballroom and headed for the corridor to the ladies' room. Her white satin gown swayed on her body with every step, and she delighted in the way it made her feel like a débutante. "Only a few more years," she whispered with anticipation. And in the meantime, I'll have Charlotte give me tips on the finer points of courting.

Reaching the end of the hallway, she turned the corner. Then she saw him. His presence brought Natica to a sudden halt, mid-step, in the corridor.

Standing near the elevator was the man who always seemed to be watching her. The one her mother called 'Absent Absinthe Oliver.'

He looked up, startled by her appearance, and after a moment's hesitation, gave her a smile. Natica offered him a shy smile in return. She knew she should continue walking to the powder room, but her curiosity regarding this man overrode her common sense. Natica hesitated, battling with her thoughts. She wanted to speak with him but knew how angry that would make her mother – although she still could only suspect why.

The 'Oliver' man seemed to sense her impulses and took a step toward her. For a moment, panic seized Natica and she was tempted to dash into the bathroom. But something made her stay, and she watched him approach as if in a slow-motion picture show.

"Hello, Natica," the man said, walking up. "My name is Oliver. Oliver Belmont."

Belmont! Natica's mind raced as she struggled to put the pieces together. Her mother and she had both had the name 'Belmont' when she was a little girl.

"How do you know my name?" she asked cautiously. "Have we met?"

He cocked his head and gave her a gentle smile. "Not officially, no. But how could I miss noticing such a lovely young lady at society's parties?"

A cautious smiled crossed her face. "Thank you," was all she could think to say. She found herself enamored by his appearance and wondered why. It wasn't his fine-tailored clothing, but something about his eyes. Deep brown eyes that somehow seemed so familiar to her, though she really couldn't remember from where.

"Natica!" Charlotte was approaching from the ballroom with several of her friends gabbing away beside her. "Come here at once!" she called down the corridor.

Natica turned to her cousin, and then looked back at Mr. Belmont. Their eyes locked a moment, and a sense of understanding passed between the two. Torn between her curiosity at discovering more about this man and the fear of being reprimanded, she moved to join her cousin.

"Excuse me, sir." Natica curtsied.

"Of course." He gave a slight nod, releasing her from his company.

Charlotte caught up to her wearing a stern expression. When Natica glanced back, Mr. Belmont had disappeared.

"I told you not to talk to that man!" Charlotte whispered as her friends filed into the powder room. "Your mother will be furious if she gets wind of this!"

"Why, Charlotte? He seems nice enough. But no one will tell me why I'm to avoid him."

"Just never you mind why and do as you're told." Her cousin took her hand and led her into the ladies' room.

Obediently, Natica followed, her mind spinning from the encounter. Charlotte and her friends tended to matters in the washroom, giggling and joking with each other the entire time. Natica followed them to the mirror so she could smooth her hair, but she could not get Mr. Belmont out of her mind.

Why did he look so familiar to her? She'd only caught brief glimpses of him around Newport and New York. Pushing away her thoughts, she pulled the comb from her pocketbook and assessed her appearance in the mirror.

It was then that realization seared through her like lightening, as an involuntary gasp escaped her lips.

Her eyes.

Her deep brown eyes.

She suddenly knew where she'd seen Mr. Belmont's eyes before.

They were exactly like her own.

Amidst the revelry of Charlotte and her friends, Natica was hit with a startling epiphany.

Could it be possible? Could this man be her father? Her *real* father?

It would explain everything. It would explain why her mother didn't want her near him and why he was always spoken of with such disdain. And why society's mothers had whispered around her when she was a young child as though she had committed some unknown crime. And particularly why she'd been taught to write her name as 'Belmont' when she was five and then re-taught to write it as 'Rives' a year later.

An icy numbness descended over her as she pondered the possible answer to this mystery. Should she say something to Charlotte? Natica glanced at Charlotte in the mirror and inadvertently caught her cousin's eye.

"What's wrong with you?" Charlotte asked, as her friends exited the powder room leaving the two alone. "You look funny." Studying her, Charlotte seemed to realize what was going through Natica's mind.

"What did he say to you?"

"Nothing," Natica answered. "He only introduced himself. His name is Oliver Belmont.

"Oh, no." Charlotte grimaced, trying to decide if she should mention the situation to Aunt Sara. "Anything else?" she interrogated her charge. "I told you a hundred times not to talk to that man."

Natica spun around from the mirror and faced Charlotte. "Why?" she demanded. "No one will ever answer that question for me. He's always skulking around wherever I go, but no one will tell me why."

"Some things are better left unsaid," Charlotte warned her. "Let sleeping dogs lie."

Natica struggled with her conjecture. Should she tell Charlotte she was putting the puzzle pieces together? Or should she pretend to be ignorant of this man's identity? Before she could decide, Charlotte grabbed her hand and led her out of the powder room. "Come on. I'm taking you back to your mother," she announced, as if to wash her hands of the entire event. "And if you're smart, you won't say anything to her about meeting Mr. Belmont. She'd probably forbid you to go to any more parties for the next five years!"

Following Charlotte from the washroom, Natica's thoughts were a jumble of questions and possibilities. But one thing was certain.

She wasn't as innocent and naïve as everyone thought.

Could it be that her mother had married Oliver Belmont and actually been through a divorce? And she was the child from a previous marriage? That would explain so many things, including why, when a child, she'd sometimes caught her mother with tears in her eyes when she'd not been invited to a special society dinner among the set. Divorce would be a shameful thing and would've dismissed her mother from many functions – but could it possibly be true?

It was too much for her young mind to decipher, this puzzle from her past, and her stomach churned as she returned to the ballroom with a million unanswered questions.

Chapter Nineteen

Five months later
April 8, 1899
Newport, Rhode Island

The coach drove down the rain-soaked Newport street, pulling to a stop in front of Trinity Church. Climbing out of their ride, the two sisters headed down the walkway to the entrance.

"April showers bring May flowers," Sara quipped.

"Thank goodness." A grin appeared on Jane's face. "Though predictable, it's nonetheless wonderful to see the bulbs flower each spring."

"So true."

"I feel good about making this donation to the church." Jane turned up the collar of her coat to ward off the cold drizzle descending over town. "I miss Mother and Milly so much. This feels like a worthy way to honor their memory."

"I'm excited to hear the new chimes. I'm sure they'll sound beautiful." A nostalgic smile crossed Sara's face as they entered the rectory. "We can think of our family every time they ring out during services."

"I'm especially looking forward to seeing the stained-glass windows," Jane added.

"It seemed as though they took forever to be delivered. It's a shame they weren't installed in time for Easter last week." She turned to Jane. "Let's stay for Sunday's service so we can hear the bells at Mass. We can head back to New York later that afternoon."

"I like the idea. It's still Easter season, if not actually Easter Sunday."

"So true." Sara nodded. "I'd stay longer, but it's still so cold here in Rhode Island, and I don't want to be away from the children too long."

"They're in good hands with Bridget and Anna," Jane assured her. "When I heard our donations were delivered, I couldn't bear to wait until late May to see them."

"Or hear the chimes," Sara added. "Not to mention meeting the new priest."

The ladies headed down the hall to the church office. "Now that we've received these memorials for Milly and Mother, perhaps we should consider purchasing one for Gus too," Jane suggested.

"That sounds like a great idea."

They walked into the office, bringing a halt to their conversation.

"Good afternoon, ladies." The rosy faced priest, Reverend Henry Morgan Stone, greeted them. "You must be Mrs. Rives and Miss Whiting."

"Yes, sir," Jane replied.

"It's nice to meet you, Reverend," Sara said, politely extending her hand. "Welcome to our congregation. I understand you'll be giving your first pastorate this Sunday."

"Yes, I am." He nodded, offering a warm smile. "I'm really looking forward to serving Trinity Church. It has such a rich history and wonderful parishioners."

"That's very true." Sara nodded. "Even George Washington once sat in pew 81."

"So I've been told," Reverend Stone replied, while shuffling through some papers on his desk. Lifting an invoice, he handed it to Sara.

"Here is the order for your stained-glass windows. And this one is for the bells," he added, passing them a second invoice. "We'll go over to the sanctuary in a moment so you can see them yourself, but I must say, the windows are very beautiful."

"We're anxious to see them. They were ordered from the famous Whiting and Bell firm in England," Jane said. "We've had high hopes as they're renowned for their excellent craftsmanship."

"No relation to your own family?"

"No, sir," Sara answered. "It's just a coincidence."

"I see." Reverend Stone nodded. "Everything has been installed, including the eight-bell chime in memory of your sister, Amelia Whiting Davis.

"Wonderful." Sara gave a glance toward the church. "When will they first be used for services?"

"I thought we'd ring them now for your benefit." he offered. "A test run, if you will. Then, if you approve, it will be my pleasure to ring them during every Mass in your sister's memory starting this Sunday." Reverend Stone smiled. "You've provided me with a memorable way to mark my first service as Trinity Church's new priest."

"Indeed," Sara said.

"Well, I'm excited for you to see the windows. If you'll follow me."

The three exited the church office and headed into the main sanctuary. Reverend Stone led them through the front doors and down the center aisle.

"There is your sister Amelia's window." He pointed to the side of the church, where Sara's eyes landed on the colorful glass depiction of the Virgin Mary. "I think your choice of Mary was perfect." Continuing, Reverend Stone directed their attention to the window next to it. "And that is Saint Ann, mother of Mary, installed in memory of your own mother, Mrs. Whiting."

"They are simply beautiful," Jane said in awe.

"The craftsmanship is outstanding," Reverend Stone commented. "And well worth the wait from England."

"You called for me, sir?" Sammy Langdon, the church caretaker, walked up the aisle.

"Yes, Sammy." Reverend Stone beckoned him to join the group. "This is Mrs. Rives and Miss Whiting."

"Hello, Mrs. Rives," he greeted cordially. "Miss Whiting."

"Do you mind giving a test ring to the new chimes? I thought we'd give the ladies a short demonstration before Sunday's services?"

"Certainly," he agreed with a slight bow of his head and excused himself from the sanctuary.

Sara walked around the unique closed box pews in the historical church, moving toward the stained-glass windows for a closer view. Reaching the side aisle, she noticed Jane following her.

"These are so beautiful, aren't they, Sara?"

"Yes. And as you said, a wonderful way to pay tribute to our family."

"I'm sure these windows will last much longer than any of us." Her chuckle was interrupted by the beautiful sound of the chimes ringing out from the church tower over the Newport community.

"Ah, there we go." Reverend Stone joined them in the side aisle. "They sound absolutely divine."

Sara's heart grew warm at the music of the bells. It gave her a sense of peace and a small modicum of closure at the loss of her family members.

"They're as lovely as I'd hoped, Reverend Stone," Sara said softly.

Jane nodded her agreement. The three fell quiet as they listened to the chimes finish their song, the music fading over the city-by-the-sea.

When the bells stopped, Sara and Jane had a last glance at the stained-glass windows and headed back to the sanctuary entrance. Reverend Stone held the door for them as they stepped back into the late afternoon daylight. The sky was beginning to clear over the damp city streets, showing patches of blue. The sun emerged from behind a cloud with bold beams, and Sara felt the weather redeeming in some strange way as the rain clouds dispersed.

"I can't thank you, ladies, enough for your generous donation to our church," Reverend Stone acknowledged. "And if there's any way I can serve your family, please don't hesitate to contact me or my secretary."

"It was our pleasure, sir," Jane said, shaking his hand.

"We'll see you on Sunday," Sara added while following suit. "I hope your tenure at Trinity Church is a long and fulfilling one."

"Thank you so much for your kind words," he said and headed back into the rectory.

Walking down the sidewalk, Sara and Jane saw their waiting carriage. As they stepped up to board, Sara glanced at the brightening sky.

"Jane!" she cried excitedly. "Look! A rainbow!"

Jane followed her glance and gasped. "Oh, how lovely!"

"And how absolutely perfect!" Tears welled in Sara's eyes. "It's almost as if heaven itself has witnessed and approved of our donation."

"Or Mother and Milly are sending a sign," Jane whispered, reverence in her tone.

The two women paused, gazing at the colorful beauty that embraced the skies over the Newport harbor. Filled with a sense of completion and contentedness, they dallied longer on the sidewalk.

"Do you think life goes on?" Sara asked wistfully.

"We're promised a place in heaven, if that's what you mean."

"No. Not in heaven, exactly." Sara wasn't sure what she meant. "Do you think we ever get a chance to come back and do things again? A second chance, if you will. A chance to make what was wrong, right again."

"Like reincarnation?" Jane asked skeptically. "I've heard tales of it from India, but offhand, I don't know anyone who's been a princess in a previous lifetime. Besides, I've got enough to deal with in this lifetime." She gave Sara a quizzical look, trying to fathom what was going on in her mind.

Sara blushed, suddenly self-conscious, and the two sisters fell silent, watching until the rainbow faded into the blue sky of the afternoon.

One month later
May 14, 1899
New York, New York

"I think we'd make a great team, Bill, and I agree the Democratic Party can benefit from our joining forces."

Smoke filled the interior of the plush executive offices, floating lazily in the air. Taking a long drag on his cigar, Oliver looked at Mr. Bryan across the room, where he sat perched on the corner of his heavy mahogany desk.

"Let's not beat around the bush, Oliver. You know I'm looking for a running mate," he admitted. "And I also need to raise more campaign funds. I think you might be the perfect man to fill those shoes. The election is next year, and it's past time to start the stump." He glanced over his horn-rimmed glasses. "By the way, I saw the article in your paper, *The Verdict*. Quite a pontification, if I do say so myself."

"I'm guessing you approve?" Oliver asked. "I tried to stick to the opinions we've previously discussed."

"Yes. It sounded good, although perhaps a bit dramatic, if not grandiose."

"Drama is part and parcel of politics, isn't it, Bill." Oliver threw him a mischievous smile. "Besides, one of the benefits of owning your own newspaper is that no one can tell you what you can or cannot say – or how to say it, for that matter. If you decide to add me as your running mate, this format could prove a useful addition to the traditional whistle-stops."

Mr. Bryan flicked his cigar ashes into a tray. "Not only for us but for the Democratic party as a whole. You did well taking over the campaign for the east end of town. That freed me up so I could cover a more extensive area."

"I'm glad you approve," Oliver said. "Politics seems to agree with me, and I hope you do decide to add me to your ticket." He snuffed out his cigar. "And, of course, I'll be able to make generous fiduciary contributions to the cause."

"That would give the campaign a great boost."

Oliver got up to leave. "Let me know." He walked over and shook Mr. Bryan's hand. "I'll be staying in New York for at least another month unless you decide before then to add me as your running mate. Then I'll probably stay in the city on a more permanent basis, especially if we win the election."

"Good to know," the senator said with a nod. "I'll be in touch,"

Oliver left Bryan's offices feeling very gratified. *"Politics can actually be kind of fun,"* he thought as he reached the sidewalk.

Five weeks later
June 21, 1899
Newport, Rhode Island

It had been over two seasons since Mrs. Vanderbilt had given a party at The Breakers, and Charlotte had been anticipating the evening ever since her invitation had arrived. The dinner party, planned only for young people, would include a cotillion and informal dancing. In lieu of a chaperone, her friend, Marie Winthrop, accompanied Charlotte, the two ladies arriving together in the Whiting's finest carriage.

"There's been so much talk about the new cottage," Charlotte said. "I'm looking forward to seeing it with my own eyes." Wearing her pink silk gown from Paris, Anna had fixed her hair in a Gibson girl style. Her blond curls piled high, a few ringlets were left to fall around Charlotte's face in a very becoming manner.

"I've seen the cottage from the street," Marie replied. "But I've never been inside. I'm so glad our names were included on the invitation list."

"I was thrilled when mine arrived," Charlotte said. "By the way, your gown is *so* lovely."

The elaborate orchid gown brought out the blue in Marie's eyes, and the bodice, finished with tiny, hand-sewn beads, was delicate and quite becoming.

"Thank you. I've been saving this one for a special occasion!"

Pulling up under the porte-cochère, the driver jumped down and assisted them from the coach. Entering the foyer, the two were greeted by a footman who escorted them to the receiving line. The banquet hall was filling with young people from the set, a thrum of exciting building with each arriving guest. Charlotte felt a bit nervous but drew on her training in etiquette as she and Marie caught their first glimpse of the mansion's fabulous interior.

The Great Hall opened into an immense expanse above her head. Exquisitely decorated, the room was completed with massive crystal-and-gold chandeliers suspended grandly from the ceiling. An elegant staircase fit for a queen's promenade led to the second story. With a quick glance upward, Charlotte noticed that the upstairs gallery had an open hall set with marble pillars and ornate ironwork railings. Valuable artwork adorned the walls, and Charlotte knew the home had set a new precedence among the other Newport cottages. Remembering her manners, she tried not to stare, instead feigning a confident smile. The two ladies followed the butler into the banquet hall, their shoes tapping lightly on the marble floor as they moved.

The bronzed and gilded banquet hall was full of merriment, and Charlotte quickly spotted their friends; Anna Sands, Lily Olerichs, and Elsie Clews. Elsie was clearly flirting with John Livermore. Robert Gerry was laughing at the three as he listened in on their conversation. Charlotte felt a lot more at ease in the palatial house at the sight of friends joking and enjoying themselves.

"Welcome, Charlotte," Mrs. Vanderbilt greeted her as they reached the front of the receiving line. "We're so glad you could attend tonight."

"Thank you, Mrs. Vanderbilt." Charlotte flashed her brightest smile and curtsied. "I appreciate the invitation."

"And Miss Winthrop..." Alice Vanderbilt welcomed. "It's so lovely to have you both here."

"Thank you for the invitation," Marie said with a curtsey.

"Mrs. Sloan and Mrs. Twombley, my sisters-in-law, are sharing the hostess duties with me tonight." Mrs. Vanderbilt waved at the ladies beside her. "And, of course, you know my daughter, Gertrude, now Mrs. Whitney."

Charlotte and Marie curtsied again for the women sharing hostess duties.

"Let us know if there's anything you need," Gertrude said.

"Have you been to The Breakers before?" Mrs. Twombley asked politely.

"No. This is my first time," Charlotte said.

"Mine as well," Marie added.

"I must say, it certainly lives up to all the praise I've heard," Charlotte was quick to add.

"Thank you, my dear." Mrs. Vanderbilt seemed pleased to know the gossip around town had been positive regarding The Breakers.

How could it not be, Charlotte thought. The house was a palace.

"We'd hoped to entertain a lot more, but with Mr. Vanderbilt ill since his stroke, we've tried to keep things quiet for him," Mrs. Vanderbilt said.

A merry round of laughter erupted from one of the tables, and Charlotte glanced over at their friends, already seated in the ballroom.

"The footman will show you to your table." Mrs. Sloan nodded to the servant.

"Thank you," Charlotte said.

The two ladies curtseyed one more time and followed the footman to the same table where Lily, Anna, and Elsie were sitting together. Everyone was dressed in their finest party clothes, and Charlotte smoothed her skirt a bit self-consciously. Her pink silk and chiffon gown was every bit as pretty tonight as it had been in the shop.

Thinking back to her preparations earlier that afternoon, Charlotte nervously fingered her diamond necklace. She'd been heading to her chamber to get ready for the dance when Aunt Sara had called her into the master bedroom. Charlotte joined her in the suite, surprised to find her aunt riffling through a large jewelry box. She was holding a sparkling diamond swan necklace with a far-away expression on her face. Charlotte had felt like she was intruding on a private moment when her aunt noticed her standing in the threshold.

"Come in, Charlotte." Sara motioned for her to sit on the bed. "You've caught me day-dreaming..."

"That necklace is beautiful, Aunt Sara."

"It was a gift from my family when I made my début." A listless expression crossed her aunt's face. "That seems like such a long time ago." Glancing at her niece, she put away the diamond swan with a fond smile. "Tonight is your first party alone in society, and I think it's time to give you this."

Reaching inside the jewelry case, Aunt Sara handed her a black velvet box. Opening it, Charlotte was met by the brilliant dazzle of a diamond necklace with matching earrings. The style was classic and stunning, and Charlotte released a tiny gasp at the sight of the jewels.

"These were your mother's," Aunt Sara said softly. "I've been keeping them for you for all these years."

"They're beautiful!" Charlotte replied in awe. "These were my mother's?"

"Yes, dear, and I know she wanted you to have them one day. Now that you're a young woman, I think it's time they were yours." Aunt Sara smiled, watching as Charlotte gingerly touched the jewels. "I think you should wear them to the Vanderbilt's tonight."

Peals of loud laughter erupted from her friends, quickly jolting Charlotte's mind back to the party. Arriving at their table, the two ladies gracefully took their seats. Charlotte had never been more aware that appearances were everything, and thanks to Aunt Sara, she knew she looked her very best – down to the diamonds.

"Charlotte! You and Marie are finally here," Lily said. "You're just in time. We're having the most fun listening to Robert tell us of his escapades at Harvard."

"You don't believe all those crazy tales, do you?" John Livermore overheard her. "He just wants you to think he's a scalawag. We all know

he would never rock the boat at school. His father would kill him."

"What do you mean?" Robert demanded good-naturedly. "It's all true, I tell you." But the Cheshire-cat grin on his face said otherwise.

"Have you seen the favors?" Elsie piped up from across the table. "They are *so* fabulous. I can't wait till the cotillion starts so we can make our choices. It's going to be a hard decision."

"What kind of favors are there?" Marie asked.

"Writing sets, telephone sets, gold-topped smelling bottles..." Anna recited.

"Parasols, and much more," Lily broke in. "It's quite wonderful."

"I can't wait to see them for myself." Charlotte smiled. Relaxing into her chair, she happily realized she knew nearly everyone at the dance. Susan Webster was in attendance, as well as Miss Cushing. And Miss Grant was there too, shooting a flirtatious glance over her fan directed toward Harry Gray, who didn't seem to notice at all.

Taking in the party, Charlotte's eyes locked with a handsome young man sitting at the next table. He smiled and gave her a nod of greeting. Charlotte blushed, a little embarrassed when she realized the gentleman had been watching her!

Turning back to the friends at her table, she reached for the crystal glass and took a sip of ice water. "Who is that?" she whispered to Marie, casting a discreet glance his way.

Marie peeked subtly in the direction Charlotte indicated and turned back to her friend. "That's Henry Havemeyer, Jr.," she whispered. "And he seems to be very interested in you." A coy smile danced across her face.

"He's very handsome." Charlotte blushed. "If I do say so myself."

"We'll have to arrange a dance for the two of you," Marie plotted. "I'm sure you know the Havemeyers. They're a fine family. Quite wealthy from sugar, I've heard. Maybe there's a romance in store for you?" she added coquettishly, batting her eyelashes at Robert.

Mrs. Vanderbilt entered the banquet hall looking majestic, with Gertrude, Mrs. Sloan and Mrs. Twombley at her side. Apparently, all the guests had arrived, and the dinner was about to start. Gertrude and the older women took their place at the table near the front of the hall, and the footmen, as though having been given some secret sign, began to serve dinner.

With a deep breath, Charlotte stole another glance at Henry Havemeyer. Dare she dream of a future with this handsome gentleman? Surrounded by the glittering gold of the beautiful mansion, she felt as though anything were possible. And taking her place here tonight at one of society's most esteemed tables, she felt butterflies of excitement flutter in heart, thrilled to begin the adventure of courting.

Chapter Twenty

Three weeks later
July 10, 1899
Tuxedo Park, New York

The Rives home in Tuxedo Park was brightly lit. The dining room tumbled with laughter and high spirits as the family gathered together for the first time in as long as Sara could remember. Jane, Charlotte, and Natica sat on one side of the long table, and on the other side sat Bayard, perched next to Mildred. The small children were seated close to Sara, so that she could keep an eye on their manners. On the other side of the children sat George Jr, George's son by his first marriage. He had graduated from college at Princeton in the class of 1896 and was following in his father's footsteps in foreign service. Junior had brought a lady with him to introduce to the family, and Sara had quickly ordered the staff to prepare for a fancy dinner party.

"It's so nice having everyone home!" The joy in Sara's voice was unmistakable. "I can't help but wonder if there's a special reason?"

Junior looked at his lady guest, Betty Hare, and took her hand in his. Sitting in the chair beside him, Betty looked petite and delicate, her thick brunette hair piled on her head in an attractive coiffure.

"Well…" he began. "I suppose this is as good a time as any." Junior paused for drama as the table fell quiet. "I've already discussed things with father." He smiled across the table at George. "And, well… I've asked Betty to marry me – and she said 'yes'!"

Clapping and cheers of joy rang out through the dining room.

"This is wonderful news. A toast!" George raised his champagne glass. "To a long and happy life!"

"Congratulations!" Sara exclaimed, overjoyed for the young couple. There was going to be a wedding in the family!

Jane, delighted by the announcement, raised a glass with the others. "To a long and happy life together," she repeated. At fifty-five years old, the graying Jane looked more like a grandmother than an aging aunt.

Glasses clinked as everyone cheered at the couple's good news.

Sara caught George's eye across the long table and sent him a warm smile. True to his word, her husband had made every effort to set things right between them, even giving up his New York apartment, much to her relief. Trust grew between them again, and Sara discovered the true meaning of forgiveness. Together, they had turned over a new leaf in their marriage.

"I'm going to arrange an engagement dinner right away and invite your family over for a proper celebration!" Sara was eager to help with the wedding, even though she was only officially Junior's stepmother. "Have you set a date yet?" she asked.

"We're thinking of April twenty-fifth next year," Betty announced. "My mother thinks we'll have plenty of time to prepare for the wedding in a year."

"I couldn't agree more," Sara said with a jovial nod.

"Spring weddings are always the nicest," Jane added.

The Rives' Tuxedo housekeeper, Agnes, brought in trays overflowing with delicious food. Dishes loaded with roast beef, mashed potatoes, and gravy, not to mention exquisite vegetable casseroles and hot rolls, were served by the domestics. It was the perfect meal for their homey family reunion.

"Do I get to be in the wedding?" Mildred asked her stepbrother.

"Absolutely!" Betty told the girl with a warm smile.

"There is a perfect job for a seven-year-old girl in our ceremony." Junior pointed out in an official tone. "Betty and I hoped you would be our flower girl."

"Oh! That's wonderful!" Mildred clapped her hands, smiling at Sara when she heard the happy news.

"Sorry, little stepsister." Junior turned to Natica with a laugh. "You're a little old for the job."

"Do stop teasing me." Natica smiled good-naturedly. "I'm seventeen and going to be married soon myself."

Everyone laughed at her words as the revelry around the table grew infectious.

"You!" Charlotte scoffed. "If anyone is getting married next, it's me!" Then, as an aside, she said, "But you can be in my wedding if you want."

"Really?" Natica seemed appeased by the idea.

"What about me?" young Bayard piped up with a mouth of mashed potatoes.

"Don't talk with your mouth full. I taught you better manners than that," Sara gently reprimanded her young son as everyone laughed at his potato-covered face.

"You're a bit too old to be the ring bearer," Junior explained apologetically.

"I'm almost ten!" the boy announced proudly as he swallowed his food. "Is ten too old, Mother?"

"Yes, I'm afraid so," Sara answered, smiling at his innocence.

"We haven't made any other decisions about our ceremony," Betty interjected. "Except that we're holding the wedding at Grace Church with the breakfast afterward at my father's house on East Seventy-Fifth. That's about all the plans we've made for the actual wedding, except, of course, for acres and acres of flowers."

"You can't have a wedding without flowers," Jane stated conclusively.

"After the nuptials," Junior continued, "we thought a nice bridal tour in London would be the perfect place for our holiday. Betty and I love the stage, and you know how wonderful London theatre is."

"I think that's a marvelous idea," George said, glad to see his son so happy. He had taken his mother's death hard, but now he was moving on, building a wonderful new life for himself just as Sara had predicted years ago.

"It sounds to me like you've made a good start on your arrangements." Sara encouraged them. "And I'm sure your mother is right, Betty. A year is plenty of time to make all the wedding plans. The most important thing is that the two of you are happy."

Junior wrapped his arm around his fiancé. "We're very happy, aren't we?" He gave her an adoring look, and for a second, it looked as though he was going to kiss her right then and there but remembered his manners.

Betty blushed at his affections. "Yes, Mrs. Rives." She sighed. "We're very happy."

"What more could we ask for?" Sara said, with another warm glance at George. He smiled back with a happy glint in his eye, and they finished dinner, enjoying the simple pleasure of their growing family.

⁂

Two months later

September 15, 1899
New York, New York

Oliver hated funerals, but it was important to make an appearance at the church service. He and Alva had sent a huge spray of flowers, but she was *persona non grata* with the Vanderbilt family, so Oliver had attended the funeral alone. After the service, he'd headed to Delmonico's for the reception.

"Thank you for coming," William said, taking the chair beside him at the banquet table.

"I'm really sorry about your brother," Oliver offered. "Society certainly won't be the same without him."

"Thank you, Oliver." William gave him a forlorn glance. "It's a sad affair, but Alice had her hands full caring for him after his stroke a few years ago. I think Cornelius is a lot better off now. All the money in the world can't erase complicated health issues."

Oliver just nodded. He knew William was right. Disease and injury were the chief enemy of the wealthy set. It was the one problem that could not be fixed by throwing cash at it.

A waiter brought Oliver a fresh scotch and offered one to William as well, which he accepted. "I thought Cornelius was doing better," Oliver said. "I heard he was going to the office occasionally."

"Yes, he was." William frowned. "He was even preparing to entertain a bit. Alice was getting the house ready for a dinner in honor of Prince Cantacuzène. He was recently engaged to Julia Dent Grant, and my brother was having a party for the new couple. Everyone had arrived in New York for the celebration, which was scheduled after a Vanderbilt board meeting."

"What happened?"

"Apparently, he sat up in bed in the middle of the night and announced to his valet that he was dying." Willie shook his head in glum disbelief. "And that was it. He was gone. Died of a massive brain hemorrhage."

"I'm sorry, Willie," Oliver repeated.

"Yeah, well...." William's voice drifted. "He didn't die without making a strong statement about Neily's marriage to Grace Wilson, which, you know, he staunchly disapproved of."

"What do you mean?"

"The will was read a few days ago in the library at The Breakers." He paused and took a sip of his drink, shaking his head. "He didn't completely disinherit Neily, but half a million dollars is a paltry sum compared to what the rest of the children received. Can you believe it?"

"How very unfortunate." Oliver grimaced. "I didn't think he'd go through with it." He thought back to all the times his own father had made the same threats, but no one ever took their parents' warnings seriously. The children of the wealthy thought of it only as their parents' last resort to manipulate their offspring.

"I hope he truly loves the girl." William shot Oliver a glance. "Because Neily and Grace are going to have a difficult time keeping up in the style they're accustomed to."

"What did the old guy do with his money?"

"Of course, a large bank account has been set aside for Alice," William said. "But the bulk of his fortune is going to Neily's little brother, Alfred. Somewhere in the neighborhood of forty million. It reminds me of what my grandfather did to my own father. Giving the bulk of his fortune to my dad caused him a lot of problems among the rest of the family."

"I remember they sued him for their share."

William nodded. "Isn't wealth grand?" Sarcasm dripped from his voice as he drank his scotch.

"Come on," Oliver urged, rising from his chair. "I think you need some fresh air and a cigar."

William glanced up at Oliver, heavy grief weighing him down.

"Good idea," he agreed and grabbed his drink to follow.

<hr>

One month later
October 4, 1899
Tuxedo Park, New York

The suave motorcar pulled to a stop and parked in front of the Rives' home. Silencing the engine, a young gentleman jumped out and climbed the porch steps to ring the bell. Sara and George sat in the parlor, waiting for Agnes to announce their visitor.

"Mr. Henry Havemeyer has arrived," the housekeeper said in a formal voice.

George got up from his chair to greet the young man. "Welcome, Henry." He shook his hand. "Please come in."

"Thank you." Henry fidgeted with his hat. "Good evening, Mrs. Rives." He nodded politely.

"Hello, Henry." Sara gave him a warm smile. "Won't you sit down? Charlotte will be ready in a few minutes. You know the way young ladies are when they're getting dressed for a ball."

"You'd better get used to it now," George joked. "It only takes them longer as they get older."

Henry seemed to relax as he sat on the French Provincial divan. "I don't mind waiting." He grinned a bit shyly. "Especially not for someone as lovely as Charlotte."

Sara surveyed the young man, recognizing the admiration written on his face.

"In fact..." He toyed with his hat nervously. "I'm glad for a chance to talk with you privately." He glanced up at George and Sara.

"As you know, I'm working my way up in my father's sugar refinery business. We have a large holding within the industry, and I've been learning all the 'ins and outs' of production."

"Ah yes, the sugar trust your family is so famous for." George tried to ease the young man's nerves. "You cannot bake a cake without sugar, Henry. It's an important staple in the kitchen."

"How true," Sara concurred with a nod.

"Well, sir..." Henry glanced at Sara. "Ma'am..." He paused and took a deep breath. "I would like your permission to marry Charlotte," he said, quickly adding, "I'm in love with her. I was going to propose at the ball tonight, but I wanted your approval first."

Surprised silence fell around the room. George gave Sara a searching glance, which she returned. Henry and Charlotte had been courting for a while, but an engagement seemed off in the distant future.

"Will you take good care of our girl?" George asked pointedly. "Treat her with kindness and consideration?"

"Absolutely, sir," Henry said vehemently. "I will love and cherish her all of my years if you'll give your blessing on our engagement, of course."

Sara shot George an indiscernible nod of approval.

"Well then, Henry..." A smile crossed George's face. "Mrs. Rives and I would be delighted to welcome you to the family."

"If Charlotte accepts your proposal, that is," Sara was fast to add.

It appeared there were going to be *two* weddings in the family!

The young man beamed just as a commotion was heard at the top of the staircase. A few moments later, the three turned when Charlotte entered the room looking fabulous – with Natica close behind.

"Charlotte..." Henry stood as she entered. "You look beautiful."

And proudly, Sara agreed with him. Clothed in a silver satin gown, the young woman looked like a princess, sparkling in her mother's diamonds. Glancing at Natica, Sara could see her daughter was taking in every facet of the courtship.

"Well," Henry said, composing himself. "If you're ready?" He held out his arm for Charlotte.

She wrapped her dainty fingers around Henry's strong arm, glowing with the hope and joy of youth. "I'm ready." She smiled at her family as the couple turned for the front door.

"I want to know every detail of your evening," Natica ordered in a bossy tone.

Charlotte grinned at her cousin. "We'll have breakfast together. How does that sound?"

Natica seemed satisfied with the answer and nodded 'okay' as Sara glanced at George. Smiling, they both knew that the young ladies were going to have much more to talk about in the morning light than either of them suspected at the present moment.

As the door closed, Sara moved to peek through the large bay windows, watching as the motor car disappeared, like so many years, and faded into the night.

Chapter Twenty-One

Three weeks later
October 6, 1899
Tuxedo Park, New York

The train station bustled with people anticipating a fun day at the Goshen Horse Show. Along with a coaching parade and a series of horse races, the show touted a fabulous orchestra with over thirty members to entertain the guests. *"They've added a new feature this year,"* Sara had told George. *"A special luncheon is to be served on the grounds. Won't that be lovely?"*

Tickets for the event were in high demand, and the Erie Railroad had scheduled special trains to run between nearby towns and the fairgrounds to accommodate the increase in travelers to the show.

Catching the train at Tuxedo Park where the family had been spending the summer, Sara planned to meet George at the Goshen train station. *"I'll join you after the board meeting this morning,"* he'd said. *"There's a late morning train leaving out of Manhattan. I should be at the fairgrounds by early afternoon."*

After collecting her ticket, she stowed it in the pocket of her handbag, grabbed her satchel, and proceeded to the waiting platform.

The clear skies and warm temperatures promised a lovely day, although the wind was brisk, and Sara had to hold her hat against its strength. Ladies in fancy frocks and gentlemen smoking cigars gathered on the platform to wait for the train. Checking the time, Sara glanced at her watch as she heard the whistle blow from the approaching engine.

The loud chugging of the train, accompanied by the clack of wheels on the tracks, grew deafening as the locomotive slowed and pulled into the Tuxedo Park station.

As the engine drew near, Sara bent down, reaching for the satchel resting at her feet. Before she realized what had happened, the bumping block of the locomotive struck her, knocking her onto the station platform.

Slamming her head hard against the wooden floorboards, Sara's vision blurred. Stunned, loud thunder roared in her ears. The train station swirled and swayed in a cacophony of chaos. Faces contorted in her vision, shouting and leaning over where she lay on the platform.

"Is there a doctor on the train? We need a doctor!" a gruff voice shouted above the noise.

A man's face came into focus. "I'm Dr. Dennis," he said. "Try to stay still. Are you experiencing any pain?"

Moving her lips, Sara tried but couldn't form words from her thoughts. Struggling, she studied the man's face as it faded and disappeared into a black void.

The sharp scent of smelling salts pulled her out of the faint, and she shook her aching head, working her way back to consciousness.

"Mrs. Rives, I'm Doctor Rushmore."

"What happened?" she whispered in a hoarse voice.

"You were hit by the train. Fortunately, you were not thrown on the track. But you've got a nasty bump on your head."

"You were very lucky," Dr. Dennis added, relieved to see Mrs. Rives speaking. "You could have been seriously injured."

"Can you move?" Dr. Rushmore asked.

"I think so..."

"Let's try to get you up."

The two doctors gave Sara a hand, gently lifting her to a standing position. The world wobbled and reeled, but she steadied herself. Her head throbbed from the impact, and she gingerly touched the swollen bump, trembling from the shock of the accident.

A police officer walked up, joining the doctors. "Mr. Lorillard, Jr. has insisted Mrs. Rives be brought to his cottage immediately."

"I think that's a good idea." Dr. Rushmore nodded in agreement. "I can better examine her at his home and let her rest if need be."

"Let's get you into the coach, ma'am," the police officer said. Taking her by the arm, he guided her into the carriage, followed by Dr. Rushmore, who climbed in beside her.

"It looks as though you have the matter under control," Dr. Dennis acknowledged. "Let me know how she recovers," he added, taking his leave.

The police officer closed the carriage door and signaled to the driver. Immediately the coach took off for Pierre Lorillard's cottage, carrying the injured Mrs. Rives.

⁂

Later that evening...

"Thank goodness you weren't seriously hurt," George said with evident relief. "I got here as quickly as I could. Luckily the trains are running on time between the fairgrounds."

"I'm feeling much better," Sara assured him, touched by his attentiveness. "I'm sorry you had to miss the horse show."

"Oh, bother the horse show," George said, taking her hand in his. "There will always be another fair, but there is only one Sara Swan Rives." Leaning in, he gave her a light kiss on the forehead and wrapped his arm around her in a protective hug.

"You scared me to death. I don't know what I'd do if I lost you..."

Chapter Twenty-Two

Nearly three months later
December 31, 1899
New York, New York

Much effort had been focused on decorating New York to ring in the new year – and, in fact, the new century.

The twentieth century.

The city streets were alive with people, in spite of the cold weather, heading to parties and churches to worship and celebrate. 1900 was being heralded as a new age of prosperity and advancement. New York took great pride in holding an entire weekend of festivities to mark the occasion, and the city did not disappoint.

Twinkling lights were strung through tree branches lining the avenues as far as the eye could see. It was a wonderland of electricity, a testament to developments in science and technology. Visitors to the metropolis were delighted by the dazzling decorations.

Fireworks were planned for midnight, and crowds gathered in the streets and on bridges, anticipating the performance. Churches held mass and services, all poised to ring bells simultaneously over the homes and halls of New York, precisely at midnight, to proclaim the shift into the new century. The excitement was palpable, swelling in the hearts of all with the furor of new hope.

Taking Sara's hand, George stepped away from the window on the second-floor ballroom of Delmonico's. Around them, the orchestra played, dancers swirling with renewed optimism, all looking forward to the promise of a new era.

"You look lovely tonight," George said. "You know, Sara, the older you get, the more beautiful you are."

"Thank you," Sara said, touched by his words. "What a sweet thing to say."

"I'm only telling you how I feel."

A butler stepped up, and George took two glasses of champagne from the tray, handing one to Sara.

"A toast," he said, "to my beautiful wife."

They chimed their glasses together and sipped the old vintage.

"The city certainly is beautiful. Everyone is so happy."

"Yes, the mood is contagious." George smiled. "Only a lunatic could be glum tonight."

"I hope the new century brings prosperity and peace to us all," Sara said, giving him a sheepish grin. "I suppose I'm being idealistic, but I still believe there's hope for a better world."

"That's why I love you. Even when life seems dim, you hold on to your optimism – with a smile and a kind word, I might add. It gives me faith in the future."

Blushing at the compliment, Sara wondered if it were true. Knowing she'd stumbled into despair many times, somehow, she *had* quietly picked herself up to face another day.

He turned back to the window and pulled her close beside him, wrapping his arm around her shoulders. They stood together, gazing over a brilliant and festive New York. The occasional sound of a firecracker popped in celebration, echoing between the buildings lining the street.

"We've made it, Sara."

A quiet fell between them.

"Yes, I suppose we have, George."

Their eyes locked, and Sara drifted into the pool of affection that he focused on her. She felt the intensity of George's love, and her heart quickened, overcome by the power of her emotions.

"I love you, George." Her voice was barely a whisper baring her soul, but she knew it was true. She'd found lasting love for George.

"Oh, Sara." George hugged her, touched by her sincerity. "How long I've dreamt of hearing you say those words again." He pulled back. "I love you too, my dear. Truly and deeply."

Attention in the ballroom shifted to the immense wall clock, the minute hand edging toward the midnight hour. The orchestra stopped playing, replaced by the sound of gentlemen and ladies chanting down the time in unison.

"Ten, nine, eight..."

George reached for their champagne glasses on the nearby table and handed her a coupe, effervescent bubbles bouncing over the rim.

"Five, four, three, two, one... Happy New Year!"

The crowd cheered with deafening exuberance. Bells clanged and chimed over the New York streets. The windows rattled from the boom of fireworks, while confetti fluttered through the ballroom. The orchestra kicked into *Auld Lang Syne*, and voices rose to sing along with the familiar tune.

Leaning in, George kissed Sara slowly, with unrestrained passion. He pulled back and looked into her eyes. "Happy New Year, my love." He raised his glass and toasted against hers.

"Happy New Year, George." She sipped on the toast and leaned into his arms. Warm and safe in a changing world.

Chapter Twenty-Three

Four months later
April 24, 1900
New York, New York

The classic gothic architecture of Grace Church loomed high above Natica in a display of buttresses and formal arches that left her feeling small. Magnificent stained-glass windows filtered colored light over all those who'd congregated today for her stepbrother's wedding. She gazed at the church, lavishly decorated with satin ribbons and bushels of fresh flowers, casting their fresh, perfumed scent into the air.

Sitting next to her mother in the pew, Natica watched as Mildred slowly led the bridal procession. Her little sister looked sweet in her pale-blue dress and matching poke bonnet, trimmed with blue ribbons and pink flowers. Carrying a large willow basket that overflowed with delicate roses, Mildred smiled like a little lady as she ceremoniously followed young Master Philip Roosevelt down the church aisle, scattering flower petals along the way. The young boy was wearing a white sailor suit, serving as ring bearer for the bride and groom.

Natica glanced at Junior, who waited anxiously near the altar for the appearance of his bride. His best man, Arthur Street, stood by his side, flanked by Mr. Montgomery and Betty's brother Meredith, who were both serving as groomsmen. Natica scrutinized Bishop Hare, whom she'd overheard was the bride's uncle. She thought he was a funny-looking man with a big nose. The bishop stood at the front of the cathedral, ready to perform the ceremony with the assistance of Reverend Dr. Huntington, the current rector of Grace Church.

Strains of the Bridal March filled the massive building, and a feeling of awe passed through Natica as she turned with the other guests to see the bride enter the sanctuary. Betty seemed to glow with joy, taking the long walk down the aisle on her father's arm. Her white satin gown was trimmed with fine lace, and her tulle veil was pinned to her blond hair by a crescent diamond, a wedding gift from Junior to his new bride.

As the procession played out before her, Natica remembered that Charlotte would soon marry in July, and true to her word, her cousin had invited Natica to be one of her bridesmaids, along with Lily Oelrichs. The gowns they'd picked out were absolutely gorgeous, and Natica could barely wait for the summer wedding planned for *Swanhurst* during the height of the social season.

She glanced across the aisle where Charlotte sat next to Henry with the Havemeyer family. Soon after Charlotte's nuptials, Natica knew it would be time for her to make her own début into society. She'd finally be able to go to the parties and balls that, at present, she was too young to attend. Watching her stepbrother marry under the magnificent eaves of this majestic cathedral, Natica pondered the mysteries of the début ritual known as 'coming out'. What unspoken secrets might this advance into womanhood reveal to her? *"Will I find true love? Will I live happily ever after?"*

Glancing at her mother, standing proudly with her young brother Bayard at her side, Natica casually wondered if her mother had ever conceived of any career for her daughters other than marriage. Or did her mother simply follow, unquestioningly, the traditions that had been set for decades of women. Traditions which predestined a life filled with the responsibilities of wife and a mother, as well as a society hostess.

"Here's your rice." Interrupting her thoughts, her mother handed her a bundle of the grain wrapped in white tulle.

The ceremony concluded with the declaration of the couple as husband and wife. Everyone watched the happy newlyweds return down the aisle, arm-in-arm, smiling amidst the crowd of relatives and well-wishers that filled the church. Following her family out to the street, Natica cheered on the newlyweds, then joined the guests throwing rose petals and rice on the joyous couple as they escaped into their carriage.

"That was a beautiful ceremony." Natica heard her mother say to George. "I have so many happy hopes for the two of them."

"None the least of which is being blessed with a grandchild?" George teased her.

Natica watched her mother smile at the thought. "I suppose we should be off to the reception," she said, herding the family toward their carriage. "Charlotte is riding with Henry, and Mildred is riding in the bridal procession."

As Natica got comfortable on the coach seat, she keenly felt the absence of Charlotte. After she married, Natica would be the eldest child at home, a realization that brought both joy and trepidation to the young woman's heart as the carriage headed down Fifth Avenue to the bridal breakfast.

One month later
May 25, 1900
New York, New York

Finishing up some agreements in the plush offices of the New York Central Railroad, William's eye caught the engagement announcement on the pages of the *Times* strewn across his desk. Giving it a read, he saw it was simple and to the point.

Havemeyer – Whiting Wedding

NEWPORT, May 24. – Announcement has been made that the wedding of Miss Charlotte Whiting to Henry O. Havemeyer, Jr., will be on July 11 at Swanhurst, the Newport home of Mr. And Mrs. George L. Rives, Miss Whiting being their niece. It is understood that the young couple will go abroad immediately after the wedding.

"*Another wedding at Swanhurst,*" he thought. Dim memories of witnessing Sara and Oliver speak their vows intruded like an unwanted visitor. William shook them away as he considered his own children, now married. With Charlotte approaching her wedding day, William knew Natica was not far behind in entering society. "*Where have the years gone?*" he wondered fervidly? So much had changed, though he tried to deny it.

William stared absently at the newspaper while reviewing the years in his mind, with visions of Alva and their marriage, the children – and the nasty divorce that had ended it all. "*The picture had ended much better for Oliver, but certainly not at all good for Sara, although she does seem happy enough married to George.*"

"A call for you, sir," William's secretary Johnson said from the doorway. "And your motorcar is ready to take you to the train as soon as
you're ready."

"Thank you, Johnson." William grabbed the phone from the cradle and quickly returned to business, answering the call from his banker.

※

One month later
June 24, 1900
Middletown, Rhode Island

The sound of horses whinnying met Oliver's ears as he approached the stables at Gray Craig. He loved the smell of hay and alfalfa, and the hot summer air was pungent with the scent of it. Breathing deeply, he entered the darkness of the equestrian center and paused to let his eyes adjust to the room.

"Harvey!"

"Over here, sir," his manager called out.

"Where is that Indian animal keeper and his interpreter?" Oliver asked as he found the man preparing buckets of food for the horses.

"They left a while ago to feed the monkeys, sir," Harvey told him. "They should be back any minute. Or would you like for me to send for them?" The stable hand knew his boss could be impatient sometimes – and also unpredictable.

"Ah, here they are now, sir." Harvey glanced at the door behind Oliver to see Sahib enter the stables with Mr. Matthews, the interpreter.

"Ah, Matthews. Just the man I wanted to speak with. Do you mind interpreting for a bit between Sahib and me?"

"Of course not, sir."

"Come in to the office and sit down for a minute," Oliver offered, leading the way.

Mr. Matthews spoke to Sahib in his native Hindi, and the two men followed Oliver into the office. Mr. Matthews obediently sat in one of the leather chairs while Sahib remained standing.

"I was wondering," Oliver began. "If it's at all possible to train my chimpanzee?"

"Of course, sir, we've already done so in many ways."

"I don't mean in the usual ways." Oliver waved. "Something more extraordinary."

"I'm not sure what you mean, sir."

Sahib stood quietly, watching the two men converse.

"I had this idea... As a way of entertaining my guests," Oliver said. "Do you think you can train my chimpanzee to, say, smoke a cigar? Or sit down to dinner with guests?"

"Well, I'm not sure." Mr. Matthews seemed doubtful, but he turned to Sahib and spoke to him for a few minutes while Oliver waited for the answer. He might not be fluent in Hindi, but Oliver could tell by Sahib's gestures that there might be some possibilities.

"He says it can be done with steady training, sir," Matthews informed him. "Although he cautions us to remember that the animal comes from the wild and therefore can be fickle at times. It's quite possible he could wreak havoc in your house and upset your guests in the process."

Oliver smiled at the possibility. "I'm willing to take that chance." After a minute, he got up from his seat and fished through the pockets of his jacket. Standing over the manager, Oliver handed him several cigars. "Would you mind starting the monkey's training at once?" It was more of a command than a request.

"As you wish, sir. At once." Matthews spoke to Sahib, and the two got up to leave the stable office.

"Be sure and keep me posted on your progress," Oliver called after them.

"Certainly, sir," Matthews replied, ushering the Indian out of the stables.

Chapter Twenty-Four

Three weeks later
July 11, 1900
Newport, Rhode Island

Thank goodness the weather was perfect: blue skies and lots of sunshine. Checking her watch, Sara noted it was a few minutes before noon. A honking horn pulled her attention to the driveway as the Training Station Band drove onto the grounds, right on schedule. The lawn at *Swanhurst* was crowded and buzzing with the jubilant guests invited to Charlotte's wedding to Mr. Havemeyer.

Outdoor garden parties were all the fashion this season and Sara was delighted to see her plans come together with fabulous success. A large tent had been erected on the grass for the wedding breakfast and filled with round banquet tables. All the decorating had been carried on in the same fashion as if the wedding were held in a fancy ballroom – complete with tablecloths, china, crystal, and huge centerpieces of *American Beauty* roses.

A peek at the *Swanhurst* piazza filled Sara's heart with joy. The wedding party was seated at a long table, laughing and talking with guests. Charlotte looked lovely and happier than Sara had ever seen her. Dressed in a Princess-style gown, delicately trimmed with fabulous Renaissance lace, Charlotte made a beautiful bride. And it was clear her beauty wasn't lost on her new husband, the handsome and successful Mr. Havemeyer, who obviously adored her.

"Mother!" Natica called out as Sara approached from behind the house. Wearing her bridesmaid's gown, Natica looked lovely in her simple pink chiffon dress, thrilled to be part of the wedding party. "We have a slight problem!"

"We do?" Today's wedding ceremony had gone off smoothly, without the slightest hitch. Sara wasn't about to let anything ruin the day, and her nonchalant smile relayed as much to Natica.

"What's the problem?" Sara shouted to be heard over the band, which was starting up a jaunty tune for the benefit of the bride and groom.

"The wagon that's meant to carry the band in the wedding procession has lost a wheel!"

"Is that all?" Sara grinned, not very troubled. "Can it be repaired?"

Natica had to shout above the music while the happy crowd danced and laughed on the estate grounds. "I don't think so, but maybe we could substitute the fish wagon?"

"I'm sure that would be fine." Sara laughed. "As long as it doesn't smell of fish. Do whatever it takes to get the wagon ready."

Moving across the lawn, Sara noticed George sitting at a table with Rear Admiral Luce and Lord Pauncofote, smoking a well-earned cigar. George had proudly led the bride down the aisle in the *Swanhurst* parlor earlier that day, delivering Charlotte to the altar in the wedding procession. Now, he was in his element, hosting his associates after fulfilling the duties of Charlotte's deceased father.

Several servants dashed about keeping the trays and pitchers full of food and drink for the guests, while others working the small bar were busy filling glasses with champagne and spirits.

Walking across the yard to check on the children, Sara's diaphanous gown floated behind her. She spotted Anna keeping an eye on Mildred and Bayard, who were playing ball with the younger set on the side of the house. It appeared they were having as much fun as the grown-ups. Heading to the piazza, she went to check on the bridal party.

"I see you're all enjoying yourself," she whispered, hugging the bride.

"Oh, Aunt Sara! This is the happiest day of my life!" Charlotte beamed.

The joy written on her niece's face made Sara wish that the girl's mother and father were alive to see their daughter so happy. She'd done her best to give Charlotte a proper upbringing. Sara hoped Gus and Florence were watching from heaven with approval.

"The garden wedding was a fabulous idea." the bride told her aunt. "It's so *en vogue*. Everyone is completely enjoying themselves."

"We're all very happy for you, Charlotte," Sara said, with a quick glance at the sunny sky, "And happy it didn't decide to rain today."

"The wedding couldn't be more perfect."

"It's almost three o'clock," Sara noted with a glance at her watch. "If you're going to catch the steamer, you should think about getting ready to leave soon."

Leaning in, Henry overheard the advice. "Why don't you gather your things, sweetheart, and we'll get ready for the procession?"

"Good idea." Charlotte smiled. "But the party has been so lovely, I hate for it to end. The day went by much too quickly."

"Oh, Charlotte, the fun is just beginning." Sara flashed her a knowing smile and left the newlyweds to their guests.

Heading back across the yard to the driveway, Sara reached the front of *Swanhurst* where she found Natica joking with Lily Oelrichs and Perry Tiffany. They were laughing and fooling around as they helped Tommy Ruecock pull the fish wagon into line. Natica seemed to be having the time of her life. It did Sara's heart good to see her daughter surrounded by so many friends.

Lean and strong, she was becoming very good at tennis. The teenager spent many a summer morning over at the casino practicing her swing. Natica had quite a name for herself around Newport when it came to being the one to beat in the game. Turning, the girl noticed her mother's return and flashed a bright smile.

"They're ready!" Natica called, and Sara waved back in acknowledgement.

The coaches stood in line, finally organized for the procession down to the Newport wharf. The bridal carriage was first in line, followed by the fish wagon ready to transport the Training Station Band. Apparently, the musicians planned on entertaining the newlyweds for the entire trip down the hill to Commercial Wharf, and they piled into the wagon, playing all the while.

When the bride and groom emerged from the front door of *Swanhurst*, cheers and applause rose up from the crowd, gleefully pelting the newlyweds with rice and slippers. Charlotte and Henry ducked, laughing as they rushed through the throng and climbed into the open carriage – as even more rice continued to rain down on them.

John McCormack, on summer break from college, jumped to the top of the bridal coach next to the whip and hung a slipper filled with rice to the back of the vehicle just as it started pulling away. Another private coach joined the convoy carrying Mrs. Oelrichs and Mrs. Phelps, intent on riding in the procession. People headed for their own coaches and motorcars, all set on following the newlyweds down to the Newport wharf.

"Come on!" George appeared out of nowhere. "We don't want to miss out on the fun." He pointed to their open carriage, Owen at the reins, ready for the short trip into town.

"I'm coming!" Sara called, completely caught up in the excitement. Gathering her skirts, she jumped into the coach beside George.

The wedding party was a veritable parade of autos, carriages, and wagons as it moved through Newport. Loud music rose from the band, filling the city streets with gay tunes. Sara hummed along when she recognized '*She Was Happy Till She Met You*', smiling at George all the while. Next, the band played 'Mendelssohn's Wedding March' which clearly advertised to any casual observer what all the hullabaloo was about.

Soon the bridal coach approached the pier, where Sara could see a large crowd of spectators gathered on the wharf. "Look, George!" She pointed at the harbor. "It seems everyone in Newport has come out to watch Charlotte's wedding."

Chuckling, George noted the crowd. "I think your wedding celebration is a success, my dear. I'm sure this will be in every newspaper from here to New York by tomorrow morning."

"Wonderful!" Sara laughed happily. "I want to read all about the good news!"

Owen parked the carriage near the ferry, and Sara and George climbed down, pushing their way through the crowd toward the newlyweds. When Charlotte and Henry emerged from their ride, a fresh shower of rice rained down heavily on the couple. The torrent was so great the bride sought shelter under a freight shed. Sara and George moved toward the gangplank to wish the couple a final goodbye.

"Oh, Aunt Sara!" Charlotte beamed with joy. "You've been like a mother to me. Taking care of me when I was a child, nursing me through illness, teaching me how to act like a lady." She wiped a tear from her eye. "How will I ever, ever thank you?"

"Sweet Charlotte..." Sara brushed away her own tears. "Seeing you so happy is all the thanks I'll ever need."

"And you too, Uncle George." Charlotte hugged him. "Thank you so much for stepping into my father's shoes over the years – and for escorting me down the aisle today. This has been the most wonderful wedding celebration ever."

A loud horn sounded from the boat as sailors pulled up ropes.

"We've got to go, Char," Henry urged.

The bride threw her arms around Sara for a final hug, then, taking Henry's hand, she followed him onto the vessel.

The band kicked into a loud rendition of '*I Don't Want No Cheap Man*' as the newlyweds boarded, cheered on by the crowd. Then, as the Fall River Line steamer moved from the wharf, the strains of 'Lohengrin's Wedding March' once again played sweetly over the Newport harbor.

Sara and George stood hand-in-hand, watching along with the crowd as the boat grew smaller and smaller over the ocean.

"Go with God," Sara whispered.

PART TWO

Natica

Natica Caroline Belmont Rives

Chapter Twenty-Five

Two weeks later
July 27, 1900
Newport, Rhode Island

With so many exciting things happening, Natica almost forgot to get her little sister a gift. *"Mildred's birthday is fast approaching, and I want to give her something nice,"* she thought. *"And I know Mother is planning a birthday dinner to mark the occasion."*

Leaving a note on the dining room table, Natica made a quick decision to go into town and do a little shopping. Mindful she'd get a lecture about going out alone, she brushed aside the thought, impatient for an outing.

Walking to the foyer, she pinned her straw hat in place, arranging it on her head with a stylish tilt. Checking her appearance in the large gilt mirror, Natica fussed with a few brunette tendrils, then pinched her cheeks for color. Happy with her efforts, she smiled and grabbed a lace parasol from the umbrella stand near the door.

Moving at a leisurely pace, she strolled down Webster Street then turned onto Thames, headed for the shopping district. A few blocks further, Natica entered the *'Daniel E. Sullivan Shop'* in the Brick Market, intent on finding something nice for Mildred.

The store was filled with everything from furniture and lamps, to clothing and toys. Natica found her way through the shelves, pausing to admire a lovely rabbit-hair muff. It had a matching hat, but Natica wasn't sure she liked the style. *"I think a hat and muff would make a better Christmas gift."* So, she decided against it. Moving on to the toy shelf, she found beautiful porcelain dolls and checker games. A miniature tea set caught her eye, and Natica lifted it off the shelf for closer inspection. With its tiny china pieces all neatly packed in a miniature picnic hamper, Natica made up her mind it was the perfect birthday gift for Mildred and went to find a clerk.

Across the aisle, she spotted a mannequin wearing a beautiful hunter-green day-coat. Distracted, she went to give it a closer look.

"My début is set for November," Natica mused, fingering the velvet coat. "And I can barely wait." She did her best to fight off her impatience.

She recalled her mother voicing misgivings about the date, suggesting they might wait another year. *"I'll be an old maid if she keeps making me wait,"* Natica agonized silently. She'd already been to so many dances and parties, it wasn't as if she was an unknown among society. Quite the opposite.

"Can I help you find something, miss?" A perky brunette clerk walked up behind Natica. Wearing a starched white blouse and black skirt, she smiled cordially.

"I'd like to purchase this," Natica replied and held up the tiny tea set.

"Very nice," the middle-aged woman politely answered. "If you'll follow me over to the cash register." The clerk led Natica around the shelves and took her place behind a glass display counter filled with alarm clocks and egg timers. She turned to Natica, reaching for the tea set.

"Is this a gift?" she asked. "Would you like me to remove the sales tag?"

"Yes, please." Natica smiled. "That would be nice."

She watched the woman take off the price tag and wrap the present in tissue paper. Placing the tea set in a box, the cashier wrapped a pink-satin ribbon around it, tied it off in a lovely bow, then placed the box in a paper shopping bag. The clerk perched a pair of half-glasses on her nose, then started punching buttons on the cash register. Bells chimed from the machine as she rang up the sale.

Casually, Natica let her eyes meander over the shop's wares. That's when she spotted him – again!

Mr. 'Absent Absinthe' Oliver Belmont.

Belmont was talking to a clerk with his back turned to Natica. He hadn't noticed her, but she was certain it was him. His short height, his wavy brown hair, and fine tailored suit – it was him all right. Natica crouched a bit and turned back toward the clerk while noting that Mr. Belmont was at the jewelry counter.

"That will be ninety-eight cents," the clerk announced, shaking Natica from her thoughts.

Fumbling for her wallet, Natica realized her hands were trembling. What was it about Mr. Belmont that caused this unnerving effect on her? She handed the cashier a dollar and took her two pennies change. Placing the coins in her purse, she lifted her bag from the counter and glanced around for an escape route.

"I don't want to talk to Mr. Belmont," she decided. In fact, she absolutely did not want him to see her. And if her mother found out about this, in light of the fact that she was unchaperoned, she would really be in trouble.

Spotting a door at the back of the store, Natica made her way toward it – but along the way, something made her stop.

Why was she running away like a scared bunny?

"Perhaps it's time I do the opposite," she whispered, summoning her courage. She – Natica Caroline Rives – was going to march over to Mr. Belmont right this minute and demand an explanation. Or perhaps, she should start by revealing her suspicions to him – that she believed he was her father.

Her *father,* for heaven's sake!

Then, once that was settled, she could ask him what had happened to cause such a terrible rift – a riff that had severed their father-daughter relationship to the point of complete eradication.

Spinning on her heel, Natica was determined to confront him. Nearing the jewelry counter, the clerk stood alone, busying himself with merchandise in the glass showcase.

"Can I help you, miss?" the salesman asked, looking up through glasses that made his eyes appear large.

"No..." she stammered, glancing left, then right. "No, thank you."

Mr. Belmont was gone. Searching the store, Natica saw he was nowhere to be found.

"I'm not sure if I'm happy or disappointed," she whispered, returning outside to Thames Street.

"Well... If not today, then one day soon!" Natica resolved. It's long past time she had the truth. And if it comes down to it, she'd visit him at Belcourt and see to it herself!

With new confidence, she headed back to *Swanhurst* just as the chimes at Trinity Church rang out the noon hour.

Ten days later
August 6, 1900
New York State

The 12:15 train had left the station as scheduled and soon was traveling over the New York countryside headed for Tarrytown. Natica tried to distract herself with the scenery while struggling with her confusion and grief. How could this have happened to her stepbrother? It just wasn't fair!

She glanced across the luxurious train car reserved especially for the family, disheartened by the grim faces: Aunt Jane, Charlotte, and Henry, her mother, stepfather and siblings, all sat quietly, dressed in mourning black. Mrs. Hare was talking to her brother, Bishop Hare, with red, tear-stained eyes. Bishop Hare had traveled in from Dakota, just like he'd done to perform Junior's wedding. No one could have ever guessed he would be back only three short months later to bury the young bride.

"We were summoned to London, where they were on holiday," Mrs. Hare whimpered. "And when we got there, Betty was already so near death."

"Typhoid fever can act quickly," Bishop Hare said quietly, holding her hand. "I'm sure the doctors did everything in their power to save her."

"I just can't believe she's gone..." Mrs. Hare released a soul-wrenching sob while dabbing at her eyes with a crumpled handkerchief.

Grief was thick, the burden of sadness oppressive, weighing heavy in the chugging train car. Her mother whispered something to George, who sat next to Junior, holding vigil over his bereaving son. Her stepbrother's face was blank, his eyes hollow, staring off into space with no sign of emotion.

What a horrible turn of events! *"I just want to scream at how unfair life can be,"* Natica brooded. One minute she was watching Mildred scatter rose petals down the wedding aisle, and the next, she was mourning her new sister-in-law at her funeral – in the same church! How could this be?

If a funeral could be beautiful, Natica decided that Betty's had been so. A white cloth embroidered with a purple and silver edge had adorned her coffin. Although there weren't many floral arrangements in the church, her casket had been piled with wreaths made of white and pink roses. Sadly, Natica remembered Betty's fondness for flowers. The full choir singing '*I heard a Voice from Heaven*' and other hymns had been almost too grim for Natica to endure, but for her stepbrother's sake, she found the strength to get through the service.

"They were just finishing their bridal tour." Mrs. Hare wept softly as she spoke. "And were getting ready to return to the states when Betty got ill. They were unable to reduce her fever..." The woman broke down in a fresh round of tears.

"There, there Mary," Bishop Hare worked to comfort his distraught sister.

Natica saw the bishop glance over at his brother-in-law, his expression etched with sympathy for the man. Mr. Hare seemed lost in thought, his face hidden under the brim of his hat while he stared down at his polished shoes.

"He's just walked his daughter down the aisle," Natica thought. *"And now he's faced with the horrible task of laying her to rest."*

There was little anyone could do to console the grieving hearts on this train.

"The family didn't want her buried in Wappinger's Falls, where most of the Rives are interred in the family plot." Mary spoke again, looking to him for understanding. "And the Hare family is interned in Philadelphia, which is too far for me to visit, as well."

"I think the Sleepy Hollow cemetery was a good decision." Bishop Hare assured her. "Why don't you try to nap a bit before we get to Tarrytown."

Natica watched as Betty's mother shook her head 'no', wiping her eyes yet again. "I'll only have to wake to this nightmare," she whispered.

The train rumbled down the tracks to its destination, rocking the passengers in a gentle sway. A desperate ache filled her heart as Natica took in the sad faces gathered for the somber journey. The thought of her sister-in-law lying in her beautiful coffin at the back of the train was an unspeakable reality she was forced to come to terms with, like everyone else on the train.

To think a bride could die so soon after her wedding, Natica decided, was a crime and punishment that no one should ever have to face.

No one.

Not ever.

⚜

Four days later
August 10, 1900
Newport, Rhode Island

The mood around the *Swanhurst* parlor was tense, despite the bright sunlight filtering into the room.

"What do you mean I can't make my début in November?" Natica cried, tears of frustration forming in her eyes. "You promised me I could finally come out!"

"I'm sure you can understand how Betty's death has changed things." Sara reasoned with her. "It's just not proper for you to make your début while the family is in mourning."

"Betty's death has been horrible," Natica conceded. "But I had my heart set on having my debut after my birthday."

"I'd prefer if you waited until next spring, or at least until after Christmas in New York. I promise I'll make it up to you with a wonderful party."

Discouraged, Natica got up from her chair and went to the parlor window. Silently, she stared out over the *Swanhurst* grounds. Working hard to remain calm, she tried a different tack. "There must be a solution that'll work for both of us, Mother. Maybe we could have a small gathering – nothing fancy. That way, I could at least begin receiving invitations to a few balls."

"Natica, you're only now coming up on your seventeenth birthday." Sara reminded her. "Another year isn't going to make that much difference." She looked at her strong-willed and often-stubborn daughter.

"It makes a difference to me!" Natica moaned, throwing her hands in the air. "Most of my friends have already débuted! I'm being left out of so much fun!"

Their discussion was interrupted by the sound of the front door closing. George came in, taking off his hat, and joined them in the sitting room.

"How did it go?" Sara asked him. Grateful for the timing of his arrival, she hoped for some support in dealing with Natica's contention.

He held up an envelope and set it on the coffee table. "I was able to get the tickets for Alaska," George told her while removing his jacket. "We'll cross the country by train. I've scheduled the trip for several months, so we can stop and sight-see along the way."

"We're going on holiday!" Natica asked, incredulous. "Now?" She walked back from the window. "Mother, please tell me this is a joke."

"Yes, Natica." Sara kept her voice low. "We thought it would be best to take Junior on a trip to help him get over Betty's death. You and the children will be coming as well. It'll help everyone get over this tragedy."

"But I don't want to go on holiday! Not *now*. August is the high point of the summer season."

"Don't you think it'll shine poorly on you if you're out at parties so soon after Betty's death?" George asked, quickly assessing the scene in the room.

"Perhaps." Natica shrugged. "But I think enjoying the season will help me adjust to her death much easier than some boring two-month train ride across the United States."

"Regardless of your opinion, we are going," Sara ordered. "So, you'd better start packing your things for an extended trip."

"Please, don't make me go!" Natica begged, frustration getting the better of her emotions. Bursting into tears, she ran from the parlor and headed upstairs to her chambers. George and Sara looked at each other as they heard her door slam hard.

"She'll get used to the idea." George sighed as he sat down on the sofa. "At least, I hope so. Natica could make for a very disagreeable traveling companion if her foul mood persists."

"I know." Sara frowned, pressing a hand absently to her temple. "But I'm in a tough position. I really can't blame her for being disappointed, but the funeral has changed everything. The family is in mourning, and we must observe the proper protocol in respect to Betty's memory."

"I completely agree. We're all having a rough time coming to grips with her death."

Swiveling in his chair, George noticed Jane walk in from the dining room. Sara followed his gaze and smiled weakly at her sister joining them in the parlor.

"I was in the breakfast room and couldn't help but overhear," Jane admitted. Dressed in black, Jane wore a simple linen day-dress.

"She doesn't want to go to Alaska," Sara said, releasing a heavy sigh. "I understand her summer plans are spoiled but aren't everyone's?"

"It is terrible, but Natica's young and anxious to join in with her crowd. I remember how you were at her age." Jane pointed out, her eyes twinkling at the memory.

"It can't be helped." Sara sighed, taking a seat on the sofa beside George.

The three grew quiet, each contemplating the situation. The sound of birds singing in the trees outside trilled into the parlor from the yard, the sweet songs offering a pleasant distraction from the conflict in the room.

"I have an idea," Jane spoke up. "Why don't you let Natica stay here with me for the summer? The rest of you go ahead on your holiday. I'll look after her while you're gone."

George was the first to speak. "I like the idea." He turned to his wife, nodding his agreement.

"I'm not sure I do," Sara countered. "If I know Natica, she's going to want to attend as many parties and picnics and fox-hunts as she possibly can. She'll need a constant chaperone."

"I'll go with her. I'm not that old that I don't still have friends among the set," Jane admonished with a lift of her chin. "And the girl has already been through so much, enduring the hardship of the funeral. It's not healthy for her to dwell on such a sad state of affairs when she's got so many happy things on the horizon. Bridget can go along with you, and Anna can stay behind to help look after Natica. You should let her stay. I promise I'll keep a close eye on her."

"I like the plan," George repeated, leaning onto the sofa back. "Think about it, Sara. We'll get Junior and the kids out of town for a break, and Natica can focus on being a social butterfly. I think it's a marvelous idea." He gave his sister-in-law a grateful smile.

"I'm still not sure." Sara shook her head. "Natica can be willful and hard to handle sometimes."

"And you were never willful at her age?" Jane needled with a tinge of sarcasm, making her point. "Let her stay with me here at *Swanhurst*. We'll be fine."

"Do you really want to be traveling with an unhappy teenager?" George asked his wife. "You should really think this through. If you ask me, Jane's come up with the perfect solution."

Sara released a long sigh. "Okay, okay. You've talked me into it."

A triumphant grin broke across Jane's face. Her niece was going to be delighted to discover she'd persuaded her mother into letting her stay on in Newport.

"If she gives you one bit of trouble..." Sara began.

Jane interrupted, holding up a hand to stop her. "She'll be no trouble at all, Sara."

"Are you certain you want to saddle yourself with such a responsibility?"

"It'll be fine. Anna will help out."

"If you're sure..."

"I'm quite sure. Should I tell her, or do you want to do it?"

Sara grinned at Jane, obviously pleased with herself. "Go ahead and tell her."

"Thank you," Jane said, heading for Natica's chambers. "It'll be my pleasure."

"Thank goodness that's settled," George said, returning his attention to the travel documents. Spreading the papers on the coffee table, he showed them to Sara to further discuss the specifics of their travel plans.

Chapter Twenty-Six

Two weeks later
August 27, 1900
Middletown, Rhode Island

"Natica!" Cathleen waved, the lace sleeve of her yellow gown fluttering in the breeze. "Over here!"

The picnic at Oakland Farm was in full swing when she and Aunt Jane had arrived in Middletown. Filled with happy faces, all ages of guests enjoyed the country setting, and the weather couldn't have been more perfect for a picnic.

Strolling beside Natica, Aunt Jane wore a casual, black cotton gown befitting her age. Natica didn't mind having her older aunt chaperoning her during the summer. She thought her aunt very sweet – and there was no question she'd done her a huge favor by talking her parents into letting her stay on in Newport for the summer. Just that fact alone had endeared her to her Aunt Jane.

"Go on, dear." Jane shooed her from under her summer hat. "I'm going to be with the other ladies." She pointed to a set of picnic tables under the shade of towering oak trees across the yard.

"Thanks, Aunt Jane." Natica flashed a wide smile and took off across the grass to join her friends.

A soft wind blew from the ocean under a sky filled with white, fluffy clouds that occasionally hid the sun. The breeze had little effect on the August heat, a bit unbearable as of late due to the humidity.

Sauntering across the lawn, Natica wore a lovely violet cotton-gauze dress that fluttered in the afternoon air, accenting her feminine figure. She smoothed a wayward curl up into her bun, tucking it under her straw hat. Her mother had strictly informed her that she was no longer permitted to wear her hair down her back like she had as a little girl.

"A proper lady must wear her hair in a more modest style," her mother had said, teaching her how to fix the coiffure. But Natica wasn't very good at the task, so Anna usually did it for her. Anna had a real talent when it came to styling hair.

"Cynthia was just asking about you," Cathleen said as Natica reached their picnic table.

"We weren't sure if you were coming to the party," Cynthia added, looking lovely in a mint-green lace dress. A matching half-bonnet covered her thick, blond curls. "I heard your family went on holiday, and we thought you'd gone with them."

"Lucky for me, I got to stay in Newport," Natica announced with a happy chirp. "My parents wanted me to go to Alaska! Can you believe it?"

"They might as well have taken you to Siberia," Laura said, wide-eyed. Standing at only four-and-a-half feet tall, she gave the appearance of someone much younger than her eighteen years, which bothered her to no end. Laura was the daughter of Elisha Dyer, who'd married a distant cousin of the Swan family.

"I know!" Natica frowned. "My Aunt Jane offered to stay with me. I could just kiss her for saving me from the terrible fate of summer in no-man's-land."

The three young ladies chatted around the gingham-covered picnic table. Plates loaded with shortbread and peanut butter cookies, as well as watermelon and fresh picked blackberries, were offered in platters and bowls. An icy pitcher of lemonade looked too delicious to refuse in the afternoon heat. Natica accepted a glass from the servant tending the tables and sipped the sweetly-tart drink. Shimmying onto the bench, she took her place next to her friends.

Startled, Natica glanced up to see Reggie Vanderbilt rush over, grab a cookie off the table and shove it in his mouth. Wearing a polo outfit, his light-brown hair was slicked back and parted in the middle.

"Hello, ladies!" Arthur and his brother William came jogging up behind Reggie, also dressed for polo.

Cathleen shot the gentlemen an impish look. "Hello, Reggie. What are you gentlemen up to?" she asked in a sugary voice.

"We just signed up for the polo match," Arthur said, his eyes shining with fun. His heart-shaped face was boyish and handsome, making him popular with the débutantes. "I'm going to beat the pants off of Will and Reggie, both."

"Good luck trying," Reggie taunted with a challenging grin. "I've beaten you in every match this summer."

"Ah, but not by much," Arthur countered with an easy chuckle.

"You cheated," Will joked good-naturedly. Resembling his brother, Will was equally as handsome, although a few inches taller than Arthur, with a more muscular physique.

"Listen to this abuse, ladies." Reggie waved at his friends. "Do you hear what I have to put up with? Spreading lies about my sportsmanship like that. They're just sore losers."

He was certainly suave, Natica thought, tossing him a coquettish glance. Reggie smiled back at her, then at Cathleen, and grabbed another cookie.

"Are you ladies going to come over to the polo field and watch the match?" Reggie asked.

"We wouldn't miss it for the world," Cathleen cooed, vying for his attention. There was no doubt the girls were enjoying a chance to flirt with three of the wealthiest, most eligible bachelors in town.

"Are you going to eat every single cookie?" Cynthia harassed Reggie playfully. "Leave a few for the rest of us."

"I thought ladies didn't eat sweets," Arthur countered. "Something about preserving your waistline."

"Don't you worry about our waistlines," Natica advised. "We have that well under control."

"So I've noticed." Will gave her a devilish look, and Natica blushed in spite of herself.

"Let's go." Arthur slapped Reggie playfully. "We'd better head over to the stables and make sure our horses are ready for the games."

"Okay." Reggie nodded. "Alfred should be over there already. He's entering the match, too."

Alfred was Reggie's older brother, and the two seemed inseparable. *Oakland Farm* had been sold to their father, Cornelius, by Oliver Belmont several years ago, and the young men often visited to enjoy the riding ring and open land.

"Did you know Mr. Belmont brought in some of his best horses for the match?" Arthur asked. "And he said we could ride any horse we want. First come, first pick." He laughed and started off toward the stable. "Come on... I don't want Alfred grabbing the best animal."

Natica came to attention at the mention of Mr. Belmont. Was it Oliver Belmont they were referring to?

"Wait up!" Reggie grabbed a few more cookies and ran after him, with William in hot pursuit.

"Ladies..." Will waved goodbye as the two left the table chasing after Arthur.

"My, my..." Cathleen chuckled. "I think it is going to be a wonderful picnic, after all."

"I couldn't agree more," Natica said, watching the gentlemen disappear in the direction of the barn.

***

Two days later
August 29, 1900
New York, New York

The plump maid took the coat and, smiling warmly, led Natica into the parlor. The servant's uniform was completed with a tiny maid's cap, perched properly on the crown of her head. "Mrs. Havemeyer will be right down," she said in a formal tone. "Please make yourself comfortable."

"Thank you," Natica answered. Sitting on the velvet divan, she removed her lace gloves and placed them in her handbag.

"I hope my arrival before noon isn't too early to call," she worried silently. *"But we are family."* Natica had made the decision to talk with Charlotte, and she simply could not wait until two o'clock for proper visiting hours. While she waited, Natica admired the gorgeous home Charlotte and Henry had built on Fifth Avenue. Lovely furnishings, valuable paintings, and objects d'art filled the house in keeping with fashionable society.

"Natica!" Charlotte wobbled into the room wearing a fancy white muslin gown. Her creamy complexion glowed under golden locks, giving her the appearance of an angel. "What a nice surprise!" She gave her cousin a warm hug. "Miss Watson, will you get us some coffee?" she instructed the maid, aware that her cousin preferred it over tea.

"Yes, ma'am," the maid replied, leaving the room on a curtsey.

"I'm so sorry I haven't visited more often," Charlotte apologized. "But as you can see, I am well along in my confinement." The bump on her belly was clearly evident under her cousin's dress.

"You look wonderful, Charlotte," Natica complimented. "And I'm excited to meet my new little cousin when he or she arrives."

"Thank you." Charlotte beamed as the maid returned with the coffee service.

Pouring the hot brew, the servant moved to open the windows wider to allow a breeze, then disappeared into the depths of the large house.

"How are you feeling?"

"I'm doing fine," Charlotte assured her. "But I feel as big as a barn. It gets challenging to move around at this stage of pregnancy."

"I'm certain it's best if you lead a quiet life for the time being," Natica replied, brushing a stray hair from her eye.

Thinking back to Charlotte's mother's death when they were both young girls, Natica knew her cousin had grown up without her mother's loving guidance. Although her own mother had done her best to be a maternal substitute for Charlotte, Natica surmised her cousin was filled with an unspoken need to nurture her own children. A need that was greater than one felt by most women.

Pausing, Natica searched her mind for a way to broach the conversation.

"Are you enjoying your summer?" Charlotte asked, glancing over her cup. "I'm sure the sadness of Betty's loss has delayed plans for your début."

"Yes, it has." Natica shrugged. "Mother postponed the ball. But I've been attending events without the formal introduction of a coming-out party. It's not as though I'm unknown among the set."

"True. I heard Aunt Sara wanted you to go to Alaska with the family."

"Yes," Natica said. "Thank goodness for Aunt Jane. I'll be indebted to her forever for saving my summer. And as far as the formality of a coming-out ball, I'm fine skipping the whole affair. I've been receiving invitations as if I were properly introduced."

"How lovely for you." Charlotte smiled. "Has anyone caught your fancy?"

"I've met several interesting gentlemen, I'm just not sure about a future with them. The last thing I want to do is commit myself to a life of unhappiness by marrying the wrong man or worse yet, end up divorced." She whisked her eyes across the room at her cousin and reached for her coffee. "There seems to be a plague of divorce these days."

Catching her glance, Charlotte intuited a deeper reason for the visit. It wasn't unusual for Natica to stop by from time to time, but this morning there was an aura of seriousness about her.

"It's true, divorce is becoming more common among the set. But it's no reason to think you'll end up unhappy. Call me old-fashioned, but I still believe marriage is a wonderful thing. Henry and I are very happy, and the upcoming birth only adds to our joy."

"I'm sure this is a wonderful time for you." Natica smiled, working to gather her courage to tread into forbidden waters. "I suppose there's another reason for my visit." She floundered, searching for the right words. "I've always been able to talk with you, Charlotte, and I thought you might be able to answer a few questions for me."

"Questions about what?"

"Well…" she hesitated, growing insecure. "About *me*."

"You? I don't understand."

"I was on my way to the library to search through old issues of the *New York Times*, but that seemed like such skullduggery." Natica laughed nervously, summoning her nerve to continue.

"Go through the *Times* in search of what?" Charlotte asked, puzzled where the conversation was heading.

Taking a deep breath, Natica answered, "About my father."

The room fell silent, an awkward tremor in the air. Charlotte slowly put her coffee cup on the table. "I see." She tilted her head, meeting Natica's eye. "You want to know about your father?"

"Mother won't say a word about him," Natica blurted, her words running together. "She keeps telling me George is my father. But I know he's not my *real* father, but my stepfather. And quite honestly, Charlotte, I'm sure I've put the pieces together. But I need someone to confirm my suspicions once and for all and tell me the truth. I'm sure you can understand how important it is for me to know what really happened."

"You place me in an uncomfortable position, Natica. Perhaps you should have this conversation with your mother. I have no desire to damage my relationship with Aunt Sara over something that happened a long time ago."

"You, of all people, should know that's impossible. Mother refuses to broach the topic, vehemently changing the subject whenever I ask about it."

"I suppose that's true…" Charlotte frowned. "So, tell me, what are these pieces you think you've put together."

Natica leaned toward her cousin as if sharing a dark secret. "Every time I turn around, that man Oliver Belmont is watching me. At the horse show, at the casino, in the shops – any time I'm out in public. Yet, he always keeps his distance. And he's never in attendance at any of the same balls or parties as our family. As a child, I was aware of the whispers around me and Grandma's constant reference to 'Absent Absinthe Oliver'." She glanced at her cousin, trepidation giving her pause. "I've come to believe that Oliver Belmont is my father."

The clock ticked loudly on the mantle, echoing over the mute room. Charlotte released a deep sigh and leaned back on the divan.

"Your mother is going to kill me for this," Charlotte said bleakly. "But I can see you're not going to be happy until you find the answers you're looking for." She paused, then gave Natica a slight nod. "You're right in your conjecture. Oliver is your father."

Natica's breath caught in her throat. She'd felt certain she'd deduced the truth, but having Charlotte confirm her theory was unnerving.

"And my mother and he are divorced?"

Charlotte nodded 'yes' then fell quiet, not sure how much she should tell her cousin.

"What happened?" Natica implored her. "Why did they get divorced?" Sensing Char's hesitation, she urged her on. "I'm sure this was all in the newspaper. Either you tell me, or I'll find out for myself."

"Calm down." Charlotte reached over and touched her hand warmly. "I just don't want to upset you."

"As if not knowing who my real father is, is not upsetting enough?" Natica cried. "Please, Charlotte, tell me what happened."

Begrudgingly, Charlotte began the tale of her aunt's protracted engagement to Mr. Belmont, sharing how after more than a year, the couple was finally permitted to wed. Natica listened closely as her cousin relayed the information of the honeymoon, shared by her grandmother and two aunts who'd followed Natica's mother and Oliver to Paris, joining them in the honeymoon suite. She continued the lurid story of physical abuse and French dancers as gently as she could, trying to focus on the facts and not the gossip. After all, in spite of his inexcusable conduct, Oliver was still the girl's father.

"So, my father disowned me after the separation. And as a result, our family wouldn't allow him to see me," Natica concluded. Struggling with her emotions, the truth smacked her senses like a steel mallet. Natica was both overwhelmed and empowered to realize she had Belmont blood pumping through her veins. Maybe Oliver wanted to know her. Maybe he regretted the separation, and that was why he watched her.

"Yes. They thought he was a bad influence on you with his wild ways." Charlotte nodded. Concerned the shock of the truth might be harder to take than Natica let on, she asked, "Are you okay?"

"Yes," Natica assured her cousin with a brave smile. "I'm okay. It's just as I thought, for the most part." Natica reached for her pocketbook to take her leave. She wanted to run away and find a place to hide while she came to terms with the reality of her birth.

Charlotte rose from the sofa with Natica. "Are you quite sure you're okay?"

In reply, Natica stepped over and gave her cousin a warm embrace. "I promise, I'm fine." She paused. "Thank you, Charlotte, for finally telling me the truth. I know it took courage. And I won't breathe a word of our conversation to anyone."

"I hope I've done the right thing."

"I would have discovered the truth somehow. I'd much prefer it was from you."

Leaving Charlotte's home, Natica wasn't sure what she was going to do now that she knew the facts. Maybe nothing, but there was satisfaction in finally having the whole story.

Watching her cousin's departure through the window, Charlotte grew unsettled. "I hope I've done the right thing," she murmured again.

Chapter Twenty-Seven

Two weeks later
September 12, 1900
Newport, Rhode Island

"Natica..." Jane called up the steps. "It's time to go."

"Coming..."

A minute later, her niece appeared at the top of the stairs looking more beautiful than any débutante had a right to. Jane paused at the sight, reminding herself she was in charge of the girl until her parents got back from their holiday. She knew that might prove to be a challenge tonight at Mrs. Astor's ball, with Natica looking so attractive.

"I'll be right down," Natica called.

Jane returned to the sitting room, where she waited for her niece. A few moments later, Natica whooshed into the room in a pale-yellow ball gown covered with flounces of matching lace and tulle. Her hair was pinned up in an intricate weave of curls, and her mother's borrowed diamond earrings sparkled in perfect accent, as did the matching necklace.

"You look like a princess!" Anna sighed, following her into the room. "Absolutely gorgeous!"

"I agree," Jane said. "You certainly do justice to Mr. Worth's gowns."

"I'm so excited! I feel like a real lady tonight," Natica said, spinning around in her dress. Wisps of sheer fabric fanned out around her body like the soft petals of a rose.

Troubled after her talk with Charlotte regarding her birth father, Natica had decided to do nothing about it for the time being. Pushing it to the far corners of her mind, she instead focused on her social schedule.

Turning to her maid, she asked, "Do you have my gloves and fan?"

"Here they are." Anna handed her the accessories. "More flowers have arrived, and these came for you as well." The maid handed her several cards. "You can add them to the others. I think the gentlemen are beginning to notice you, miss."

Natica took the calling cards, hastily checking the sender. "This one is from Reginald Vanderbilt," she told them. "He's requested a place on my dance card." A dreamy feeling wrapped around Natica's heart at the thought of Reggie.

"And the other is from William Burden," she announced. Natica wasn't sure what she thought about him, although he *was* handsome and came from a prominent family.

"And so, the night begins!" Jane said with a chuckle. "Come on, let's get going. It's rude to be late."

"I'm ready if you are," Natica said, following her aunt to the front door.

"Have a wonderful time," Anna called after them. The maid stood on the porch, watching as they disappeared into the coach. She just knew her mistress would cause a stir at the party tonight.

"She's so beautiful." Anna sighed, closing the door behind herself.

Two weeks later
September 29, 1900
Newport, Rhode Island

Summer slid into autumn with simple ease. Evidence of the passing days was apparent by the cooler temperatures amidst a changing kaleidoscope of vibrant New England leaves. Society took note, and one by one, Newport visitors returned to their life in America's growing metropolises until only the residents of the city-by-the-sea remained in town.

The footman hauled the trunks into the foyer of *Swanhurst.*

"Would you mind carrying those up to our rooms?" Sara called politely, walking into the house.

"Yes, ma'am," the footman replied, heaving the trunks upstairs.

She removed her fancy hat and hooked her cloak on the coat rack near the entrance. A chilly autumn wind blew into the house through the opened door, reminding her that winter was fast approaching.

Meeting Sara in the foyer, Jane and Natica greeted her with a hug each.

"Alaska is far more beautiful than you would ever guess," she announced. "It was lush and green with snow-capped mountains that are quite a sight in the middle of the summer."

"I'm glad you had a nice holiday." Jane smiled. "You're home just in time for tea."

"How is Junior?" Natica asked, her brown eyes filled with concern for her stepbrother. "Did the trip seem to help him at all?"

"I don't know." Sara shook her head sadly, taking a seat on the sofa. "I can only hope so." She accepted the cup offered her by Jane, steam rising over the brim. "We did what we could to take his mind off of Betty's death, but it's going to take some time."

"Where's George?" Jane asked. "Did he stay on in New York?"

"Yes. He had a meeting at Columbia University, but I suspect he really wanted to stay close to Junior."

"Probably a good idea," Jane replied, setting her tea on the table to cool.

"So..." Sara assessed Natica. "Tell me about your summer. Did you have a good time?"

"Oh yes, Mother." Natica perked up at the question. "I went to picnics and clam bakes and dances..." her voice trailed off with a sigh. "It was fabulous."

"You didn't wear your aunt out, I hope." She glanced at Jane and grinned.

"Not at all," Jane assured her. "I had a wonderful time myself. And your daughter is quite the belle of the ball. I had to keep a close eye on her with all the gentlemen competing for her attention."

"You don't say?" Sara smiled. "You remembered your manners, of course."

"Of course. I was a perfect lady. You would have been proud of me."

Although they'd only been in Alaska for a few months, Natica looked older to Sara. Her new hairstyle lent her daughter a mature appearance, as did her fashionable Parisian day-gown.

"Are there any gentlemen I should know about?" Sara inquired, peaking a brow. "Anyone in particular who caught your fancy?"

A silly grin covered Natica's face, and she blushed. "No. No one special."

Sara felt her maternal instincts take over. "Why do I find that hard to believe?" She looked at Jane, who just shrugged. "Hmmm..." Sara narrowed her eyes dubiously. "You two aren't telling me something."

"Well, I did receive flowers and calling cards for dances."

"From whom?" Sara scrutinized Natica for answers. "You haven't made your début yet. It's a little soon for you to be filling your dance card."

Ignoring the reprimand, Natica answered. "From Mr. Vanderbilt and Mr. Burden, to name a couple."

"Which Mr. Vanderbilt?" Sara knew the large family had many young cousins and sons entering society.

"Reggie," Natica answered simply. "And Will sent some too – William Burden. He has a brother, Arthur, you know." She tried to act nonchalant, but that was hard to do under her mother's penetrating gaze.

"I see," Sara answered. "Wasn't Reggie courting your friend Cathleen Neilson?"

"I don't know if they're actually courting," Natica said lightly. "But Cathleen does seem to like him, if the way she flirts with him is any indication."

Sara listened to her daughter, deducing much more from the conversation by the girl's undercurrent of secrecy. It was obvious to Sara that both William and Reggie had caught Natica's eye. She decided not to prod her any more than she already had and sipped her tea, letting the conversation grow quiet.

"By the way..." Sara changed the subject. "Now that the summer season is over, I'm thinking of taking you to Paris for a month before the holidays hit. I'm sure you'll like that more than Alaska." she chuckled playfully. "I think we should do some serious shopping for your début next season."

"Oh, Mother!" Natica grinned, clearly delighted. "That would be so wonderful. The dresses we got at Mr. Worth's last year were simply perfect. One just cannot find such marvelous outfits here in the States."

"So true." Sara chuckled, amused by her ebullience. She knew the Rives family did not have the countless millions of other families in town, but they were still quite rich, rich enough to outfit her daughter in fabulous garments, as fine as any seen among the set.

"Why don't you come along, Jane?" Sara invited. "We'll return long before Thanksgiving, in plenty of time for the New York season."

"Hmmm..." Jane tapped her lip with a finger, considering the offer. "I think I might pass this time. You two run along to Paris."

"I don't want to stay too long," Natica hedged. "I've got a social calendar to keep."

"How about two weeks?" Sara asked. "Plus a week by steamer each way, we'll only be gone a month. We can attend a Paris masquerade ball or a party with the 'set' to keep your social calendar up-to-date." Sara met her daughter's eyes. "How does that sound?"

"That sounds perfect," Natica answered. "Absolutely perfect."

"Then it's settled," Sara agreed, finishing her tea.

Five days later
October 4, 1900
New York, New York

Flicking her wrist, Natica turned the page of *Harper's Bazaar* while checking the time on the large wall clock. The quiet library loomed high above her head in a splendor of magnificent architecture. Tall arched windows filtered in the late morning sun, dusting rows and rows of books with hazy light. Sitting at the carved and heavy wooden library table, she occupied her mind with the magazine while she waited for the librarian to return with the newspaper editions she'd requested from the back room.

Unable to restrain her curiosity, Natica had surrendered to the urge and headed to the library to see what she could find out about her parent's divorce. It had taken her over an hour to ferret through the card catalog searching out any articles pertaining to the Belmont family. Starting her search in 1882, a year before her birthday, she discovered several city newspapers listed articles, and the more she dug, the more she found.

"Here you are, miss," the librarian said, setting the stack of periodicals on the table in front of her. Wearing a red sweater and glasses that hung from a silver chain around her neck, the prim woman carried herself with a matronly disposition.

Pushing aside the magazine, Natica pulled the pile of newspapers toward her with a cursory glance. "Thank you."

"Let me know if you need anything else," the librarian said. "When you're done with these, please drop them off at my desk so they can be filed and returned to storage."

"Yes, of course," Natica answered.

The woman left Natica to her work, and she slipped a paper from the top of the stack, an edition of the *Harrisburg Telegraph* from May 19, 1883. Turning the pages, she spotted a story about her mother's honeymoon in Paris in the society section.

'*Shortly after their arrival in that city, the young husband went on a week's visit but stayed away six weeks, his companion* en voyage *being, some assert, a French ballet dancer whose acquaintance he had made during a former visit to Paris. The bride of a few months, thus deserted, returned to Newport, her homecoming causing more of a flutter than her wedding. The bride's friends were opposed to the wedding, but she was blinded by love. Now she sees clearly, though too late, through the disguise which gave her lover the appearance of a man but revealed him in his true character as a sensual hypocrite. Girls give heed to a mother's counsel, even though love whispers sweet words and swears eternal fidelity, her eyes can penetrate the mask of the hypocrite when your own love-blinded can see only the hero of your virgin dreams.'*

Stunned by what she'd read, Natica continued her search through the papers, finding another article in *The New York Times*. November 1, 1883, she read, realizing that was only several months after her birth. Opening the paper, she perused the pages until she found what she was searching for. There, in black and white, the article's headline read:

'Why They Remain in Newport'

Gulping, Natica plunged ahead, taking in the entire account spelled out in great detail.

'It is generally believed that several well-known New York ladies are residing here for the purpose of securing divorces from their husbands. It is admitted that Mrs. Oliver Hazard Perry Belmont, née Whiting of New York, is determined to apply for divorce. To this day, Mr. Belmont has never been permitted to call upon his wife or child.' With rapt interest, Natica finished the article. *'... It looks as if he intends to show fight.'*

Pausing, she closed the newspaper and stared up at the ornately carved and coffered ceiling of the library, lost in silent contemplation.

"It's all true," she thought. *"Every bit of it is true."*

Personal accounts were one thing, but this was the published word. Even though she'd already heard the awful tale from Charlotte, it was still a shock to see the story in print, publicly relating the events that had delivered her mother to scandal.

And she was the product of that short marriage. Natica leaned her elbows on the wooden table and rubbed her eyes, her mind filled with a thousand questions. Who was it that prevented her father from visiting? Her mother? Her grandmother? Probably both, Natica decided. But in the end, did it really matter? Her mother had remarried, and George had adopted her, raising her as one of his own. Her heart filled with a new love for her stepfather, who'd been so good to her over the years.

What was she going to do? Whether or not they acknowledged her, she still had a birth father and the bloodline of a very influential family. Could she be a part of the Belmont clan? Did she *want* to be a recognized member of the Belmont family? Natica was smart enough to know she was lucky to be a member of the Rives family and cautioned herself against growing impetuous or confrontational. After all, this had happened nearly twenty years ago.

Opening the New York *Tribune* dated December 10th, 1890, she found a copy of her grandfather's last will and testament published when she was only seven years old. August

Belmont had added a clause to the document, and she quickly realized it pertained to herself and her mother.

'*But no person shall be entitled to take, under the provisions of this article, as issue of my said son, Oliver Hazard Perry Belmont, except such issue as he may have by some wife whom he shall hereafter marry.*'

Clearly, her grandfather had specifically protected his will against Natica or her mother staking any claims for the Belmont money.

As if. They had money of their own, she fumed.

Shivering, Natica buttoned her sweater closed as the words gave the stock to the animosity generated between the two families.

Stacking the papers into a pile, she rose from her chair and carried them to the librarian's desk. Numb from the shock of the knowledge she'd gained, Natica returned to the table. Pushing in the chair, she grabbed her pocketbook and headed for the exit on Fifth Avenue with a million thoughts running rampant through her mind.

Two weeks later
November 11, 1900
Paris, France

The Arch de' Triomphe loomed large over the Paris café where Natica and her mother were having brunch. From where they sat, they had a perfect view of the beautiful city.

"This is one of my favorite cafés," Sara told her daughter. "I used to come here with my mother and sisters years ago. I love the way the elm trees line the Champs Elysees." Taking in the view of the romantic city, Sara announced: "There's simply nowhere else like Paris."

Mother and daughter admired the scene, looking as though they entirely belonged in France. Wearing stylish gowns and lovely hats, their good taste and fine breeding were evident to any observer.

After her trip to the New York library, Natica had thought long and hard about Oliver Belmont. Knowing what had happened, she worked to come to terms with the reality of her birth father and the hardship he'd brought down on her mother. Some days it troubled her greatly; other days, not so much. Now, watching her mother closely, she considered telling her what she knew. It bothered her to keep her discovery a secret from her mother, but Natica didn't want to create a conflict or deal with endless lectures. She decided to let the matter slide. Ultimately, her life was free of past scandals, so why stir up the dirt? Besides, it was a beautiful day, and they were in Paris. She was a welcome guest at all the best society balls and had a wonderful stepfather who adored her. Ultimately, Natica had decided to let bygones be bygones – at least, that's how she felt today.

"It is beautiful, Mother, and so nice to be back," Natica agreed, taking in the lovely view. "I forgot to mention I received a note from my friend Cynthia Roche before we left. She's supposed to arrive with her family at the end of the week."

"That will be nice," Sara said, while reviewing the daily specials. "The two of you can shop together – with a chaperone, of course."

"Of course," Natica acquiesced. "But I want you to come to Worth's dress shop with me. I trust your judgment more than my own when it comes to knowing what looks best."

"Thank you, Natica." Sara met her daughter's eyes. "Am I mistaken, or did you just compliment me?"

Natica gave her a crooked smile, shrugged, then changed the subject. "I'm so glad for the chance to practice my French. Grandma would be proud. We don't speak it around the house as much since she passed away."

"Your grandmother loved France." Sara's eyes misted with memory. "She decorated the house in furniture and fabrics she brought home with her from Paris. She would have spoken French all the time if we'd let her."

Sara couldn't resist the fond thoughts of the family visits to Paris. Those were joyous days filled with operas and parties, not to mention hours of shopping with Jane, Milly, and her mother. She glanced at Natica and saw Oliver's eyes, then remembered the afternoon on the rue so close to where they now sat. The rue where Natica's father had proposed marriage to her that summer day so many years ago – a proposal not endorsed by his parents. Sara was determined Natica would not end up married to a selfish man like Oliver.

'Now is not the time to dwell on the past,' she thought. "When do you want to go to Mr. Worth's?" she asked Natica. "Is after lunch too soon?"

The predictable delight erupted from Natica. "Not a moment too soon!"

Five months later
March 4, 1901
New York, New York

Resting in the leather office chair, Oliver loosened his tie and leaned back with a sigh. "Well, brother, let's have a toast."

"Congratulations, Oliver," Perry cheered, clinking his crystal glass against his brother's. "It appears we have a common vocation in politics." Removing his suit jacket, he hung it on the back of his chair and sat down across from his sibling.

"It appears so." Oliver smiled, relaxing as he drank the aged scotch. "It's going to take some time to get used to being called 'congressman', but I'm up to the challenge."

"There are quite a few perks to the job." Perry grinned. "I'm certain you'll discover that yourself, once you start your term."

An easy chuckle escaped Oliver. "I'm sure that suits me fine."

⚜

Four months later
July 9, 1901
Newport, Rhode Island

Lounging at the table under the covered patio, the three ladies were catching up on news. Gathered for the May's luncheon party, they'd just served themselves at a fabulous buffet of tempting summer foods. Berries and salads were offered with grilled chicken and sea bass, sending delicious smells wafting into the air. Elegant guests, dressed in their finest afternoon outfits, leisurely chatted at tables arranged under the old shady trees on the lawn. The manicured yard, blooming with hydrangeas, offered an open view that swept majestically down to the sea.

"I can't believe she asked me to be in her wedding. Isn't it just wonderful?" Isabel May gushed with delight. Slim and fair-haired, she wore a simple gown with a square-front yoke, adorned with tiny, embroidered pink flowers.

Recently back from New York, Natica was happy for a chance to catch up on the news with her friends, only now hearing about the engagement.

"Are you certain it's not just a rumor?" Cynthia cautioned. "You know how gossip spreads."

"I assure you this is *not* gossip." Isabel nodded her head vehemently, her flaxen hair bobbing in rhythm. "Cathleen told me herself. It's a fact. Reginald Vanderbilt has proposed marriage – and she's accepted."

Pleased for Cathleen, Natica was well-aware there was now one less bachelor up for grabs. She'd started to have some misgivings about Reggie anyway, as he seemed to drink an awful lot of liquor. But apparently most men did, she thought sourly.

"If you're certain of it, then there will be a formal announcement." Natica pointed out, her excitement growing. A Vanderbilt wedding was sure to be a spectacular affair. "Do you know if they've set a wedding date?"

"I think they're planning it for April next year," Isabel said between bites of salad. "I'm not really sure if they've chosen the exact date. Mrs. Vanderbilt was against the idea at first, but not because she didn't approve of Cathleen. She just thought the two were a bit young to marry."

"Is that a joke?" Natica laughed. "Isn't Reggie twenty-two?"

"That's old enough in my book," Cynthia said, nibbling on a bowl of strawberries in a very elegant manner.

"Mine too," Natica agreed. "Cathleen's mother will be very happy to know her daughter is marrying into such a prominent family. Are they having the ceremony here or in New York?"

"Nothing's been set yet, but Cathleen mentioned they were thinking about having it here in Newport if they can find a suitable location. There was some talk of them renting Arleigh from Mrs. Pratt for both the ceremony and reception," Isabel said. "I'm sure you'll both receive invitations. I'm so excited! It will be the event of the season."

"I'm still enjoying this summer," Natica countered. "By the way, my mother has finally set the date for my début. Officially."

"That's wonderful!" Cynthia clapped, hearing the news, the lacy bell sleeves of her dress swaying rhythmically. "We'll have the best time – and you'll finally be allowed to court."

"How fun!" Isabel cheered along. "When is the party?"

"It's set for July twenty-seventh at the Atlantic House." Natica worked to hide her enthusiasm. "She's having a huge celebration and plans on inviting everyone. Guests are attending from New York, Boston, and family from Columbus."

"I can hardly wait!" Isabel chirped in support. "Do you have a dress yet?"

"Yes, of course." Natica leaned closer. "It's *so* fabulous! And all the rage in fashion – white silk with a stylish collar and tiny beads embroidered on the bodice. We got it in Paris – along with a hundred other beautiful things."

"It sounds *so* lovely," Cynthia cooed. "You'll probably have every man in Newport trying to steal a dance with you."

"I certainly hope so." Natica smiled devilishly. "After all, that *is* the point."

The three ladies lapsed into a clamor of laughter that echoed off the patio and rolled down to the sea. So many exciting things were happening, and they were going to be a part of it all.

Chapter Twenty-Eight

Ten days later
July 19, 1901
New York, New York

The afternoon air was cooling down as evening settled over the dusty city, bringing much needed relief from the hot afternoon sun. It had been a long, tiresome day. Dinner at Sherry's might be just the thing to unwind, George decided, entering the upscale restaurant to meet his friend.

"I'm glad you could join me," he said, shaking Howard Hunt's hand in greeting. "Dining alone is never much fun."

"I was glad when you called." Howard smiled warmly. A stout man, he matched George in height, but carried a much heavier frame. Flecks of silver showed in his full head of thick black hair, while well-trimmed sideburns demonstrated his fastidious nature. "My family is summering in Newport, so I've been focusing on work. If you've been as busy as I have, then we both need a drink."

"Agreed." George nodded, following the maitre'd to a dining table near the bar. The restaurant was crowded and a little noisy with the sounds of clinking glasses and dishes rising over the murmur of diners. They sat down and ordered scotch, while they reviewed the chef's specials.

"How is your family?" George asked Howard. "Everyone doing okay?"

"Yes, things are well," Howard told him. "Susan is doing fine, as are my two children. Howard Jr. will be going off to Yale in the fall, so we all have high hopes for him."

"Always an exciting time for a young man," George noted, purposely avoiding the subject of Junior.

The delicious smells stirred his hunger, and he decided on a grilled steak for a main course. Their waiter stepped up and delivered the drinks, then politely took their food order. Heading back to the kitchen, the servant left the men alone to talk.

The conversation was light as George and Howard were both weary from their work-day. Sipping their drinks, they chatted about their families and social engagements throughout the meal. The waiter returned periodically, delivering courses of soup, salad, entrée, and dessert to their table.

"Are you going back to Newport?" George asked him. "I hear there's going to be a wonderful ball held at Aquidneck House in the beginning of August. My wife is looking forward to it."

"I may take the train up," Howard replied. "If I can finish this contract for new turbines and seal the deal in time. A few weeks off would be nice before autumn hits."

"I couldn't agree more." George nodded, reaching for his glass. "It seems like time is moving faster every day. I can barely keep up."

"It's hard sometimes, but I don't mind working," Howard admitted. "I know many men in our set prefer the leisure life, but I like the challenge and the feeling of accom-plishment when I put together a successful business deal."

"Or win a big case," George added.

The dining room settled into quiet as the evening wore on into night, the temperature cooling to a more comfortable climate. Several patrons left the restaurant, leaving many of the tables vacant.

"If you'll excuse me for a minute." Howard rose from his chair, laying his napkin on the empty dinner plate.

"Of course." George nodded. He watched Howard disappear around the corner and sat back in his seat with a sigh. It had been a good day.

"Hello, George."

Spinning toward the bar, George was both surprised and annoyed to see Oliver Bel-mont addressing him.

"Hello," George said dryly, irritated by his appearance.

Oliver's eyes were bloodshot, his clothing a bit rumpled for the early hour. He looked as though he'd been drinking here at the bar all day.

"I know we've never really spoke," Oliver said, taking a seat at his table without an invitation.

Anger rippled through George at the man's audacity. It was hard to disguise his dislike for this man. "We don't really have much to talk about now, do we, Oliver?"

"Actually, we do," Oliver disagreed, giving him a cocky smile. "We have Natica to talk about."

George shot him a stern look at the mention of the girl. "I don't really see where *my daughter* is any concern of yours." George accented his words to drive the point home. How a man could abandon his pregnant wife – in a foreign country no less, George would never understand.

"I saw in the newspaper that Natica is making her début in a few days."

"That's no concern of yours, Belmont." George's lips formed a tight line of barely disguised irritation.

"But it is." Oliver insisted. "Everything the girl does is my concern."

"Actually, Oliver, that's where you're wrong." George leaned across the table to be sure he heard every word. "I do not want you anywhere near my family. You gave up that right when you disowned the girl and abandoned her mother. So, I would appreciate it if you'd continue to keep your distance." George leaned back, working to keep his temper in check.

"I understand that's your position," Oliver argued. "But no one really knows except for Sara and me what happened on our honeymoon. The only important thing is that I have a daughter from..."

"No! Oliver, you're wrong!" George interrupted him sharply. "You do *not* have a daughter. You have William's wife, that's who you've got, and a reputation that brings nothing but embarrassment to all who associate with you."

"I want to see her!" Oliver blurted against his criticism. "I want to talk to Natica and tell her I'm her father."

"You've gone mad!" George almost shouted, his face turning red. Their discussion was beginning to draw glances from the surrounding diners. George tried, but found it challenging, to contain his anger. "I am her father," he said in a low growl. "You will stay away from Natica – and Sara, or I'll place a restraining order against you to guarantee that you do."

"She's not a little girl anymore," Oliver continued vehemently. "She has a right to know that I'm her father. I'm a congressman now and..."

"You should have thought about that before you disowned her as a baby and left her mother in a web of scandal to raise the child alone," George reminded him harshly.

"Believe me, George, I regret that more than anyone. The way things turned out with our marriage was a nightmare. But I was a young man then. I've changed. If I could go back and do things differently, I would. I want another chance to know Natica."

"The best thing you can do for the girl is stay away from her," George spat. He grabbed his scotch and finished it in one gulp, slamming the glass on the table. "Now. If you'll excuse me, this conversation is over."

Oliver started to speak again, but in the face of George's animosity, he abandoned his efforts. Rising from the chair he sauntered to the bar. As he passed, George reached over, roughly grabbing his arm.

"I mean it, Oliver." His eyes shot daggers into the man. "You stay away from my family, or I'll make trouble for you with the authorities just in time for your little stint in congress. I don't care how rich you are."

Clamping his jaw tight, Oliver smirked but said nothing. With a quick move, he jerked his arm back and smoothed the fabric of his suit, giving George a sardonic smile.

Running a hand over his beard, George caught his breath, just as Howard returned. "Let's get out of here," George said. He got up and threw a few bills on the table.

Howard gave him a confused look but nodded, following George out of the restaurant.

———

Two days later
July 21, 1901
Newport, Rhode Island

Anna walked into the *Swanhurst* sitting room, her face hidden behind a fabulous bouquet of white lilies and roses embellished with baby's breath.

"We've gotten another delivery for Miss Natica," she called, searching for an empty space to place the flowers.

Sara joined her, entering from the dining room, her floral print skirt flowing around her feet. "Here's an empty vase if you need it for a bouquet." she offered. "I think we're going to have to start putting some of these on the dining room table."

A happy laugh escaped the maid. "Miss Natica will have to dance all the way into tomorrow if she's going to fill all these requests for her company tonight."

"Has she seen these flowers yet?"

"No, ma'am." Anna smiled, shaking her head. "She said she wanted to sleep late this morning. I suppose Miss Natica wants to be sure she has the energy to make it through her début."

Walking in from the kitchen, Jane glanced around the room. "The house looks like a flower shop. I remember when this happened for your début!" She gave Sara a fond smile. "We had the same problem trying to figure out what to do with all your bouquets."

"It's a lovely problem to have," Sara noted. She was proud that her daughter was so popular among the set but worried that she was growing up too fast. Sara couldn't help but notice the younger generation was much more risqué than her generation, throwing wild theme parties and cavorting until all hours, leaving tales of debauchery in their wake. And now, with the telephone and motorcar, coupled with the arrogance and ignorance of their age, it was hard not to want to keep the girl home until she was thirty!

"Be sure to keep the cards together with the flowers," Sara instructed. "So that Natica knows who sent what."

"Yes, ma'am," Anna answered. "If I'm not needed here any longer, I'll get back to pressing Miss Natica's gown."

"That will be fine," Sara said. "Is Bridget with the children?"

"Yes, ma'am. They went to the park a while ago," Anne called from the hallway. "Bayard had a softball game."

Sara glanced at the clock. "It's only eleven-thirty."

"What time does the party start?" Jane inquired.

"Dinner will start at ten o'clock. The florist is going over around noon to decorate." Sara looked a little overwhelmed. "I'm expecting almost one hundred guests tonight."

Jane chuckled at her sister. "You sound just like Mother."

"Do I?" Sara laughed, catching herself. "I suppose I do..."

"Yes, you do," Jane said, shaking her head in amusement.

It was true she'd challenged her own mother's views on courting and marriage as a young woman. But these were modern times, and now that Sara was a mother herself, she understood her responsibility – in fact her *duty* to carry on the tradition for her own daughters the way her mother had done for her and her sisters.

Sara paused, memories flooding her mind of her dream of contributing something more to the world, as Edith did with her novels. In the end, especially after the tribulations of the divorce, Sara had surrendered to her role as mother and matriarch in lieu of other interests, gaining new appreciation for her mother's efforts.

After a moment, Sara smiled at Jane. "I'll take that as a compliment."

One month later
August 15, 1901
Newport, Rhode Island

Bellevue Avenue was crowded with people out for an evening stroll. Newport hoteliers, currently invaded by travelers, gave word they had not a single hotel room for guests who'd come to the city without first making a previous reservation.

The August weather was sticky and thick, as was typical for late summer, and many were out to escape the heat of their rooms. Excitement filtered through the throng, seeking entertainment for the summer evening. An acclaimed performance by a New York chamber music group was opening at the casino theatre, and people crowded the box office trying to get tickets for the eight o'clock show.

Joining the fun, the three débutantes ambled down the sidewalk dressed to impress for their evening promenade. The young ladies were often seen around town and had been dubbed 'The Gigglers' by the older set because they were always laughing. Cynthia, a blond, Gwen with her honey-brown hair, and Natica, a stunning brunette – made quite a vision as they walked along, joking and discussing the latest gossip.

"Don't you find these promenades rather boring?" Natica asked her friends.

Their dresses swished and flowed as they sashayed along Bellevue wearing fancy wide-brimmed hats and toting lacy parasols.

"Not at all," Gwendolyn proclaimed. "I rather like the outings." Gwen was Arthur and Will Burden's cousin. She'd just gotten back to Newport from boarding school in London. "I enjoy an evening stroll. Besides, this is the way things have always been done."

"All true, but occasionally I do grow weary of it," Cynthia noted. "In the end, nothing really changes."

"Indeed." Natica nodded in agreement. "It's so important and yet somehow so frivolous."

"I must admit the rules of etiquette do grow tiresome," Cynthia added. "Don't share this with anyone, but I'm always trying to ditch my chaperone."

"Your secret's safe with us," Gwen assured her with a tiny smile. "We do have to follow a strict regime of etiquette. Wear this, don't wear that. Do this, don't do that. It's exhausting."

"I have an idea," Natica said. She turned to her friends with a devilish sparkle in her eye. "Let's shake things up and do something mischievous."

"Oh no." Gwen groaned.

"What did you have in mind?" Cynthia asked with open curiosity.

"Oh, I don't know..." Natica scrunched her eyes in thought. "Nothing really harmful. Just a little fun to shock people out of their routines."

"You could always run down the street in your pantaloons." Cynthia joked. "I'm sure that would cause a stir."

The three of them laughed at her suggestion. "That's a little extreme." Natica objected. "My mother would lock me in my room for the rest of my life."

"Mine too." Gwen smiled. "Or worse. She'd send me back to London on the next steamer."

"I have an idea!" Natica's eyes grew wide with excitement. "Follow me." She waved her friends into an alley beside the Audrain building. "I've come up with the perfect prank."

"Tell us!" Gwen urged, getting in the spirit of things.

"Let's unpin our hair and let it flow long down our backs like we did when we were schoolgirls." She pointed to an old wooden crate. "We can toss our hats there for safekeeping."

"Oh, I love the idea!" Cynthia cheered. "It's perfectly harmless but will certainly liven things up."

"What do you think?" Natica asked Gwen. "Are you game?"

"Sure. Let's get silly and do it."

The three erupted into a profusion of giggles as they discarded their hats and proceeded to remove the hairpins from their coiffures. In a few moments, the three were standing in a circle, each with their waist-length hair flowing in the evening breeze.

"Ready?" Cynthia asked her friends.

"Ready!" Gwen said.

"Ladies, let's turn some heads!" Natica took them by the hand and led them straight into the middle of the evening promenade on Bellevue Avenue.

It was only a matter of seconds before they began to receive shocked glances from prim and proper gentlemen strolling with their priggish wives. Whispers and disapproving looks were thrown their way as the young ladies sauntered down the avenue with heads held high while tossing their long tresses into the breeze.

Unable to suppress her merriment, Natica giggled in chorus with Cynthia and Gwen, delighted by the ruckus they were causing in the crowd. The three teenagers completely ignored the impropriety of their actions and indulged in their prank with impish delight.

As the débutantes neared the casino box office, the fervor grew far more noticeable. People stopped, appalled, and openly stared at them. Churchgoers and mothers turned, gasping at the girls in horror as if they'd committed some unspeakable crime.

"Look!" Commodore Hanson shouted. "It's 'The Gigglers'. They've let their hair down in public."

"Shameful!" A woman dressed in black openly chastised their behavior.

A murmur went up from the crowd, buzzing at their escapade. Fighting the urge to stick out her tongue at the oglers, Natica chuckled with abandon. Reaching the corner of Memorial Avenue, the three made the turn and took off running in their fabulous Parisian dresses, hooting and giggling as they circled their way back to the alley behind the Audrain.

"Oh, that was too much fun!" Cynthia cried, catching her breath from the run.

"It certainly beats boarding school," Gwen added, trying to stop laughing.

"Did you see their faces?" Natica asked between chortles. "That will definitely give them something to talk about."

"For a very long time!" Cynthia added with a wink.

Chapter Twenty-Nine

Nearly two years later
April 14, 1903
Newport, Rhode Island

"Congratulations to you both!" Natica smiled at the bride and groom as they received their guests. Wearing one of her new gowns, she'd given special attention to her appearance for today's wedding reception.

"We're so happy for you," Cynthia chimed in, standing at Natica's side. Her lovely fuchsia-pink dress brought color to Cynthia's glowing cheeks.

Arleigh Estate had been rented from Mrs. Pratt for the wedding, and the decorators had done an outstanding job. Following the bride's instructions, they'd created a forest wonderland for the refined guests invited to today's celebration. It was said over twenty thousand flowers had been provided by the florist.

"Thank you, ladies." Reginald smiled, looking dapper in his white topcoat, a tea-rose boutonniere neatly pinned to the lapel.

"I'm so glad you're both here to share the day with me," Cathleen said, glowing with joy. Her white satin gown was layered with delicate sheer chiffon, and the high bodice and sleeves were constructed from the finest quality antique lace. "The wedding gifts you sent are beautiful. All the presents are on display in the library if you want to see them."

"I'm sure they're wonderful." Natica smiled. She could only imagine the expensive and extravagant wedding gifts the couple had received. The gossip around town said the Vanderbilts had hired a plain-clothes detective to guard the wedding treasures.

Noticing the receiving line growing longer, she urged Cynthia on, not wanting to hold Cathleen up chatting about gifts.

"We'll talk with you later." Natica nodded toward the line.

"Thank you so much." Cathleen waved graciously and turned to the next guest.

With Cynthia at her side, Natica moved on to the ballroom leaving the bride and groom to greet the long queue of guests.

"I suppose you and I are the only two unwed débutantes remaining from our group of friends," Cynthia noted glumly.

"We've got plenty of time to marry," Natica assured her. "I, for one, do not want to rush into marrying someone who might turn out to be a horrible husband just for the sake of having a lovely celebration."

"I know you're right," Cynthia said. "It's just that weddings are so much fun. I can't help but daydream about being the complete center of society's attention, even if it is only for a day or two."

The ladies milled through the happy reception, stopping to talk with friends as they crossed the room to the buffet tables. Weaving their way to the hors d'oeuvre display, they grabbed a few puffed crab pastries, crudités, and other elegant appetizers.

"Hello, Natica." Michael Vincente appeared beside her holding a coupe of champagne. "Does your mother let you drink spirits?" he asked, handing her the glass.

Stepping from behind Natica, Cynthia batted her eyelashes. "Hello, Michael," she said, jumping into the conversation. "What my mother doesn't know won't hurt her."

He glanced at Cynthia and grew flustered. "Hello there, Cynthia. I didn't see you standing with Natica." He glanced at the coupe glass in his hand. "I'm afraid we need more wine."

Gallantly he handed his coupe to Cynthia and with a quick swoop, grabbed another glass from a tray carried by a passing butler.

"There you go," he said, a gleam in his eye. "Champagne for everyone."

"Thank you so much." Natica grinned, impressed by his little display.

She found Michael very handsome. Tall and muscular with light brown, wavy hair, his deep, amber-brown eyes were flecked with gold. Dressed for the wedding in his dinner coat, he looked even more attractive. Cynthia continued fluttering her eyelashes at him, and Michael seemed a little embarrassed by her effort.

"This is an amazing party," he said, glancing at the guests. "Of course, we all knew it would be fabulous."

"That's so true," Natica agreed. She quietly examined his features as he talked, finding it difficult to take her eyes off him. "Our friend Isabel is one of the bridesmaids."

"The bride and groom gave the attendants such beautiful gifts," Cynthia told him, her blue eyes bright. "Diamond earrings for the ladies and diamond tie-pins for the gentlemen."

"That does sound nice," he conceded. "But not unusual for the Vanderbilts."

Taking a sip from his wine, he met Natica's eyes. "I was wondering if you might honor me with a dance later?" he asked casually.

Cynthia began to frown when she realized Michael's attention was directed at Natica.

"I would like that very much." Natica smiled. The romantic timber of his voice was not lost on her.

"Hello, William." Cynthia perked up at the appearance of Will and Arthur Burden.

"Hello, ladies."

"Isn't this just a lovely wedding?"

"Quite." Arthur nodded. "But I'd expect no less for old man Vanderbilt's son."

The brothers made quite a handsome pair dressed in their formal wear.

"I've been to Mrs. Pratt's cottage before," Will told them. "But it's never looked like this. I've never seen so many flowers in one house."

"What's a wedding without flowers?" Cynthia quipped. "Cathleen loves flowers. I'm sure she wanted to make today memorable."

"She's certainly succeeded in doing that," Natica said.

Will seemed to be watching her closely, making her feel a little self-conscious with Michael still standing beside her. Will threw a fast look at her companion and quickly realized he had some competition.

"I was wondering if you had any room left on your dance card?" Will asked Natica pointedly.

"I've got room on my dance card." Cynthia perked up.

"Well then, perhaps you'll promise *me* a dance." Arthur jumped in to help his brother.

Cynthia paused and gave Arthur her sweetest smile. "That would be lovely."

"And you?" Will returned his attention to Natica while Michael took note with consternation, clearly aware of his advances.

"I think I may have one open spot," Natica answered, her eyes darting back and forth between the men.

It was almost amusing watching the two compete for her affection. Courting is fun, Natica thought, especially when so many exciting bachelors are showing me favor. With a smile, she took another sip of her champagne and prepared for a long night of dancing.

The next week
April 22, 1903
Newport, Rhode Island

Throwing the newspaper aside in anger, Alva bristled at the announcement. William had successfully petitioned the court to amend his divorce decree, allowing him to remarry. Worse than that – the wedding was to take place tomorrow in London. But the bride's name remained a mystery, as were the details of the ceremony.

The maid poured tea and handed it to her mistress. Alva sipped it and grimaced. "This is tepid," she reprimanded. "How many times have I instructed you to make certain the tea is hot before you serve it to me!"

"I apologize, ma'am," the maid said, flushing in embarrassment. Gathering the tea service, she hurried to the kitchen for a fresh, hot pot of the Darjeeling brew.

Alva's thoughts returned to William's wedding, and she wondered why there was such mystery regarding his bride. "Whoever she is," Alva grumbled, "she's certainly earned my wrath." Her eyes grew dark and brooding while she considered the matter.

Though they'd divorced years ago, and Alva was now married to Oliver, she still felt dominion over William as the mother of his children. "I can't wait till he starts running around behind her back," Alva murmured with new animosity. His dalliances were rumored to have focused on her old friend Consuelo Yznaga, now the Duchess of Manchester. That news had quickly brought a sharp end to their friendship.

"The new Mrs. Vanderbilt will soon come to know the special joy of marriage to the philandering Willie," she attested, her pug-like nose red with anger.

The maid returned with fresh tea prepared by the cook. She poured a new cup and handed it to Alva, steam rising from the surface of the brew.

Sipping daintily, Alva let out a howl. "My mouth is burned!" she shouted, glaring at the frightened maid. "How hard can it be to make tea properly!" Disgusted, she shook her head, taking her foul mood out on the harried domestic.

Two weeks later
May 9, 1903

New York, New York

A warm breeze floated over New York; the sunny day was perfect for the annual coaching parade through Central Park. Although the sport had always been popular, it was particularly so this season. Public coaching lines, offering trips around the city and to nearby towns, were booked solid for the summer. Private carriages made a statement of their own with regular convoys around the metropolis in a public display of finery.

Colonel Jay, the president of the Coaching Club, had arranged for a full promenade today. Eleven very fine carriages joined him for the drive from Central Park to One-Hundred-and-Fourth Street. There, they'd circled the horses and returned to the park, disembarking for a break to enjoy the lovely day before proceeding to a luncheon planned at an eatery in the Bronx. Each carriage was fully loaded with passengers, all of whom were wearing fabulous attire in a great show of wealth, refinement, and good taste.

Climbing down from her carriage, Natica turned toward the street. *"I'm surprised to see such a large group convened for today's promenade."* Twelve coaches lined the street, each with at least six passengers riding inside, along with six more perched on the outside, making a total of nearly one hundred and fifty people in attendance for today's event.

Pulling at her leather gloves, Natica strolled through the group with her cousin, Evelyn Parsons, by her side.

"I must admit, I'm enjoying myself immensely," Natica said to her companion. Looking splendid in a ruby-red gown, Natica's stunning hat was jauntily perched on her head, a fashion statement matched by all the ladies.

Natica recalled the note from Evelyn that had arrived last week inviting her to ride along with Evelyn's family in the annual parade. Natica had readily accepted the offer. The two ladies found amicable companionship in each other, their friendship growing stronger by trust and shared confidences.

"I'm so glad you could join us today," Evelyn said with a wide smile. "I wasn't sure if you already had plans or not." She raised a silk parasol over her head, shadowing her eyes from the sun.

"As it turns out, my calendar was open." Natica smiled, observing the abundance of young men in the group. "And this will give us both the perfect opportunity to meet new people."

The ladies shared an appreciative glance. As they walked behind their coach, Natica heard Mr. Hatten instruct a young woman on the particulars of managing a four-in-hand.

"Lately, women are showing new interest in coaching," Evelyn remarked. "I understand that lessons are now offered specifically for ladies, teaching them the proper way to handle a horse and carriage."

"Yes, I know," Natica returned. "I've scheduled several private lessons myself." Relishing the chance to break into a male dominated convention, Natica had signed up for the instruction.

"Have you, indeed?"

"I have. I seem to be catching on to the art of driving, but admittedly, I've still got a lot to learn."

The ladies strolled past the coaches, neatly parked along the street. Leafy trees provided shade from the sun, leaves flickering light on the sidewalk from the gentle breeze. Men and women meandered over the grass, a veritable fashion show of fine apparel and jewels, all on display for the afternoon outing. The picturesque scene was worthy of an artist's paintbrush.

"There's Jonathan Post," Evelyn noted with a nod in his direction. "I must admit, he makes my heart beat a little faster." Blushing, she turned to Natica and asked, "Would you mind if I go over and talk with him for a few moments?"

"Not at all," Natica answered, noting the sparkle in Evelyn's eye at the sight of the handsome man.

Evelyn left Natica's company, strolling nonchalantly toward Mr. Post, who was now leaning against a fat tree trunk smoking a cigarette. A horse whinnied close to Natica's ear, and she turned in response to pet its soft nose. The chestnut-brown animal nuzzled her, obviously hoping for an apple or a carrot, and she wished she had one to spoil the lovely bay.

Laughter rose from a group of men, and she glanced in their direction. She stood riveted as she noticed him, standing near the side of a coach, alone, inspecting the fine ride.

Oliver Belmont.

Straightening her spine, Natica watched him silently from behind the horse, trying to decide what to do — years of mystery and confusion welled up inside her, bolstered by the revelation of the truth she now knew.

"Now is the time," she decided, reflecting on the Belmont family, lost to her by his hedonistic behavior – behavior that had negatively impacted her life and her mother's social standing. Fighting against her temper, she took a deep breath and marched toward him. Coming up behind Oliver unnoticed, she reached his side and smacked him hard on the shoulder with her leather gloves.

Surprised by the blow, Oliver jumped and turned toward her. His eyes flashed with recognition, and he smiled warmly at his estranged daughter.

But Natica did not return his smile, staring at him coldly.

They stood that way for a heartbeat.

"I know who you are." Natica confronted him, her voice low and harsh. "And I know all about your little marriage and Paris honeymoon with my mother."

The smiled faded from Oliver's face. "I don't know what they've told you..."

"*They* didn't tell me anything. But I discovered the truth just the same."

"There are many versions of the truth. Why don't you give me a chance to explain my side of the story?"

"Don't bother. What I haven't heard first-person, I've read in old newspapers."

"The newspapers!" he scoffed. "Only a fool believes all that propaganda."

"Are you calling me a fool?"

"Of course not. I'm only asking for a chance to discuss this further."

"No, thank you. I'm not interested in your explanations. I hope that's clear enough for you."

"You're not being fair."

"Fair! Skulking in the shadows since I was a small child! Watching me from the fringes of a crowd! Weren't you concerned about frightening me? Didn't you think I'd get suspicious?"

"I only wanted to catch a glimpse of you. Please, listen to my side of the story."

"I feel certain you've managed to put quite a spin on your side of the story with twenty years' worth of practice." Natica narrowed her eyes but maintained her composure. "Suffice it to say I know that my grandfather, the *great* August Belmont, completely disowned me from the Belmont family, quite legally, I might add, in his will. I think that speaks volumes, don't you?"

Inflexible and tough, Natica challenged him.

Oliver started to speak again, and she stopped him, pushing her open palm close to his face. Father and daughter grew silent, staring at each other like dueling opponents.

"I have nothing more to say to you. I only wanted the satisfaction of letting you know I'm aware of the scandal you delivered to my mother, not to mention smearing the Whiting family's honorable name – and branding me with a reputation nearly as bad as a bastard!"

"Please, Natica, give me a chance to explain."

"Thanks, Pops, but no thanks! That ship has sailed."

Spinning on her heel, Natica returned to her carriage, feeling somehow absolved of his sins and empowered by her own self-respect. It felt good to finally confront him, and her satisfaction brought a modicum of closure to years of questions.

Returning from her chat with Jonathan, Evelyn strolled up beside her, oblivious to Natica's turmoil. Her easy smile hinted at an enjoyable conversation with the attractive Mr. Post.

"We're leaving for the luncheon now, Natica. Let's return to our carriage."

"Of course."

Following her friend, Natica threw a glance over her shoulder, taking great pleasure in the fact that the pretentious Mr. Belmont had retreated, disappearing from sight into the coaching crowd, like he'd done so many times throughout her life.

Two months later
June 18, 1903
Newport, Rhode Island

A stuffy chauffeur wearing a starched uniform and cap sat at the wheel of the Packard, driving the débutantes through town. The early summer day was picture-perfect, and a buzz of activity surrounded the casino, even at this early hour.

"I was getting quite bored," Payne said. "I thought I'd die of tedium if I didn't find some fun to occupy my time before tonight's ball."

Sitting in the back with Natica, Payne's long face was not as lovely as others, but she more than made up for it with her fine costumes and elaborate hats. Payne wore her dark hair short with a Marcel wave, preferring a more modern style.

"I'm glad you called," Natica said. "I didn't have any plans for lunch."

"It's a small diversion." Payne toyed with her lace gloves. "I'm so excited to meet the prince tonight, in town from Spain. I've heard so much gossip about him it's hard to keep my curiosity in check. He's said to be very handsome."

"I suppose we can form our own opinion tonight," Natica said. "Who knows if the rumors are true? That's why it's called gossip!"

Pulling the car to a stop in front of the casino, the driver parked and came around to open the door for the ladies. Surveying the crowd as she climbed from the vehicle, Natica noted a little girl around seven milling around the well-to-do group. Apparently alone, she stood on the sidewalk, looking distinctly out of place in her worn and ill-fitting clothes.

"What is that little waif doing on the sidewalk?"

"Where?" Payne asked. Catching sight of the girl, she paused. "She looks like a little beggar if you ask me."

"Well, it's all an accident of birth, don't you think?" Natica asked.

"I suppose..."

"I have an idea. Let's spoil the child, shall we?"

"What do you have up your sleeve this time?"

"Why, candy, of course!"

"Candy?" Following Natica's gaze to the sweet shop, Payne's eyes lit up. "Yes, of course. Candy."

Sharing a glance, the two silently agreed on a visit to the confection shop and approached the girl on the sidewalk.

"Hello," Natica said with a friendly smile. "What's your name?"

"Amy," she replied. Her brown eyes were large and round as she assessed the ladies. "Do you have a penny to spare?"

Laughing, Payne said, "We can do better than that."

"How would you like a treat?" In an easy move, Natica took the girl's hand and led her across the sidewalk.

"Oh yes!" Amy's smile grew wide at the offer. "For me?"

"For you," Payne assured her, opening the door to the confectioner's shop.

Once inside, a clerk greeted them with a bright smile. "How can I help you, ladies?" The man's white shirt was perfectly pressed, his gray hair curling around a black visor.

"We'd like to buy this youngster a bag of candy," Natica said.

"A very large bag," Payne added. She was never one in favor of moderation.

"Excellent." The clerk nodded. He reached for a paper sack and held it up. "Is this large enough?"

"Don't you have something bigger?" Natica asked, peering over the counter.

"This is the largest I have." the clerk replied, pulling a bigger sack from the shelf under the cash register.

"Tell the man what you would like," Payne urged the girl. "And don't be shy about it."

Immediately the little one began pointing at taffy, jellies, caramels, and lemon drops, arranged like jewels behind the glass counter. Smiling, the clerk loaded up the bag. He seemed to be enjoying the fun as much as the débutantes. It didn't take long for the sack to fill to the top with sweets. Natica paid the clerk, and the three returned to the avenue.

"Now, be on your way." Payne smiled, handing the girl a quarter for extra measure.

"Thank you!" Amy called after them with a wave.

Payne and Natica headed toward the casino for lunch, leaving the little girl on the sidewalk beaming under the load of her candy sack.

"Now that was fun!" Payne giggled.

"I imagine she's going to have a hard time explaining that to her mamma." Natica chuckled, delighted by their impromptu diversion.

"Indeed, she will." Payne grinned.

Four months later
October 3, 1903
New York, New York

Snuffing out his cigar, Perry glanced at Oliver slumped in the leather chair, his glum face replacing the usual smile.

"Don't let it get you down, little brother. There will be other elections." Convening in Perry's walnut-paneled New York office, the two discussed the outcome of the recent vote.

"I know." Oliver shrugged, a stubble of beard showing on his face. The two had been up all night, awaiting the election results. "I was certain we'd at least win the democratic vote. I thought we made such good running mates." He reached for the newspaper to read the article one more time as if by reading it, he could discover where the failure rested.

"In the Congress conventions held by the Democrats of New York and Richmond counties last night, the surprises were the turning down of Perry Belmont and Oliver H.P. Belmont in favor of Timothy D. Sullivan and William R. Hearst, respectively."

"We did a great job in the thirteenth district," Oliver grumbled, rubbing his chin. "I can't understand how we lost the nomination."

"I can," Perry scoffed, meeting Oliver's eye. "Hearst is a wealthy man, Ollie. I'm sure he knows people in high places."

"And we don't?" Oliver argued. "This is an election of the people."

"Indeed," Perry said, sarcasm evident in his tone. "At least you had a good run for the past three years representing the city. Now you'll have time to devote to a more leisurely life."

"I suppose." Oliver shrugged. He hated losing, but perhaps it was time to return to his thoroughbreds back in Newport.

———

Three months later
January 21, 1904
New York, New York

Coaches pulled up to the palatial house one-by-one delivering guests to the evening party. Taking George's hand, Sara walked beside him to the grand entrance of Carrie's new home, accompanied by Natica. The three were warmly greeted by solicitous footmen.

The home had been modeled after a French palace, and Sara had to admit, the building was easily as grand as any European castle she'd ever visited – but she'd expect nothing less from the Astor clan, especially with the precedent set by Alva Vanderbilt.

Constructed of Caen stone on the outside, the grand hall revealed itself upon their entrance to be built of white marble. Colorful tapestries lined the walls, hanging over gilt furniture covered in rose-colored fabric. Large palms and boxwood trees brought fresh life to the cold stone hall. Crystal vases were filled with tulips, daffodils, and hyacinths, infusing the fragrance of spring over the arriving guests. Letting her eyes travel, Sara noted an exquisite marble staircase wrapping around the main foyer as it rose to the second story. Carrie stood regally at the head of the stairs, greeting guests to the housewarming party, with Mr. Wilson and her mother at her side.

"Carrie looks lovely," Sara murmured to George as they took their place in the receiving line.

"Yes, she does." George nodded, looking quite dapper himself in his white dinner jacket. "And she seems happy."

"What an amazing house," Natica breathed. "It's nearly as grand as the Vanderbilt's house."

"Perhaps that's the point," Sara said to her daughter. "We both know the Astors prefer to be the pinnacle of the set especially when it comes to competing with Alva."

Mother and daughter smiled discreetly at the jibe while the line moved steadily forward. It took nearly twenty minutes before the three finally reached their hostesses.

"Mr. and Mrs. George Rives," the footman announced. "And Miss Natica Rives."

With a bright smile, Carrie took Sara's hand. "I'm delighted to see you, Sara." Smiling at Natica, she added, "And my goddaughter – you look positively lovely."

"Thank you." Natica blushed. Reveling in the compliment, Natica curtseyed on cue. Her dark brown hair had been braided and woven into a lovely up-do, tiny wisps left to fall over her ears. Her green velvet gown hugged her young curves to significant effect.

"What a fabulous party," Sara proclaimed, offering a curtsey as well. "Hello, Mrs. Astor." Sara curtseyed again for the matriarch. "It's lovely to see you again."

Though regally dressed, the years were showing on the woman's wrinkled face, and Sara thought she looked weary. The rather obvious wig was styled in a mode that seemed too young for her aging complexion, adding to her drawn appearance. Adorned with a treasury of diamonds, the jewels appeared to weigh on Mrs. Astor's aging frame.

"Hello, Sara." Mrs. Astor smiled. "Welcome, Mr. Rives." With a fond eye, she turned to Natica. "What a beautiful belle you've grown to be."

"Thank you," Natica said modestly, her chestnut eyes brilliant in the lamplight.

George bowed elegantly to the hostesses. "The house is quite spectacular! You must be pleased with the results." He could be very charming in these situations, a skill developed from his years in politics.

"I assure you, I am." Carrie sighed. "One has no idea the extent of work involved in building such a place until you've been through it." In an aside to Sara, she whispered, "Never again."

The two chuckled at her admission like the old friends they were.

"Tonight, I am more than ready to mark the completion of such an undertaking," Carrie announced. "We've planned a wonderful celebration, including a lovely musical program in the main hall, followed by supper in the dining room."

"We're looking forward to it," Sara said, noting the growing receiving line. "Well, we won't detain you any longer."

"You must join us for a private luncheon to afford us more time to catch up." Mrs. Astor offered, "You must come as well, Natica."

"That would be lovely," Sara readily agreed.

"We'll set a date," Carrie promised. "In the meantime, please enjoy a glass of champagne and hors d'oeuvres until the recital begins. The footman will lead you to the ballroom."

"Thank you." Sara smiled, giving the women a final curtsey.

The footman led them down a back staircase, equally as grand as the front, delivering them to a vast white and gold ballroom. Passing by walls lined with mirrors in keeping with the French decor, the footman escorted them to their table.

Taking their seats, the sound of the musicians tuning instruments reached them as it drifted through the hall. Sara noticed Natica wave to a friend seated nearby, then the girl grew quiet.

Following her daughter's line of vision, Sara caught sight of a young gentleman. Handsome and refined, he bowed his head, acknowledging Natica with a smile.

"I believe you have an admirer," Sara whispered.

Spinning to face her mother, Natica's cheeks went pink with embarrassment. "I suppose I do."

It was unusual for Natica to be so demure. Sara decided she'd better check into the identity of the young man who had obviously found favor with her impetuous daughter. It was her duty to make sure only the most eligible bachelors found their way into Natica's heart.

Chapter Thirty

Nine months later
October 27, 1904
Newport, Rhode Island

The cool autumn air hinted at winter as it blew the sailboat across the Newport Harbor. Natica pulled the thick wool coat snugly around her for warmth while looking out over the vastness of the sea. The sun had just slipped below the horizon, the sky turning a bright fire-orange. Brilliant hues reflected off the water in a sparkling palette of sunset color.

"It's going to get cold fast now that the sun has set," Jonathan Post shouted. Tall and muscular from long hours on his sailboat, Jonathan wore a denim bucket cap over his sandy-brown locks. Calling to the gentlemen, he instructed them to hoist the sails so they could catch a stronger wind.

"How long will it take to get to Rose Island?" Natica asked Cynthia.

"Oh, it should take less than an hour," she answered, her eyes beaming with fun from under a satin bonnet.

Eight daring teenagers had plotted together for the evening sail to the lighthouse and abandoned fort, reportedly haunted, said the locals. Arthur and Will Burden, along with Michael Vincente, had persuaded Jonathan to let them use his sailboat. The ladies, although a bit cautious about being on the island after dark, decided after a lengthy debate that it would be a harmless, albeit spooky escapade.

The journey to Rose Island was less than a mile, and the friends were looking for a bit of Halloween fun. Throwing caution to the wind, Natica, Cynthia, Evelyn Blight, and Gwen had climbed in the boat with the gents just before sunset.

"We'll be there in twenty minutes," Michael told her, overhearing the question. "Just in time for dark."

"You're not scared, are you?" Jon taunted, tying down the rope from the mainsail.

"No. We're not scared." Evelyn smirked. "There's no such thing as ghosts." Taller than the other ladies, Evelyn was strong and more daring than most her age.

"No such things as ghosts, eh?" Michael cocked his head, a tendril of hair falling over his eyes. "You just keep telling yourself that."

"Don't worry," Arthur assured them, puffing up his chest. "We'll protect you."

"That's what I was worried about," Natica ribbed sarcastically, causing the ladies to burst into tittering laughter.

The sailboat made good time in the night wind, and soon they pulled up to the old dock on the far side of the island. They didn't want the keeper currently living in the lighthouse to notice them, as he'd be sure to chase them back to Newport.

An eerie mist was rising from the ground. Blending with the sea fog, it swirled and settled over the island brush as, one by one, the teenagers climbed onshore. The men unloaded the lanterns they'd packed, then torched them to life with a match. Fooling around and flirting, the young people laughed amongst themselves as they headed down the worn path toward the half-finished remnants of Fort Hamilton.

The construction of Fort Adams had made a garrison on Rose Island unnecessary, and the project had been abandoned half-finished, leaving shadowy walls and rooms left to decay in the elements.

"We'd better not let old man Curtis see us out here," Jon said in a low voice, referring to the lighthouse keeper. "Or he'll chase us out faster than a brush fire."

The lighthouse suddenly ignited with a flash, ready for the night's duty, and the group instinctively crouched behind the bushes, growing silent. Wind rustled through the grass, and after a moment, they realized they hadn't been spotted. Rising from the cover of the hedges, the friends continued their walk to the old citadel, enjoying their Halloween mischief.

Will found a spot hidden from view behind two crumbling walls of the fort. "Why don't we build a little fire here?"

"That sounds good." Michael kicked at some wood with his leather boot. "Curtis won't see it from here." Catching Natica's eye, he added, "We should tell ghost stories. Maybe that will bring the spooks out."

Cynthia laughed nervously at the idea and stepped closer to Arthur. "Will you protect me?" she asked coquettishly.

"Of course," he murmured, a glint in his eye. "You're perfectly safe with me."

Natica laughed at the obvious come-on, watching the couple openly flirt. She could be mistaken, but it seemed as though Arthur and Cynthia were getting very chummy these days. Natica wouldn't be surprised if there were an engagement announcement just around the bend.

In a few minutes, the men had started a crackling fire while arranging makeshift seats out of blocks and debris for the group to sit on. The young women stepped up to the fire, gathering closer for heat.

"Are you cold?" Will asked Natica, easing his tall frame onto the log next to her.

"No, I'm fine." She smiled, thankful she'd worn a thick coat.

The sunset had long dissolved into a blue-black sky, and stars were growing bright, sparkling overhead.

"I heard the spirit of the last lighthouse keeper still roams the island," Jon told them in a spooky voice. "He sneaks up behind you and..." He jumped at Gwen, who recoiled with a squeal. "He grabs you!" Jon finished with a wide grin. The ladies giggled nervously while the men laughed openly at his shenanigans.

"I've got a story for you," Michael offered, fighting off a laugh as he spoke.

"Oooh..." Gwen urged. "Won't you tell it to us?" She folded her legs under her long skirts and wrapped her arms around her knees.

Nodding, Michael began his tale in a mysterious voice. "Once upon a time, the fort here on Rose Island housed a small garrison of military men to overlook the storage of artillery stockpiles. Many had left sweethearts behind on the mainland when they'd entered military duty. One soldier missed his betrothed tremendously. At night, in the primitive conditions of the island, he yearned for her even more. Unable to endure another day without his beloved, he decided to sneak off the island after dark and steal an evening with his lady."

"Like we did?" Natica asked mischievously. She noticed Jonathan pull out a flask and take a long swig from the bottle.

"Exactly like we did," Michael confirmed, his face animated. "But before he could row the boat away from the dock, he was spotted by a soldier on night watch who mistakenly thought he was a British spy. All the men were supposedly in their barracks, and the watchman, thinking he was protecting the fort from invasion, shot the AWOL solider, who died instantly."

"How dreadful!" Gwen recoiled with a gasp, her eyes wide.

"And so sad!" Cynthia chimed in.

"Indeed, it is a sad tale," Michael said. "And now, it's said the soldier's spirit roams the island for all eternity, trying to get back home to his sweetheart."

"Woooooo..." Arthur waved his arms, mimicking a ghostly moan.

The ladies giggled again, enjoying the tale of phantoms and spirits.

"Very good story," Jonathan complimented, passing the flask around the circle.

"Thank you." Michael made a wide bow in response to his friends' applause.

"I've got another scary tale," Will began in an eerie voice.

The stories continued into the chilly autumn night until the young people tired of their fun and broke off into couples. Arthur and Cynthia strolled into the dilapidated fort hand-in-hand while Will seemed to hover close to Natica. She couldn't help thinking he was a little jealous of Michael's obvious attentions. The two had developed a bit of a rivalry where she was concerned. She liked Will well enough. His family certainly had the wealth and respect of the set, and her mother encouraged her to let him court her. But Natica had felt herself growing more attracted to Michael over the summer. As fall descended on Rhode Island, she caught herself thinking about him often, especially when she was drifting off to sleep at night.

When her mother discovered she was seeing more of Michael than Will, she'd tried to dissuade Natica from getting serious with him. Michael's family was also a respected member of the set but not near as wealthy as the Burdens.

"His father is an astronomy professor at Cornell University," she'd told her mother. *"Michael comes from a most respectable family."*

"I just think you could do better," her mother had insisted.

Perhaps Michael's family was not as financially successful as her mother would have wished. Regardless, it was her life, and at the present moment, Natica was growing more enamored with the handsome Michael.

The fire crackled, sending sparks into the smoky air. Evelyn seemed interested in Will's affection and moved over to sit beside him on the log. Timidly, she asked, "Do you believe in ghosts?"

Her efforts to divert the young man away from Natica were successful, and Will and Evelyn became engaged in their own conversation. Jonathan and Gwen chatted beside them near the fire. Michael took advantage of the moment and pulled Natica up from her seat with a tug of his hand.

"Let's go explore a little," he coaxed. "Before we head back to town."

Giving him a coy glance, she got up from her makeshift seat. "As long as you'll protect me from the ghost soldier," she said in an alluring tone.

"Oh, I promise you're safe with me," he assured her, smiling.

The two made their way through the remnants of the old buildings as a night wind blew over the island. Natica shivered in the lowering temperatures, the cold of winter edging into the autumn breeze. Michael seemed to notice and boldly put his arm around her in a swift, easy move.

"Sir. Are you taking liberties with me?" Natica challenged, calling him on the move.

"Absolutely." Michael sighed, leading her further behind the tumbling fort, and away from their friends. When they were hidden behind a collapsing wall, he quickly pulled her into his arms.

"Natica..." he whispered. "You're so beautiful." He gently brushed her face with his hand.

At first, she resisted his advances, her upbringing reminding her of a lady's proper conduct. But then, gazing into his handsome eyes in the rising moonlight, she allowed herself to ease into the allure of his embrace. They stood that way for a moment, gazing into one another's eyes, until Michael leaned in and kissed her gently. Natica couldn't help enjoying the softness of his lips.

Pulling away, he assessed her reaction to his daring move. Realizing Natica was open to his advances, he kissed her again — deeper this time.

Natica enjoyed the velvety feel of his lips and escaped into the pleasure he offered, allowing herself to ease into a tighter embrace. She knew it was growing late, and their friends would be missing them, but Natica didn't care. Time stood still for her as she returned Michael's ardent kiss on the dark island. After a few moments they paused, and Michael instinctively took a step back from her – just as Will walked around the corner of the falling structure.

"There you are!" Will shouted, a little annoyed that Michael had managed to get Natica alone. "We're getting ready to head back to Newport. Have you two seen Cynthia and Arthur?"

"No," Natica answered softly, burying her hands into the deep pockets of her coat.

Michael and Natica joined his search for the missing couple, following him between the ruins of the fort.

"There they are." William spotted his brother off in the shadows with Cynthia. "Come on!" he called. "We're heading back."

The couple emerged from the darkness, falling into step with the others.

"Have you seen any ghosts?" Michael asked devilishly.

"Only you, if you don't behave yourself!" Will joked with an offhanded glance his way.

Assembling with the others by the campfire, they gathered up their few belongings.

"Let's get back to the boat," Jon said, kicking out the fire. "It's getting late, and we've got to get these ladies home before their parents discover we're not at the casino dance."

With one last glance around the island, Natica savored her contentment, still warm from Michael's kiss. Falling in line behind Gwen and Evelyn, she discovered both Michael and Will flanking her as the group retraced its steps down the path to the dock.

It was apparent that the young men were competing for her attention, and they continued to do so all the way back to Newport.

A week later
November 3, 1904
Newport, Rhode Island

"Everything is just about done," Sara announced with a sigh. She took a seat on the sofa next to Jane in the library, where she was reading the newspaper and sipping chamomile tea.

"It's the end of another summer season at *Swanhurst*." Jane looked up, reading glasses perched on her long nose. "I still get a little sad when we close the house up."

"I know what you mean," Sara said. "It's like we're packing up our memories."

Pointing at the paper, Jane shook her head in disgust. "Can you believe that woman?"

"Who are you talking about?" Sara leaned over for a closer look at the article Jane was reading.

"Alva, of course," Jane said. She smacked the paper lightly with the back of her hand.

"What's she done, now?" Sara asked. "Other than throwing another extravagant party."

"The caterer is suing her," Jane announced. "He claims Alva is refusing to pay the bill from the last party. Apparently, she was unhappy with his service and wouldn't write him a check."

"That's the most ridiculous thing I've ever heard." Sara frowned. "If the food at Alva's party was anything less than fabulous, everyone would be talking about it. Instead, I've heard only the opposite."

"Me, too." Jane openly scowled. "Alva owes the caterers nearly two hundred dollars. That's nothing to sneeze at."

"With all her money, that's a drop in the bucket."

"But not for the caterer," Jane pointed out. "Alva has more money than she or her heirs could ever spend. She wouldn't be such a tightwad if she had to cook the food herself. She's getting too imperious for her own good."

Sara laughed outright. "Alva, cook?" she asked sarcastically. "I'm sure she doesn't even know how to boil water."

"She'd never refuse to pay her dressmaker," Jane joked. "For fear she'd be wearing last year's fashions."

"Could you imagine the gossip?" Sara chuckled at the thought. "I can see the headline now: 'Wealthy Millionairess Wears Same Dress Twice.'"

"It would be delicious," her sister admitted with a mischievous smile.

"Indeed, it would. It's easy to see why Alva and Oliver are disliked so much, considering the way they treat people so poorly."

"Mother... we're home!" The children's calls echoed through the manor house.

"Mother..." Bayard and Mildred entered the library with Anna.

"We just got back from the park," Mildred announced. Wearing her play dress, her hair was tied up in pigtails that bounced over her ears when she moved.

"Did you have fun?" Sara asked, giving each a hug.

"I went on the sliding board ten times," Mildred said proudly.

"Ten times!" Jane praised. "You must be tired out after all that."

"No, but I'm hungry."

"Me too," Bayard joined in. "I was playing softball with the boys." At fourteen, the youth was lean and muscular. His play clothes were soiled with dirt from the ball field.

"Bridget will get you some lunch," Sara told them. "Cook's been very busy in the kitchen baking ham and macaroni with cheese. Later this afternoon, we're going back to the city. How does that sound?"

"Great!" Bayard cheered. "I love riding the train."

"We're on a schedule." Sara smiled at her son. "So run along and get some lunch."

The boy nodded, then ran off behind Anna and Mildred for his afternoon meal.

Left alone in the library again, Jane folded the paper and set it on the table.

"I suppose that's my cue to get dressed," she announced. Rising from her seat, she headed for her chambers to finish packing.

Six weeks later

December 20, 1904
New York, New York

A fresh snow had fallen over the city, just in time for Christmas. The holiday spirit was evident in the happy mood of New York's residents as they looked forward to the yuletide celebration. The new snow only added to the fervor and excitement.

"I can barely wait till Christmas morning!" Evelyn Blight's nose was red from the cold. "I have all my gifts wrapped and ready, and Mahlon just got in from London. I'm dying to know what he got me."

"I'm sure he bought you a fabulous gift," Natica said, jumping on the toboggan behind her friend. She was buried under layers of cotton and woolen clothes, her hair hidden under a mink hat. "Probably a gorgeous piece of jewelry."

"Oh, that would be wonderful!" Evelyn's eyes took on a dreamy look.

"Hold on tight!" Cynthia called from the front of the sled and pushed off down the hill.

"Wait!" Gwen cried, grabbing onto Evelyn sitting in front of her – and not a moment too soon. The toboggan took off down the slope amidst squeals of delight.

With the holidays fast approaching, everyone was in a celebratory mood. Arthur and Will waited with Jonathan and Michael at the bottom of the knoll in Central Park. The fresh snow had proven irresistible to the friends, who decided to go sledding rather than ice skating.

The toboggan flew to the bottom of the slope, gliding to a smooth stop in front of the waiting men. The young women jumped off, laughing in excitement.

"Have you ladies had enough?" Jonathan asked. He rubbed his cherry-red nose with the back of a leather glove. "Why don't we get some lunch and hot cocoa?"

"That sounds wonderful," Gwen agreed, barely recognizable under layers of wool. "My fingers and toes are getting frostbite."

"Well, we can't have that now, can we?" Jonathan said, his voice frisky.

Michael threw a snowball at Will, and Arthur retaliated. The guys broke into a skirmish while the girls stood off to the side, trying to avoid getting in the line of fire.

"Natica," Cynthia whispered with a wave of her hand. "Come over here."

Following her friend, Natica joined her behind the meager shelter of an old oak trunk that blocked the wind a little.

"What's up?" Natica asked, giving her a questioning glance.

"I've got to tell you the news or I'm simply going to burst!" Cynthia's voice bubbled with excitement.

"Tell me what?" Natica urged. "What's happened?"

"Arthur has proposed to me!" she quietly exclaimed, trying not to let the others hear.

"Oh!" Natica covered a gasp with her fur mitten. "When did this happen?"

"Last night," Cynthia told her. "And both our parents approve. It appears I'm getting married!"

"Congratulations!" Natica squeezed Cynthia's hand. "That's wonderful news. Why all the secrecy?"

"My mother wants to keep it quiet until an announcement can be printed in the paper. Please say you'll be a bridesmaid. I really want you in my wedding."

Natica laughed. "It seems that's become my new vocation. Much to the jest of the set, I'm becoming a professional bridesmaid."

"You could be a bride if you wanted." Cynthia squinted her eyes playfully.

"What do you mean?"

"Don't be so dense." Cynthia scowled. "It's no secret Will adores you. Why don't you marry him, and we'll have a double wedding!"

"You must have lost your mind tobogganing down that hill."

"My faculties are quite fine," Cynthia insisted. "If you'd stop for a minute and think, you'd see that it's true. He's only kept his distance because he's uncertain of your affection for Michael. You should forget about Michael and marry Will," she stated authoritatively, watching Natica for a reaction. "He'll be able to provide you a much better life, and..." she paused for effect, "we can be sisters-in-law!"

"I see you've got things all planned out for us. You must be in cahoots with my mother. She just finished telling me almost the same thing."

"Well, then..." Cynthia gave a sharp nod. "That's because it makes perfect sense."

"What are you two whispering about?" their friends asked, gathering near the tree.

"Are we going for that hot cocoa?" Michael interrupted, his cheeks chapped red from the wind. "Or are we going to stand here in the cold and freeze?"

"Let's go," Jonathan said without waiting, and started for the carriages parked on the street. "I think I may need a little bourbon in my hot chocolate," he shouted to the others as they followed him for cocoa and the warmth of a fire.

Chapter Thirty-One

Three months later
March 17, 1905
New York, New York

In the privacy of her bedchamber, Mrs. Astor riffled through her desk for a fresh piece of stationery. The mid-day sun shone through her wide window, reminding her she had the entire day stretching out before her with no actual plans in place. Moving through her daily routine, she'd dressed in a simple but elegant house-dress, the color of spring leaves, while fighting against a nagging loneliness.

"Perhaps I'll send a few notes," she thought. Writing helped her pass the time, as these days she received few callers. Browsing through her address book, the sound of the rifling paper echoed through the isolation of the lonely room. *"How I miss the old days,"* she thought, reviewing the names in the notebook. *"The fancy parties and the companionship of my friends."* It became evident by the markings and notations in the book that many of the old guard had passed away with the years.

Pushing aside some old letters in the drawer, Mrs. Astor lifted the invitation from her ball in January.

Mrs. Astor

At Home.

January Ninth, Ten O'Clock.

The card was simple, succinct, and to the point, just as she liked it. *"This ball had been wonderful. One of my best."* And yet, she'd become bored by the social frivolities of the evening. Although such activities had occupied her attention for most of her life, nothing was quite the same anymore, yet Mrs. Astor couldn't quite pinpoint exactly what had changed. Glancing at the card again, she remembered her guests' faces, smiling and talking in the ballroom. *"I'd had my quota of merriment for one night,"* she recalled. Quietly leaving the party, she'd retired to her chambers at the early hour of one o'clock, unnoticed by her dancing guests.

With a forlorn grin, Mrs. Astor reflected on the vulgar antics of the set these days. *"Dinner with dogs and monkeys."* She recoiled at the image. *"How gauche! The smell alone should prove offensive."* Pushing away the thought in disdain, she returned her attention to her letter, finishing it with a flourishing signature. Placing her writing supplies back in the drawer, she rose from her desk, shivering, and pulled a woolen shawl over her shoulders.

"Perhaps I'll go down to the library and read for a while. The newspaper should be here by now."

She left her room feeling a bit unsteady and headed down the corridor toward the marble staircase. *"The new house uptown will be ready soon,"* she reflected. *"Perhaps I should install an elevator? I think I'll talk with the architect about adding one."* With her hand on the railing, she trod the steps with care, keenly aware of the limitations placed on her body by age. Halfway down the smooth stone steps, a sharp pain seared her eyes, and she rubbed her forehead with a free hand. The old matriarch wobbled perilously, her vision blurred. Unable to regain her balance, she slipped, falling swiftly to the bottom of the majestic staircase.

Lying prostrate on the cold marble floor, Mrs. Astor's head was covered with sticky, scarlet blood.

"My life can't end like this." Struggling to summon the servants, society's aging queen could only moan, and quickly slipped from consciousness under the palatial foyer of her grand fortress.

Seven months later

October 7, 1905

New York, New York

The opera season was in full swing, and as was usual among society, the performance was always followed by an exquisite ball. Tonight's soiree was at the Waldorf Hotel.

Dressed in the requisite formal attire, George and Sara entered the ballroom along with Natica. A very handsome family, the three turned heads as they moved between the tables.

The hotel was bustling with elegant guests wearing their jewels and finery, and the Rives family greeted friends while proceeding to their reserved seats.

"The theme this year is autumn woodland," Sara noted. "And I must admit, the effect is magical." She took great delight in checking out the florist's creations designed for tonight's soiree.

Each event so far this year had been unique and grand, creating a parade of beautiful and dreamlike environments designed for the party season. Tree branches painted black held an array of colorful faux leaves, creating an enchanting autumn forest. Pumpkins, gourds, and hay bales added to the effect, their musty scent making Sara nostalgic.

"Autumn is my favorite time of year," she told George. "I just love the colors and the scent of the leaves."

"Here's our table," George said with a nod toward the decorations.

Taking a chair beside him, Sara turned her attention to the bevy of dancers headed for the ballroom floor, prompted by the orchestra's new song.

"Natica seems to be enjoying herself," George noted with a glance at the dance floor.

Sara watched as her daughter joined her friends for the cotillion. Natica's rosette-lace dress floated around her in a most alluring way, and a knot of prospective suitors vied for her attention, unnoticed by Natica, as she laughed with the other débutantes.

"I wish she'd dance with William Burden. He's such a good catch." It was no secret Sara preferred the young man as a match for the girl. "I'm getting the distinct impression Michael Vincente wants to monopolize Natica's time. He's claimed frequent dances with her."

"Maybe Michael is just a passing fancy," George said, rubbing his mustache. "If you push her too much, she might do something rash just to spite you."

Sara grimaced at the thought. "I can't help myself," she admitted. "I want her to have a happy life, and sometimes you've got to put practical considerations before affection. She's been out in society for years now and still hasn't decided on a husband."

"She's certainly been a bridesmaid in enough weddings the past couple of seasons," George joked good-naturedly. "Think of it this way. When she finally marries, she'll have had a lot of practice on the precise way to walk down the aisle during the ceremony."

"I would prefer the next time Natica walks down the aisle, she's the bride, not the attendant." Sara frowned at George, and he smiled back.

The Hungarian orchestra finished their song, and the dancers regrouped for the next tune. Sara watched as Mr. Burden escorted Natica onto the ballroom floor. Holding himself straight and tall, Will, in his finely tailored evening clothes, had a powerful presence. Apparently, he'd reserved a space on Natica's dance card after all, much to Sara's relief.

George shook his head, wearing an amused smile. "Well," he said as he got up. "While you decide Natica's fate, I'm going to join the men for a cigar."

"That's fine. And I'm going to visit with Charlotte for a bit." Sara gathered the flounces of her beige taffeta gown and rose from the table. The full skirt of her dress flowed around her ankles, accented with delicate, golden butterfly appliqués; they seemed to flutter as she moved. "I noticed her with Henry sitting across the ballroom. I'll join you back here later."

George nodded and walked off in search of the gentlemen as Sara wove her way through the tables, heading for the other side of the ballroom.

"Sara!"

She glanced back to see Edith sitting at a table with a few women. As she walked over to join them, she couldn't believe her eyes. Edith was chatting with Carrie and their old friend Elizabeth Slater.

"Oh, my goodness!" Sara exclaimed in delight. "This is just like old times."

"Only we're the old ones!" Edith laughed, age crinkling her smile.

"We're not *that* old," Carrie chided, giving Edith a mock frown.

Elizabeth got up from her place and came around to greet Sara with a friendly *La Bise*. The two women stood looking at each other, assessing the changes the years had made in their appearance.

"You're still so beautiful," Elizabeth complimented Sara.

"I could say the same about you!" Sara said as they each took a chair at the table.

"The only one missing is Anita," Carrie said. "I was so sad to hear of her passing."

"Her life ended much too soon," Sara agreed somberly.

The ladies grew quiet thinking of their friend, Anita, and the good times they'd all shared together in their younger days.

"In any event, I'm happy I bumped into all of you," Sara said. "It seems we always just miss each other with our busy schedules."

"I know," Edith agreed. "I've been traveling between France and upstate New York for the past few years working on my novels."

"Tell her your news," Carrie urged. Blonde hair framed her face, rising from the nape of her neck into a high upsweep. "Wait until you hear this!"

"Tell me what?" Sara quizzed, looking back and forth between her friends. "What's happened?"

"Something wonderful," Elizabeth promised. "Tell her, Edith!"

Smiling, Edith announced, "My latest novel is going to be published any day now."

"That's fabulous news!" Sara exclaimed. "You did it!" She clapped her hands together lightly in delight. "What's the title?"

"*The House of Mirth*," Edith announced, proud of her accomplishment. "It was very successful as a serial in *Scribner's*, so the publisher decided to release it as a novel. I'm certain the 'set' will hate it, as I couldn't help indulging myself in a subtle commentary regarding my perception of society."

A laugh escaped Sara. "You? Subtle?"

"It's a blatant comment on the sins of the wealthy." Elizabeth disclosed. "I followed it in the magazine."

"Better be careful," Carrie warned, raising a tiny brow. "Or you'll end up like Ward McAllister: outcast from society." Carrie referred to Mrs. Astor's former escort.

"Since Mr. McAllister committed the unforgivable sin of publishing the names of the Four Hundred in his book," Edith said, "most people have distanced themselves from his company."

"He was an arrogant fool," Carrie stated, barely disguising her distaste for the man. "He seemed to think he'd personally created the rules of propriety after flying around Europe visiting royal courts. His constant criticism of the set became his demise. If McAllister had remained discreet and been satisfied as an escort to my mother, all would have been well."

"He died alone at his club in disgrace," Sara said. "A disgrace he brought on himself, I might add."

"His funeral was well attended," Edith added. "But I think guests came more out of pity than admiration."

Turning to Carrie, Sara asked, "How is your mother? I heard she took a terrible fall in March."

"Yes, she did, and it's been perfectly awful."

"Oh, dear." Sara sighed. "I'd hoped it was nothing serious."

"I'm afraid it was quite serious. She injured her head and has not been the same since. The doctor thinks a stroke caused her fall."

"How very dreadful," Edith said.

"For the most part, she seems as fine as ever. But occasionally, she lapses into episodes straight from the past, addressing friends long gone as if they were sharing tea together. It can be quite disturbing to watch."

"I'm so sorry to hear that," Sara said sympathetically. "Perhaps I should visit. Do you think it will help?"

"I'm not sure." Carrie frowned. "You could try your luck, but don't be surprised if she mistakes you for someone else. Hopefully you'll catch her on a good day."

The discussion was interrupted when a balding butler approached the table with a tray of fresh drinks. The four women each accepted a glass of champagne.

"In spite of Mrs. Astor's hardship..." Sara smiled. "I think the occasion of our reunion tonight deserves a toast."

"I agree." Carrie nodded. "It's been a lifetime since we've all been together."

Chiming their coupe glasses together, the ladies sipped and chatted, delighted to share common memories of the past along with news of their growing families and Edith's work, of course.

"Is that Natica?" Elizabeth asked, glancing at the dance floor. "She's even more beautiful than I'd heard."

"And very headstrong."

"Is she engaged yet?" Carrie asked. "I'm sure she's had a lot of prospects."

"Maybe too many." Sara sighed. "She seems to enjoy being courted more than the idea of marriage."

"How is your son?" Elizabeth asked Carrie, gracefully changing the subject.

"He's a grown man now," Carrie announced with a half-smile. "Marshall Jr. will turn twenty next month. I don't suppose it'll be long before he marries."

"He's definitely at that age." Sara agreed. Turning to Elizabeth, she said, "I've heard you have two children."

"Yes, a son and a daughter. Although I lost an infant son at birth, which broke my heart." A shadow passed over Elizabeth's face. "But I've got two healthy children to keep my mind off the heartache."

"I suppose I'm the only one who is childless," Edith realized. "My writing was much more important to me than the allure of motherhood."

"Children or not, we're all very proud of you," Sara told her fondly.

"I'm sure you've heard William Vanderbilt remarried," Elizabeth mentioned. "Apparently, Anne Rutherford caught his eye."

Sara took pause at the talk of William's marriage. It was only a matter of time before he returned down the aisle. "He doesn't strike me as a man that likes to be alone," she said casually.

"I suppose he grew weary of the young débutantes," Elizabeth suggested.

"Him?" Edith scoffed. "Never. He's probably still carrying on behind Anne's back the way he always did. A leopard doesn't change its spots, you know."

"Agreed," Carrie said in an acerbic tone. "And Oliver Belmont's been very visible, making a name for himself in New York politics. Does it bother you to talk about him?" she asked Sara belatedly.

"Not as much as it used to." Sara shrugged nonchalantly.

"It's easy to understand how he lost the current nomination. I, for one, would never vote for such a scoundrel."

"Nor I." Edith scowled. "But it will make for interesting fodder for my next novel. I hope to have the last word when it comes to Oliver Belmont," she announced to the others.

"How do you propose to do that?" Sara inquired with trepidation.

"As we all know, truth is stranger than fiction," Edith said, her coffee-brown eyes sparking with intrigue. "It's easy enough to change a name to protect the innocent, with a letter missing here or a letter added there. And maybe an off-handed story about a wealthy scoundrel who takes off with a French dancer and abandons his wife."

"Oh no, Edith," Sara worried aloud. She felt mildly concerned about Edith using her experiences with Oliver as inspiration for her novels. But perhaps it would afford her some satisfaction with its commentary on the conduct of her first husband.

"Not to worry, Sara…" Edith leaned in closer to her friend. "But do keep in mind, the pen is mightier than the sword."

⚜

One month later
November 3, 1905
Newport, Rhode Island

A crowd of reporters worked to get closer to the lady equestrians, tablets and pencils in hand. The horse snorted, and Natica patted the animal, working to calm her mount from the chaos surrounding them.

"Miss Rives! Miss Rives!" a bespectacled man wearing a deerstalker hat called to her. "Why have you decided against the side saddle?"

Smiling, Natica turned to him, amused by the stir her ride was causing. "Sir, you try riding on half a saddle and tell me if you find it a stable position to gallop a horse, especially in a fox hunt."

"Yes, but what about the propriety of a woman riding astride?" he countered. "There are many who find it an abomination to the feminine sensibilities."

Laughing outright, Natica climbed atop her horse. Wearing a riding habit of slacks, she easily slid into the cross saddle and grabbed the reins.

"The times are changing, sir, and so are the rules. Women are just as capable of riding the hunt astride as any man. I'm sure you'll find we're not the delicate, helpless creatures we've been made out to be."

"Can you elaborate on your position?" he pressed.

In response, Natica gave a call to her horse and took off across the field, leaving the reporter scribbling furiously on his tablet.

Chapter Thirty-Two

One week later
November 18, 1905
New York, New York

The new Astor mansion on Fifth Avenue was ablaze in electric light as guests were received by the matriarch. The house, decorated in pink and gold, was resplendent in a flourish of hundreds of pink roses displayed in pure gold vases.

Joining Mrs. Astor in the receiving line was her daughter, Mrs. Wilson, keeping a close eye on her mother. Carrie stood adjacent to the guest of honor, Prince Louis of Battenberg. He looked rather daunting; his uniform abundantly adorned with campaign metals arranged in a line across his breast coat, while a gold-fringed sash fell over his shoulder with regal aplomb.

The German prince had enrolled in the British navy, rising through the ranks to admiral. He'd gone on to marry the granddaughter of Queen Victoria, securing his place in both the German and British aristocracy. Tonight's dinner was planned for his benefit, and Mrs. Astor had pulled out all the stops to throw a dinner party fit for a European prince.

Standing on the edge of the receiving line were four lovely débutantes, specially selected to display the poise and beauty of American girls for the prince's benefit. And what a lovely sight they were, each dressed in a different hue gown of the same design. Pink, yellow, green, and blue, they brought youth and beauty to the party in a wispy rainbow of color.

"I understand there are only seventy-nine guests invited." Evelyn Burden whispered to Natica from behind her pink silk fan.

"What about the Four Hundred?"

"Evidently, since Mr. McAllister publicized the set, there's been a change in the list. Many were cut," Mabel Gerry said, leaning into the conversation. "We're quite lucky to be included tonight."

"It's true," Alice Roosevelt added. "The list has been reduced to only seventy-nine. The Four Hundred is a thing of the past." She kept her voice low while her eyes focused forward on the room.

"Clearly, the standards for the set have remained magnificent." Natica pointed out. "This is as close to a European salon as I've ever seen in America. I suppose Mrs. Astor wanted to prove a point in that regard."

"Without question, not that an Astor ball isn't always perfect," Evelyn said. Lowering her fan, she smiled sweetly at a passing guest. "I'm sure the dinner will be superb, with all the proper trappings and accoutrements, not to mention special epicurean delights." Speaking quietly, she watched the guests parading through the queue.

"No doubt." Natica nodded. "Well, ladies, I suppose we've reached a pinnacle with tonight's party. Mrs. Astor has shown us great favor."

"No question about it," Alice agreed.

The whispering came to a halt as a couple approached the prince for introductions. The ladies returned their attention to the duties of receiving guests for the new set of the 'seventy-nine'.

Three months later
February 10, 1906
New York, New York

The reading lamp filtered light onto the history book George was reading as Sara sent the children up to get ready for bed with Anna.

"I'll be in to say goodnight in ten minutes," Sara told them, herding the children toward the stairs.

"Can't we stay up later than nine o'clock?" Mildred pleaded, while pulling the ribbons from her hair. "I'm twelve years old now, and I don't need a nanny."

"I couldn't agree more, Mother," Bayard complained heartily. The boy was becoming a young man, recently celebrating his fifteenth birthday. Taller now than Sara, he very much resembled his father.

"I'll be the judge of that," Sara told them with a pat on their backs. "Now go upstairs and get ready for bed. You've got classes early tomorrow, and you need to get your rest."

"Okay," they groaned in unison. Surrendering to their mother's instructions, the two headed to the second floor, whispering to each other.

Walking back to the parlor, Sara sat in the chair next to George. "They're getting to the age where they resist my authority." She sighed.

Wearing a smoking jacket, he relaxed in the overstuffed chair. "What child doesn't? Be happy they're normal," he told her, glancing over his book.

She smiled back at him as Bridget entered the room carrying a calling card. "You have a guest," she announced, smoothing the front of her apron. "Mr. William Burden would like to speak with you."

George took the card and shot Sara a puzzled glance. She just shrugged, somewhat curious about the young man's visit.

"Show him in," George instructed with an easy smile. A minute later, Will stepped into the warm parlor, removing his bowler hat.

"Good evening Mr. and Mrs. Rives. I hope I'm not intruding," he apologized. His heavy topcoat was speckled with snow flurries; he removed it and handed it to Bridget, along with his hat.

"Not at all, Will," Sara welcomed him. "Please have a seat." She motioned to the sofa. "Can we get you some refreshments?"

"No, thank you, ma'am," he replied nervously. "I won't take up much of your time."

"To what do we owe the honor of this visit?" George asked. "Nothing serious, I hope."

"No, nothing serious." William smiled quickly. "My family is doing fine, and my mother sends her greetings."

"Tell her we said hello," Sara replied. "We'll have to invite them to dinner one night soon."

"I'm sure she'd like that." The young man nodded, growing silent.

Sara and George waited expectantly for him to speak. He obviously had something on his mind, but he seemed hesitant to begin.

"I've come about Natica," he said abruptly. "As you know, I've been courting her."

"Yes." Sara's eyes were warm. "She seems fond of you."

"And I am very fond of her." William sat forward with sudden confidence. "Fond enough to ask for your permission to marry her. That's why I've come tonight," he admitted. "I would be honored if you'd give me your blessing."

George threw a quick glance at Sara, who tried to remain nonchalant.

"Does Natica know you're here?" Sara asked quietly.

"No." Will grinned sheepishly. "I wanted to talk with you first. St. Valentine's Day is almost here, and I thought I'd invite her out for a private dinner before going to the Coaching Club dance. And since it's Cupid's favorite day, I wanted to propose marriage. But not without speaking with you first, of course."

Sara gave the young man a pleasant smile. George caught her eye, and she signaled with an imperceptible nod. Sara recalled Henry Havemeyer had acted much the same way when he'd come about marrying Charlotte. Like a stage performance with a well-rehearsed script, the words and the sentiment were the same.

"This is a bit unexpected..." George began. "But Mrs. Rives and I both think the world of you. We'd be delighted to have you in our family."

Relief flashed on Will's face as he broke into a wide smile. "That's wonderful. I was hoping you'd approve."

"Of course, Natica is the one to ask," George pointed out.

"Yes, of course, she is." Will nodded quickly. "But she'd make me the happiest man in the world if she agreed to marry me."

He got up from his seat and gave them a tiny bow. "I'll not take up any more of your time." He walked over and shook George's hand.

"Take care of yourself, young man." George smiled. "And good luck with your proposal."

"Thank you, sir," Will said, preparing to leave. "Have a good evening, Mrs. Rives."

"Good evening, William," she replied.

Bridget magically appeared in the parlor holding Will's coat and hat and led him to the front foyer.

"Well..." George stated the obvious after he left. "This shall either be very good news or very sad news for Natica, depending on her feelings for the young man."

"I think it's wonderful news," Sara said with a broad smile. "I'm glad he finally decided to make his move. The Burdens are a very respected – and wealthy family. Natica's lucky to have won his affection."

"This may be true, but remember, Sara, you're not the one marrying the young man."

"I understand." She folded her hands under her chin. "But as her mother, I still have a say in matters pertaining to her future."

"I'm almost afraid to ask what that means." George gave her a suspicious glance and returned to his history book.

"I'm going to say good night to the children," Sara announced absently, lost in her thoughts.

Leaving the parlor, she headed for the steps to the second floor, all the while mulling the ways she would convince Natica of her good fortune.

Two months later
April 9, 1906
New York, New York

The city was chilly today. The afternoon sun struggled to break through springtime storm clouds with little success. A harsh wind blew through the streets with gusts that spoke of passing winter days in spite of the April date.

"Have you given William an answer to his proposal yet?" Sara asked her daughter. She patted a napkin over her lips and placed it on the table beside her empty lunch plate. The maid quickly took the plate and returned to the kitchen.

The two had just arrived back in New York after spending a few weeks in Paris – and Natica still had no plans for marriage. At twenty-three, the girl remained a favorite among the eligible bachelors, but Sara was growing concerned at her daughter's resistance to matrimony.

The trip to Europe had been Sara's decision, made in an effort to separate Natica from Michael Vincente.

"How nice to find the Burdens were also in France," Sara said. "It gave us a chance to visit." She couldn't help indulging in a bit of matchmaking where her daughter was concerned. Sara had hoped the absence of Michael would make the girl focus her attention on Will, who clearly adored Natica. He was patiently waiting for an answer to his marriage proposal.

Natica set her napkin on the table, evading her mother's eyes. She'd been trying to avoid this conversation for weeks. *"Is it too much to hope that Michael would offer a proposal of his own?"* she wondered. Which, she silently affirmed, she would quickly accept. Lately, she'd been troubled as Michael seemed to keep his distance from her. Natica wasn't sure if she'd offended him or if another débutante had caught his eye.

"No," Natica said simply. "I haven't given Will an answer yet. Isn't it enough that I danced with him every night in Paris?"

"I suppose, unless you're leading him on," Sara admonished. "May I ask what you're waiting for? Will is a great catch, and you shouldn't keep him hanging. He might find another to take your place if you hesitate too long."

"What if I decide I don't want to marry him?" Natica asked her mother curtly. "Or to marry anyone – ever?"

Sara's shocked expression told all. "You can't be serious? What you're proposing is a lifetime of solitude as a spinster on the fringes of society. Or perhaps you'd like to join a convent and become a nun?" She fought the impatience rising in her voice.

"I'm perfectly serious, Mother," Natica said firmly, her amber eyes kindling with indignation. "Marriage is a lifetime commitment, and I don't want to find myself trapped with a man that makes me unhappy."

"There are ups and downs in every marriage," Sara pointed out sharply. "Just as there are in life. A couple must make a promise to work through the hard times. Then, together, they reap the benefit of the joys they share. Will is devoted to you, and he wants to make you happy. I don't see why you keep focusing on the possibility of divorce."

"Don't you, Mother?" Natica fought her anger, threatening to burst like a bomb on a battlefield.

Sara looked at her daughter, confused and angered by her nonchalant attitude toward Will's proposal.

Biting her lip, Natica fought back her words. Should she confront her mother about the scandalous divorce that had terminated her first marriage to Mr. Belmont?

In a tone of authority, Sara continued. "I suggest you accept Will's engagement. Today is not soon enough. You've been leaving him hanging since February."

"I'm done with this conversation." Natica got up from the dining room table to escape the argument, but Sara followed her daughter into the sitting room.

"Don't walk away from me, young lady!" Sara ordered, confronting Natica in the gloomy light. "Do you think you'll always be a young débutante with men clamoring for your attention? If you're not careful, you'll wind up with no suitors at all."

Coming to a halt, Natica turned to her mother in a wave of fury. "You cannot order me to marry Will Burden – or any man for that matter. It's my life and my decision."

"That may be true, but I have many more years of experience. Besides, I'm certainly entitled to my opinion," her mother declared harshly. "There are many considerations for a good marriage, and you can do no better than marrying into the Burden family."

"I like Will just fine, but that doesn't mean I what to *marry* him. Besides, what if my heart belongs to another?" Natica snapped. She stepped further into the parlor, distancing herself from her mother.

"Do you really imagine you're the first woman to think she's in love?" Sara shook her head in frustration. "Or that being in love will make your life or marriage any easier?"

"I suppose that's where we differ in our opinions!" Natica shouted. Walking to the foyer, she headed for the staircase. "*I* think marriage should be about love. *You* think marriage should be about money and social status, with love as an afterthought." Her emotions got the best of her, and in a furious voice she asked: "How did that work out for you, Mother? And your little loving marriage to Oliver Belmont? That certainly brought you years of happiness."

Sara recoiled in shock, offended by words that hit like shrapnel, splintering her senses. "What do you know about such matters?"

"I know a lot more than you think!" Natica spat. "Do you really think you could hide such a scandal from me? When were you going to tell me that Oliver Belmont is my father? My *real* father?"

"I don't care what you think you know. It takes more than paternity to make a father. Oliver abandoned you. He doesn't deserve to be your father or to have any contact with you."

"I'm an adult now, and that's *my* choice." She shot her mother a furious look. "Because of your past, and your divorce, I don't belong to *any* family. I'm not a Rives. I'm not a Whiting. And I'm not a Belmont, either! Who am I Mother?" she demanded in a loud bellow. Catching her breath, she composed herself, then announced in an even voice, "Whether or not I speak with Oliver Belmont is *my* decision. Not yours!"

"That's where you're wrong," Sara ruled, adamant. "As long as you're living in my house, I'll make sure you don't make the same mistakes I did at your age. And that's why I strongly suggest you marry William Burden!"

"Or what?" Natica taunted. "Are you going to lock yourself in your bedroom and refuse to eat? Or perhaps threaten suicide like Alva did until Consuelo agreed to marry the Duke? I thought you had more character than that!"

Natica's words stung Sara with the pain of a hundred wasps. Yet, in the throes of her temper, Sara suddenly and clearly grasped Alva's motivation to go to such extreme lengths for the sake of the family.

"How dare you speak to me that way!" Sara frowned at Natica, while toiling to recognize her own daughter beneath the fury of her verbal onslaught. "It's almost the start of the summer social season. If you're not careful another lovely lady may come and steal Will right out from under you. How will you feel then, Natica?"

Hot tears began to flow down the girl's face. "Please..." she begged through sobs. "Don't rush me into something I'm not ready for."

"When exactly will you be ready?" Sara asked crisply. "You'd do well to think long and hard about accepting Will's proposal – and the sooner the better."

With a heavy bawl Natica turned and ran up the stairs, disappearing into the depths of the house. Sara walked back to the parlor, trembling from the harshness of their confrontation. She'd resented her own mother meddling in her affairs, but Natica was far more headstrong than she had ever been!

"Well... That did not go very well, but I had to say *something*," Sara murmured. "Before it's too late."

Chapter Thirty-Three

Ten days later
April 19, 1906
New York, New York

The lovely warm day delivered the promise of spring, with dogwood and crabapple trees broadcasting a gorgeous display of pink and white blossoms over the streets of New York. Fallen flowers left a trail of color on the sidewalks, and George looked forward to summer as he trekked through the petals littering the path.

"Papers! Get your papers here." the newsboy called above the noisy avenue. His black knickers were held up with green suspenders, one falling from his shoulder haphazardly as he shouted. "Extra, extra! Earthquake strikes San Francisco! Read all about it!"

A small group clustered around the boy as George walked up, anxious to read the news. Throwing the youth a coin, George grabbed the newspaper from him, and stared at the headline.

"Good heavens," he whispered. Reading on, the article revealed over seven hundred people were dead, and the count was expected to rise. Fires were raging through San Francisco, and many people were still missing. "This is horrible," George said, watching the news whip through the crowd.

Another voice shouted from across the street doing battle with the newsboy's chant. A distinguished gentleman in a three-piece suit wore a signboard that read 'Return to the Bible'.

"Repent now, sinners!" he yelled to anyone within earshot. "The rapture is upon us!" His urgent bellow continued without pause. "Repent! Repent before your soul is lost and left behind!"

Tucking the paper under his arm, George turned away, continuing the short walk home. But his enjoyment for the beautiful spring day was squelched by the ranting of the religious zealot and the sad news from California.

～ ⚜ ～

Two days later
April 20, 1906
New York, New York

The quaint café was located off Madison Avenue, a favorite place for locals who appreciated specialty coffee drinks. Natica enjoyed the espresso as it was the best outside of Paris.

When Anna came to Natica's chambers to help her dress this morning, she'd delivered a letter sent to *Swanhurst* by Michael Vincente, inviting her to meet him for coffee. Sending a response confirming the time, Natica gave special thought to her outfit today. Perusing her wardrobe in the armoire, she chose a flowing navy-blue skirt and a high-necked lace blouse. Catching her appearance in the full-length mirror, she approved, thinking the attire gave her a casual, yet attractive, look. Finishing it off with a wide-brimmed hat, she left her bedchamber and headed for the café.

"His note sounded important," Natica thought, as she left the house on schedule for their rendezvous. There was a lightness in her step as she entered the coffee shop, looking forward to spending time with the man who'd captured her affection.

"Hello, stranger," Michael greeted her from a table in the corner. With a wave, he summoned Natica to join him. "Finally back from Paris, I see."

"Yes." Natica gave him her most dazzling smile. "My mother thought it best to spend time with the European set."

"Did you have a nice trip?" he asked, his wavy brown hair falling over his forehead in a most endearing manner.

"Nice enough, but the parties can become tiresome. How about you?"

"It was lively around here. New York is the city that never sleeps. There is always something happening." Growing serious, he met her eye. "But I didn't ask you here to talk about the social season."

"Oh? Then why did you ask to meet me, Michael?" Her heart fluttered in anticipation, anxious to hear the words she'd dreamt of. Dare she hope he was finally going to bring up marriage?

Shifting on the wooden chair, he grew uncomfortable. "I know we've shared some special moments together." He paused, his demeanor growing serious. "But I thought you should hear it from me. I mean..." He stuttered, "I didn't want you to hear from someone else."

"Hear what? Have I missed out on some news?"

"Natica, I heard William Burden proposed marriage and I was certain your parents approved, especially after they took you off to Paris. It's no secret my family is respected, but we don't have the wealth enjoyed by most in the set." He fiddled with his coffee cup and grimaced. "There's no way I can compete with the Burden family. I felt certain your parents dissuaded you from our growing fondness."

"My parents can't dictate who I'll marry," Natica said, straightening in her chair. "Even if they think they can, I won't have it."

"Regardless." He fidgeted. "You should know, I'm engaged to Miss Potter now."

His words sunk into her mind, and she faltered. Natica could not have been more shocked if he'd slapped her across the face. Catching her breath, she quickly regained her composure, and smiled lightly. She didn't want Michael to know how badly the news hurt. Her heart ached, but she remained seemingly calm to any casual observer.

"Well then, I suppose congratulations are in order." She forced a smile.

Releasing a pent-up sigh, Michael offered her a weak grin. "I wasn't sure how you'd react to the news."

"I'm very happy for you both," she lied. "Well – now that you and Miss Potter are betrothed..." Rising from the seat, Natica grabbed her handbag. "It's clear we have nothing more to say to each other. Good day, Michael. I wish you well."

"Natica, wait..." Michael called after her, but she was already out the door of the café, without ever having enjoyed an espresso.

Six weeks later

June 11, 1906
New York, New York

There wasn't an empty pew in all of Grace Church. The church overflowed with lilies and daisies, perched in large vases at the altar and tied to the pews for added accents. The New York house of worship was filled with elite witnesses present for the nuptials of Arthur Burden and Cynthia Roche.

The bridesmaids would lead the procession two by two, unaccompanied by the ushers, who stood in a line with the groom at the front of the church. Taking her place beside her cousin, Evelyn Parson, Natica stood tall, holding her bouquet, ready for the ceremony to start. Catching herself daydreaming, she focused on the flurry of activity going on around her. Cynthia made a lovely bride in her exquisite gown and antique lace veil, and she was clearly jubilant to be marrying Mr. Burden today.

Smiling sweetly, Natica kept up her performance of happiness for the couple, but she felt no true joy today. Her heart had been broken by Michael, though she realized it wasn't really his fault. *"If we'd only been allowed to court without all the propriety of dowries and family pedigree,"* she thought. *"I know we could have found a lifetime of happiness."*

But that wasn't going to happen now. Michael's marriage to Miss Potter had been announced in the papers. *"Clearly,"* she decided to herself, *"It's time to focus on my own future."*

Pondering William's marriage proposal, she had come to terms with the reality of the union, deciding to accept his offer. Cynthia and she would be sisters-in-law, and life would go on as it always had, cradled in the luxurious life of America's aristocracy.

The organ began to play the Bridal March, and Evelyn turned to her. "We're first. Are you ready?"

"Yes." Natica nodded, taking her place beside Evelyn. Step by measured step they moved down the center aisle of the church, while Natica smiled freely at the guests attending today's nuptials.

Five months later
November 1, 1906
New York, New York

The butler delivered the folios to Mrs. Astor in the parlor as requested, listing the Astor inventory of dinnerware. Thomas Hade had been her trusted servant since 1876 and had assisted his employer over the years in choosing the perfect china and silver service for her dinner parties and balls.

"As you requested, ma'am," he said, placing the folios on the tea table beside her.

"Oh wonderful, Hade." Mrs. Astor smiled, reaching for the books. Her gray hair was pulled back in a tight bun, and she wore no jewelry, except for her diamond wedding ring, which she continued to wear regardless of Mr. Astor's passing many years previous. "I'm planning a huge opera ball, and everything must be perfect."

"Of course, ma'am." He helped her peruse the inventory, going through the pages of the catalogue with her.

"I think I'll use this pattern." She pointed to the picture. "The same as when Prince Battenberg visited." She smiled at the servant. "This gold set has always been a favorite. I'll have to use the matching gold utensils. Nothing really speaks of affluence the way that gold does, don't you think?"

"Of course, madam." Making a notation in a tablet, the butler went through the party preparations with Mrs. Astor as he had many times over the past thirty years. Sadly, he listened while the old woman chatted on about the guest list, making certain August and Caroline Belmont were sent an invitation. Mr. Hade knew full well Mr. and Mrs. Belmont had both passed away years before, but made no mention of this to the confused matriarch.

Mrs. Astor's dementia had grown more severe, and she talked as though it was 1880 again, the height of her reign over society. The family, specifically Mrs. Wilson, had instructed the butler to carry on as always with the intention of keeping her mother appeased in her elderly years.

"But do not follow through with any of her plans," Carrie had ordered Mr. Hade. "I'm afraid there will be no more dinner parties or balls with Mrs. Astor in such a condition."

"This will do nicely," Mrs. Astor said, pointing to the set of gold tableware in the inventory book. Looking up, she smiled at the butler. "Make sure everything is made ready as the dinner is Friday. Have the invitations been sent?"

"Yes, ma'am."

"Very good. That will be all for now, Thomas. We'll work on the menu tomorrow."

"Yes, ma'am." Taking up the catalogues, the butler bowed and left the sitting room, his heart filled with a deep melancholy.

One month later
December 8, 1906
Lakewood, New Jersey

The nurse came over to the bed and removed the thermometer from Natica's mouth.

"Your temperature is normal, miss. Are you feeling any better today?" The nurse, Lillian Wade, had come highly recommended. Recently hired by the Rives family, she'd accompanied Natica to the spa at the Lakewood Hotel.

"A bit," Natica lied, feeling as listless as ever. She pushed herself up in bed while the nurse plumped the pillows.

"Why don't I open the curtains?" Wade offered. Walking to the window, she pulled the draperies wide. "It's much too gloomy in here."

Watching her efforts, Natica caught the view outside of an overcast sky. Dark winter clouds hovered over Lakewood like a specter, and that suited her mood just fine.

"Can I get you anything?" the nurse asked, handing her a glass of water.

The doctor diagnosed the girl with a new ailment called 'New Yorkitis.' Just exactly what type of illness 'New Yorkitis' was seemed unclear to the nurse. In her professional opinion, the young lady seemed to be suffering more from a mental malady rather than a physical one. The stress of living in the modern and bustling metropolis was blamed for her illness. Still, as she surveyed the young woman in bed, her aptitude and experience caused her to think the actual malady plaguing Natica was simple melancholy.

"No, thank you." Natica smiled at the woman standing over the bed. "I think I'm going to try to nap before I go down for my hydrotherapy treatment."

"That sounds like a good idea," the nurse agreed. "Your appointment isn't for a few hours." Pulling the blankets over her charge she asked, "Do you think you'll be okay for a bit? I was going to dash over to the pharmacy and fill your prescription. It won't take long."

As Natica had been unable to sleep well the past few nights, the doctor had prescribed her an awful-tasting elixir to cure the problem. "That's fine." She waved her away, anxious for some privacy. "You go ahead while I nap."

Grabbing her cloak from the coat stand near the door, Miss Wade nodded. "Okay, then. I won't be more than a half-hour. If you need anything before I return, ring the front desk."

"I'll be fine," Natica assured her, watching the nurse leave the suite. The room fell quiet except for the sound of the wind buffeting against the windowpane. Outside, she could hear crows squawking in the nearby oak trees.

Natica turned on her side working to get comfortable, when her thoughts returned to the upcoming year. *"Christmas will be here in a few weeks,"* she thought. But try as she might, Natica couldn't seem to get into a holiday mood. William and she had announced their engagement right after Thanksgiving but had asked their families for some time before they publicly disclosed the news to society in the papers.

"And so I can adjust to the idea myself."

Her mother had been very pleased to hear that Natica had accepted William's proposal, convinced their argument had prompted the decision. No one knew the real reason she'd accepted the proposal, except perhaps, Michael Vincente, who had indeed married Miss Potter in a quiet wedding last week.

"Maybe my mother was right. Maybe Michael was never as fond of me as I imagined." Ultimately, she'd decided her attraction to Michael was nothing more than a schoolgirl's infatuation, and she'd pushed all thoughts of him aside in favor of a more mature relationship with Will.

"Will's family is certainly in favor of the marriage," she said softly, thinking how Mr. and Mrs. Burden had eagerly embraced the match. There had been a private engagement dinner at the Rives' New York home, and as winter set in, Natica warmed to the idea of building a life with Will.

And yet, as the days drifted by, her energy seemed to wane. *"I'm not feeling well,"* Natica had told her maid. Taking to her bed, she remained there day after day, a sense of despondency settling over her. Growing lethargic, Natica eventually succumbed to illness.

Her mother had called the family doctor who'd diagnosed a terrible case of 'New Yorkitis'. He'd suggested Natica be sent to the spa for some rest and water treatments, which were proving to be a very successful cure for the malady.

She picked up a framed photo of Will sitting on her bed stand. *"He's very handsome,"* she thought, running a fingertip over the frame.

"William is sweet," Natica whispered. "He'll be a good husband to me, and I'll never want for a single thing."

She couldn't help but feel flattered at the way he'd returned to her, determined to get an answer to his proposal. He'd grown particularly insistent after Cynthia had married his brother, Arthur. Natica had once again filled the role of bridesmaid for her friend, and again for Evelyn Blight and Mahlon in October. Watching all her friends marry, her mother's words of caution had started to glare at her with truth. Cynthia and Arthur seemed so happy, so why should she think marriage to Will would deliver her anything less?

"He adores me," Natica said softly, staring at the photograph, and she knew it was true. And she was falling for him as well. Maybe, in time, she'd learn to love him back in equal measure.

The door to the suite opened and Miss Wade walked in carrying a paper sack and a large floral box.

"You've had a delivery," she announced.

Walking to the bed, she set the box on Natica's lap. Removing a dark-brown bottle from the bag, the nurse read the instructions on the label and went to the kitchenette for a spoon.

Untying the red ribbon on the box, Natica lifted the lid, and was greeted with the delightful vision of two dozen passion-red *Eternity* roses, their lovely scent quickly emanating through the room.

"These are so beautiful," she cooed, feeling better every minute.

An envelope was nestled among the blooms addressed to her. She pulled out the card and read:

> *Coming to visit next week.*
> *I miss you and hope you're feeling better.*
> *Sending all my love,*
> *Forever yours, William*

"Did you get any rest?" Miss Wade asked. "I know I wasn't gone long."

"Actually, I'm feeling a little better." Natica smiled. Throwing aside the blankets, she sat up on the side of the bed, the ruffles of her lace nightgown sweeping the floor. "I think I'll go down to the restaurant for a light lunch before I head to the spa."

Assessing the sudden rejuvenation, Miss Wade glanced at the roses, then back at Natica. "I think that's a marvelous idea," she said, happy to see her charge improving. "I'll put these in water for you."

"Thank you." Standing, Natica brushed her hair back into a ponytail. "Can you please put them on the nightstand? I want to enjoy their fragrance while I sleep."

"Of course," the nurse answered lightly, watching Natica head to the dressing room.

Chapter Thirty-Four

Five weeks later
January 14, 1907
New York, New York

Gripping the newspaper with unnecessary force, Oliver read the article again. Rumors had been circulating since late last summer; now they appeared to be true.

MISS RIVES ENGAGED
Favorite of Mrs. Astor to Marry W.D. Burden
Tells it at Lakewood.
Special to The New York Times

LAKEWOOD, N.J., Jan 13 – Announcement was made to their intimate friends here to-day of the engagement of Miss Natica Rives, daughter of Mr. and Mrs. George L. Rives, to W. D. Burden, son of Mr. and Mrs. James A. Burden. Miss Rives is taking the baths at the Lakewood Hotel, and her fiancé came down by automobile on Friday to spend the weekend. When they returned from an automobile ride this evening both smilingly admitted the truth of the report.

"Yes, we had intended to make a formal announcement when we returned to New York," said Miss Rives, "but the news is out now. It's true."

Miss Rives is one of Mrs. Astor's favorites in the younger set. Her fiancé is a brother of Arthur Scott Burden, who recently married Miss Cynthia Roche. Miss Rives broke down as a result of too active participation in social affairs last summer and was quite ill for several weeks. She came to Lakewood to recuperate and has been taking the 'water cure' treatment to which John D. Rockefeller and I.H. Harriman submitted last season. She will return to New York next week.

Oliver glared at the newspaper. "Daughter of Mr. and Mrs. Rives, indeed," he fumed. His hand had been forced when he and his family had disowned the girl, and now, as she prepared to marry, he found it a bitter pill to swallow.

A very bitter pill indeed.

"I know you want to go to her wedding, Oliver." Alva had written in her most recent letter from England. *"But her family will never allow it. Why don't you come to London and visit Consuelo and me? It will probably be best if you just leave New York behind during the nuptials."*

"Perhaps she's right," he sadly conceded, finally laying the paper aside.

———※———

One month later
February 8, 1907
New York, New York

The crackling fire lent a cozy warmth to the Rives' parlor. Roses, delivered earlier to Natica, sat in full display, arranged in a cut-crystal vase sitting on the coffee table.

"Thank you so much for the flowers." Natica smiled, her eyes shimmering in the firelight. "I can tell you've discovered my weak spot for roses."

"I plan on sending them every day." Will chuckled. "In fact, I'll plant you your very own rose garden, if you'd like."

Laughing, Natica caught his eye. "You spoil me."

"Perhaps." He grinned. "But I take it as my personal responsibility to do so. In fact, I have another gift for you."

"Oh? Do tell." Natica leaned toward him expectantly. "Please, don't leave me in suspense."

Enjoying the tease, Will rose from the divan and walked back to the foyer. He returned carrying a rather large box, the lid slightly ajar.

"You'd better hurry and open it," Will advised. "Or the surprise might be spoiled."

He set the box on the divan beside Natica. Lifting the top, she saw a tiny bundle of white fur. A Pomeranian puppy gazed at her with adoring brown eyes.

"Oh!" Natica's face lit up. "How adorable!"

As she lifted the puppy from the box, it licked her nose, wagging its tail with unrestrained exuberance. Natica broke into happy smiles. "I love him! It *is* a boy, isn't it?"

"Yes, a little boy – and it looks like he's quite fond of you, too. Of course, he's going to need a name."

She considered for a moment, then an idea popped into her mind. "Snickers! I'm going to call him Snickers. Oh, Will, what a sweet gift. Thank you." She planted a light kiss on his cheek.

"I thought he could keep you company. Dogs are said to be man's best friend – and woman's too."

"Well, I certainly hope so," Natica said laughing, while the puppy slathered her with affection.

Sitting down on the divan beside her, Will petted the little rascal, glad to see his gift had brought the reaction he'd hoped for.

⚜

Two months later
April 10, 1907
New York, New York

The inhabitants of New York bustled about the city attending to business, the warm spring weather delivering a welcome end to the dark nights of winter. The Rives and Burden families shared the excitement and preparations of the upcoming nuptials, emphasized by the newspapers, who printed frequent articles about the affair in the society pages.

"It's so unfortunate that Will's father passed away right before the wedding," Sara commiserated with Jane. Sitting at the desk in the drawing room, she was busy finalizing arrangements for the celebration. Reviewing the orders for flowers and the caterer, she checked the guest list one last time. "No one wants to start a marriage under a shroud of mourning."

"I think your decision to have a small reception at home will keep things proper," Jane assured her from an adjacent chair. "How's Natica been feeling?"

"Better, I hear," Sara noted. "She's driving in today from the Hotel Netherland to look in on the preparations, but she's limiting her visits."

Now in her forty-sixth year, Sara retained her loveliness, her complexion showing few wrinkles to betray her age.

"Any idea what's ailing her? I heard she received an anonymous letter that was quite vicious regarding her character."

"Wasn't that terrible! Especially since she's dealing with the recent death of Will's father."

"Who would do such a thing?"

"Natica thinks it's a former secretary she was forced to dismiss. George is over at the Burden home now discussing it with Will."

"Well, I hope the police are able to put an end to it. Rumors are circulating in the papers that Natica's going to postpone the wedding due to illness."

"That's ridiculous. In any event she's said nothing to me." Sara looked up from her paperwork. "I think Natica's just exhausted. She wants to stay at the hotel out of sight of the reporters so she can rest up for next week's wedding."

"I think that's a good idea." Jane nodded. "But you'd think she'd want to have more of a hand in the ceremony. You've been making all the decisions regarding the wedding."

"I don't mind attending to the details while she recuperates," Sara said. "Besides, that's a mother's job, isn't it? I'm happy to do anything I can to help this wedding move forward. Finally, Natica will be starting a new life. She's almost twenty-four, and most of her friends are already married with children."

"We both know you can't put a time limit on marriage," Jane reminded her. "Remember Milly? Who would have thought she'd have become a bride at forty-eight?"

"I certainly don't want Natica to wait until mid-life to marry." A frown crossed Sara's face. "I just hope she recuperates in time for a happy wedding day."

"I'm sure it will be picture perfect."

"Pictures!" Sara jotted in her notes. "I've got to call Bradley Studios and make certain they have the date and time correct for the wedding. Not to mention the location. I don't want them showing up at the wrong church."

"Relax, will you?" Jane begged. "You're starting to make me nervous."

"Sorry," Sara apologized, smiling sheepishly. "I think we'll all rest a little easier once this marriage is a *fait accompli*. I know I will, anyway."

Jane shook her head and chuckled, watching her sister continue to review the details for the fast-approaching wedding day.

"It won't be long now," Jane said, caught up in the anticipation. "One more week and Natica will be a bride."

One week later
April 17, 1907
New York, New York

Her cousin, Evelyn, helped Natica put on the tulle veil, securing it with the diamond hair clips custom-made for the occasion. The exquisite hairpiece cascaded in coronet fashion down the side of her veil in a glitter of jewels.

"You look absolutely beautiful," Evelyn told her, serving as the bride's one and only attendant.

Natica met her eyes in the mirror. "Thank you." She loved her wedding gown. Chiffon was layered over white Liberty satin in a billow of tucks set with delicate lace. The diamond engagement ring sparkled on Natica's finger, and she felt beautiful, the way a bride should.

Today was the day. She was going to be married in a short while and never be Natica Rives again. Like every bride before her, she would surrender her individuality to her husband and heretofore be known as Mrs. William Burden.

The door to the bedchamber opened and Cynthia came in to join them. Dressed to the nines in a powder-blue evening gown, she was flushed with excitement. "How's our lovely bride-to-be holding up?"

"I'm good, but I've got a bad case of butterflies in my tummy," Natica answered. Turning on the chair, she asked, "Are you upset with me for not inviting you to be my bridesmaid?" It had become such a joke about her always being the bridesmaid herself that Natica decided to keep her attendants limited to only one, her cousin.

"Of course not!" Cynthia assured her. "I'm just happy we're going to be sisters-in-law. Arthur is tired of hearing me talk about it."

Natica's mother had seen to all the wedding preparations, including the church decorations of palms, roses and Easter lilies, as well as flowers for the Rives' home where the reception would be held later this afternoon. Her mother assured her everything was set.

"I heard you've decided not to leave immediately for a honeymoon," Cynthia said.

"William and I are going on an auto tour for a few weeks first. Later this year, we've planned a honeymoon in Europe. Will says everything is ready, and all the plans are set in place."

"How lovely for you both."

But now, Natica realized, it was time to get married. She got up from the chair and went to view herself in the full-length mirror in her bedroom at the Rives' New York home.

A rustle at the door brought her mother, Aunt Jane, and Charlotte into the chambers where she was dressing.

"Oh, Natica!" Charlotte cried. "You look gorgeous!" She smiled at her cousin from under the brim of a yellow peach-basket hat.

"And so do you, Evelyn," Sara said to the maid of honor. Wearing layers of white chiffon, Evelyn's outfit was finished by a yellow leghorn hat, adorned with a large blue ostrich feather.

"Thank you, Mrs. Rives." Evelyn smiled sweetly. "Your gown is quite lovely, too."

Sara had picked a silver satin dress, embroidered and trimmed with matching lace. Perfect for the mother of the bride.

"If the fashion show is complete," Jane stated, with a glance at Natica, "I believe your stepfather is waiting to escort you to the church."

The group headed downstairs to the front entrance where George waited, pacing the parquet floor of the foyer. Cynthia, Charlotte, and Aunt Jane kissed Natica's cheek in a whirlwind of affection. Sara finished with a tidy hug, so as not to mess the bride's hair or wedding gown. Evelyn fluffed Natica's dress and veil, ready to assist her out to the carriage for the ride to Grace Church.

"Well..." Sara sighed. "Are you ready?"

Natica smiled at her mother with firm resolve. "I'm ready."

"Okay then. We'll catch up with you at the church."

With a nod, the group headed outside, her attendant bustling over her gown as Natica climbed into the bridal coach. Last in the carriage, Evelyn sat beside Natica. George took the seat opposite the ladies wearing a formal tuxedo dinner suit. Made popular at the fancy dinners in Tuxedo Park, the name had stuck.

"You look nervous," Natica teased her stepfather.

"I suppose I am, a little." He grinned. "You'd think I'd be used to this, as I did the honors for Charlotte."

"I don't imagine it's something you get used to." Natica smiled kindly.

As the entourage neared Grace Church, the clamor of crowds pressed against the carriage. Adorned with streamers of white ribbon and flowers, it was easily spotted as the wedding coach when it pulled up in front of the church.

Police worked to push back the throng, consisting primarily of young women anxious to glimpse the bride. George alighted first from the coach, followed by his stepdaughter, who took his arm. Evelyn followed, seeing to the bride's train as they made their way through the crowd.

Roses rained down on Natica, tossed at her from bystanders, as George led her to the entrance of the sanctuary. Police circled the bridal party, but the crowd grew aggressive, grabbing at Natica's lilac bouquet and gown. Growing frightened, she appealed to the officers for protection. The bluecoats formed a strong line, pushing the encroaching women back with some force in an effort to get the bride safely into the church. Clearly, Natica's popularity in the newspapers had instigated the unruly interest in her nuptials.

Once inside the church, Evelyn again fussed over Natica's gown, preparing her for the trip down the aisle.

"It appears our efforts to keep things quiet have failed." Natica frowned. "I hope the Burdens aren't too upset about the crowds."

Patting her hand, George smiled. "Don't worry about that now. Your groom awaits, my dear." He paused, surveying his lovely stepdaughter. "Shall we?"

"Yes, we shall."

George led Natica to the top of the aisle, where they waited for the organist to begin the strains of the Bridal March. The blast of music echoed through the sanctuary, and Natica took a deep breath. Smiling, she held tight to George's arm as he led her down the aisle toward the altar.

Chapter Thirty-Five

Two months later
June 11, 1907
Virginia Beach, Virginia

Speeding down the highway in their new motorcar, Natica tucked her hair snugly under her scarf, pulling it tight against the wind. She thought the convertible was great fun and the newlyweds were enjoying the sights as they headed to Florida for a vacation.

"Arthur and Cynthia have already arrived in Saint Augustine," Will told her while maneuvering the car through a turn. "They said the weather's been gorgeous."

"I'm excited to join them." Natica smiled. "We'll have such fun. The ocean is so warm and beautiful in Florida. Perfect for bathing."

"Very true." He glanced at his new wife, his eyes filled with devotion. "Not at all like the cold waters off New York. I thought we'd stop in Myrtle Beach for a night. It's on the way. What do you think?" Will asked.

"That sounds lovely." Natica gave him an alluring glance.

She'd grown quite smitten with Will, perhaps even falling in love with him. Or maybe she'd been in love with him all along and hadn't known it. In any event, their wedding night had been both romantic and terrifying, but William had been patient, and took his time, gently persuading her into a passionate mood. Natica discovered that she enjoyed marital relations with him, and each time they made love, she became more relaxed – except for one problem.

She didn't want to get pregnant. Not yet, at least. Natica knew she was expected to deliver a male heir, but there was plenty of time for that. As the days wore on, she'd waited anxiously for the appearance of her monthly cycle. She'd breathed a heavy sigh of relief upon its arrival. *'Much better late than never,'* she'd decided.

Unbeknownst to her husband, Natica had visited her doctor and asked about ways to avoid getting pregnant – much to the shock of her physician. In a clipped voice, he'd given her a few methods to try, chief of which was abstinence. Finishing his short speech, he'd advised the newly married girl *"that there was no foolproof method to avoid pregnancy, even in the twentieth century."* The doctor went on to lecture her on the duties of a wife to provide children.

Her efforts to evade pregnancy and the doctor's visit were her little secrets, and she vowed to keep them from Will for fear he'd misunderstand her motives. She wanted children – just not yet. And she wasn't going to be forced into something she wasn't ready for.

"You look beautiful today," Will said out of the blue. "Not that this day is any different from the others. How are you feeling?"

"Fine." She smiled. "Just tired from traveling."

"It's a lot more fun to go by auto than train, don't you think?"

"Oh, yes." Natica nodded her agreement. "We can stop if we want and sightsee anywhere along the route."

"That's the beauty of it," Will said. He glanced at a roadside sign advertising a restaurant. "Hungry?" he asked, pointing toward the billboard. "That restaurant's only ten miles ahead. Why don't we stop and have lunch there? Take a little break."

"That sounds nice," Natica agreed with a smile. "I think I'm ready for some lunch."

"Perfect," Will said, dropping his foot harder on the accelerator pedal. "Let's see how fast this car will go."

And the newlyweds sped off, due south, down the Virginia highway.

Six weeks later
July 26, 1907
Newport, Rhode Island

Immense tables had been set throughout the banquet hall of Belcourt with much style and fanfare, befitting the gothic ballroom. Oliver stood in the small balcony, overlooking the guests in attendance for his little impromptu party, set to begin promptly at twelve noon. Among the fifty or more curious visitors were Lispenard Stewart, Miss Sherman and Mrs. Mamie Fish, who always showed interest in unusual entertainments. Society's new resident comedian, Mr. Lehr, was also present. Although not very wealthy, he'd made a name for himself by escorting Mrs. Astor to parties after McAllister's fall from grace, although Mrs. Astor herself was absent from the scene today, due to her continued ailing health.

"They're all in for quite a treat," Alva said, joining him on the balcony. Her brocade dress was a touch too fancy for a noon party, but she'd worn it nonetheless, as she never missed an opportunity to outshine the other cottagers. "When are you going to announce our special guest?"

"As soon as the breakfast begins." Oliver gave his wife a conspiratorial smile. "I want to be sure everyone has arrived for the performance." He kept his excitement at bay, anxious to introduce the set to another of his eccentric diversions.

He'd heard the casino had been crowded with an afternoon party, but it held insufficient charm to keep the curious from attending his own party at Belcourt, and the casino had quickly emptied. Bailey's Beach was also forgotten today during the bathing hour, and Oliver was happy to see his luncheon attended by the most prominent residents of Newport's summer season.

"This is certainly going to make the newspapers," Alva declared, tossing him a clever smile. "And it'll probably start a new fad."

"But they'll see it here first," Oliver gloated, enjoying the suspense. "Where is Eli?" Elisha Dyer, Jr. had been chosen to introduce the guest of honor.

"He arrived a while ago by automobile," Alva told him. "Everyone is waiting in the stable with your Indian servant." She glanced at her diamond watch. "Shall we tell the servants to begin?"

"Yes," Oliver said, nodding toward their table at the front of the hall. "Let's take our place with our guests."

Oliver leaned in and spoke quietly to a servant standing nearby, waiting at attention for orders. The man disappeared, and Oliver led Alva downstairs to their waiting seats. When they entered the banquet hall, the room fell quiet. The guests sat perched in their chairs, curious, waiting impatiently for the appearance of the promised entertainment.

With a nod of Oliver's head, the festivities began. An army of footmen dressed in full Belmont regalia appeared carrying silver trays laden with gourmet delicacies. Without a word, the men began serving the meal. Oliver noticed his Indian servant, Sahib, standing near the doorway awaiting instructions.

Rising from his chair, Oliver announced in a loud voice: "Ladies and gentlemen, please welcome our guest of honor: Consul, the chimpanzee."

Murmurs and nervous laughter erupted in the room as Mr. Dyer and the animal keeper stepped to the front of the hall before the diners, escorting a monkey dressed in full morning costume. He had a frock coat and a white waistcoat, looking more human than anyone could have imagined.

The chimpanzee was led to a table where he promptly sat down and began enjoying the elegant meal, unaware that it had been prepared in his honor.

The guests smiled, delighted at the performance, and the chimp appeared to thoroughly enjoy the attention, as well as the meal served to him. He had sufficient skills to properly use the knives and forks, as well as to drink from a glass. Consul was offered champagne like a typical guest, which the monkey seemed to really like. The diners were thoroughly entertained by his genteel antics.

After the simian finished his lunch, Oliver went over to join Consul, offering the chimp an expensive black cigar. The primate bit off the end like a pro, but after taking one taste, threw it away. The guests, amused by his antics, howled and chuckled from their seats, occasionally breaking into applause.

Trying again, Oliver handed the chimpanzee a cigarette. The chimp took it, and using a lighted match offered by the trainer, he lit the smoke himself. Consul evidently preferred this much more than the cigar, and puffed on the cigarette with skill, much to the pleasure of all.

The party grew louder, and the group more raucous as the liquor began to take effect. Returning to Alva's side, Oliver and she milled around the ballroom, enjoying the praise from their guests.

"This has been such fun!" Mamie Fish told her hosts, her round face looking grim even when she smiled, an effect created by her long jowls. Wearing a wide and outlandish hat, the brim hosted an entire bowl of fake fruit. Not a pretty woman, and rather tall, Mrs. Fish delighted in being outrageous. "I must invite Consul to a party at my house."

Alva's lips turned up in a crooked smile, and she winked at Oliver. The fad had already started, just as she'd predicted.

"I think we should have Mr. Lehr entertain with Consul as well." Mrs. Fish glanced at the gentleman. "What do you say Harry?"

"Oh, no," he scoffed, holding up a hand in objection. Lehr was a handsome man, who wore his hair slicked back from his face. Tall and quick to smile, he was well-liked, despite being low on funds. "I have too many engagements already planned this summer to be entertaining a chimpanzee."

"Well, perhaps elephants would be more to your liking?" Mrs. Fish teased, enjoying his discomfort.

"Elephants!" Oliver perked up. "What a splendid idea! There's plenty of room here at Belcourt for elephants."

Mr. Lehr gave them both a nervous smile. "I think I'll leave the animal shows in your capable hands," he insisted, rising from the table. "If you'll excuse me."

"Of course." Alva bowed her head. After he disappeared down the hallway, she turned to Mrs. Fish with a chuckle. "I think you scared him off, Mamie."

"The old geezer has no sense of adventure," Mrs. Fish declared. "But I must say your party has given me fresh ideas for entertainment."

"Indeed." Oliver shared another private smile with Alva. Taking her hand, he moved on through the dining hall, visiting tables and chatting with the afternoon guests.

Six months later

January 5, 1908

New York, New York

The Burden family's New York mansion was alive with society guests welcoming the newlyweds home from their holiday in Europe. Electric lighting illuminated the mansion and grounds, chasing away the darkness for the evening party. Flowers and Ficus trees decorated the home in a style fit for any upper-class ball. Natica's mother-in-law was busy ordering the servants around, while mingling with the elite and well-dressed guests.

Viewing the party from the top of the staircase, Will turned to his bride. "Are you ready to face the music?" His eyes shimmered with happiness in the lamplight.

Weary from travel, Natica was nonetheless excited to see her friends and family. "You make it sound like a firing squad," she joked nervously. "It's not as if we don't know these people."

"True." He assessed her proudly. "Only there's one major difference. Now you're my wife."

She blushed as Will offered his arm, and together they descended the wide staircase. Natica felt like a queen with her long sweeping gown flowing behind her in waves of rose-pink crepe-de-chine fabric. Will, handsome in his white tuxedo, gave her a reassuring smile as they joined the waiting guests.

Mrs. Burden saw them enter the ballroom and hurried to greet them. "At last, our guests of honor." She took Natica's hand with a smile. "You look lovely, my dear."

"Thank you." Natica smiled graciously. She felt a peaceful confidence tonight, happy to be back in America.

"I hope your room is satisfactory?" Mrs. Burden wore a jewel-laden tiara over her silver hair, her dark-green gown one of the newer, more fashionable styles.

"It's lovely." Natica nodded. "I was very comfortable, thank you."

She and Will had private adjacent bedrooms, as was the custom, each with a private bathroom. Entrances opened from each bedchamber to a small servant's hallway, giving them access to each other. This allowed for confidential liaisons between the newlyweds without the prying eyes of the home's occupants. Natica was accustomed to the wealth afforded by her own family, but there was no question marrying Will had moved her a step higher into the echelons of the American aristocracy.

"Are the two of you ready to join me in the receiving line?"

"Of course, Mother," Will said congenially. "Natica and I are looking forward to welcoming everyone."

Natica could see her husband was proud to finally assume the position of prominence that their marriage provided him. He was no longer a Harvard schoolboy, but now, a husband.

"Natica!" Her mother appeared at her side dressed in a navy-blue satin evening gown. "You look wonderful. How are you? How was Europe?"

"We had a wonderful tour," Natica told her with a quick hug. "Did you get my letters?"

"I did." Sara smiled. "And I relished every word."

"I'm sorry I didn't have time to stop by and visit. I was tired when we got home yesterday afternoon. All I wanted to do was sleep."

"I completely understand. Charlotte and Henry are here – Bayard and Mildred, too. They can't wait to see you." Sara informed her daughter. She was so proud of Natica, she had to resist the urge to squeeze her. "When you're rested, I want to host a party for the two of you. Maybe at Sherry's or Delmonico's?"

"That sounds perfect," Natica answered. "I'll help you with the details if you'd like."

Moving to the front of the ballroom, Mrs. Burden hushed the orchestra and turned to speak. The dinner guests settled, focusing their attention on their hostess. Growing quiet, they waited for her speech.

Seeing the party was getting underway, Sara squeezed Natica's hand. "We'll talk later," she whispered, and returned to her table where George and the family were seated.

"Ladies and gentlemen..." Mrs. Burden began. "Thank you so much for coming tonight. May I introduce tonight's special guests, our newlyweds, just back from Europe. My son William, and his new bride Natica: Mr. and Mrs. William Proudfit Burden."

Applause filled the room and Natica felt more like a celebrity than a new bride. It was easy to understand why so many women struggled to reach the pinnacle of marriage among society. The attention was intoxicating.

"The receiving line is over here," Mrs. Burden quietly instructed, walking over to rejoin them. In an easy move, she led the newlyweds to their place at the side of the ballroom.

One by one, Natica smiled and greeted her friends and family. Cynthia and Arthur were first in line, with Natica's bridesmaid and cousin, Evelyn, in tow. The Vanderbilts were well represented by Alfred and Elsie, who greeted her after Gertrude and Harry. Natica was happy to see Reggie and Cathleen also in attendance. And, of course, Charlotte and Henry were there, too, with her brother and sister, Bayard and Mildred. As the line swirled by Natica in a cacophony of congratulations, she skillfully stepped into her role as a new wife—a role she'd been prepared for since childhood.

Dressed in a bright red gown, Mrs. Stowe stepped forward, a profusion of feathers bouncing from her hat. "Congratulations!" she clucked. "Any news of an heir yet?" The old woman smiled coyly at the newlyweds.

An embarrassed laugh escaped Will, who gave Natica a nervous, side-long glance. "We hope to provide a new heir at the earliest possible moment," he offered, hoping to appease Mrs. Stowe's curiosity.

The woman held her chin in the air and continued to smile at the two. "Good. Good." She grinned, raising an expectant eye to Natica.

Blushing at the old lady's boldness, Natica looked away, feigning interest in the remaining guests in the receiving line.

Babies.

An heir.

Her head was spinning with the demands of duty and expectations. But Natica presented a bright and happy face to their guests. Standing tall beside her husband, she graciously received each one.

Chapter Thirty-Six

Seven weeks later
February 20, 1908
New York, New York

Evening fell over New York, draping the city in a cloak of darkness. February cold edged into the house, kept at bay by the furnace and fireplaces. The Burden home was quiet, and Natica escaped to her room to finish her mystery novel. She'd been under the weather for several days and felt unusually tired. *"Food upsets my stomach and I really have no appetite,"* she thought. But lying around had only delivered a plague of boredom she sought to overcome by escaping to her books.

Climbing the steps, she headed to her bedroom. *"How easily Will and I have settled into a steady routine,"* she ruminated. *"I thought it would take longer to find a regular rhythm to our life after the honeymoon."* But, in fact, her new life had brought comfort and security as she and Will grew closer with each passing day. *"I am quite enjoying our secret rendezvous in his suite at night."* She smiled to herself. Natica had learned to embrace her womanhood, and with time, the newlyweds found intimate companionship together – their marriage flowering in a garden of genuine affection.

Reaching her room at the end of the hall, she headed for the bed. Stacking the pillows high, Natica got comfortable snuggling in with her novel, when a gentle knock sounded at her door.

"Come in," Natica called.

Her maid, Emma, opened the door, her tiny frame blocking the light from the hallway. The twenty-year-old servant looked weary, her hair falling loose from under her cap.

"It's nine o'clock, miss. I wanted to know if you had any final instructions before I turn in for the night?"

"Has the doctor sent over my prescription?"

"Yes, ma'am," Emma told her with a slight nod. "It looks like a high-potency vitamin. He wants you to start it in the morning with breakfast. Are you feeling any better?"

"Yes, a little." Natica shifted under the blankets, her long brown tresses pulled back in a braid.

"By the way, this letter came for you earlier." The maid pulled an envelope from the pocket of her apron and handed it to Natica.

"Thank you," she said, taking the note. Flipping the envelope over, she saw it was addressed to her but bore no name revealing the sender. Slipping the letter between the pages of her novel, she decided to wait and read it later when she was alone. "Is Mr. Burden home yet?"

Will worked all day at his family's manufacturing office where he'd assumed an executive position after their honeymoon. Her husband frequently presented her with invitations they'd received to parties and balls, but Natica waved them away much to Will's disappointment. Her interest in social functions had waned for the time being. Instead, she chose to stay in her room with her novels and the sole company of her Pomeranian puppy, Snickers.

A few weeks ago, a steady niggling in her mind caused her to become suspicious she was pregnant. Secretly, Natica had gone to visit her doctor, and he'd confirmed her hunch.

She was with child.

Shocked at first, the idea was growing on her, and tonight she planned to share the news with Will. Natica felt certain he would be delighted.

"Yes, ma'am. I heard him come in as I was walking up the steps," the maid said.

"Thank you, Emma. If you'll fix the drop-light, I think I'll read a while longer."

"Yes, ma'am." The maid went about fixing the lamp for her mistress. Placing it on the nightstand, she attached the green rubber tube to a gas-line bracket four feet above the bed on the wall. Although the main rooms of the house had been outfitted with electric lighting, most of the upstairs rooms still relied on the old-fashioned gas lines for the lamps.

"If that will be all?"

"Yes, that's all for tonight. But please be sure not to disturb me before ten o'clock tomorrow morning. I want to get a good night's sleep."

"Yes, of course, miss. As you wish." The maid curtseyed. "Good night," she said, and pulled the door closed.

Natica lifted the book from her nightstand, only to be interrupted by another knock at her door.

"Come in."

"Hello, my sweet." Will smiled as he entered, his brown hair brushed back from his face. He'd removed his tie and his dress shirt was unbuttoned at the top, revealing the dark curls of his chest hair. Tiny wrinkles around his eyes showed his fatigue, creasing when he smiled at her.

"How is my bride feeling this evening?" The mattress sunk under his weight as he sat on the bed beside her. Tenderly taking her hand, the newlyweds exchanged a light kiss.

"I'm feeling much better," she told him. "I thought I'd stay up and read for a while." Natica studied his handsome features, keenly aware of Will's devotion. What more could a woman ask for? "You look tired. How was your day?"

"Fine. Fine..." Will glanced at Snickers sleeping on the floor next to an open window. "Are you sure you want to leave this window open in the middle of winter? I'd hate to see you catch another cold."

The napping puppy raised his head, as if knowing it was the subject of conversation.

"It was getting a little stuffy in here," Natica explained. "So, I cracked the window for some fresh air. I'll close it before I go to sleep," she promised.

Will glanced at the lamp on the table. "We're planning on putting electricity through the whole house this summer. Then you won't have to bother with these gas lines anymore."

"I don't mind," Natica assured him. "As long as I can see my novel to read, I'm happy."

The two sat in companionable silence as Natica summoned her courage. Taking a deep breath, she plunged ahead.

"Will... I have something to tell you."

"Oh?" he asked, a frown line forming between his eyes.

"I went to see my doctor," she said, catching his eye. Natica couldn't stop herself from grinning, and she let the moment swell, dangling the suspense with elegant mischief.

"And..." Will looked at her expectantly. "Is everything okay?"

"Yes, everything's fine. Except for one small matter." She loitered over the words. "It appears we are going to be parents."

Will's jaw fell open at her announcement. "Are you certain?" he whispered.

"The doctor said that's the reason I've been so tired as of late and why food is so disagreeable."

"Oh, Natica!" He leaned in and hugged her, his brown eyes glistening with joy. "This is the most wonderful news! I can barely breathe!"

She blushed, enjoying his elation. "Do you mind if we keep the news between us for a few more days?"

"Why the secrecy?"

"No reason. It just seems so special. I want to savor the idea before we tell our families."

"As you wish," Will agreed with an easy shrug. "But please, don't make me wait too long. I'm certain I'll burst from excitement." A silly grin teased his lips, and he rubbed his forehead in thought. "We're going to need to get the nursery ready – and a name! We need to come up with the perfect name for our little addition."

Chuckling, Natica shook her head lightly. "Yes, we'll need to choose a name, but we have plenty of time for that."

"How far along are you?"

"The doctor said around ten weeks. We've got a while to go."

"I can barely believe it's true." He smiled, clearly overwhelmed with the happy development.

"I assure you, it's true."

"Well then, you need your rest. I'll leave you to your novel," he said, getting up from the bed. "I'm so glad I checked to see if you were awake before I turned in, although I'm sure I won't get a wink of sleep."

They laughed together then lingered in an affectionate hug.

"Don't stay up too late," he ordered gently. "And make sure you close that window."

"I will." She nodded, pleased to know she'd made him so happy.

"Good night, then."

"Good night Will," Natica said. "Sleep well."

Will leaned down and kissed her lightly on the lips. "Sweet dreams, Natica," he whispered, and walked to the door. With his hand on the brass doorknob, he hesitated, and turned back toward his wife.

"What is it?"

"I just wanted to say…" Will paused for a moment, his eyes sparkling like bright evening stars. "I wanted to tell you that I love you, Natica."

"I love you, too," she responded, knowing it was true.

"Sweet dreams," Will repeated, leaving her alone in the quiet room.

Watching the door close, Natica wrestled with the responsibilities of love and marriage and children. Thinking back to the day she and Payne had bought the poor child candy, Natica was grateful for all the material comfort she enjoyed. Yet, deep in the very core of her soul she felt something was lacking in her life, yet the cause remained elusive. A phantom of melancholy tried to edge itself into her spirit, working to haunt her happiness, and steal her vivacity.

Perhaps a baby will cure the problem, she considered, and reached for her novel.

"Yes, I'm certain this baby will bring me much joy."

Opening her book, Natica leafed through the pages to her bookmark, when the letter slipped into her hand. *"I forgot about this,"* she thought, and opened the note with curiosity. Unfolding the paper, she looked at the bottom of the page for the sender.

A quiet gasp escaped her when she saw it was from Oliver Belmont. With some trepidation, she began to read.

My dearest Natica,

I have hesitated to write, as you've made your position quite clear. Yet, I cannot stop myself from reaching out to you in an attempt at reconciliation. I suppose it is too late to correct the errors I have made in my youth, but it is not too late to ask for your forgiveness. As your father, I have often wondered what life would have been like if I could have raised you as a Belmont. Now, you are a beautiful woman, married, and most likely looking forward to starting a family of your own one day soon. It would be presumptuous to think I could be a part of that idyllic vision, and yet, in my heart the yearning to be a grandfather persists, just as my yearning to be your father compelled me to watch you through the years, though sadly, from a distance.

I am genuinely sorry for our estrangement and take full responsibility for what ultimately is my own loss. If you could, through some miracle, find forgiveness, or at least tolerance of my company, I would be greatly relieved. I know I cannot make up for years lost, but if you would give me half a chance, I should like to, in some small way, offer you the consolation of a father's lasting love for his daughter. Despite what has happened, you have always held a special place in my heart, and regardless of your response to my letter, you shall continue to do so throughout every day of my life.

Sincerely, your father,

Oliver Belmont

Folding the letter closed, Natica pondered his words, finding them touching and quite sincere. Rubbing a hand over her belly, she thought of the love she already felt for the child growing inside her, so innocent and helpless. Natica was forced to acknowledge her maternal instincts and yearned to protect and provide the little one with a wonderful life.

"Perhaps my father had to grow into his own parental instincts," she thought. *"But do I really want to see him?"* Rubbing the bridge of her nose, Natica found herself softening to

the idea. After all, she'd never actually heard his side of the story. Not that it would matter at this point. Or would it?

"The least I can do is meet with him and hear what he has to say for himself," she decided. Pushing the letter inside the envelope, she stuffed it into the back pages of her novel. With an impulse toward forgiveness, Natica made up her mind to write to her father in the morning. *"I think I'll invite Oliver to meet for lunch,"* she thought. *"Although it best be somewhere off the beaten path, so as not to be seen."* She didn't want to upset her mother, but perhaps it was time she met for a discussion with her father. Perhaps they could even develop some type of relationship.

"Better late than never," she thought, returning to the pages of her mystery story.

Chapter Thirty-Seven

The next morning
February 21, 1908
New York, New York

A break from winter's frigid temperatures had brought a clash of seasons, causing a terrible storm. Thunder and lightning arced over the New York skyline, and the wind howled as the deluge dashed against Sara's carriage, blurring the view through the windows. The scene took on a surrealism that wrenched her emotions, and she struggled to remain calm. A hard rain was falling, unrelenting in its fury. The dark sky was tinted an eerie, greenish-yellow glow under the torrent of rain from black, heavy clouds.

But Sara was oblivious to it all. Turmoil and disbelief contended for their place in her mind as her coach roared through the New York streets, splashing through the puddles and mud.

Rubbing her temples, Sara prayed like she'd never prayed before. "Dear God, let it be a mistake." A flux in the phone line, a simple misunderstanding...

The rain grew harder, more furious. A sudden squall swooped down and smacked against the side of the carriage. The coach tilted, rising off one wheel, then shuddered as it slammed back on the hard stone road.

"We should pull over, ma'am," the driver yelled down, "It isn't safe."

"Go faster, Jonathan!" she ordered. "It's urgent!"

And the whip did as instructed, yelling to the frightened horses.

When at last the Burden mansion came into view, Sara edged anxiously on her seat, impatient for the carriage to pull up to the curb. The horses whinnied and Jonathan yanked the reins hard, grinding the coach to a stop on the storm-soaked streets.

Sara jumped out, stumbling in her rush to reach the front door, impervious to the cold rain pelting her face. She rang the bell, then rudely entered the mansion, not waiting for an answer. She was met by the surprised look of an English butler.

"Where is she?" Sara demanded, dispensing with formalities.

"Mrs. Burden is in the parlor," he informed her grimly.

"Natica! Where is Natica?" Sara headed across the foyer where mere weeks before she'd watched her beautiful daughter make an entrance.

"Sara..." Will's mother approached from the parlor, weeping. "I'm so sorry. I'm so sorry..." She shook her head, wiping her nose with a handkerchief.

Sara's eyes darted around the home, searching. Focusing her glance up the staircase, she took off as fast as she could move. On the second floor she was met with the horrific scene of the coroner pulling a sheet over her daughter's body. Several police officers stood nearby, ready to roll the gurney down the hallway. Dr. Lyle and Dr. Kinnicutt stood off to the side, overseeing the body's removal.

"Stop!" Sara sobbed, running for the gurney. "There must be some mistake!"

A police officer stepped from the shadows of a doorway, blocking her path. "I'm sorry, ma'am, you can't go down there."

"The hell I can't!" she shouted, shoving him away without propriety. She ran toward the coroner, Mr. Shrady, the medical examiner who'd been called in to investigate. Tall and balding, the aging man looked up as she approached.

"There must be some mistake," she insisted, shaking her head in denial. "There must be some mistake!"

"You shouldn't be here, Mrs. Rives," Mr. Shrady said softly, his face grim. "We've already identified her body. I'm very sorry." He paused, his jaw clenched. "The official cause of death has been ruled accidental asphyxiation by gas. We weren't sure at first if the girl had committed suicide or not."

"What are you saying?" Sara demanded, appalled. "Natica would never take her own life. She was so young, and newly married. She had everything to live for!"

"Yes, ma'am. That's true." Shrady nodded, working to calm Sara. "But it's no secret the girl had a bad case of melancholy. Please try to understand, Mrs. Rives, it would be remiss if we didn't investigate the situation thoroughly." He continued cautiously, "We found her dog by an open window alive and well. That leads us to believe it was accidental."

Sara turned from him and stumbled toward the gurney, sobbing, the strength ebbing from her body. But she had to see for herself if it was true. Another police officer moved to stop her, but Coroner Shrady waved him off, and the policeman let her pass.

Sara lifted the sheet and there she was.

Her beautiful baby girl.

Motionless and cold white with death, laying still on the gurney. So beautiful, even to the end.

"This can't be happening," Sara cried weakly, wanting to refute death's claim on her daughter's life.

"Someone call the girl's father," Coroner Shrady ordered urgently. "Tell him to come at once."

Dr. Lyle walked over, a witness to Sara's grief, and took the sheet from her hand, gently covering Natica's body again.

"I'm sorry, Mrs. Rives," he said softly. "We did everything we could. It was simply too late."

"How could this happen?" Sara demanded between sobs. "How did this happen?"

"Her lamp came loose from the wall connection, filling the room with gas fumes. The maid found her this morning when she went to serve her breakfast at ten o'clock. We believe she died in her sleep about three or four hours earlier."

Sara crossed her hands against her heart as if to protect herself from the agony. She watched, dazed, as the medical technicians rolled Natica's body to the elevator. She followed, and tried to fit inside the car, but the attendants objected, waving her off. In response, Sara headed for the steps, crazed with grief. Rushing down the staircase, she met them on the first floor, staying as close to Natica as they would allow, while the paramedics wheeled her body outside to the waiting ambulance.

Passing the parlor, Sara saw Will. Hunched in a chair, he was bent over, covering his face with his hands, weeping without restraint. Mrs. Burden was openly sobbing, while cuddling the Pomeranian in her lap. Sara paused, watching the dog, knowing he'd escaped a terrible fate, and wishing the same had been true for Natica. Turning, she followed the gurney outside into the fury of the storm, not wanting to be separated from her daughter for a moment.

Fighting against reality, Sara stood on the sidewalk, her clothing soaked with rain, a somber witness to the horror playing out before her. A streak of lightning sparked across the sky in a jagged line of blue-white fingers, matched by a tremendous echo of thunder. The ground rumbled under her feet, but Sara was unaffected, watching transfixed as medics loaded Natica's body into the ambulance. She stood motionless, paralyzed, her hair matted against her face in the wet gale. Numb with anguish and disbelief, she turned when a carriage roared to a stop in front of the Burden home.

Fury filled her veins when Oliver Belmont climbed from the coach. He glanced toward the ambulance and headed for the vehicle, presumably to see the awful truth for himself.

Sara leapt toward Oliver across the sidewalk, blocking his path. "How dare you show your face here!" she shrieked. "You have no right to be here!"

"I have every right to be here!" Oliver shouted above the thunder. "Natica is my daughter! Do you hear me, Sara? She is *my* daughter!" It was hard to discern his tears from the rain covering his anguished face.

"You abandoned your daughter!" Sara wailed. "Abandoned her! None of this would have ever happened if it weren't for you!"

"How do you imagine that to be true?" he defended wildly, rainwater dripping from the brim of his bowler hat. "I tried to reconcile with you after Paris. I tried to get you to come home to me at Oakland so we could raise our daughter together. But you refused!"

Oliver took a step toward her with outstretched arms. "Try to understand, Sara. I was young, and in spite of what you think, I loved Natica from the start."

"You beat me when I was pregnant!" Sara screamed, smacking away his hands. "You could have killed her before she was even born. I could never trust you after that. I had no choice but to protect her from your ugly temper and your drunken outbursts."

"I'm sorry. I didn't know you were pregnant," Oliver cried.

"That's no excuse for such abhorrent treatment!"

"This is your fault. Yours and your stubborn mother who wouldn't leave us to live our lives in peace. Always meddling..."

"How dare you speak poorly of my mother!" Sara battled. "She protected us from you and your selfish, narcissistic ways!"

"And then you pushed Natica to marry that Burden man." Anger rose in Oliver's voice as he accused her. "Just like your mother, you were willing to sacrifice her happiness for social status!"

"Where did you hear such nonsense! Of all the nerve!" Sara's anguish turned to rage. "What do you know of the matter anyway? Natica married Will of her own volition – and she was happy. Her marriage gave her a chance to finally move past the shame *you* saddled her with by deserting us in Paris!"

Oliver stepped toward the ambulance again and Sara threw her body in his path.

"No!" she screamed again. "You are *not* her father. You will never be her father! And now it's too late to try to make things right, Oliver!" She stepped closer, screaming in his face. "It's too late!"

Sara's body writhed with sobs. "Go away!" she shouted. "Go away and never show your face anywhere near me. You are a miserable excuse of a man! You care about no one but yourself."

"Mr. Belmont, perhaps you should leave." A police officer approached the two quarreling on the sidewalk.

"And don't you dare think about coming to Natica's funeral!" Sara wailed. "Or I swear I'll have you arrested for trespassing!"

A fresh onslaught of rain battered the street. Movement caught her eye, and Sara spotted George running toward her like an apparition in the eerie light of the storm, the hem of his raincoat flapping in the wind.

"My God, what's happened?" he demanded, reaching Sara as she stumbled on the sidewalk.

"George..." Sara wailed. "Natica's dead."

"Oh, dear God..." He stared at her in disbelief. His focus shifted to Oliver standing nearby. "Belmont!" George growled, his eyes dark and angry. "I told you to stay away from my family!" George took a step toward him, livid with rage, poised to strike Oliver hard, while struggling to help Sara. "Haven't you ruined enough lives?" George demanded over the wind.

The policeman stepped in again and took Oliver's arm. "Sir, perhaps you'd better leave." He gently pulled him away from the scene.

Livid with frustration, Oliver shook in anger, glaring at Sara and George. Lightning cracked open the sky, scattering a flash over their pained faces. A boom sounded from across the way as the bolt struck an old oak, sirens wailing to life from a nearby fire station.

Abruptly, Oliver shook his arm free of the policeman, and returned to his coach. Sara watched him climb inside, the carriage disappearing down the avenue in gray shadows.

George worked to lead Sara to her coach, out of the storm, his arm wrapped tightly around her waist, supporting her weakened body.

"No!" Sara fought against him, sobbing. "I can't leave Natica! I can't leave Natica!" She struggled against George, then slumped faint in his arms.

George caught her, breaking the fall. "I need a doctor!" he shouted to the medics. Carrying Sara, he fought his way against the wind and rain back toward the shelter of the Burden house.

The next day
February 22, 1908
New York, New York

Oliver placed a call to *The New York Times*, *The New York Sun*, *The New York Herald*, and every other newspaper he could think of. "Sara can keep me away, but she can't stop me from telling the world Natica was my daughter," he murmured to himself, grief-stricken.

"*New York Times*: obituaries," a man's deep voice came over the phone line.

"Yes. This is Oliver Belmont," he announced, sitting at the desk in his study. "I'd like to print a very large obituary in tomorrow's paper. Money is no object."

"Yes, sir. Of course," the voice replied over the telephone line. "How would you like it to read?"

And Oliver told him precisely how he wanted the announcement to be printed.

Mrs. William Proudfit Burden, formerly Miss. Natica Belmont Rives, died on February 21 at the residence of her mother-in-law, Mrs. James A. Burden, 908 Fifth Avenue. Mrs. Burden was a daughter of Mrs. George L. Rives, nee Sara Swan Whiting and on the paternal side, a granddaughter of the late Mr. and Mrs. August Belmont and a great-granddaughter of Commodore Matthew Calbraith Perry, USN, of international fame. Her marriage to Mr. Burden, a son of the late James A. Burden took place in Grace Church on April 17, 1907. She was a namesake of Lady Lister-Kaye (Natica Yznaga) a sister of Consuelo, duchess of Manchester.

Two weeks later
March 6, 1908
New York, New York

Fresh snow had fallen over Manhattan, blanketing the city in white purity. Watching from her bedroom window, Sara breathed in the quiet evening, pulling her velvet robe tighter against the cold.

"Two weeks," she whispered. "Two weeks of hell since Natica died." She wondered if her daughter was cold, buried under the hard late-winter earth.

Moving away from the window, she went to sit at her desk, her hair hanging limp around her pale face. Stacks of letters and cards of condolences were piled haphazardly over her writing space. Lifting one of the envelopes, she flipped it over to see the sender. Mrs. Astor. She threw the unopened letter back on the pile and sat back with a sigh.

"I can't seem to find the strength to read these," she realized solemnly. *"Let alone write a response."* The funeral had been beautiful, in a sad and mournful way, and the set had been sympathetic to the family's loss, sending countless flower arrangements and cards.

The pain intensified when the coroner revealed Natica had been pregnant. Sara was grateful for the support of friends, but it did little to heal the anguish of losing her firstborn to such a senseless accident. The fact that Natica was pregnant with her unborn grandchild made the loss completely unbearable.

The press had printed a three-page article detailing Natica's life, her marriage, and the specifics of the gas leak. A large photo accompanied the story, displaying her youth and beauty for all the world to see. The Burden family bore the guilt of the faulty gas line, and it was said they'd immediately begun work on installing electricity throughout the home to prevent any further disasters.

But for Natica, it was too little, too late.

Sara's eyes were red and sore from crying an unending river of tears. Brushing her hair from her face blindly, she thought of her other children, and realized she must find a way to escape her grief and carry on. Bayard and Mildred needed her, and more than ever, she needed the comfort of her children. "But how to go on..." Sara whispered, staring at the pile of letters on her desk. "How to go on..."

Chapter Thirty-Eight

Three months later
June 10, 1908
Hempstead, Long Island

The corridors of Brookholt were quiet, save for the melody of a song sparrow floating in through an open window. Dr. McCosh, Dr. Bull, and Dr. Langheart were speaking quietly as they approached Alva.

"How is he?" she asked anxiously, wringing her hands with worry.

"The operation for the appendicitis itself was a success," Dr. McCosh explained somberly. The older of the three doctors, his black hair was flecked with silver. "But unfortunately, there have been complications."

"What type of complications?" Alva found it hard to remain calm while listening to the doctor's prognosis.

"I'm afraid he's developed an infection. Peritonitis has set in," Dr. Langheart informed her, his voice gentle but serious. "His general weight is high, and he was in poor health when the appendicitis first struck last week. I'm afraid the situation is dire."

"Mrs. Belmont," Dr. Bull said gently, regarding her through thick glasses. "We don't think he'll make it until morning." The doctor paused, then added, "I'm sorry."

"Don't be ridiculous. I'm sure he'll recuperate. Is he conscious?" Alva asked. "Can I see him?"

The three doctors exchanged an astute glance but said nothing to the contrary.

"It's fine if you want to sit with him for a while," Dr. Langheart said. "Although he's not conscious at the moment. There's a chance he may come around, but I wouldn't count on it."

Alva got up and headed for Oliver's room, hesitating for a moment with her hand on the doorknob. Summoning her courage, she entered the chamber, the room dark, the curtains drawn against the bright daylight. A nurse worked over Oliver, checking his vital signs. Alva sat in the chair next to his bed and prayed with all her might, hoping against hope for a miracle.

And that is the way things remained. All afternoon and into the evening, the doctors and nurses came and went, while Alva kept vigil. She lost track of time, thinking back on the gay days they'd shared together, fighting against the finality of his illness. Using her lace handkerchief, she dabbed away the perspiration on his forehead, and Oliver stirred. Alva's heart leaped with joy, hoping it was a sign of improvement.

He opened his eyes and gave her a weak smile. "Alva..." Wan and pale, the simple effort to speak seemed too great for him.

"Yes, Oliver. I'm here." She staunchly hid her grief, taking his hand to comfort him.

A faint smile appeared on his face, and he gazed lovingly at his wife. "Alva..." he repeated sweetly.

His eyes were glassy and bloodshot with fever; Alva watched him closely for signs of improvement – but found none. Oliver's attention was drawn to something beside her. She turned to where he was looking but saw only the empty room.

"Natica..." He smiled with joy. "You've come back to me."

A chill ran up Alva's spine, and she looked again at where Oliver was gazing but saw nothing.

"It's me. Alva..." she told him, thinking him delirious from fever.

Oliver looked back at her and grinned. "I see you, Alva," he whispered weakly. "And I see Natica, too. Can't you see her? She's standing right beside you."

A glass bottle fell to the floor from a table near where he looked, crashing against the carpet, unbroken. Alva jumped, wondering what had caused the bottle to fall.

A broad smile covered Oliver's face. "At last, Natica and I will be together. I finally get to be with my daughter. I finally get to be with my daughter..."

Oliver's voice trailed off as he lapsed back into unconsciousness. Frightened by his vision of Natica, Alva shuddered. The phone rang, startling her, and she quickly grabbed it for silence, not waiting for a servant to answer the ring.

"Hello," she answered. "Who's there...?"

But no one replied.

The sound of static echoed over the telephone wire, hollow and empty.

Alva held the phone away from her ear, frightened, and quickly replaced the phone in its cradle. She raced from the darkened room in search of the doctor.

The physician returned with her to the sick room and checked on the patient. Finding no pulse, he pulled the sheet over Oliver's head.

"I'm sorry, Mrs. Belmont," Dr. Langheart said. "He's gone."

The sound of her quiet tears filled the room as the doctor reached for the telephone to call the undertaker. Turning, she left for the privacy of her Brookholt bedchamber, pondering Oliver's last words.

"Perhaps father and daughter finally *are* together," she whispered, wondering unabashedly about the afterlife.

Three days later
June 12, 1908
New York, New York

NEW CLAIMANT FOR BELMONT'S VAST FORTUNE
Texas Woman Says She is the Rightful Heir and is Coming to Fight for Her Rights
SAYS NATICA RIVES WAS A CHANGELING
Has Letter Purporting to be from Belmont and Locket Containing Pictures with which She Hopes to Prove Her Contentions.

NEW YORK, June 12 – While funeral services were being held today over the body of O. H. P. Belmont, fashionable New York society is convulsed by a report from Galveston, Texas that a second real heir to the Belmont millions, a woman, will leave there tomorrow to fight for the estate.

The woman says her name is Louise Whiting Belmont Clarke. She declares that Natica Rives, wife of millionaire William P. Burden, was a changeling; that she was no more the daughter of O. H. P. Belmont than of her step-father Rives, whose name she took, and that she had no real claim to the wealth of the dead capitalist.

As evidence of her claim, the Clarke woman has in her possession a copy of a letter alleged to come from Belmont to a detective agency in which he says that his daughter is lost to him forever and that her place has been filled in the family circle so far as to the outside world is concerned.

The Clarke woman exhibits a gold locket with two portraits, one of them, she says, that of her mother Sara Whiting Belmont, and the other of herself at the age of 4 years.

"Once in New York," she said, "I will find many who know I was living at least up to six years ago. I have seen reverses and I am to blame, but I can surely prove that I am the daughter of O. H. P. Belmont.

New Castle News,
New Castle, Pennsylvania

Later that same day
June 12, 1908
Newport, Rhode Island

Frowning as she read the newspaper, Sara bristled at the absurdity of the claim. *"Everyone in the set is familiar with such attempts by con artists and frauds,"* she thought. *"Always doing their best to convince the world of their lies."* But it hurt more knowing it was her own daughter whose good name was being smeared by the little imposter. And the woman had wasted no time to stake her claim – as outrageous as it was.

"But the joke is on her, the little fraud," Sara thought. She knew Oliver's father, August Belmont, had strictly specified in his will that no money from the Belmont coffers would ever go to descendants from their marriage.

Taking a breath to calm herself, Sara turned the page and saw the list of current obituaries. She read the article again, Oliver's name among the recently deceased in New York. She'd heard he'd taken ill with appendicitis, but she wasn't sure how serious his condition was.

"It's over," she whispered, laying the newspaper on the sitting room table. "It's all over."

The sacred triangle of the family: father, mother, and child.

Oliver, Sara, and Natica.

"I am the only one who remains now," she whispered.

Her first marriage was gone – just a memory. A wave of release passed through her soul, mired by so much loss. But with simple tools like faith, hope, and forgiveness, Sara was gaining new wisdom born of her bereavements. And with this new wisdom, she gave herself permission to move beyond the tragedies delivered by life, consciously focusing on simple joys.

Shaking herself from her thoughts, she walked through the breakfast room to join George and her teenage children having lunch outside on the piazza. Pausing, she stood in the shadows of the doorway, taking in the beauty of the *Swanhurst* lawn on this lovely summer day. A breeze fluttered the branches of the old beech tree, a constant witness to their lives over the years.

Sara watched her family, unseen, as they talked and laughed together while realizing that, somehow, life goes on. She thought of Jane, a spinster, and the many widows in the set, their loneliness etched into their faces. Somehow, Sara knew she'd been given a second chance. In that moment, all the joys and sadness of the past years scattered into the wind while she listened to the happy laughter coming from Mildred, Bayard, and George.

And Sara realized how deeply she loved them all.

"The past is past," Sara whispered and went to join them. Closing the door behind her, she courageously stepped into the future.

And in that ending, Sara found a new beginning.

Chapter Thirty-Nine

Eight years later
November 30, 1916
New York, New York

Day by day, the years slipped by with the change of each season, and life took on a new purpose and a new rhythm for Sara. She'd focused her energy on raising her son and daughter, and the two grew into adulthood, bringing much pride and solace to George and Sara.

Now, here it was, Thanksgiving Day. The dining table was heavily laden with roasted turkey, stuffing, and mashed potatoes. Yams, broccoli, and asparagus were carefully arranged on a silver serving platter, looking like a savory work of art. Passing the cranberries, Sara grinned, enjoying the holiday celebration with her family.

Junior had joined the military and moved to Austria, where he took a new bride, Gisela Preinerstorfer. In a recent letter, George had received pictures of his three grandsons, and Sara suggested they visit, but not until after the war. Europe was in a violent upheaval, but Junior insisted on staying in the military to assist with the conflict. *"I can't help but worry about them living on the outskirts of the battle zone,"* she thought. And at night, she said extra prayers for their protection.

New York society was forever changed with the passing of old Mrs. Astor, who died a few months after Oliver in October 1908. *"Gone are the genteel days when she reigned as America's queen,"* Sara mused. She was now replaced by less stringent modern standards of conduct and entertainment. On the surface, society remained refined and proper, but Sara knew in her heart that nothing would be the same without Mrs. Astor.

A year later, in November of 1909, Jane took her final breath.

"I'm ready," she'd told Sara. *"I've endured enough of the trials and tribulations of life. I'm tired and ready for a rest from the world."* Sara had teased her at the time, thinking her sister was indestructible.

She wasn't.

Bayard went off to college at Yale, and Mildred made her debut into society, creating a stir among the eligible bachelors of the set. *"It didn't take long before both of them fell in love."* Sara thought of these things tonight while gathering with her family for Thanksgiving dinner.

Smiling across the table, George raised his wineglass. "It appears we're going to have *two* weddings next year."

"I believe history is repeating itself," Sara said thoughtfully. "Much the same way that Junior and Charlotte married, only months apart."

"I suppose that's true." George smiled. "Our children marry like the creatures on Noah's ark – two by two."

Laughter and smiles broke out around the table. Mildred sat close to her fiancé, Fred. His great-grandfather was the famous poet William Cullen Bryant. Sara wondered if Frederick shared his talent for stanzas and verse. Regardless, she was delighted with the match.

And Bayard, he'd fallen for Helen Hunt. The Hunts were another well-respected New York family, and the two seemed quite smitten with each other. What more could a mother ask for?

"I'd be quite happy to help with the wedding arrangements if you'd like." Sara offered. "Have you made any plans for the ceremony?"

Mildred reached for Fred's hand. "As a matter of fact, we've decided on Saint John the Divine," she answered. "In the Whiting Chapel. Wouldn't that be splendid?"

"That sounds lovely," Helen said, turning to Bayard. "We should do the same! Not everyone has a family chapel in such a magnificent church."

"That's fine with me." Bayard nodded. "I'm sure you ladies can work out all the details. Just let me know where and when, and I'll be there with bells on my shoes."

"I second that notion." George chuckled.

Watching him across the table, Sara realized the years were wearing on George. And most assuredly on me as well, she thought, returning her attention to the party.

Mildred Sara Rives

"Let's move to the parlor, shall we," Sara suggested. "We can discuss the wedding plans over coffee and pumpkin pie."

———— ❧ ————

Five months later
April 12, 1917
New York, New York

Society
Miss Mildred Rives Becomes the Bride of Frederick Marquand Godwin.

The marriage of Miss Mildred Rives to Mr. Frederick Godwin took place at noon yesterday in the Whiting Memorial Chapel of Saint John the Divine in Morningside. The bride was given away by her brother, Mr. F. Bayard Rives, who will marry Miss Helen Leigh Hunt on June 1st in the same chapel. The bride's father, George L. Rives, has been ill.

———— ❧ ————

Three months later
July 4, 1917
Newport, Rhode Island

The Newport harbor was dotted with sailboats, the beaches swarming with bathers out to enjoy an ocean swim before the evening's Independence Day fireworks. Bright sunlight sparkled off the waves and slid across the sea onto the house at the corner of Webster and Bellevue Avenues. *Swanhurst* sheltered the family from the hot sun, where they'd all gathered together on the piazza to enjoy the holiday. Sitting around the table, they enjoyed lunch in easy company.

"The pictures came out so perfectly," Mildred said, her stylish haircut bobbing as she spoke from under the brim of her straw cloche hat. Cuddling the album of wedding photos under her arm, she was anxious to share them with her mother and father.

"I can't wait to see them." Sara smiled, her graying hair styled in a pretty updo. "Did you and Helen get your photos back yet?"

"Another week or two," Bayard replied. Handsome in his brown trousers and white button-down shirt, he relaxed in the wicker porch chair. "The photographer claims he's overwhelmed with work from all the recent weddings."

"He promised they'd be done soon," Helen added. "But it's hard to be patient." Happiness filled her eyes while she sipped on iced tea, the breeze fluttering the skirt of her cotton sundress.

"I think you'll find it well worth the wait," Fred assured them from across the table.

"Do you want anything, Dad?" Mildred asked George.

Looking over, George smiled at his daughter. "Some lemonade would be nice." Gray and frail, George showed clear evidence of his decline. Sitting in a wheelchair, he was covered with a cotton blanket, despite the summer heat.

Concerned over her father's health, Mildred doted on him, ever mindful of his comfort. Walking to the buffet, she poured him a glass of lemonade and placed a paper straw in the goblet to make it easier for him to drink. Carrying it over, she took the chair beside him at the table, tending to her father with solid devotion.

Reaching for the photo album, Sara said, "Don't make me wait another moment. It will be like reliving the day all over again."

"You're going to love them." Mildred smiled, her eyes wide. "There wasn't a bad one in the bunch."

⚭

Six weeks later
August 23, 1917
Newport, Rhode Island

Trinity Church was packed to capacity, every pew occupied. Many who could not find a seat stood at somber attention in the foyer or along the nave. All the summer residents were present, as were the Governor of Rhode Island and his wife, Mrs. Beeckman.

Countless flowers and wreaths filled the church, displayed around the pews, pillars, and pulpit of the sanctuary in colorful floral profusion. The mahogany casket was covered with dozens of bright red *American Beauty* roses, an apt memorial for a devoted American.

The organ began to play, and George's funeral commenced with full pageantry. Sara stood flanked by Mildred and Bayard, watching through tears from behind the black veil of her hat.

Chapter Forty

Seven years later
May 22, 1924
New York, New York

Standing at the second-floor window of her New York home, Sara looked down over the city from her bedroom. Neon lights flashed over shops and marquees while automobiles roared down the street, hurrying to and fro in the busy night. It was nothing like the New York she'd known from her youth.

Removing her robe, she walked to the bed and pulled back the fluffy cotton blankets. Laying on the soft mattress, Sara snuggled to get comfortable. It had been a long day but one she'd thoroughly enjoyed. Pulling the blanket over her shoulder, she grinned, thinking how much joy her grandchildren brought to her life.

Mildred had two daughters with Fred; Lizzie and Milly – while Bayard and his wife, Helen, had a boy and a girl. Bayard had named his son George, after his father, and his daughter was named Margaret – Maggie, for short. The four little ones had scrambled around Sara all afternoon in the parlor, playing games, stacking blocks, and reading storybooks. Their lives were simple and carefree, and Sara delighted in the company of their youth and innocence. Children say the funniest things, she thought, fluffing the pillow under her neck.

George had passed away a month after Bayard's wedding, and he'd missed the uncomplicated joy of their grandchildren. Sara thought Mildred's daughter, little Lizzie, resembled her grandfather. *"Although, of course, she is much prettier."*

George had left a legacy in politics as well as with Columbia University. Still, more importantly, he'd been a wonderful husband and father, and Sara knew he'd have been a fabulous grandfather if he'd lived to see the day.

But he hadn't.

Her thoughts wandered back to her first Newport ball, dressed in her golden gown, excited to finally be courting. She remembered her grandfather, Judge Swan, his grand portrait hanging in the *Swanhurst* foyer, and the snow globe, a treasured gift from him when she was a child – broken years later in her time of despair. Her thoughts streamed through her mind to a vision of her father, bouncing her on his knee while he told her she was his gift from the angels. Her father, riding high atop his mighty horse, proud and strong, galloping down the *Swanhurst* driveway. Mildred and Bayard had a lasting heritage that would carry the family into the new century and, hopefully, far beyond.

Unbidden, visions of her life passed through her mind, some happy, some not so much. Yet, somehow, none of it really mattered anymore. She sighed, knowing she'd risen like a phoenix from the fires of scandal to once again find her rightful place among society. And she'd carried her children into the fold of America's aristocracy for another generation.

Overcome with fatigue, Sara yawned. Weary to the core of her bones, she reached to turn off the lamp, bringing the room into pleasant darkness. Closing her eyes against the world, she sighed, yearning for *Swanhurst*, the home where she'd been born.

"Perhaps I'll head back to Newport tomorrow," she thought, craving the quiet. Honking horns and sirens permeated New York as Sara drifted off in a dream, the noise replaced by the gentle rustling sound of the leaves on the old copper beech trees blowing in the ocean breeze.

Weightless, she floated, drifting deeper and deeper into the details of the lucid and colorful dream. She was home at *Swanhurst*. The family was sitting around the dining room table, and her heart burst with joy as she realized they were all there!

Jane and Milly. Gus and Florence. Her father and mother – even her grandfather was there, sitting at the head of the table. Everyone was laughing, toasting glasses as they gathered for a family meal.

Elation filled her heart when Sara noticed Natica. She turned toward Sara, smiling, looking young and beautiful.

"Here she is now," Natica greeted. "America's daughter has finally come home."

Part Three

Swanhurst

Swanhurst
Newport, Rhode Island

Chapter Forty-One

One week later
June 24, 1924
Newport, Rhode Island

Heavy wooden chairs were arranged before the lawyer's huge cherry-wood desk. Cigar smoke hung in the air, circling over the middle-aged attorney's head. Wearing a black suit, his deep-set eyes were serious as he pulled a set of papers from a manila folder.

Mildred fidgeted with her glove, distracted when Bayard was ushered into the office. He removed his dark brown fedora and offered her a grim smile, taking the seat beside her.

"Now that we're all here," Mr. Hanner said. "We can proceed with the reading of the will."

The lawyer's voice droned on as he read the legal stipulations of Sara's last will and testament. "You will both receive $250,000, which will be placed in trust and dispersed throughout your lifetime." He looked at Mildred over his spectacles, "And you, Mrs. Godwin, shall take ownership of *Swanhurst*, the family home. It's been passed from mother to daughter for several generations, and now it will be your property."

Mildred nodded, not offering any comment.

"May I advise you to prepare your own will as soon as possible, bequeathing *Swanhurst* to your own daughters."

"Is that absolutely necessary?" Mildred asked.

"I think so, yes." The lawyer nodded. "Your mother has added a stipulation that the house be donated to the Newport Art Association in the event of your early demise. It's just a legal precaution," he added. "Once the home is yours, a new will ensures the house is kept in the family for your own daughters."

"I understand." Mildred nodded, gathering the papers he offered.

"The documents will be filed immediately. Let me know if you have any questions or concerns." He reached to shake Bayard's hand across the desk.

With an arm across Mildred's shoulder, Bayard ushered his sister from the office.

"It's just the two of us now," she whispered.

"I know." Bayard nodded. "I know."

One month later
July 27, 1924
Newport, Rhode Island

Swanhurst brought Mildred a mixture of joy and sadness these days. It was hard to walk through the house, filled with memories of her mother, without feeling a sense of loss.

The funeral at Trinity Church in New York was nearly as crowded as her father's had been years before. The next day, her mother's body was transported by train for burial at Island Cemetery with the rest of the Whiting family.

Now, Mildred struggled against her grief, missing the sound of her mother's laugh. Fred and the kids shared her sadness as they grew accustomed to life without Grandma Sara. The family loved *Swanhurst*, and they'd decided to remain in Newport after the funeral to spend the summer like many Swan and Whiting generations before them.

Working to return normalcy to their lives, Mildred went through the usual motions of day-to-day life. Today the weather had been perfect for the beach, and Mildred took great delight in watching her two daughters, Lizzy and Milly, play in the sand with their buckets and shovels. Fred leaned back in a beach chair beside her, eyes closed against the bright sun. He stirred and looked at his watch.

"It's getting late," Fred said, sitting up. He picked up a Panama hat from the blanket and pulled it on his head to block the sunlight.

Nodding, Mildred stood up, squishing her bare feet in the sand. "Come on, girls. It's time to go," she called, pulling a knit dress over her bathing costume.

The two children ran over and helped their mother load their belongings into the beach bags while Fred folded the beach chairs, slinging them over his shoulder. Returning to the parking area, the family piled into the new Ford, slamming the doors closed.

"I want to run into town and pick up a few things," Mildred said. "Then we'll grill hot dogs for dinner. How does that sound?"

"Yummy!" Lizzy cheered from the backseat.

"Yay!" Milly echoed.

"Steak for you." She smiled at Fred.

"Thank goodness." He smiled back, eyeing his wife with amused adoration.

As he drove the car into town, Fred pulled out a pack of cigarettes. Rolling the strike wheel on his gold lighter, he lit the smoke and passed it over to Mildred. *"God, I love her,"* he thought, feeling like the luckiest man in the world.

Smiling, Mildred took the cigarette, puffing on it as Fred lit another for himself.

"What's that look for?"

"What look?" he asked, feigning an innocent grin. "Can't a man look at his wife without raising suspicions?"

"I suppose..." Mildred laughed, returning his affectionate glance.

The car rumbled through the narrow streets, and in a few minutes, they were surrounded by the hustle and bustle of downtown Newport. Fred maneuvered the car into a parking spot on Thames Street in front of the Brick Market and braked to a stop. Mildred jumped out and opened the car door to help the girls climb from the back seat.

"Where are your shoes?" she asked her daughters.

"I don't want to wear my shoes." Lizzie pouted, her cheeks red from the sun.

"Me either," Milly chimed in.

Too tired to argue, Mildred just shook her head at the girls.

Rolling his eyes, Fred ushered them onto the sidewalk while buttoning his shirt closed.

"You look like a couple of waifs." Mildred chuckled. "I'm certain our barefoot daughters are about to create a scene in this conventional town," she whispered to Fred as they entered the market.

"Or maybe they'll start a new fad." Fred chuckled, enjoying the prank.

Moving past the front display, the two caught sight of a prim old woman. Dressed in black from head to toe, she wore a hat with too many ostrich feathers jutting off the brim. Her jaw dropped at the appearance of the girls running through the shop barefoot, clearly aghast at the sight.

"Well, I've never..." she started, then caught sight of Frederick towering over her and stopped mid-sentence.

Fred looked sternly at the old woman, then took Mildred's arm and led her down the adjacent aisle, husband and wife sputtering into giggles like schoolchildren.

"I believe Milly and Lizzie have caused a ripple in the status quo," Fred whispered.

Holding a hand over her mouth to squelch her laughter, Mildred nodded. "And I'm so glad for the opportunity."

✦

Three years later
December 22, 1927
New York, New York

Pacing the parlor, Fred paused, glancing out the bay window at the snow-covered grass of the *Swanhurst* yard. Mildred had been in labor for hours, and the suspense was driving him crazy.

A son?

A daughter?

He remembered the birth of Milly and Lizzie, both born here at *Swanhurst*. *"I should be used to this."* he thought and took up his pacing again. "But Mildred had been younger then," he murmured, running a worried hand through his dark brown hair. "And I've heard childbirth can become more difficult for women with age." Now thirty-three, it had been six years since Mildred gave birth to Lizzie, their youngest.

A ruckus from the upper floor reached Fred's ears, and he stopped mid-stride. Unable to contain his patience a moment longer, Fred climbed the stairs to the second story of *Swanhurst*. He stood in the hall as a nurse came out carrying sheeting covered in crimson blood. He reeled at the sight, growing concerned.

"Is everything all right?" he asked the nurse.

The woman kept walking toward the stairs, her white dress swaying as she moved. "The doctor will be with you shortly."

Taking up his pacing once more in the hallway, Fred grew steadily more disturbed by the moaning coming from the birthing room. There was an urgency rippling through the house, one he didn't recall at the previous births. A feeling of foreboding wrenched inside him, and he tried to relax, telling himself all was well. The nurse returned upstairs wearing a fresh apron and carrying clean sheets.

"Can I see my wife?"

"It's best if you wait here, Mr. Godwin." the nurse answered curtly. Entering the bedchamber, she left Fred in the hall staring at the door, helpless.

Fred could hear the doctor ordering the nurse in a sharp tone. Muffled sounds escaped the room, mingling with Mildred's whimpers. He fought the urge to enter the bedchamber, rationalizing to himself that it was best to wait and let the doctor do his work unfettered. After an eternity, things grew quiet behind the door, and Fred wondered why he didn't hear a baby cry. Finally, the nurse re-emerged from the bedroom, followed by the doctor, his face grim.

"I'm sorry, Mr. Godwin," Dr. Tomley said. "I'm afraid we've lost them both. There were complications with the umbilical cord. I tried my best to save your wife, but the bleeding was too severe."

Staring at the man, Fred struggled to speak. His heart crushed in his chest, shocked by the doctor's words. He faltered, staggering as if from a decisive blow. Studying the man's face, Fred saw the ugly truth clearly written in his dismal expression.

"Was it a girl or a boy?" he finally asked, his voice a faint whisper.

"It was a son," Dr. Tomley informed him quietly. "I'm very sorry for your loss," he repeated, excusing himself to the washroom.

Rubbing his hands over his face, Fred labored to cope. Mildred couldn't be gone! She was the love of his life! He floundered, falling into a nearby chair, his devastated sobs echoing through the halls of *Swanhurst*.

"How on earth am I going to tell Milly and Lizzy that their sweet mother is gone," he wondered. *"How will they ever get by without her love?"*

Epilogue

Six months later
June 1, 1928
Newport, Rhode Island

Swanhurst was bustling with people congregating on the lawn for today's dedication festivities. A complete program had been prepared, including speeches, classical piano selections by Mrs. Rooney, and a violin performance by Miss Sadie Taber. Rear Admiral William S. Sims and Mr. Theodore Green of Providence made the principal addresses relative to the dedication, and Miss Price read a poem she wrote specifically for today's celebration.

"Today, the Newport Arts Association graciously accepts the donation of *Swanhurst Manor* as a memorial to Sara Swan Whiting." Admiral Sims addressed the group, dressed in full military regalia.

Bayard listened to the presentation with mixed feelings. His mother had always supported the arts, but *Swanhurst* was the family home. After today, it would become a public building used by students, teachers, and supporters of the arts. Never again would *Swanhurst* host a family dinner. Never again would a family member be born, married, or die within its hallowed walls. Struggling with his emotions, he listened to the dedication observance conclude in a chorus of applause from the guests.

Walking across the lawn, he decided his mother would have thought it a wonderful ceremony. Moving between the folding chairs, he considered the changes brought on by the passing of his sister. The family lost *Swanhurst,* but he was grateful, at least, that the house would bear his mother's name in memorial for many years to come.

People clustered in groups, happy to have a building devoted entirely to the arts, and conversation buzzed through the assembly on a current of excitement.

Heading for some refreshments on the piazza, two women caught Bayard's eye, chatting together on folding chairs under the shade of the old beech trees. He smiled, recognizing his mother's friends Mrs. Edith Wharton and Mrs. Carrie Wilson. Making his way through the crowd, he approached them.

"Mrs. Wharton?" he asked politely. "Mrs. Wilson?"

"Yes." Mrs. Wharton looked up from under her attractive blue hat and smiled.

"I'm Sara's son, Bayard Rives." He smiled and extended his hand to each of the women. Mrs. Wharton had become quite famous for her novels. The latest, *The Age of Innocence,* had garnered her a Pulitzer Prize.

"Oh, Bayard!" A wide smile covered Edith's face. "You're a grown man now, I see. Please sit with us." She patted the chair beside her.

"I imagine this has been a hard day for you," Mrs. Wilson offered. The older woman was delicate and lovely, despite her age. "I know *Swanhurst* has been in the family for many years."

"Yes, ma'am, it has." He smiled politely as he sat down with the ladies. "It's like losing another family member. My mother died a month before her sixty-third birthday – June 20th of '24. *Swanhurst* has been passed from mother to daughter since it was built in 1851 by my great-grandfather Judge Swan," Bayard continued proudly. "Mildred inherited the house, but since she didn't survive, my mother's will designates the manor to be donated to the Newport Art Association, together with an endowment of one hundred thousand dollars. With Mildred gone, the provisions of Mother's will must be followed by law."

"The only stipulation is that the house retains the name of *Swanhurst* for future generations as the *Sara Swan Memorial.* I'm sure it will bring much joy to the artists and musicians of the city." He paused and met their eyes. "Did you enjoy today's dedication?"

"Yes. It was wonderful." Edith nodded approvingly. "I wouldn't have missed it for the world."

"I'm so sorry about losing your sister," Mrs. Wilson added. "She was so young."

"It's been a terrible ordeal." Bayard grimaced. "My brother-in-law, Fred, took the girls and moved to Scotland."

"Scotland?" Mrs. Wilson repeated. "Does he have family there?"

"Yes, ma'am." Bayard nodded.

"Take heart, son," Mrs. Wharton said. "Time has a way of healing a loss like this."

Bayard nodded, finding comfort in his mother's friends.

"Your mother had such a beautiful singing voice." Mrs. Wilson sighed, her eyes lively with the recollection. "She loved the arts – all art, whether music, painting, or theater. I think it's wonderful that her memory will live on in such a positive way."

"I agree," Bayard said. "Her love for the arts passed on to me, and I spent a few seasons in the theater at Yale. Did you get a chance to view the original paintings on exhibit in the library and parlor?"

"Yes, I did." Edith nodded in admiration. "There are some beautiful pieces on display. I especially like the work by *Marietta*. She shows great promise, but I have a soft spot in my heart for women artists."

"It does seem like they have to jump a higher hurdle to receive any acclaim," Bayard agreed.

"It can't be easy being the last of your family." Compassion shadowed Edith's wrinkled face. "It broke my heart that I didn't see your mother again before she passed."

"She is greatly missed," Mrs. Wilson added, growing somber.

"Yes." A shadow passed over Bayard's face. "She certainly is."

Edith gazed at the young man thoughtfully, and Mrs. Wilson grew quiet. A fresh breeze moved through the leaves in the beech trees as the three lapsed into silence. It was as if they were gazing through memories from years past — years of his mother's life and the years of the Gilded Age.

After a moment, Mrs. Wharton asked: "Does it make you sad? Knowing *Swanhurst* will no longer be in the family."

"I admit it does." Bayard shrugged. "The practice of passing the home down the maternal line as a dowry ensured the women of the family would always have a home and some security, which, as you know, was not always afforded before women achieved basic civil rights – like the right to vote." He glanced at the women and grimaced. "I just hope *Swanhurst* doesn't fall into the hands of a developer who decides to make apartments out of it – or worse, tear it down."

"That would truly be a crime," Edith agreed. "It is a beautiful example of early American architecture – some of the earliest here in Newport. At least for now, we know the home stands."

"I heard they're starting a choir," Mrs. Wilson said, brightening the conversation.

"Yes, I heard the same." Bayard nodded, leaning back in his chair. "*The Swanhurst Choir*. I kind of like the sound of it. We've also erected a giant granite cross in the Whiting plot at Island Cemetery in Mother's honor. I decided to use her maiden name for both dedications in a small effort to preserve the Swan-Whiting surname and its history."

With a glance across the yard, Bayard noticed the crowd gathered for today's celebration was beginning to thin. Guests departed in automobiles as late afternoon shadows began to fall around the estate. A hollow feeling grew in Bayard's chest as the finality of today's events hit home.

Edith picked up her cane and stood. "Well, I must be going," she announced. "If you're ever in France, please come and visit."

"Thank you. That's very gracious of you."

Edith turned and gave him a firm look, directly meeting his eyes. "Your mother was a beautiful and genteel woman who was dealt an ugly hand by Mr. Belmont and his family, Bayard. She stood strong and proud in the face of a cruel and judgmental society, and in the end, she overcame it all to find happiness and love. I'm happy to know she was memorialized today. Sara deserves it more than you know."

"I couldn't agree more," Mrs. Wilson added, easing her diminutive frame from the chair beside her. "Good luck to you. And best wishes to your family."

"Thank you for your kind words." Bayard fought back his tears as he watched the two women walk toward the parking area.

A cleaning crew began to pick up after the celebration, gathering trash and folding the chairs into stacks. Walking into the house, Bayard took his last tour of *Swanhurst*. Moving through the rooms felt surreal, like a dream, memories passing through his mind from days past.

Saying a brief goodbye to the directors of the Art Association, he walked to the front door and paused in the foyer. Glancing up the wide staircase, he remembered the many times he'd watched his beautiful mother descend the steps in her exquisite French gowns. The memory of melodies filtered through his mind, an echo of family weddings and dinner parties held here at *Swanhurst*. He lingered, knowing things would never be the same. After a time, he stepped outside onto the front porch with one last look over the lawn. The leaves of the copper beech trees rustled in the warm sea breeze as if whispering him a final farewell.

Lost in his thought, as he walked toward his car, a middle-aged woman rushed to intercept him on the driveway. Well dressed, with chestnut-brown hair and hazel eyes, she hurried in his direction.

"Mr. Rives!" she called. "Mr. Rives!"

"Can I help you?" Bayard asked as she reached his side.

"I'm so glad I caught you before you left." She smiled. "My name is Miss Fayol. I'm a journalist with *The Ladies Home Journal* magazine."

"Good evening, Miss Fayol," he said, shaking the woman's hand. "What can I do for you?"

"Well, I was wondering if you wouldn't mind answering a few questions for me?" The woman pulled a small notepad from her purse. "The magazine wants me to write an article about today's dedication ceremony. I was doing some research into your mother's history, and I must say, she was a very fascinating lady."

"Yes. She had quite an eventful life."

"I was hoping I could persuade you to do an interview for the article?" She flashed him a wide smile. "I'd like to give my readers a more personal insight into today's dedication with the most accurate information possible."

Bayard rubbed his chin while considering the idea. "Can you give me some time to decide? I'm unsure what my mother would've thought about me talking to the press."

"Of course, but I'll only be in Newport for a few more days. My editor can be rather impatient, and we may miss the opportunity."

"I understand," Bayard said.

"Let me give you my telephone number." The reporter jotted down her number and tore the paper from her small tablet. "I do hope you'll call me tomorrow, Mr. Rives. I truly believe your mother's story would interest our readers."

"I'll let you know what I decide," Bayard said, turning for his car.

"I appreciate it." Miss Fayol waved goodbye and walked to her car, parked further up the *Swanhurst* driveway.

Climbing into his automobile, Bayard took one long, last look at the family home. He thought about his mother's legacy, and he thought about *Swanhurst* and all that had happened here over the years.

Starting the engine, he drove to the corner of Webster Street.

Perhaps this is a story that should be told.

Turning onto Bellevue, Bayard headed for Ocean Avenue. He wanted to watch the sun set over the Newport sea one last time.

THE END

Swan Song

J.D. Peterson ©

The dance of life,
The dance of death.
With fleeting joys and broken hearts.
Repeats,
Within the tests of time.
Repeats, the test of time.
The ceremonies of our dance,
Christening,
Birthday,
Wedding and Wake.
Repeats,
Within the tests of time.
Repeats, the tests of time.
Our spirit true,
We grow to know
ourselves in greater depth.
Repeats,
Within the tests of time.
Repeats, the tests of time.
As round and round and round we step,
The dance of life.
The dance of death.
Repeats,
Within the tests of time
Repeats, the tests of time.

AUTHOR'S NOTE

Swanhurst Manor was the property of the Newport Art Association until a director took Sara's Trust to court and broke the agreement, selling the house back into the private sector. The manor survived the foreclosures, demolitions, and Real Estate developers that became the fate of many of Newport's magnificent old homes in the twentieth century. Today it still stands in its original location on Bellevue Avenue, restored by the previous owners in keeping with the original design, as a beautiful testament to a bygone era. An auction in 2013 left the fate of *Swanhurst* in the hands of new owners.

OF INTEREST

Name	Born and Died	Died in	Age
Sara Swan Whiting Belmont Rives	5-22-1861 to 6-20-1924	New York	62
Natica Caroline Belmont Rives	9-1-1883 to 2-21-1908	New York	24
George Lockhart Rives	5-1-1849 to 8-18-1917	New York	68
Francis Bayard Rives	1-11-1890 to 9-28-1969	Massachusetts	79
Mildred Sara Rives Godwin	7-31-1893 to 12-22-1927	Newport, R.I.	34
Sara Swan (Mrs.) Whiting	6-2-1820 to 6-7-1894	Newport, R.I.	74
Augustus Whiting (Senior)	7-7-1796 to 1-12-1873	New York	77
Jane Whiting	9-19-1844 to 11-10-1909	New York	65
Ameila (Milly) Whiting	1-3-1846 to 6-6-1896	New York	49
Augustus Whiting (Junior)	7-28-1850 to 7-23-1894	Newport, R.I.	43
Charlotte Adelaide Whiting Havemeyer	7-27-1880 to 10-10-1962	New Jersey	82
Edith Newbold Jones Wharton	1-24-1862 to 8-11-1937	St. Brice Sous Foret, France	75
Caroline Webster Schermerhorn Astor	9-21-1830 to 10-30-1908	New York	78
Caroline (Carrie) Astor Wilson	10-10-1861 to 9-13-1948	New York	87
William Kissam Vanderbilt	12-12-1849 to 7-22-1920	Paris, France	70
Oliver H.P. Belmont	11-12-1858 to 6-10-1908	Hempstead, N.Y.	49

ACKNOWLEDGMENTS

As I finish writing this tale, which has occupied much of my life over the past twenty years, I again wish to send heartfelt thanks to Kristine Bonner. Kris worked diligently with me to edit this manuscript. Her time and talent were a tremendous gift toward the completion of the trilogy and I will be forever grateful.

Thank you to "She-who-shall-remain-nameless" for help with branding, photos, and graphic design. I appreciate all your efforts helping me publish this novel series. You're a whiz kid.

Yet another fluke of synchronicity occurred while finishing up this last manuscript. Author Nellie Kampmann (*A Haunted History of Columbus Ohio – History Press*) discovered photos I'd been searching for of the Whiting Family while doing research at the Ohio historical society. Thank you, Nellie!

I would also like to thank David Black, author of the book "August Belmont – The King of Fifth Avenue" (Dial Press) This massive tome provided many leads and clues that helped me piece together Sara's life. It was an invaluable book to me, and one that I came to refer to as my "bible" of the gilded age.

Many thanks to John Hattendorf, Historian, Trinity Church Newport R.I. Mr. Hattendorf was able to supply missing pieces to the Whiting family line and history, as well as information regarding the bells and stained-glass windows donated by the Whiting family to the church.

For the most part, I have been able to adhere closely to history and the dates of events. Although I took liberties with history, I worked to use facts. For example, the Audrain Building mentioned in Chapter Twenty-Eight was not completed until 1903, two years after the scene took place.

Last but certainly not least, I want to acknowledge you, dear reader. Your interest and enthusiasm for Sara's story has given me much-needed energy, fueling my determination to complete this trilogy, therefore completing my task of revealing the truth about this historic scandal, with the added benefit of preserving Sara's memory.

It has taken years of work, but now that your story has been told I hope you can rest in peace, dear Sara. Rest in Peace.

J. D. Peterson

BIBLIOGRAPHY

Books

The King of Fifth Avenue - The Fortunes of August Belmont by David Black
Dial Press N.Y., N.Y. Copyright ♥ 1981 ISBN 0-385-27194-8

A Season of Splendor – The Court of Mrs. Astor in Gilded Age New York
by Greg King. John Wiley & Sons, Inc. Hoboken, New Jersey. Copyright 2009 ISBN
978-470-18569-8

The Vanderbilts and the Gilded Age – Architectural Aspirations by John Foreman and Robbe Pierce Stimson, St Martin's Press, Copyright 1991, ISBN-0-312-05984-1

Ladies and Not-So-Gentle Women by Alfred Allan Lewis. Penguin Group, Copyright 2000, ISBN-670-85810-2

Semper Eadem; A History of Trinity Church in Newport, 1698-2000 by John Hattendorf, Historian, Copyright 2001 Published by Trinity Church Newport R.I. ISBN 978-0970650-70-2

Alva, that Vanderbilt-Belmont Woman by Margaret Hayden Rector, The Dutch Island Press, Copyright 1992. ISBN-0-934881-13-8

George Rives Genealogical Notes
New York Public Library
Available online: www.nypl.org

Newspapers
The New York Times Archives (New York)

The Newport Mercury (Rhode Island)

The New York Sun (New York)

The Brooklyn Daily Eagle (New York)

The Scranton Republic (Pennsylvania)

The Reno-Gazette Journal (Reno, Nevada)

The Oregon Sunday Journal (Portland, Oregon

Photographic Credits

Artist Renderings - From photos courtesy of Columbus, Ohio Historical Society.

All other photos are in the public domain.

ABOUT AUTHOR

J. D. Peterson is an author, singer-songwriter, and artist. In addition, she is an alternative healer, certified in multiple modalities. Originally from the East Coast, Ms. Peterson lives in Southern California.

For historical photos, documents, book club questions, and more, visit:

www.americangilt.com
Join us for the Podcast:
'American Gilt and the Gilded Age'
Video Podcast available on YouTube.com

Made in the USA
Middletown, DE
29 September 2023

39777861R00179